"*The Return* is intelligent suspense at its finest. Boyd weaves an intense and surprising story, making you care deeply for the characters. If you enjoy complex and compelling drama, pick up this book!"

—MARY E. DEMUTH, author of
Watching the Tree Limbs and *Wishing on Dandelions*

"Austin Boyd delivers a perfect mix of action, drama, and suspense. This enticing novel illuminates a web of deception involving espionage and eugenics. *The Return* is a must-read that is sure to captivate its audience!"

—JENNY FRITH, RN

"I could not put *The Return* down. Austin Boyd's treatment of human clones as unique individuals was especially insightful and impressive."

—JAMES C. MOSCATO, MA, director of conferencing
and education, The Center for Bioethics and Human Dignity

"Austin Boyd's MARS HILL CLASSIFIED trilogy is a rare treat: both a gripping story and a genuine and entertaining testimony of faith. Whether surviving odd events on Mars or struggling with challenges of isolation, cultic intrigue, or geopolitical puzzles on Earth, the characters and events in *The Return* are captivating. Austin Boyd realistically depicts different paths to salvation attempted by his characters—personal ambition, technological superiority, secret spiritual knowledge, or authentic Christian faith—with many surprising turns."

—J. EDWARD CULPEPPER, PhD, pastor and writer

"In this third installment of the MARS HILL CLASSIFIED trilogy, Austin Boyd weaves all the threads together in fast-paced action that races toward the conclusion. This series grows in depth and suspense with each new addition. *The Return* will not leave readers disappointed."

—KATHRYN CUSHMAN, author of *A Promise to Remember*

"What serious Christian hasn't wondered if his or her faith could withstand a bombardment of chaos, despair, and the depths of sheer hopelessness? The enemies the characters confront are beyond our world and imagination. They triumph as well as inspire. You'll cheer with their victories, sorrow with their despair, and enjoy every page."

—DALE CRAMER, author of *Winds of Fury, Circles of Grace*

Books by Austin Boyd

It Only Takes A Spark

The Evidence

The Proof

The Return

Nobody's Child

H_2O

THE
RETURN

A NOVEL

MARS HILL
CLASSIFIED
BOOK 3

AUSTIN BOYD

LIVING
INK
BOOKS™
Writing Worth Reading™

The Return

© 2007 by Austin Walker Boyd Jr.

Living Ink Books, an imprint of AMG Publishers
6815 Shallowford Road
Chattanooga, TN 37421

Print Edition   ISBN 13: 978-0-89957-830-9   ISBN 10: 0-89957-830-6
ePub Edition   ISBN 13: 978-1-61715-385-3   ISBN 10: 1-61715-385-0
Mobi Edition: ISBN 13: 978-1-61715-386-0   ISBN 10: 1-61715-386-9
ePDF Edition: ISBN 13: 978-1-61715-387-7   ISBN 10: 1-61715-387-7

Cover design by Daryle Beam of Brightboy Design, Inc., Chattanooga, TN

This novel is a work of fiction. Names, characters, places, and incidents are either the product of the author's imagination or are used fictitiously. Any resemblance to actual events, locales, organizations, or persons, living or dead, is entirely coincidental and beyond the intent of either the author or publisher.

Unless otherwise identified, all Scripture quotations in this publication are taken from the HOLY BIBLE: NEW INTERNATIONAL VERSION® (NIV®). Copyright © 1973, 1978, 1984 by International Bible Society. Used by permission of Zondervan Publishing House. All rights reserved.

Other versions include: *THE MESSAGE* (MSG). Copyright © 1993, 1994, 1995, 1996, 2000, 2001, 2002. Used by permission of NavPress Publishing Group; and the *King James Version.*

Published in association with the literary agency of Leslie H. Stobbe, 300 Doubleday Road, Tryon, NC, 28782.

Printed in the United States of America
1 2 3 4 5 6 7 8 9 10 –B– 16 15 14 13 12

For my family:

To my growing children, Austin, Andrew, Alexander, and Alice—real-life inspirations for the Wells family, their characters, joys, and challenges. I am so proud of each of you.

To my patient and enduring wife, Cindy—my hero in real life and the inspiration for Amy Wells. Thank you for the many silent sacrifices you've made on my behalf.

ACKNOWLEDGMENTS

AS AN ATHLETE IMPROVES under the guidance of good coaches, I've benefited from the mentoring and wise insights of many editors and friends who helped prepare *The Return* for publication. Dave Lambert (Howard Books) served as my developmental editor through all three novels of this series. He pointed out many large and small problems in my writing, and shared blunt but compassionate criticism. His thirty-page reviews were the highlight of my writing process, providing a roadmap for important modifications. I've grown immensely in the craft of fiction under his tutelage.

Linda Nathan (Logos Word Designs) deserves special mention for her spiritual insights as we refined the life and dialogue of my characters. Linda has been with me from the start of my novel career, patiently pointing out my faults and encouraging me in my successes that I might improve as a writer. Jeff Gerke (Marcher Lord Press) was a huge help, showing me corrections to plot and structure during early drafts. Karen Ball (www.karenballbooks.com) critiqued the first chapters, pointing out revisions to speed up the plot and add tension. These good friends are all accomplished novelists as well as freelance editors.

Kay Campbell of the Huntsville Times, and my journalist son, Andrew Boyd, were major contributors to the bonus article "Deceived!" that appears in the back of this book. Kay and Andrew have stretched my thinking through their piercing insights during many talks. Their enthusiasm for balanced journalism was the inspiration for the unique postscript to this novel.

Many friends provided frank criticism of the smooth draft manuscript. Thank you all for the important inputs you provided: Dr. Ed Culpepper; Richard Mabry, MD; Colonel Teresa Ortiz, U.S. Army;

Sam Whatley; Bill and Nancy Slagle; Dr. Carolyn Boyd; Kelly Lynn, MD; Pam Erwin, RN; Kegan Smallwood; Rev. Jim Moscato; Mary Ellen Harris; Deanna Wood; Jenny Frith, RN; Dave Coy; Beth Beck; Debbie Gehrisch; Cynthia Peterson; Kathleen Burgess; Connie Krueger; Gretta Russe; Daniel Tillinghast; Heather Lozano; Jackie Strange; Beth Self; Sandra Lee Smith; Lizette Vega; Catherine Leggitt; John Clarke; Nancy Ellen Hird; Rev. Dale Clem; Matthew Eppinette; and my dad, Walker Boyd.

I am indebted to Kris Wallen, Kate Epperson, and Rod Morris of the NavPress editorial department for their work to release the first edition of this book. Thanks to my agent, Les Stobbe, whose wisdom about the publishing market and his openness to God's leading brought my writing to the market. Thanks, also, to my publicist, Rebeca Seitz (Glass Road Public Relations), who so ably promoted news of my book and established my national speaking platform. Finally, thanks to Publisher Dale Anderson, Senior Editor Rick Steele, Warren Baker, Trevor Overcash, and the rest of the AMG Publishers team for giving this out-of-print series a new life. I'm thrilled to be part of their vision to share truth through fiction, and bring the Gospel to every corner of the Earth.

Jesus used parables to share truth. He is the master storyteller, and His spirit is the inspiration for the stories I am privileged to share with you, the reader.

Austin Boyd
304 Broad Armstrong Drive,
Brownsboro, Alabama 35741
www.austinboyd.com

1

THE SMALL POINT OF LIGHT moved toward them, an unhurried but relentless advance across a lifeless red plain. Not an out-of-the-ordinary sight on Earth, perhaps—a slow vehicle crossing the high desert. But this was Mars. And until moments ago, eight Martian astronauts, along with all of mankind, had thought those explorers were the sole living beings on this forsaken, desiccated planet.

"The glint's still headed straight for us." Rear Admiral John Wells, known to his crew as "Hawk," pointed at the computer display, consternation knitting his brow. "At the current speed of advance, it'll be here in three days. Tops."

John heard the quickened breathing of the seven other astronauts gathered around him in the quiet of the Martian morning. Hemmed inside their tight cylindrical home, the crew formed a tense circle in the mission operations center of their laboratory module.

"You've only seen those reflections at sunrise, right?" Martin Oswald, their lanky flight engineer, better known as "Oz," winced as he plucked hair from the side of his head. The guy's nerves had gotten so bad the bald spot was hard to miss now.

Colonel Melanie Knox nodded and looked up from a data terminal, her small frame bristling with energy. "Satellite surveillance picks up a glint as it crosses the horizon every morning. But only at low sun angles. There's no mistake—something's out there. I woke you because I wanted you all to see for yourselves." She studied her wide-eyed crewmates and waved a hand across the screen. "Whatever it is, guys, it's closing in on us."

John's crew conferred an hour later in the dining area of the habitation module. Everyone but John nursed a mug of coffee as they debated the next step.

"Houston's probably flipping out right now. And no one knows what we're dealing with." Dr. Deborah Readdy sighed and pushed a frazzled jumble of wiry strawberry hair over her shoulder. "It looks like a vehicle in this image. But it's too blurry to be sure."

Deborah tossed a glossy printout onto the scuffed plastic of their eight-person dinner table. All eyes riveted on the photo's fuzzy detail of what looked like a silver box. Behind her, a large wall monitor displayed expanded video images of the silver thing overlaid on a map of the deeply eroded Nirgal Vallis region of Mars.

This was their home, a rugged land of ravines and gullies, hundreds of miniature Grand Canyons coursing across the pockmarked face of bone-dry Mars. A lonely planet, distant from all John had ever known and loved, and proving more barren by the day—until now.

"That thing's blurry because we're taking the pictures with a *weather* bird, Deborah," Oz said as he peered at the photo. "The satellite's twenty-one thousand kilometers above the planet. It's not designed for high-resolution imagery." He slumped in his seat, bony shoulders spiking up under a loose, blue NASA jumpsuit. "Shoot, I'm surprised Melanie saw that reflection at all. We're alone, right, John? No secret manned missions?" He tossed a crumpled juice packet at their commander. "And no aliens?"

John caught the trash ball one-handed and shook his head. "You know as much about this as I do, Oz." He stared at the glossy photo. "Deborah's right. NASA freaked when I told 'em."

"Is it any wonder?" Melanie said. "We've got no idea what we're dealing with."

"There won't be any better imagery to help us. Mars Surveyor won't be in orbit 'til we're long gone." Jake Cook spoke for the first time that morning. The big man's deep voice reverberated like a bass drum in the gleaming white habitation module. "So, what do we know? Something big, of unknown origin, is headed our way."

Jake pulled the glossy image toward him, then leaned over the table, resting his large frame on his elbows. "We have two choices. Either we intercept this thing and deal with it. Or we sit on our hands and wait for it to arrive. In either event, we have to make some quick decisions when we meet it . . . them . . . whatever." Jake sat up, leaned back in his chair, and waved a hand at the airlock. "Remember, we aren't armed, and our only transportation off this planet is unguarded, a kilometer away."

His comment touched a nerve. No one ever considered guarding anything on Mars. They all started to talk at once.

"Jake's got a point." Melanie stood up to focus the group's attention. They quieted as she pointed a cursor at the track prediction on the screen. "We can't even lock the doors. I'd rather *act* than wait." She turned toward John, her gentle brown eyes demanding a response.

The crew geologist, Dr. Robert Witt, spoke with an aggravating nasal tone. "You're delusional. All of you. We know we're alone, right? It's probably a glint in the camera lens at sunrise." He huffed. "Just a blip. Nothing to get excited about."

John raised a hand for silence as the others railed at "Geo," their crew skeptic. He surveyed the four men and three women waiting for his pronouncement. *Navy Rear Admiral John Wells, commander of the third manned mission to Mars—"Hawk," America's most experienced astronaut.* That's what the news ticker said once when he was on camera. It was time to command. "Put a lid on it, folks. Geo's point's as valid as any other right now."

John turned toward the blurry silver image on the big screen, resting both elbows on the table, his chin perched on his folded hands. The crew waited for him to speak. It was a tense silence.

Maybe it is *a figment of our imagination,* he thought. A noisy ventilation fan rattled in the background, distracting him. After five hundred dusty days on the Red Planet, things broke down much too often. *Can't afford major failures now. Four more months to go . . .*

When they'd begun this odyssey nearly seventeen months ago, everyone dreamed of water and ice on Mars, assuming they were alone on a planet shaped eons ago by rivers and lakes. They came looking for microscopic life, fully expecting to find it. The equipment functioned perfectly and failures were minimal. Lately, however, John spent half his time fixing broken stuff, the planet was bone dry and devoid of life everywhere they'd drilled, and now a vehicle appeared to be crossing this dusty rock headed toward them. Somehow, he sensed, their mission was about to be severely tested—much like it was the first time he'd come here.

"I agree with Mel," John said at last. "If something's out there, we can't let it get to us first. I'll coordinate the details with Houston and we'll head out today to investigate. Blue team, suit up. Gold team stays here."

He looked at Melanie, his second in command. "Be prepared to get your team out of here fast, Mel. You might not get much notice."

John moved slowly down the ten steps from the airlock, thinking about the next ten hours. His foot settled into the sugar-like dust of Mars, a familiar squishy sensation that affirmed he was outside. His hard bulky suit fit like a well-worn glove, and he took a deep breath of the dry recycled air, glad to be outdoors despite the circumstances.

It felt good to be afoot again for the first time in a week. The inside of his Mars suit smelled like a locker room after a year and a half of hard use, but the rigid torso fit like he was born into it. And, in a manner of speaking, he *was* born for this—space exploration, his lifelong passion. He looked into the distant amber sky above a rust-red rocky plain pocked with craters and ridges. A deep gorge ran west. He never wanted to forget this experience—standing on the face of another planet nearly two hundred million kilometers from Earth.

Seven years ago, John had floated in his suit, attached to his crippled ship, Epsilon, staring into the void of space as he passed Venus. Alone. A terrifying isolation. Yet the chill of the loneliness back then couldn't compare to the apprehension that gripped him now. He prayed for calm, but an inner voice, the quiet whisper of God's guidance, urged him on: *Go!*

A salmon-colored disc, surrounded by a halo of fine dust particles, shone in the morning sky. John stared beyond the team of four astronauts, his eyes on a distant, rugged, and increasingly ominous horizon.

"You ready, old man?" Jake let out a belly laugh as John gazed into the sun. "If you're not up to this, we can grab you a wheelchair."

John smiled, knowing his old friend couldn't see his grin. The sun's reflection glinting off the gold-tinted visor of his helmet was too bright. "I'm older, Mr. Cook, but definitely wiser. Be glad the shrinks gave me a thumbs-up to keep an eye on you pups. You'd have never made it this far without me."

"You're probably right, Methuselah." Jake patted John's backpack.

"Methuselah?"

"Yeah. Like that old geezer in the Bible. You're the oldest man on Mars."

Methuselah. Noah's grandfather. A sudden rush of memories ripped at John's heart, and he saw Amy, a petite brunette with a Bible picture book, reading about the ark with his young sons on a late summer morning while they all watched a torrential rainstorm. Baby Alice rolled on the floor in a layette, and the aroma of Saturday's breakfast of bacon and biscuits lingered in the air. That recollection of family warmth turned to ice in an instant, replaced by memories of their funeral. His wife and four children, ripped from him six years ago next month. Body parts raining down in a hail of burning aircraft wreckage.

John grunted as if he'd been kicked in the gut. Gritting his teeth, he shoved the pain of this daily mental hell deep inside. His raw grief compartmentalized yet again, the old pilot joined his team.

"You okay, pal?" Jake studied John from his position beside the rest of the crew.

"Yeah. Fine. I'm ready." John stepped forward, a checklist in his gloved hand. His loss was like acid rising in his throat. Forcing it back down didn't soothe the burn. "We've got a unique mission today, ladies and gentlemen." Three suited astronauts stood before him next to a large rover that reminded John of a California strawberry packer, six huge wheels suspending a glass-walled cab two meters above the ground.

John read from the miniature video screen on his data tablet. "Eighty kilometers round trip. Our primary target is probably some kind of vehicle, based on the image. Should take us ten hours, give or take an hour. That, plus—" he paused—"whatever we'll need to respond to the approaching visitor."

"Visitor?" Oz exclaimed. "Thought you said we're alone, Hawk?"

John shrugged. "Call it a target, then."

"Yeah. 'Target.' I like that." Oz sounded both pleased and anxious. "Are we armed?"

"You know we aren't. So give it a rest, Oz." Jake was tense, too. "We need to get going. Oxygen supplies and fuel checked out fine, John. Melanie did the rover preflight for us."

Melanie nudged John in the side. "I'd be glad to lead the team and let *you* stay here."

John smiled. "Thanks, Mel, but I need you to stay and hold down the fort." If John gave her the word, Melanie would leave without them, taking half of the Mars crew aloft to their return vessel in orbit—to safety. "You got the keys?"

Melanie nodded at his playful question, then laid a gloved hand on his arm, the top of her helmet barely as high as his shoulder. She held on for a long moment, her shiny visor hiding a normally expressive face. "Be careful, John. I want us to leave this rock *as a team.*"

"Twelve o'clock!" Jake exclaimed loudly as they crested a low berm four hours later. He leaned between Deborah and John, pointing toward a bright object that lay directly in front of the rover.

John's heart skipped a beat. *It can't be!*

Startled, Deborah braked hard, pitching John forward. Jake grabbed at the seats to keep from spilling over the control console. Oz held onto the back of John's seat, craning his long neck to see the brilliant point of light fifty meters beyond them.

"Closer?" Deborah asked as Jake urged her to continue.

John nodded, unable to form a word.

Vertigo gripped him; his head spun. A tsunami of nausea rolled through John's gut. Everything he'd held sacred, including proof of the alien fakeries he thought he'd exposed long ago, all exploded before the glowing object just beyond the ridge's crest. A familiar golden sphere lay in the dust, shimmering with an intense luster. There could be no doubt now.

We're not alone. . . .

Jake and Oz stood with John outside the rover, near an orb the size of a large orange, shimmering gold. The glow intensified as John approached it. No one spoke; even talkative Deborah was silent, sitting at the controls of the rover behind them.

Impossible.

"There's no dust on it, Hawk." Oz photographed the scene, kneeling to get within a couple of meters from the globe. "No tracks that I can see."

Maybe it landed here, John thought. Of all places on Mars, for whatever reason, the globe lay directly in his path.

John's heart beat so hard he was sure Jake, Oz, and Deborah could hear it pounding. He fought to breathe deep, to calm down—but failed. He'd convinced himself years ago that these orbs were part of a complex tapestry of deception, instruments of someone or some nation, capitalizing on a perpetual spiritual hunger in generations of questioning people. Self-deluded people scattered across the Earth who wanted to believe in an alien race. He forced a shallow breath and shuddered.

Was I wrong?

"Looks just like those orbs you guys tried to bring back from Mars on your first mission, John." Jake stood across from him. John kneeled, his hand reaching toward but not touching the glowing sphere.

It was like the others. A perfect duplicate of the gifts that purported "aliens" had left seven years ago on Earth to announce a mysterious coming Father Race—a race that supposedly had seeded human life long ago throughout the galaxy—and on Earth.

They were a ruse, weren't they? The aliens and that weird religion burgeoning on Earth? He'd been convinced then. But here was more proof on Mars.

John leaned toward the beautiful sphere. His gloved hand hovered above the mystical ball, his heart racing.

"Don't touch it, Hawk!" He heard Deborah's voice, but her message didn't register.

I have to know.

"No, Hawk!" someone yelled on his comm link as he reached closer to the radiant sphere. "We don't know if it's safe."

It never harmed the others. John's glove shook as he lowered it, oblivious to Deborah's screams and the slam of frantic heartbeats in his ears.

Oz put a gloved hand on his shoulder to restrain him, but John shook it off.

This is my chance.

John's rubber-tipped fingers touched the orb and it exploded with a piercing blue radiance.

✦

"Don't touch it!" Amy cried as little Abe crawled toward their meager Christmas tree. Before she could reach him, their crawling baby had grabbed a low branch, and the holiday decorations were crashing down upon him.

Springing from the rug in the center of their den, John barely missed getting a hand under the toppling fir and the star atop it. Like diving for a football in the end zone, he'd only managed to get a hand on one ornament, a precious blue glass ball he'd bought for his mother years earlier that she had recently donated to their collection. The remainder of Amy's ancient handblown ornaments splintered on the floor around their babe.

"John!"

Deborah's piercing scream brought him back to Mars. Knee-deep in red dust, he grasped the blue globe between white-gloved hands. An adrenaline-driven blue jolt shot through John's eyes and down his neck, exploding shivers through his shoulder and spine. Gooseflesh rose on his arms and legs as his muscles tensed for fight—or flight.

He was now the sixth.

The first blue explosions had occurred when two silver spider crafts presented their orbs to Mars Rover eight years ago, a thousand kilometers north-northwest of where he was now. Barb Kanewski said it happened the same way when her late brother accepted the third orb from Earth's first spider visitors only twelve days later in a swamp at Cape Canaveral.

On Mars seven years ago, his late friend and Martian explorer, Dr. Michelle Caskey, had experienced the blue explosion of light as she accepted the fourth orb from alien spiders. Aliens who met her landing craft on the day she was the first human to touch the Red Planet. A month later, a fifth orb blazed in the hands of Father Malcolm Raines, greeting a group of silver spiders in the cloister of a Benedictine abbey on France's Mont Saint Michel.

Five brilliant golden orbs, each presented by tall silver spider-like visitors, followed by five blinding blue flashes when the orbs were first touched. The blaze of this sixth orb was too brilliant to watch, and John turned his head as he grasped the sphere tightly with both hands. In a moment, the blue outburst faded to an azure glow.

Why here? Why now? The inside of his clammy Mars suit suddenly felt icy cold.

John stood still, clutching the blue globe. He fully expected a towering silver spider to materialize out of thin air and spear him through the chest with its sharp-tipped leg. Alien robot landers, three meters tall, should be flying in for an eight-legged landing, or walking up single file, their deep bass voices booming at him from nowhere. That's the way it usually happened. Or maybe he should expect the tall space preacher, Father Malcolm Raines, to saunter up in flowing purple robes as he had on Mont Saint Michel, hands raised to the sky exclaiming, "Father! Our number is six!"

The events of the past eight years on Earth and Mars had seen every fashion of strange occurrence with the presentation of these mysterious orbs. He had no idea what to expect next. And no idea why he'd found one here, in the middle of nowhere on Mars.

Something would happen soon. It always did.

Moments later, John stood in response to a tug on his arm, probably Oz trying to get his attention.

"Over there!" Jake yelled on the comm link.

"I see him. But—" Deborah gasped.

"John?" Oz's voice was strangely low and subdued.

John turned toward Oz and held up the ball. "Number six!"

"No." His friend's voice was stern. "Turn around, Hawk. *Now.*"

John shuffled around, then flinched. The orb slipped from his grasp and fell into the dust at his feet.

For a moment he was back in Clear Lake City, in late October, cleaning windows for Amy. His oldest son Abe had crept through the living room in a ghoulish Halloween mask, then pressed his face against the glass. When John turned back to his task with a fresh paper towel, he'd met the bloody face with a scream—like the scream he'd just stifled.

A short humanoid stood one hundred meters away. It was dressed in what appeared to be a brilliant silver suit, like none John had ever seen before, topped with a strange trapezoidal helmet sporting two vertical antennae. The humanoid raised what looked like a hand, perhaps in greeting.

"Heart rate 145, John! Breathe!" Deborah's words pricked him, and he gasped for the breaths he'd missed. He couldn't make himself move.

Fifty years of alien images from picture books and movies mingled with pure wonder, rekindling childhood hopes that he might, of all humans, be the first to meet another life form. His dreams played at once like a mental movie in this historic encounter.

It's true. We're not alone.

In a flash, the movie strip broke, his mental film reel spinning out of control as the implication slapped him repeatedly:

I was wrong. There is life here . . . intelligent alien life.

The silver-clad humanoid kept its hand high, palm facing him. John's radio crackled, but it wasn't the usual clear radio link from his crew. The voice was like none he'd ever heard. It was high-pitched, almost girlish.

"We've been searching for you. My mother and I."

2

SONYA EDWARDS SCRATCHED at her tight Lycra bodysuit. The black fabric stuck to her lithe body like a second skin, too thin to ward off drafts of cold air blowing under the pews of the ancient convent chapel. Sonya shivered and rubbed her legs. The odor of old oak and damp stone surrounded her—the perfume of age.

A winter's afternoon sun streamed through ornate stained glass panels before her, a mosaic of red, yellow, blue, purple, and black adorned with painted images of mythical heroes from a forgotten era. The warriors and saints meant nothing to her, but the yellow cross at the mosaic's center held her gaze. Sonya focused on the warm light, sunbeams heating her stretchy garment. She stared through the shades of gold and white that framed the cross, imagining a fierce sun and endless beaches, hot days and crashing surf. An island sanctuary beckoned her far from this dirty metropolis in northern Italy.

A tall, stern woman dressed in matching Lycra stalked by. Her eyes darted into every pew, on the prowl for a sleeping teen. A chapel full of fifteen-year-old girls watched the black-suited lioness as she hunted among them for nodding heads. Once free of the threat, Sonya released a red elastic bow binding her long black ponytail. She shook out her hair and then gathered it as tight as she could. The shock to her scalp energized her. Fidgeting in the hard oak seat, she bound her long mane and pushed it over her shoulder. Despite the drafty cold, sleep pulled at her eyelids below a thin eyebrow line.

More than three hundred other tall olive-skinned girls dressed just like her sat in row after row of the old chapel, the gathering room at their convent home in Trieste. In front of the room, Father Malcolm Raines, Guardian of the Mother Seed and Principal Cleric of Saint Michael's Remnant, lectured from a copy of the book she held in her lap: *On the Origin of the World: The Nag Hammadi Library.* She knew it cover to cover, as did all her sisters. They had to.

Sonya fidgeted, and her eyes roamed back to the cross. She reached to her neck where a small silver adornment had once hung, a precious going away gift from her mother. Absentmindedly, she fondled the soft spot in her throat, imagining the tiny cross dangling from a braided necklace as she dove through crashing waves and ran in shallow tidal pools.

The patrolling black widow returned, and Sonya forced herself erect in the hard seat. Momentary rest wasn't worth public punishment.

"Thirteen ancient codices!" the tall man exclaimed, lifting a copy of the book as he strutted across the low platform. His greased and straightened black hair reflected sparkles of light as he turned. Sonya watched the sun move across the window as the giant of a man ranted. She counted the seconds, one by one, until the disc was directly in the center of the warm yellow crucifix.

"They bring us enlightenment to lead us into our new day!" Father Raines raised his hands, exhorting her and her teenage sisters to new levels of interest in the Gnostic lesson of the day. "You are—all of you—directly descended from the Mother of All Living Things."

Sonya bit the inside of her mouth, releasing a slight copper taste that mingled with a shooting pain. The bleeding sting kept her awake while the sun dipped beyond the edge of the cross in the center of the stained glass. Soon he'd be finished, retreating to Slovenia for the weekend with his executive assistant. She relished a blessed two-day break from this group instruction on "inner gods" and "higher planes of existence."

Sonya looked for something about him to amuse her. She focused on his brilliant white teeth. *They must be fake. Everything else is.*

". . . and these codices contain the saving knowledge—your gnosis—the true story of womankind. You are the original descendants of Eve, and knowledge of your Mother will provide the blessed insight you require for salvation."

Three hundred plus books rustled in unison. Sonya reluctantly flipped through her text as he recited each verse of the old manuscript.

"'After the day of rest, Sophia sent her daughter Zoe, being called Eve, as an instructor in order that she might make Adam, who had no soul, arise so that those whom he should engender might become containers of light.' Do you see? Our Mother Eve is not the embodiment of sensual nature, temptation, weakness, or the disgrace of man. She brought us the fruit of gnosis . . . the knowledge of good and evil. And you are her sacred seed."

Sonya squirmed. "Seed"—Father Raines's favorite word. She was also a "vessel," his frequent term for her and her sisters. Ripe wombs in which he would soon forge the future of mankind. Father Raines assured them all that it was the highest honor to have been raised since birth for this mission, to serve The One. Sonya stared at the stained-glass cross again, its yellow dulled to an orange as the sun faded into the west.

An honor? How she longed for anonymity, longed for her mother and brother and her old lifestyle in the western Pacific. Far from here.

Sonya watched the man's teeth, a sharp white contrast to his deep purple robes and chocolate skin. His words faded away, replaced by the memory of another day, another place, six years ago. Another dark skin, but a soothing singsong voice. She remembered her mother repeating tender words of care, and later shedding tears of great pain as they were separated.

Father Raines's teeth morphed into images of sharp-tongued men, agents of her own father, who'd ripped her away as her mother mouthed "good-bye," that last parting drowned out by Sonya's own cries. She looked up from his teeth at the orange flicker of the descending sun in the window's lower corner. Like this sun, that island chapter in her life had set. It was gone forever.

Father Raines said she was the embodiment of Eve—the mother of all wisdom. Yet Sonya didn't feel wise. She'd never felt the spiritual spark this tall mentor claimed was deep inside her. She remembered, though, the warm glow when she heard her mother's tales of forgiveness and redemption through the one called "the Christ."

Sonya struggled to bring the old stories alive, to rekindle the dim flame. She saw the robed Jesus and His disciples leaping off the pages of colorful picture books in her mother's lap. "I am the way, the truth, and the life," He'd said to her.

Her eyes dropped from the darkening cross to the loud Guardian, grim reality crushing her fond memories. *He* was her only way now.

"You are the perfect emanation of Eve," Father Raines said again. "In the coming days when you are joined with the Father Race, you shall bring forth the Pleroma, the very fullness of God."

Sonya shifted in the pew, her insides cramping as she imagined what was coming. Her sisters, most of them in fact, seemed to look forward to that day he spoke of. Sonya craved to run and to swim again. She shook her head, aching to cut the long mane dangling from her scalp like a decorated horse's tail. *One day,* she promised herself, *I'll leave this place. There has to be a way.*

MARS

John stared in disbelief at the humanoid before him, its dual antennae popping out of the helmet like long silver rabbit ears. In all his years in the space program, he'd never seen a suit like this. His pulse pounded as the visitor's words echoed in his ears: *We've been searching for you. My mother and I.* He shuddered.

"I'm John Wells."

"I know. We've been watching you since you arrived."

This can't be! John shook his head to throw off what felt like a nightmare. The icy chill in his suit returned, shivers ripping through his spine and neck for a third time. He stared ahead, hoping the figment would vaporize, then he remembered what had brought him here and looked at his feet. The orb lay in the dust where he'd dropped it. John knelt, reluctant to touch the blue luster.

This is no dream.

John grasped the orb with one hand, his rubber-tipped gloves lifting it from the red soil. He looked up as he stood; the silver visitor hadn't moved. *"We've been watching you?" It speaks English?*

"Who are you?" John asked.

"My name's Rex. My mother is sick and needs your help." He pointed beyond a low berm in the distance. "Please. Come with me."

"Rex?" John blurted out. This made no sense. "As in 'Rex Edwards'? From the commercial mission that was lost on the way here? To Mars?"

"We weren't lost. Just out of touch."

John stood his ground, dumbfounded at this queer turn of events. The suit felt warm again, the shivers gone. "I *know* Rex Edwards. You're too small. And too young." He shook his head again. "Deborah. You getting this?"

"Copy, Hawk. We're patching it live to Houston. We thought Edwards was dead. No one's heard from his mission for over a year."

"My father died last year," Rex said, walking toward John, "but not on the way here, like everyone thinks. He achieved his dream, to bring the Father Race to Mars. I know it's a lot to process right now, but my mom's dying. She needs your help *now*."

"Show the way." Deborah gunned the MSR and pulled up beside John.

John, Jake, and Oz swung onto a space version of a running board. John hung on with one hand, the orb in the other, as Deborah bumped the MSR across the rocky plain. The silver visitor somehow jogged across the landscape in a half run, half hop, a feat John never could have accomplished. The MSR and Rex crested the distant berm at the same time.

John thought he'd seen it all. *'My name is Rex Edwards. My father brought the Father Race to Mars. My mother is dying.' Now boys running in space suits. What's next?*

Below, in a shallow ravine, sat a silver box-like vehicle. John leapt off the running board, unlatched a gear locker, and set the orb in a storage tray. Its blue glow had faded. He hurried toward the strange silver contraption, unable in his stiff space suit to match the boy's speed.

"Rex Edwards was your dad?" John called out, realizing just then they spoke on the same frequency.

The figure pointed toward a hatch on the rear of the silver vehicle, then at the other astronauts. "It's a two-person lock. Come with me, Admiral."

"You didn't answer my question," John said, scaling the two-meter ladder on the rover's rear. Rex opened the airlock at the top of the ladder and extended a hand to John.

"Dad died of a heart attack a few weeks after we landed, sir. I'm Rex Jr. I'm fifteen. Can you please help us?"

"Give the kid a hand, Hawk. I'm suiting up," Deborah responded. The boy turned and entered the airlock, gesturing for John to follow.

Five minutes later, the two stood over a gaunt woman curled in a fetal position on a makeshift pallet in the center of the floor. The warm chocolate tones of her skin had a grayish ash coloring, and jet black locks lay frazzled by her head. She was unconscious. When Deborah arrived, with three of them in bulky space suits, the cabin would be crowded. There was no room for the rest of the crew.

"Any idea what her problem is?" John asked, removing his helmet. He held his breath self-consciously, reluctant to inhale for fear of infection. But once he'd opened his visor, if there was contagion, the damage was done.

"No idea, sir. First it was balance and concentration problems, and then slurred speech. Finally convulsions and tremors. When the seizures started, I left with Mom to come find you." Rex's voice cracked. "She's been comatose since this morning."

The youth stood about John's shoulder height, short like his famous dad, with close-cropped blond hair. His diminutive features were a dead ringer for Rex Edwards Sr. The same bulldog jaw and penetrating blue eyes. He looked nothing like the long, dark woman lying on the floor.

As John struggled in his rigid suit to bend over the patient, he heard Deborah rapping on the bulkhead outside. Rex Jr. moved to the control panel and prepared the airlock for her. "It's vented now, Dr. Readdy. You can step inside," he said into his suit microphone.

"He knows our names already?" she asked over the comm link as she entered the lock.

"We've studied you for months. Listened to your communications."

"Then why not just call for help?" John asked.

Rex lowered his head. "I couldn't. My mothers disabled all our communications systems before I stole the rover to find you. They didn't want any assistance. But Mom was dying, you know? I had to help her." He hung his head as he knelt by her side. "My mothers—and my dad—refused to expose our family to your team." Rex caressed his mom's face with a wet towelette, then looked up at John with wet eyes. "Can you help her?"

John put a hand to the woman's forehead and the other to her carotid pulse. "If anyone can, Dr. Readdy can. You ready yet, girl?"

"'Bout a minute," he heard in his suit speaker. "The lock's pressurizing. Keep her breathing, Hawk."

Dear Lord, what's happening here? John wondered. The last ten minutes were a traumatic blur. A confusing jumble of fear that he'd been wrong about alien life, then indications of mystical humanoid creatures. Now proof that his crew had never truly been alone on Mars. He prayed in silence for the woman before him—and her son—two strangers who bore absolutely no resemblance to each other.

True to her word, Dr. Readdy was at John's side in less than sixty seconds, unlatching her helmet as she pressed between bulky suits.

"Shallow respiration. Fast pulse," John said, sliding aside to make room for her. "Your patient."

Within a minute of her entry into the cramped cabin, Deborah Readdy had her helmet and gloves off and a space suitcase version of a doctor's bag open. Her wiry red hair, pulled back with a clip, bounced behind her as she pulled a digital stethoscope and thermometer from her case. Deborah had poise—nothing ever fazed her. She spoke her mind, let you know when you were messing up, but come a crisis, she was cool.

"Don't you have a doctor in your party?" Deborah asked, scanning the digital thermometer.

Rex answered. "All four of my mothers are obstetricians, ma'am. And none of them could figure this out. That's why I came to find you."

"Ma'am?" Deborah said with a chuckle as she looked up at the boy. "Four mothers? OBs?" She shook her head. "I don't even want to ask."

"My guess is, we'll find out," John said in a whisper. This situation was getting stranger by the minute. "What's your prognosis?"

"Comatose. And dehydrated. I brought some Ringers." Deborah pulled out a plastic bag of fluid and began to prepare an IV. "We have a long way to go. No quick diagnosis today."

John watched as Deborah knelt in her bulky suit and threaded the IV into the woman's arm. The slender black woman's shoulder-length dark hair was curled in long delicate corkscrews. Prominent cheekbones and a high forehead reminded him of Ethiopian blood.

"You okay?" she asked quietly while she taped down the IV port. "You scared me to death when your heart rate went off the chart." She looked up at him with a scowl. "And when you touched that thing."

"That bad, huh?"

"Bad. Where is it, by the way? The blue ball?" She hooked up the fluid bag, squeezing it gently to start the flow.

"Storage locker. And I'm fine. A little shook up, that's all." John looked up at Rex and pointed to the front of the rover. The control panel closely resembled their own on the MSR. "Drive this thing as fast as you dare, Rex. Follow our rover." He keyed his microphone.

"Oz. Lead us home. We need to get to base—fast."

"Copy, Hawk. We're rolling."

Rex took a seat at the control console and had the rover moving within seconds. John grabbed at a handhold to steady himself and held onto Deborah's suit shoulder as they bounced after Oz.

Deborah nodded in the woman's direction, then up at Rex, and shrugged. She mouthed the question "mother?" in silence, then spoke up. "Do you know her blood type, Rex?"

Rex caught John's eye as he turned around. "AB positive, ma'am." Then he turned back to drive, his shoulders slumped. "Her name is May. May Randall. And since you're probably going to ask anyway, she's my surrogate mother . . . the *only* mom I've ever known." He sniffled, then glanced back at John, frowning. "I don't share any of her DNA," he said as he drove. "Not that it should matter."

"Suits me," Deborah whispered, raising an eyebrow. "And it doesn't," she said out loud. "Matter, that is." She handed the Ringer's solution to John. "Hold this up."

"Got it," John replied as they bumped across the Nirgal Vallis region, dodging gullies formed millennia ago by long dry rivers. "We'll do everything we can to help her, Rex. I promise."

3

SONYA'S TALL FRAME BARELY fit in her short, narrow bunk, the four girls stacked two by two on either side of their small plaster-walled room. She shivered in the cool of the night, the baseboard heat struggling to keep the room at fifty degrees. Her sisters barely rustled under their layers of quilts. Silence embraced her.

Sonya rubbed the inside of her lip, massaging the lining of her mouth where she bit herself earlier that day to stay awake. Every one of the girls had a pet trick for avoiding the strict discipline of Miss Monique. In the dim light of the compound's tall security lamps outside her window, she could make out forms in her room.

A four-drawer dresser, shared by her roommates, stood against the far wall, filled with their daily wardrobe of black Lycra bodysuits for school and evening, and tight black Lycra shorts for twice-daily athletic activities. Only at night did she get to feel the soft caress of cotton, a white gown she'd worn threadbare. Other girls beyond the walls of their convent home probably enjoyed dresses and pants—or Sonya's dream, a set of pink flannel pajamas.

The distant security light cast a long shadow across her one picture, propped on the dresser. Despite the dark, she could see it in her mind's eye, its lights and color burned into her memory: Her mom and brother with her on a rock outcropping on a remote Pacific island.

"Your mentors," Father Raines had reminded them all, speaking of their parents using his deep, scary voice, "served the Father Race well. You have now grown beyond their care. You serve the Unknowable One with your fecund bodies and inquiring minds." Sonya hated her fertility and the mission Father Raines was preparing her for. She longed for her days frolicking in pounding surf. She breathed deep and detected faint wisps of dinner and the evening meditation incense still in the air. The cold stung her nose.

Sonya listened for a long time in the silence of the cold night, barely able to see each of her sisters huddled under their twin comforters. No one moved. She rolled over to face the cold wall and slipped her hand up to the zipper of her pillow, opening it slowly, then sliding her hand deep into a slit in the pillow's foam core.

After a minute of careful movement, Sonya pulled out a small book and a miniature flashlight and covered them with layers of opaque quilts. Pina, the maid, had warned her years ago, before Sonya understood why, to keep her book hidden from Dr. Raines. The hole in the pillow was Pina's idea, and the gentle matron had never betrayed their secret. She brought Sonya spare batteries every week. *Thank you, Pina.* She prayed as she flipped on the little light.

Under the covering, she opened a red softcover book the size of her palm. Sonya ran her hand over a gold embossed name, worn from careful readings on many evenings like this. The inscription on the inside cover bore her mother's beautiful handwriting, fluid strokes of a dark athletic woman who'd birthed and nurtured her for a biological mom Sonya had never met.

She read late into the night, the delicate ten-year-old pages almost brittle in her hands. Her mother's Jamaican-accented voice leapt from the pages of the tiny text, soothing words of spiritual comfort that made far more sense than what Sonya had heard from Raines this day.

"Flesh gives birth to flesh, but the Spirit gives birth to spirit." She moved her finger down the page, reciting the verses under her breath, then opening her eyes to confirm she'd gotten them correct. "So it is with everyone born of the Spirit."

An hour later, she recited the last words of the chapter, working to commit the thirty-six verses to memory. "Whoever believes in the Son has eternal life, but whoever rejects the Son will not see life, for God's wrath remains on him." She repeated the words once more to herself, knitting them to her heart as sleep pulled at tired eyes. She prayed for her mom and her brother, far away.

Sonya replaced the little volume and its light in the protective slot of her pillow, zipped the case, and closed her eyes. Before she slipped off to sleep, she saw her mother's tears as her father had led her to waiting men. Her mother had prepared her for this place, as though she'd known exactly what Sonya would need, planting in her a sense of everlasting hope. Hope that continued to spring from the pages of her tiny New Testament.

Sonya's father, on the other hand, had sent her here to stay. She was now in Father Raines's care, with no hope of return. Her last waking thoughts were a chilling dread that she might one day begin to believe the tall man's lies.

Rex drove the shiny rover in silence.

"Nice design," John said to spark conversation. "Drives just like ours." The rover controls were the same, but Rex's rover had upholstered walls, padded seats, and two private toilets.

"It should, sir," Rex said, his voice tight. "Dad used your control design but liked his cab layout better." He kept his eyes straight ahead.

John watched the lights of their remote outpost draw closer, now only a kilometer away. The distant sparkles seemed to float above the frigid, rocky ground, glowing in different colors. It reminded him of his boyhood home where a sea of fireflies hovered over damp hay fields at night in West Virginia. Or his children helping him hang lights on their home in Clear Lake City. But that home back on Earth was an empty shell of a house now; no one waited for him. *They're all dead.* A little more of John died at the thought, as it did every day. He buried the pain and tried again with the boy. "Quite a sight, huh?"

Rex nodded.

"Yeah. Pretty amazing," John said. He decided to shut up. He wasn't getting anywhere.

The surface outpost for the past two NASA missions to Mars was an eclectic assortment of hardware spread across three hundred meters of dusty real estate. That distance didn't include the two nuclear power systems positioned a kilometer north of the camp, or the Mars Ascent Vehicle, known as the MAV, a kilometer to the west.

The second manned mission to Mars, launched four years ago, brought the core of this community: the surface laboratory and the nuclear power plants. Flying unmanned for months, the cargo missions landed in the Nirgal Vallis region, an area of ancient river-cut valleys south of the eastern end of Valles Marineris, a seven-kilometer-deep canyon as wide as the United States. Viking 1, and the first manned Mars mission that John supported years ago, had landed to the north-west, in a flatter, but more arid, region.

NASA's robotic cargo missions came to Nirgal Vallis three times, bringing supplies and habitations that would await the arrival of the first long-duration manned mission. Two nuclear power plants, each robotic, had crawled a kilometer north of the landing site, stringing out their power cables as they trundled across dust and rock, hiding on the far side of a low ridge, to provide nuclear electric power for the coming crews.

John saw the squat cylindrical laboratory in the distance as Rex navigated between shallow ravines toward the outpost. Shaped like a short soda can, the white laboratory hung suspended inside a tall cage atop four large wheels. Four extendable legs stabilized it.

The first crew's habitat had been their spaceship from Earth. John and his crew repeated that feat five months ago, flying across the solar system in their Martian house. Now there were two of the squat white habitation facilities, joined to either side of the laboratory.

Two habitats, one laboratory, a methane generation plant, and their MAV, all of them lit like an automobile dealership, shone through the dark night. John made out the US flag and the NASA "meatball," America's historic logo of manned space exploration, on the lighted side of each module. Five structures, awash in brilliant white beams, shone in the brutal Martian cold like beacons of homey warmth.

"It's . . . beautiful," Rex said at last.

"Beautiful?" Deborah asked, standing up behind him and watch-ing their approach. "Don't know if I'd go that far. But it's home. For the next four months at least."

"My father built all of this," Rex said, suddenly chatty. "I remember learning about every system, every design, as Dad won the contracts to construct the Mars base. I watched one of these modules launch from Baker Island. To me, it's *beautiful*." He never turned around.

"How do you intend to get his mom into the Hab?" Deborah asked, putting a hand on John's shoulder.

"My rover adapts to your pressurization ring," Rex volunteered without eye contact. "We designed it that way."

"Why?" Deborah asked. "You planned to come see us?"

"No, ma'am. But Dad wanted our systems to be compatible. Just in case."

John looked up at Deborah, and she shrugged, lifting one eyebrow in that special way she had of silently asking "can you believe this?" She turned back to her patient. "Just the same, I'd like to get a seal check before we open the airlock."

"Yes, ma'am. That won't be a problem." Rex turned to John. "Would you like to drive when we dock the rover, sir?"

John smiled. "Actually, I would. Not that I don't trust you. I just can't afford any accidents."

"I understand."

Rex brought the rover to a stop as Oz called on the comm link. "What's the plan, skipper?"

"We're docking to Hab One." He couldn't wait to get out of this smelly suit. John felt like a lobster, surrounded by the hard shell of his well-worn exploration outfit.

"They can dock with us?" Oz asked, his surprise evident.

"Rex says so. We'll give it a whirl. Otherwise, we've got to get his mom into a suit and carry her over. You dock to Hab Two and keep the crew together over there." He looked behind him at Deborah and her patient. "We've got one sick lady on our hands. We'll quarantine her for now. Seal the hatch to the Lab and isolate the air supply for Hab One."

✴

Half an hour later they had a successful mating with the habitation module, surprising everyone, John assumed, except Rex. A blast of air hit John in the face as he opened the lock to the hab module, carrying the unconscious woman, with Rex's assistance. After a day in their rovers' recycled air, the home atmosphere was a shock. The odor reminded him of a burnt almond cookie. Like on the space station, only stronger, thanks to the pungent aroma of their well-used carbon dioxide scrubbers.

Minutes later, May Randall lay on the examining table of Hab One; the first exploration crew's original habitation was now their make-shift hospital. The rest of the crew watched by video from the safety of a closed hatch and sealed air system. It was a partial quarantine, but it was all they could do.

Rex hovered by his mother's side as Deborah, John, and Sam Readdy—Deborah's physician-pilot husband—attempted to examine the unconscious woman and begin her tests. Deborah put a freckled hand on the boy's arm where he held his mom's hand.

"I need to work on her awhile, Rex. You go upstairs with John. I'll call you soon. I'm sure I can help her." She nodded toward the hatch at the base of a broad, winding staircase. John walked in that direction, hoping the boy would follow.

Rex held his mother's limp hand and caressed her forehead. He stared into Deborah's eyes, released his grip, turned without a word, and headed for the exit.

SATURDAY, FEBRUARY 22, 2020:
NAZARJE, SLOVENIA

The African-American man towered above a tall young woman, his hand grasping hers. The morning light made her Mediterranean complexion glow, and her gray-brown eyes framed by thin eyebrows and high cheeks squinted against the glare of blinding snow. She could feel the bitter Slovenian winter through the monastery's ancient wall and her Lycra skinsuit as she stood at the stone window sill.

She released his hand to wipe the fog of his breath off the cold glass. After what she'd seen last night, she sought any excuse to avoid him. For the first time in her life, including her eight years as executive assistant to Father Malcolm Raines, Monique felt cheap and used—a feeling that deepened each minute she was around him.

She pushed waist-length black hair over her shoulder and bound it into a ponytail with red elastic. Working with the long mane kept her hands out of his.

"How much longer?" she asked, nodding at a woman and a young girl walking hand in hand along a muddy path in the snow in a small garden far below. Crenellated walls stood ten meters above the two lone gray-clad females. "Six years, Father. To what purpose?"

He shrugged. Like he did when he didn't have an answer, but was unwilling to admit it. Rarely did Father Malcolm Raines not have an answer—rarely in public, that is. He was an international icon of religious freedom and independent thinking, the global leader and principal cleric of the World Inclusive Faith Church—and her mentor and boss. He *had* been her mentor—but that relationship was now tarnished beyond repair.

Arrayed in his splendid purple velvet robes, gold sash, and thin white clerical collar, Raines pushed closer to her. He pressed his face to the glass, following the figures' progress below. "It is not yet time, Monique. They must stay."

He turned to face her, but she avoided his eyes, focusing instead on the two figures. "They won't break," she said. "No matter how long we wait."

"I never sought to break anyone," he replied. "I am preserving them, not punishing them. Just as I have been instructed."

She shrugged. "Perhaps. But for six years? We—*you*—have kept them isolated from the Mother Seed, from the outside world, and from each other. Yet somehow they thrive while we wait for the time."

He turned from their bedroom window, high in the ancient Franciscan monastery's tower, and paced a thick white sheepskin rug that spanned the room, insulating them from the chilled stone. Expensive tapestries draped ceiling to floor.

Malcolm's ever-present incense burned in a corner, mixing strangely with the odor of tanned sheep hides and his pungent aftershave. Overnight she'd come to hate the potpourri stench of a sheepherding eastern mystic wearing cheap cologne, the signature stamp of another isolated weekend in Slovenia. She preferred instead the clear air of snow-capped mountains, just a pane of glass away.

Monique continued to face the window. She recognized this pensive withdrawal of his, the pout and pacing he would use to pull her to him like a magnet, knowing her old attraction to his height and strength, his command of millions of followers who hung on every word. Little did those crowds know what she'd discovered, the seamy side of Malcolm Raines. Yet perhaps they wouldn't even care.

She watched the two figures below circling their tiny lot as she pondered the past six years of weekend visits to this remote tower. They came each weekend to rest and pray as well as to monitor construction of Raines's massive additions to the imposing old monastery and Church of the Holy Mother, beautifully located on a hill above the tiny town of Nazarje. It was a new and more secure home for him, Monique, and the 321 teenage girls under his mentorship, removed from the prying eyes of gossiping Italians.

After a Saturday and Sunday morning at this window, the memories would haunt her all week at their home office in Trieste, Italy—memories of a pacing woman and child in winter, the vigorous pair working the ground in spring and summer, or playing in the tiny garden in the cool of fall. Once she'd ignored them; now she couldn't rest, wondering all day what they looked like, how they endured.

When Malcolm finalized the move from Trieste, she'd be drawn to this window *every* morning. She'd hear the two women singing every day, laughing in the summer, and hear snatches of their conversation as they paced.

She would sit in wonder, as she had for years, watching them through the glass on Sunday mornings, the two prisoners pressed into a remote corner of the garden, always looking to the east, as though listening to the town's church bells. Then they would rise and sing. Yet, despite their apparent joy, the two remained the detainees of Father Malcolm Raines, Oracle of the Unknown God and Guardian of the Mother Seed.

Monique turned her head quickly, hoping he'd decided to move downstairs to his study. Instead she caught his eye. He was watching her.

"You are concerned, Monique?" he asked, the deep baritone voice commanding and smooth. It had enthralled her for years; now the voice grated on her.

She smiled and nodded, displaying the face she knew he wanted to see. "I'm concerned, yes, for your work, and for your reputation. The prisoners are no longer an asset. Why keep them here?"

He shook his head with its perfect white teeth and salesman smile that convinced so many millions to bend their knees and open their wallets each week. He moved toward her and cornered her at the window. She tensed, dreading the probing touch of those massive brown hands. He took her shoulders in his grip.

"I have explained this, young one. I heard the voice of the Father Race. The Unknowable God instructed me to take them into my care. I have not heard any message other than this one. They are to be preserved. So we wait."

He squeezed her gently, lowering his face toward hers. Her heart sank when she looked up to meet his eyes—dull eyes with no care for the woman and child below—or, she now knew, for her. At last she saw in him what she'd sensed in her heart these past months, and what she'd finally acknowledged last night. For eight years Monique had worshipped the towering Malcolm Raines, hanging on every word and sensual touch of this self-acclaimed Priest of the Heavenlies. She'd been convinced he was Nephilim, a direct descendant of the original Father Race. Once she'd given everything for a place close to him. Now she ached to run. He pressed her tight against the cold glass.

Malcolm's lips closed on hers. The thick aroma of cologne and incense assaulted her, triggering a wave of nausea and dizziness. She turned her head, put her hand to her mouth, twisted on the cold stone sill, and slipped from under his grasp.

"Monique!" he called as she stumbled barefoot across the deep shag toward the door. "Come here! Now!"

The voice was no longer smooth, but threatening. He'd commanded her every move for eight years, but she dared not turn. Monique slung open the rough-hewn door of their tower room and dashed down the spiral staircase, chilled stone numbing her feet.

And she didn't look back. As she staggered down the curving damp steps, last night's horror reverberated in her mind: Malcolm, unaware that she watched him pore over graphic voyeuristic images of hundreds of teenage girls in their charge—the Mother Seed.

The Priest of the Heavenlies, her titan, was no longer a god-man. The raw truth assailed her, eight years of warning signs she'd ignored now falling into place like great boulders, crushing her with every revelation. She'd enabled this perversion. Whatever evil Malcolm Raines had finally become, she was his accomplice.

4

"WILL SHE BE ALL RIGHT?" Rex asked as he woke. It took a moment to get a grip on the surroundings. The fog of sleep clouded his memory of everything but his mom and her needs.

"She's resting. Let her sleep," Dr. Readdy said, laying a gentle hand on Rex's shoulder. He settled back into the soft bunk, energy sapped by bone-deep fatigue. Only helping Mom had kept him going.

The cylindrical compartment was dimly lit, and the four glass portals at ninety degree intervals were dark. *I must've slept for hours.*

The surroundings were somewhat familiar. The structure was identical, but the curved walls weren't colorful like those back home. This place reminded him of a hospital or a lab. Very NASA. Stark white. Sterile. Rex sighed, hoping he'd be able to return to the colony soon.

Rex watched Dr. Readdy gesture to Admiral Wells. "He's awake now, Hawk." She turned back to Rex. "You need rest," she said. "And fluids. You're dehydrated." She handed him a plastic squeeze bottle with a straw-like contraption on the top. "Nurse this for a while. Get it all down."

Rex took a swig, too proud to admit he was parched.

"Your mom's recovering slowly. She's asleep, not unconscious. But it's still serious." Dr. Readdy put a tiny digital stethoscope to his chest. The small metal pad was cold on his skin, transmitting the sound of his heart to her earpiece. "She's responding well to the fluids we've pumped into her. Did she drink much before she went into the coma?"

Rex nodded. "Yeah. Lots of water. The day before we met you, Mom's hands were shaking like crazy. She'd been vomiting the whole time I was trying to get her here. I tried getting her to drink, but the more she drank, the worse she got. Finally, it was like she gave up, you know? She could barely stay awake, and when she was awake, she was real edgy. Then she finally collapsed."

Dr. Readdy nodded, pulling back her scope. "She's extremely dehydrated, Rex. And hyperglycemic. Is your mom a diabetic?"

"No. Why?"

"Hyperglycemia can take several days to develop. It happens if you're not producing enough insulin to use the glucose for fuel. The sugar levels build up in the blood, and your body tries to get rid of the extra sugar through the urine. Unless you're dehydrated. The fact that she's responding so well to intravenous fluids may indicate she had another problem, one that created the blood-sugar crisis. You're sure she's not a closet diabetic?"

"I don't know, ma'am. She never told me," Rex said. "But if she was sick, Dad would've said something. Everyone who came here had to be super healthy."

"Was your Dad? Healthy, I mean?" Admiral Wells asked. He was always asking questions. Lots of them.

He doesn't trust me. Maybe my mothers were right.

"Yeah, super healthy. Weight lifter, swimmer, and all. Mom thinks the big shock from almost no exercise on the way here and then so much working out may've led to his heart attack."

That's enough, Rex decided, bothered that he didn't feel sad when talking about losing his dad. Maybe because his dad had always been telling him what to do. At least Rex didn't have to watch his father's lesson videos while he was here. That was one good thing about being away from the colony.

Rex watched the two astronauts in silence. Dad said that silence was the best idea when you wanted to keep a secret. "It keeps your enemy on his toes. So keep your trap shut," Dad had said more than once. He did.

"Got any more of that water?" Dr. Readdy asked.

Rex nodded. He'd brought enough to survive for two weeks, but used very little. "It's in the rover storage closet, ma'am. Get all you need."

"I'll pick up some samples in a minute, Deborah," Admiral Wells said, sitting down beside Rex. "Can you answer some more questions, son? It would help us to help her."

More questions. And I'm not your son.

Rex nodded. He pushed up on his elbows, leaning back against the cool bulkhead of the habitation module, sipping Dr. Readdy's orange drink. "I'm fine, sir. Long as Mom's getting better. Thank you, by the way," he said, extending his free hand toward Dr. Readdy.

She took the grip. "Call me Deborah. Everyone else does," she said with a chuckle.

Rex liked her smile; he trusted her. Her red hair reminded him of one of his mothers.

"So, Rex," Admiral Wells began, "you said your mothers or

whatever didn't call because they wanted to remain 'set apart.' Right?"

Rex shrugged. He'd known this day was coming. He'd pay for breaking The Covenant. "Yes, sir. That's right. They didn't want to call for help, and then they disabled our comms. I'm sure they didn't know I left. At least, not 'til I'd been gone awhile. I haven't spoken to them since."

"How many others are there?" Admiral Wells asked. Dr. Readdy touched the senior astronaut's arm, as though to slow down his inquisition.

"It's okay, Dr. Readdy. I understand why he wants to know." The Admiral's voice had that tone in it, not unlike his father's. It wasn't a demand to be answered so much as the quiet way the Admiral carried himself that commanded respect. Rex couldn't keep this a secret, no matter what The Covenant or his dad said. Admiral Wells and his crew deserved to hear the truth.

Rex shrugged and adjusted his position on the bunk, drawing a long sip on the bottle. "We landed a year ago, sir. A little more than that, actually. Dad planned it that way. He always built one or two more of everything that NASA bought. Habs, labs, rovers, power sources, you name it. He improved the stuff he cared most about and duplicated the rest. Eventually he had an exact copy of everything he needed to get to Mars, for a whole lot less than NASA paid for it." Rex smiled.

He watched the two adults. He'd spent months listening to these people on the radio, imagining what they were like. They seemed more interested in information and stuff than about people.

"Dad always planned to come here. That's why he worked so hard to get those NASA contracts, you know? And here we are." Rex looked away, hiding his lack of emotion. "Except Dad didn't live to see very much of it."

"He duplicated *everything*?" John asked.

"Our hab modules are just like this one. Nicer though. Nothing's white, thank goodness. Our propellant manufacturing system, the nuclear power, our life support, even the food—you name it. Same stuff you have. Only lots cheaper. Pretty smart, huh?"

"What about the rover?" John asked. "It's a different design."

"That was Dad's idea of a long-duration rover. He never liked your 'hot dog on wheels.' We also brought more food—probably better stuff, too. Gonna be here a long time."

"How long?" Deborah asked, taking notes on a digital clipboard. His own digiboard was lots newer.

He paused. *The Covenant.* Their mutual pact to never reveal their colony to outsiders, to maintain the purity of their society and their unique gene pool. His father would whip him again if he heard Rex now.

I'm a traitor. But they're saving Mom. That has to make it okay. He took a deep breath, revealing the first big secret. "We're not leaving, ma'am. Ever."

Rex saw Admiral Wells's jaw drop, his look of surprise a sure sign they'd never suspected.

"Like . . . a colony?" John asked. "How would you get supplies?"

"Dad's company is sending resupply missions. The next one arrives in late May. We've got everything we need, though. And more."

"Food, Rex! What about food? And oxygen?"

He smiled. "We've got gardens, sir. Big ones. Plenty of fresh food. Lots of oxygen. And gobs of water."

"Gobs?" Deborah asked, smiling like she was laughing at him. "Enough to last for years?"

"No, ma'am," Rex said, wondering what she thought funny. "Like, we found it, you know? As much water as we need."

Rex watched their heads rear back in shock. This was fun. The ultimate bragging rights—water, the solar system's most valuable resource.

"We brought a one kilometer drill, same as the one you've got outside. We landed five hundred kilometers east of here, where Dad was convinced we'd find water. Figured it out based on NASA mapping data, that kind of stuff. We hit a strong geothermal source nine hundred meters down. Hot water, loaded with minerals. A hot spring on tap."

The two adults just sat there, their mouths hanging open.

"It's under pressure. Shoots up. We circulate hot water for heat and then filter out the salts. The nuke makes electric power. We break water into hydrogen and oxygen, breathe the oxygen, and make methane with the hydrogen. Methane runs our equipment and powers the rovers. Bingo." He set down the empty bottle, wiping his sleeve across his mouth. "Dad thought of it all. Pretty cool."

Admiral Wells sat shaking his head. "Amazing. All of NASA's best planetary geologists couldn't figure it out, and Rex douses the big one on his first hole. Geothermal to boot." He leaned back on the stool and slapped his thigh, laughing. "We've had sixteen astronauts and two missions on this site for nearly three years. It was NASA's number-one location to find water on this entire planet, except for the poles. And all we've done is pound on dry rock." He chuckled. "You hit the mother lode on your first hole."

"Yep. Except 'mother lode' is a mining term. But that's exactly what we did." A broad smile crossed Rex's face.

"You said you have gardens?" Deborah asked. "And fresh food? How?" She leaned forward.

"Dad sent a cargo mission here loaded with four inflatable domes. The news people thought it was a hab module mission, but Dad lied. We've got twelve hundred square meters under cultivation now. A cargo mission in May is bringing another four domes. It'll double our capacity. The plants scrub the atmosphere. What we don't eat, we feed to the fish."

"Fish?" Admiral Wells exclaimed, shaking his head. "I swear, Edwards thought of it all."

"Uh-huh. Tilapia. They eat all our scraps."

"Anything else?" he asked with a laugh. "Hotels? Casinos?"

"Hotels," Rex replied with a smirk.

"You're kidding, right? It wouldn't surprise me to find a Hilton over there."

"No, sir. But he *did* invent a brick-making machine. Part dozer, part backhoe, and brick former, all in one. Dig the soil, add water, create a slurry, form bricks. The atmosphere dries 'em, and we stack 'em. Into arched vaults, like the Romans used to make. One day, we're gonna move into our hotel."

"Sodbusters, Hawk." Deborah set another orange drink in front of Rex. "His dad took a lesson out of history. Sends a prairie schooner halfway across the solar system, builds homes out of dirt on Mars, and before you know it, a little town springs up. Towns bring commerce, commerce brings development with more commerce, then lots more people, and voila! Demand goes up for more prairie schooners—wagon trains made of spaceships—and lots more work for Delta V Corporation. Even Martian real estate. Except we're not talking Oklahoma or Colorado. Bigger bucks, but the same model." She smiled at Rex, handing the bottle to him. "And I'll bet it works, too."

"It's *already* working, ma'am."

Admiral Wells shook his head, then rubbed his face with both hands.

"What, Hawk?" Deborah asked. "You have that 'I'm about to blow a gasket' look."

"I'm not going to lose it, Deb. It's just that . . . well . . . I envy Rex.

Why envy another mission when I'm the only man in history to come to Mars twice? But . . . well . . . that's the way I feel."

"Envy *me*?" Rex asked, puzzled.

The Admiral chuckled. It was the first time he'd laughed since Rex met him.

"Yes, Rex. You're building something and leaving a legacy. Making a lasting difference. We're exploring here, and that's important. I hope more missions will follow us. But in the final analysis, we're just a bunch of tuna cans on stilts in the middle of the west Texas desert, desperately trying to survive in a bone-dry wilderness."

Rex sipped on his drink, watching Admiral Wells talk with his hands, as he'd heard Navy pilots liked to do. "You know, what we're doing here is like building the Space Station. Once it was up there, and we'd floated around for a few years in the middle of nowhere, and completed the basic science, there was no compelling reason to do any more. The public lost interest. And the Station died. A hundred billion dollars were wasted because the Station was in the wilderness. You had to take up every resource you needed to survive. Just like here at our base. But . . . you guys don't have that problem." Admiral Wells shrugged, then sat forward on his stool again. "You've got water, Rex. And that makes all the difference."

Rex nodded. "That was Dad's plan, sir."

"Look. Call me Hawk. Or John. But no more 'sir' or 'Admiral,' okay?" He stood and extended his hand. "Put 'er there, Rex. You've done what a world of people, including me, only dreamed of. You colonized Mars."

John pulled on the boy's hand, helping him up from the bunk. John was starved. "All this talk about fish and vegetables makes me hungry. Ready for some vittles? They are not fresh, but at least they're healthy."

"Yes, sir. I'm hungry. Is that okay, ma'am?"

"You surely are formal, young man. Someone raised you right. It's 'Deborah,' and yes, you two go get some grub. I'll check on your mom. Hubby's probably wondering where I am anyway. Sam. But you knew that, right? He's with your mom now." Deborah patted Rex on the back as she prepared to leave.

"You got the boss's attention tonight, kiddo. Made him envious. Enjoy your meal. Keep drinking." She gave him another pat and left the compartment.

"She's right, you know," John said to Rex, pointing toward the galley area. "I *am* envious. I'd like to see your place." He led the way to a small table and went to a locker for some food supplies. When he turned around, Rex had stopped at the galley doorway. "You coming?" John asked.

"You can't, sir."

"Can't what? Eat?"

"No, sir. You can't see it. That would violate The Covenant."

John stopped, two cold dinners in hand, watching the boy, this teenager almost a stranger among his fellow humans. "The Covenant?"

"Yes, sir. We pledged to remain apart. We are the Perfect Seed."

"Perfect seed? Like genetic perfection? Raines and the Father Race? That stuff?"

He nodded. "Yes, sir. The same. Once Mom's well, we have to go back. But you can't return with us. Or visit. Ever."

"And what if I say 'no'?" John said as he turned and popped the meals into a microwave. "Let's be realistic, Rex. Your mom nearly died, and we're saving her life. We know you're out there. It's stupid to pretend you simply don't exist." He turned from the oven and motioned to the dinner table. "Sit down. Let's talk about this for a minute, okay?"

Rex hesitated in the doorway. John took a seat and waved him to a chair. "Please, sit. We've got a few minutes to kill." Rex walked over and sat down ramrod straight.

John motioned with his hands. "Something to think about a minute, okay?"

"Yes, sir?"

"You said earlier that this 'covenant,' as you call it, demands that you remain apart, separate from other missions on Mars. Right? A Martian version of the Mayflower Compact."

"Not the compact part. But, yes. To remain apart. Pure."

"Yet when your mom gets sick, you break the covenant. You cross a wilderness no other man has ever conquered, find us without using any navigational aids, and get your mom nursed back to health. If you'd stuck by the covenant, she'd probably be dead, and you'd have lost one sixth of your colony. Busted. But if your covenant says 'remain apart . . . stay pure,' the antithesis says something like 'mix with others . . . depend on your neighbors.' You did just that. You depended on others, and it probably saved your mom's life."

John leaned back, sure he'd upset the boy, but this had to be said. "Your actions are proof of the antithesis, Rex. You depended on the resources you had—a rover with no comms, a map of Mars, and no navigation support. That was a good thing."

He smiled, leaning forward again. "I'm amazed you pulled it off. You're one incredible guy." John stood to tend to the beeping oven and pulled out two steaming trays of pasta primavera. He plopped them down on the table, shoving a set of silverware and dinner toward the boy. "With a head like that, Mr. Edwards, you can have a seat on my team any day."

5

"HER NAME IS ASHERAH. We've been together a long time." Malcolm stroked the old Siamese cat cradled in his arms. "It's an ancient name. From the beginning of recorded history." He knelt to set the cat down. It alighted on three legs and ran away nimbly, one stub dangling where a front leg used to be.

"Asherah?" the wrinkled priest asked. The two walked slowly through a cavernous gothic-style hall under a towering beamed roof. The air was pungent with the smell of paint and varnish.

"Actually, her full name is 'Lady Asherah of the Sea.' The original fertility goddess. Ancient legend says she was the wife of El, the Canaanites's high god. My Asherah lost her leg fighting a ferret. She later birthed a litter of female kittens. And each one bore females—six daughters. At last count more than three hundred offspring—all females." Raines watched the Siamese navigate the slick floor with dexterity. "I admire her. Her story mirrors the Mother Seed, does it not?"

"Yes. Appropriate name." The gray-haired priest tapped a cane on the new hardwood floor and pointed left to the kitchen complex. "I'm impressed by your progress here, Guardian. It will be ready for the Mother Seed soon. Yes?"

"Very soon. All 321 of them. Perfect genetic copies, the original Daughters of Eve. They're developing well. Beyond those walls," he said, pointing to the huge hall's purple and white stained-glass windows, "hundreds of housing units will soon be ready, each apartment ideally suited to the glorious future mission."

The old priest nodded, then sighed. "For thirteen hundred years Saint Michael's Remnant has waited for the vision's culmination, Guardian. It is finally time." He stopped and tugged Malcolm's robe, his bony fingers shaking slightly. "Where is Monique? Is she ill?"

Malcolm jerked his robe from the clutching senior priest of Saint Michael's Remnant and huffed quickly away down the hall. He inhaled the aroma of new construction, the carpet and lumber, and raw sanded wood awaiting sealer. He hungered for his massive project's completion, tangible proof of his mission's coming fruition.

"Guardian?" came a warbling voice behind him. "Forgive me. Have I offended you?"

Malcolm flipped up a hand and strode out of the hall, leaving the feeble old master standing alone with a three-legged cat at his feet.

Two invalids, he thought, heading to the residence hall to check on construction progress. *An appropriate pair.*

Here he comes.

Monique braced for confrontation. This had been the first day in eight years when she hadn't shadowed his every move.

For eight years, Monique had trembled with desire every time she saw his towering frame approaching. The giant man in bright purple stood head and shoulders above the staff. A Spanish maid had once nicknamed him "Morado Grande," and Malcolm had liked the name. It sounded powerful. He never realized it meant "Big Purple." No one dared tell him.

As he stalked the hall toward her, the white clerical collar silhouetted above flowing robes against his dark brown throat made his head appear disembodied. Under those robes coursed hard muscles that had held her for nearly three thousand nights, muscles she'd seen break a man. Ham-sized chocolate hands and thick arms that snapped the neck of the only assailant who'd ever threatened them during their nightly walks in Trieste. Hands that could break her, too, if she strayed. She didn't intend to give him that chance.

His swaggering inspection of the new facility revolted her. She'd caressed that tall form for years, adoring his power and mystique. She'd been his constant companion, defender, and business assistant. *Why didn't I see it sooner?* she wondered. *He wants them all. Every girl.*

Malcolm was five rooms away. She put on her subservient face, bowing as he approached. Steeling herself, she reached out and took his hand. Her plan, finalized last night away from his side, would only work if she appeared contrite.

"Monique?"

"Yes, Father?"

"I need to know why you've not been yourself."

She looked at the floor, betting her success on her next words. A ruse she'd practiced for hours. It had to work. She looked up, meeting his eyes as she caressed his face.

"Please forgive me, Master. I strayed. I was—I *am*—envious. This facility has your complete attention. The Mother Seed occupies your many hours. Your focus on them takes you away from me." That was the sordid truth. She hadn't lied.

She nestled her head between his arm and chest, snuggling her face into his velvet robe, fighting her stomach's revolt.

"I've disgraced myself, and you, in my poor service," she said. "I want you all for myself." She looked up into his eyes. "Please, my Nephilim. Forgive me."

Moments seemed like hours. His hand was on her head, stroking the long black ponytail. A sure sign he'd accepted her contrition.

Now the great balancing would begin. Comply and submit, without losing her self-respect, until she could make her move. Whenever that was.

Monique breathed deeply and faked another smile. "Come, Father. See our progress." Before Malcolm could object, she pulled him into a suite, already labeled with a girl's name on the door, "Valerie," and a number, "217."

"See, Guardian? Preparations are complete. All three residence halls are ready for the Mother Seed. One hundred thirty-two apartments in each, for the girls and staff. I inspected all three floors of each building in the past twenty hours."

She led him quickly through the unit, before he could change his focus to her.

"Kitchens and dens are ready for each girl. Night suites," she continued, pulling him a few meters from the kitchenette to a modestly decorated and furnished room, but staying clear of the bed, "appointed as you specified. With access to learning tools and our internal data network. And here," she said, pushing open a door to a small adjoining room with a tiny crib. "Nurseries. In every apartment. For the Mother Seed and their Glorious Mission."

She took his hand, putting on her best act. Her life, and the welfare of hundreds of other girls, depended on her ability to regain his confidence.

"We're ready to receive the Mother Seed, Guardian. I trust you are pleased?"

MARS

Deborah Readdy watched May Randall's eyelids flutter, a sure sign the medication and hydration were working. She'd dripped nearly six liters of fluid into her patient, monitoring renal function and blood sugar. She pressed May's hands in her own, praying. She would come around. God would provide.

The woman opened her eyes, trying to fix her location in the dim light. "Dr. Readdy?" Her voice was weak, scratchy . . . and slurred. She didn't seem able to look at Deborah for more than a passing glance.

Deborah released her hand, recoiling involuntarily. "You know my name?"

May smiled slightly, trying to nod from the bed. "I think so. I mean, uh-huh. Is Rex safe?"

"Yes. He's asleep. Upstairs." Deborah nodded toward the hatch leading to the stairs. "John's watching over him."

"Admiral John? I mean, Wells?"

"The same. You really *do* know about us, don't you?"

"I guess I do. It's hazy." Her eyes continued to dart about the compartment.

Deborah checked May's blood pressure and released the cuff. "How do you feel?"

May touched her head. "Headache. Mouth dry." She wrinkled her face, a puzzled look like she was unsure what she'd said. "You . . . understand?"

May's eyes closed. She drifted off to sleep without another word.

MONDAY, FEBRUARY 24, 2020: MARS

"Flat affect. Inability to maintain eye contact. Slurred speech. Neurologic symptoms." Deborah pulled up some medical diagnosis pages on her terminal, pointing out symptoms to John as she surfed through the database. "She's in and out of it throughout the day. Deep fatigue. That was the last clue."

"And you checked her water?" John asked, tossing a bottle of the stuff at Dr. Sam Readdy, who'd joined them at the table.

"I checked it," Sam said. "Tastes pretty good, by the way. Beats that stuff in our water tanks, I'll say that much. But if I were bipolar, I'd be sucking it down by the gallon."

"Meaning?" John asked. His unibrow was wrinkled with that "I-don't-understand" look.

"Meaning it's loaded with lithium," Sam responded. "Super high concentrations. Every one of their people is probably zoned out, or leveled out if they have any disorders. Never seen a toxicity case like this one. May nearly died."

"She poisoned herself on the water, Hawk. That's why, when we got her on fluids, she started coming around." Deborah tapped on the computer screen.

John shook his head. The diagnosis could have taken weeks without those water samples.

"What's next?"

"Time, Hawk. Let her body flush the bad stuff, and she'll come around. Get to know Rex. You have plenty of opportunities before she can go anywhere." She waved toward Sam and the bottle. "And get a call through to Rex's mothers, or whatever we call them. They need to know about their water supply. It could kill them."

THURSDAY, FEBRUARY 27, 2020: MARS

"What happened to me?" May asked as she pushed back her corkscrew locks.

"Your blood sugar was very high. You were dehydrated, and the first thing that came to mind was hyperosmolar hyperglycemic nonketotic coma. But Rex said you didn't have diabetes. Yet you had the severe dehydration, and all the global neurological defects."

"I do *not* have that, Dr. Readdy. I'm certain there's no adult-onset diabetes. I checked that, when I still could."

"Agreed. Rex said you were vomiting before you left. And he pushed you to drink water?"

She nodded.

"So, I tested the water. I think we found your problem, but first a couple more questions. Were you on any drugs for high blood pressure? Enalapril? Lisinopril?"

"Yes. Lisinopril. But it wasn't doing the trick for my blood pressure, so I added hydrochlorothiazide. Is my blood pressure still high?"

"It wasn't when you were dehydrated six liters. But your meds validate my diagnosis."

"What diagnosis? Did you find the cause?"

"Certainly not diabetes, doctor. You were drinking yourself to death. On water loaded with lithium. The ACE inhibitors and the diuretic forced your kidneys to concentrate the lithium in your blood, and you suffered a severe bout of lithium toxicity. The lithium poisoning and the electrolyte and fluid imbalances led to confusion, and eventually tremors. Symptoms you experienced, correct?"

May nodded. "Yes. It started about two weeks after I increased the dose on the ACE inhibitor and added the diuretic."

"Then nausea and a metallic taste in your mouth, followed by discoloration of your fingers and toes?"

She nodded again. "I was taking some Aleve, too. For a strained back."

"Golly, May. You hit a grand slam. Your meds might have been fine if you hadn't been pounding down 'lithium on the rocks.' When you got nauseous, Rex convinced you to keep hydrating, and he forced you to take your blood pressure pills. He meant well, but he was pumping you full of a deadly combo of meds and minerals. When you got here, we stopped the pills and put you on IV fluids—and good water. Your body eventually took care of itself."

"We have to tell them!" May tried to rise out of the bed, then collapsed. "Tell them about the lithium!"

"We did. It's okay. They know now. Do you drink the groundwater raw?"

"No. We filter. Osmosis. That must not have worked, though."

"No problem. John says that's an easy fix. He can repair anything. If anyone on your team's bipolar or depressed, by the way, they'll be lovin' that stuff. But everyone reacts differently. Worst case, you might see a slow shuffling walk or lack of emotional expression. Maybe restlessness, or jerky face movements. Rex seems to be fine, though." Deborah paused. "He said your other crewmembers didn't want him to bring you to see us. Why is that?"

May smiled again. "I don't remember much of my last days there, but I do recall he insisted I come. I didn't want to at first." She coughed, reaching for a napkin on the tray.

"So he said. Something about a covenant."

"Yes. The Covenant. To remain apart. To be pure."

"Apart from what? Are we contaminating you? I'd sure like to know, because you're the only sick person I've seen in a year." She was tired of this Father Race heresy. Now she'd have to hear it all over again.

May took the doctor's hand. "No. You aren't a contamination, Deborah. We simply want to accomplish our mission free of external stimuli."

"You blew that. Seems to me you needed some doctor support."

"I *am* the doctor. But I couldn't heal myself." She shook her head, setting the napkin aside. "It wasn't something four obstetricians could sort out, I guess."

"Appears so."

"You probably wonder why. Four OBs, that is."

Deborah turned away, sure her effort to keep a straight face didn't cover her smirk. "I have my theories, May. But it's probably none of my business. My mission is to make you well." She turned around, handing her a cup. "Would you like some water?" she asked with a chuckle. "Without the lithium?"

"Please."

Deborah handed her the drink, unable to resist any longer. "Okay. I do wonder—"

"Yes?"

"OBs on Mars? Why not send an internist, for crying out loud? But obstetricians?" She threw her hands up. "I'm at a loss."

"A colony, Deborah. Here on Mars. We're missionaries of the

Father Race."

Deborah shook her head. "I'm sorry, but I don't buy that stuff."

"Forming a colony? Or furthering the kingdom of the Father Race?"

"Both. The Father Race tripe riles me the most. I thought we left those lies on Earth with Malcolm Raines."

"They're not lies. He's our Oracle. The Guardian of the Mother Seed. And he's right, you know."

"Look, May. Dr. Randall. Rex's mom. Forget the Father Race stuff a minute. You can appreciate my professional skepticism as a fellow doctor. I've been on this rock for over a year. A colony has no chance here. We've proven that."

"And we've proven just the opposite. We're succeeding. Hasn't Rex told you?"

"He and John spoke last night." She'd heard it all, but hoped May would answer the one question that John never asked.

"Mars isn't dry, Deborah. We have water, geothermal heat, and growing plants. We've built structures and grown fish. We came here to start a new life, and colonization includes reproduction. That's why I joined Rex's team."

Deborah's jaw dropped. May's serious. *They mean to stay here. And have babies.*

"Reproduce? I mean, except for your son, you're short a man." She hesitated. "You know what I mean."

May smiled. "Yes. I do. That was Rex Sr.'s role. Perhaps one day it can also be my son's. But for now we have the Seed. We're prepared."

Deborah stood over her, unsure she was hearing this. *They brought seed? A donor bank? Or stranger yet, embryos? Are they crazy?*

She swallowed a dozen retorts. "Let's get you ready for Rex's visit. He'll want to know you're awake."

May was quiet for a long while as Deborah worked on her, removing IVs, cleaning off tape residue, and helping the tall woman freshen up. Deborah was glad for the interlude.

"I'd like to say one more thing," May finally said. "I suspect you don't agree with us, but this is important."

Deborah met May's eyes. "Yes?"

"Rex violated our Covenant, to remain apart. But he did it to save my life. I'm indebted to him for his bravery. And his initiative."

"He was brave, all right. Five hundred kilometers of hostile planet brave."

"When his father died, we felt that any contact with you or others would compromise our mission—would compromise our belief in our mission and in him. We disabled the rover's communication system for just this contingency—in case someone would attempt contact with you, or try to run for help."

"And good thing he did. Run, I mean. You'd be dead otherwise. You realize that, right?"

"I do. And I don't fault my son."

Deborah studied May a long while, her dark arms and her face. She wanted to voice the question tugging at her, but was afraid to hear the answer.

"In answer to your unspoken question, Deborah, I am his mother."

"I wasn't—" Her face flushed.

"Yes. You were. And it's a valid question. You and I are both doctors. No secrets, agreed?" She grasped Deborah's hand.

"I was a surrogate mother for Rex and for his sister. His father paid me handsomely, and from that relationship arose a deeper appreciation of our mutual interest in this mission. I raised the children that Rex Sr. was too busy for, children I'd always wanted but never had because I was too preoccupied with my profession. It was the best of both worlds. I was the well-paid mother and mentor to Rex and his sister. And I got the chance of a lifetime to be part of this historic mission. To colonize Mars. A mission that has required huge sacrifices from all of us." She looked away, coughing.

Deborah shook her head. "Well, that explains it." She touched May's arm. "Sorry I asked."

May's lips curled into a gentle smile, her brown eyes wet. "Don't apologize." She wiped her eyes with the back of her hand. "We're here to establish a colony on Mars, and it's working. Part of our mission naturally includes having children. A mission—thank you—that you've enabled us to continue."

"Maybe. But better not try 'til we fix that water filter," Deborah said with emphasis. "You try to have babies while drinking that stuff, and you're asking for trouble. Lithium's bad news for pregnancy."

A look of shock spread across May's face. She nodded slowly. "Congenital defects. Heart valve abnormalities."

Deborah raised an eyebrow. "Not a great way to start a Father Race." She handed May another cup of water and a napkin. "Be glad we found you, Dr. Randall. If we hadn't diagnosed that water problem, your baby mission would have been a bust for sure."

6

"I DON'T MISS MY MENTORS at all," Judith said, wrapping her long black ponytail into a bun, then letting it fall free. "Life's much easier here."

Sonya thought her roommate's obsession with her long hair a bit odd. The girl had been gathering, twirling, and releasing it for the past hour. Saturday was their day of rest, and they usually spent the first half in bed.

"Video games. That's what I miss," Celeste chimed in, jumping from her top bunk. "Television. And movies. Sometimes, this is so-ooh boring." She pointed at Sonya. "D'you have any games? Your dad was rich."

Sonya smiled. "Yes, but we never played with them. We were outside whenever Mom wasn't teaching us lessons."

"Yeah. I remember," Judith interrupted. "Home schooled, sand everywhere, and a wicked tan." She winked at her roomies, then pulled her hair into a bun again.

Sonya sighed. Judith wouldn't survive beach life with her precious makeup and aversion to sweat. But she'd worship the tan that Sonya and her leathery brown brother had sported during their years in the Pacific. Sonya wondered if she remembered her life then as she wanted to, or as it really was. Life as a nine-year-old seemed so long ago. Before puberty, before Italy. Before this place.

Kristen, the silent one, spoke. "We had games. And beaches. And brothers . . . but I don't miss the boys. It's safer here."

Kristen loved this place. She called it her safe house. "No men, thank goodness, except Father Raines," she'd once said. Sonya had heard enough from some of her other sisters' secret stories to know what Kristen meant. She was glad she'd never walked the path of pain this sister had. Sonya reached over the side, dangling her hand for her friend to grasp. The two connected. They were the closest of companions.

"Does it bother you?" Kristen had asked a few months ago when they were alone together.

"Bother me?" Sonya asked. "What?"

"To be his vessel. You know what he plans to do, right?" Kristen's voice squeaked like she was about to cry. She'd made a face like a cornered pet had once long ago. Wide-eyed and desperate, with nowhere to turn.

"Yes, I know." Sonya hesitated. It was hard to voice the truth. "We'll be moms."

Neither girl had spoken for half an hour after that talk months ago. Her arm dangling over the bunk rail, she squeezed Kristen's hand. Remembering her closest sister's pain that day, Sonya wondered how Judith and the other girls could feel such glee about what was planned for them. Other than she and Kristen, her sisters were all fawning over

Malcolm Raines and their glorious role in the future of the Father Race.

An hour later, her sisters chattering on, Sonya felt a question burning a hole inside her. She had to ask them about her dream. Judith and Celeste were probably too shallow to help her figure it out. But Kristen might understand.

"Did you ever imagine what it might be like to drown in a tar pit?"

Judith laughed. She was a vapor head, just like her bunkmate.

"Tar pit?" Kristen asked, her voice high and scratchy.

"You know. Like the dinosaurs sank into," Sonya said. "Thick black stuff, with sticky bubbles rising up through it in slow motion. You can't swim in it."

"Like quicksand?" Kristen squeaked.

"Yes. But tar. Much worse."

"Why tar?" Celeste asked, genuinely interested. Maybe there was hope for her yet.

"This place is tar," Sonya muttered. "This life. I feel like I'm in a tar pit up to my neck. Something dark and sticky's trying to drag me down. To suffocate me. I dream about it all the time."

She squeezed Kristen's shaking hand. Her sisters on the far bunk had blank expressions on their faces. They clearly didn't get it. Sonya wasn't surprised.

"Do you ever drown?" Kristen asked softly. Sonya peered down at tears welling in her dear friend's eyes. She felt a twinge of guilt for scaring her. But Sonya had to know. *Am I the only one who feels this way?*

"No, I never drown," Sonya responded. "There's always a bright light just before I wake up. I'm sinking, and I close my eyes as my head goes under. Everything goes black, and I can't breathe any more. The tar has arms and hands that grab at me. It pulls me deeper, forcing something over my face. Then, next thing I know, a bright light wakes me up. I've been pulled free and, somehow, I wake up clean."

A knock on the door startled them all. Sonya released Kristen's hand.

"Free time," said a large matronly woman, her English heavily accented with a native Tuscan dialect. She caught Sonya's gaze, smiled, then tossed a tied package of towels and sheets into the room. *"Bambini! Andiamo a mangiare!"*

Time to make their beds and go eat. Sonya would talk to Kristen about her dream later.

A hairy mole dotted the edge of the heavy woman's big smile. "Meester Guardian, he gone! Pizza now! You come!"

MARS

"I'm sorry."

"For what?! You saved my life, Rex," May said. "You went against the grain—like your dad—just to save me. Please don't apologize, son."

"I broke The Covenant, Mom. We'll be news in every home on Earth."

"That's not the end of the world," May said, resting in the lab module's hospital bed. Her right hand covered Rex's; her left stroked his smooth face. He'd have to shave soon; her treasured son was becoming a man, and he would draw apart. It was the way.

"Your dad gave us The Covenant, Rex. But he also trusted us to use our heads. You did the right thing." May squeezed his hand. "Thank you."

Rex nodded, and May turned to the eight astronauts around her conferring about the next step. She smiled at Dr. Readdy. "Thank you,

Deborah. I hope I can repay the debt one day."

Deborah shrugged and smiled. "Keep that pack of colonists alive and well. That'll be thanks enough."

"Which begs the question," John began, "of when we're going to get you back home. Rex and I contacted the colony. They finally answered our calls after we broke the news to NASA. They don't like the exposure."

"No," May said, looking away. She couldn't pretend to smile any longer. *Rex is right. They'll hate me back home.* "Maybe we're all better off though, right? At least, I know I am."

"They want us to come back right away, Mom." Rex looked at Deborah. "When can she travel?"

"A few days. I'm more worried about getting her home safely than when she leaves," Deborah replied. "I'd like to go with her. Make sure she has no relapses."

John shook his head.

"What's that supposed to mean?" Deborah asked. "We're not going with her? Or 'I'm not sure'?"

"Not sure. I agree, it's dangerous to send Rex alone with his mom before she's fully recovered. But NASA's given me some strict guidance. This just got more complex."

Rex released May's hand. "What guidance, sir?"

"I'm supposed to escort you. All the way."

"I got here alone. We'll find our way home," Rex said.

May pressed his hand.

"I don't doubt you can do it, Rex," John said. "But now that we know the colony's there, we *all* have a responsibility . . . and a *desire* . . . to get you back safely."

"It's not my mom you care about. You just want to see what we've got."

"Is visiting your colony so bad?" Jake asked, his eyes locked on May. "We're in this together, Rex, so why don't we help each other out?"

"We can't!" Rex protested. "The Covenant says—"

"Enough, Rex," Geo exclaimed, the crew's vocal skeptic. Deborah had whispered about him frequently. His voice grated on May. "You broke that precious covenant thing to get here in the first place. Question now is, what're we gonna do with you? Throw you back into the wilderness or walk you home?"

"Enough, Geo," Melanie said. "We know where you stand."

"Good, no surprise if I repeat myself then," Geo said, jutting out his jaw.

"She said zip it!" John blurted. "NASA says 'go,' so we'll go. *When* we go is up to Deborah and May. You don't have to accept our escort—but we're going. When we're close to your place, and if you're feeling fine with no complications, maybe then we'll split if you ask us to. Fair?"

"You'd drive five hundred kilometers and stop before you got there?" Witt protested. "You can't be serious!"

"If he said it . . . he is," Melanie interrupted, glaring at the geologist. "And my word will always mirror his. Bet on it."

John nodded toward Melanie, then touched the sheet over May's foot. "We'll go when you're ready, May. Your decision. Can you lead us back, Rex?"

Rex looked at his mom, then at Dr. Readdy, then at his mom. She nodded and smiled. He grinned and turned toward John. "Yes, sir. I can. I'll tell my mothers."

"Then that settles it," Jake said, moving toward the bed. He patted May's shoulder. "Rest up, little lady. We're going on a road trip."

"Move the Mother Seed," Malcolm said. "It is time." Monique stood next to him, staring out the window of their tower high above the prisoners.

The snowmelt had started. She'd already seen the woman and her child on their knees in the wet slush early that morning as the church bells rang. Every Sunday they'd crouched in the same corner, listening. Heads down, like they were praying, while Malcolm snored late into the day. She'd risen early this morning, slipping out from under his grasp to watch them. When the bells ended, they'd retreated into the stone cottage at the tower's base. Now they were out for their morning walk. Malcolm watched, dispassionate.

Monique couldn't bear standing next to him. The image of the two below had seared itself in her mind since last week. Like a siren in her dreams, they called out to her, begging her to release them. Monique wouldn't have given the two a second thought even a few weeks ago.

She hugged herself, aching to be free. Every mention by Malcolm of the girls in Trieste was a caustic reminder of their private images on his data terminal. Pulled, no doubt, from his micro-miniature security cameras placed everywhere within the Trieste compound.

Monique moved away from him ever so slightly, yearning to be anywhere other than here. She felt as if her life had slammed into a dead end, seeing Malcolm for what he was, reflected in the mirror of his own lust. She was simply an instrument of his gratification. *But for how long?*

Monique had begun to question her faith in the Unknowable God. All this laboring for years for fulfillment. And for what? Did she have it, after all? *Does anything I've done for the Father Race count?* She closed her eyes and tried to listen, deep inside her consciousness, where Malcolm promised she'd find godlike insights. The silence mocked her.

Monique wondered too if he really believed what he preached, or if she was simply a mandatory adoring audience helping him to accept his own lies. She yearned to explore life, to find that happy spirit promising a better life, the hope she'd known as a child, before the orphanage. She felt chained to him instead.

"The Seed of Man is on Mars," he began, stroking his velvet robe and turning from the window toward her. "The timing of the Father Race is perfect. We can proceed."

Monique gritted her teeth. "The girls are prepared to move here, my Raksasa, where we can offer them a more permanent home than Trieste. They await only your command." She sighed, sad for so many young women who had no idea what they were facing.

"And so it shall be," he said, lifting his hand straight up in a palm-out greeting, arm extended, that had become his latest fetish. "Let it begin today." He gestured out the window. "Soon, it will be time for the Harvest. Very soon."

Monique rechecked the video controls, confirming that her boss was in his palatial Guardian's conference room two floors below. She left the security control panel at the far end of their bedroom and returned to the window to watch for the figures in the garden. She wanted one last glimpse today, before she and Malcolm returned to Trieste.

The Master of the Remnant had returned to confer with Malcolm on some pressing issue of funds for their worship center on Mont Saint Michel. *Life's all about money,* she mused. Funds flowing in from all over the globe, from seekers who wanted to be part of the Father Race, sending their DNA samples, pictures, resumes, and biographies to make sure their "seed," as Malcolm called it, was headed to the stars.

Monique knew better. Malcolm had all the "seed" he could use. One hundred million donated DNA samples later, there was no time to look for more candidates. The hopeful didn't know that, and Malcolm didn't bother to tell them. Hundreds of thousands of samples flowed in monthly to Malcolm's DNA laboratories in China, accompanied by the ten-thousand-dollar deposit each person submitted for the evaluation of his or her genetic profile, establishing an Individual Father Race Family History. The complex document purported to weave each person's story back to prehistory and, many hoped, to the Nephilim or to Eve.

"Genetic imperfection." Monique pondered the phrase as she hung in the open window's cold breeze. No more Nazi-like breeding out of undesirable characteristics. Malcolm's Chinese scientists could read DNA like a book. It was simply a matter of finding a person with perfect DNA—no defective genes representing the tens of thousands of potential diseases and physical failings Malcolm classified as "impure."

That was another reason she'd begun to question his intentions, lofty goals she'd embraced as her own, but now knew had been a cover. The perfect "seed" simply didn't exist. There were no perfect DNA samples in the hundred million or more they'd analyzed. Imperfection, it seemed, was normal. Now that she knew, and remained silent, she was a prisoner in Malcolm's web of deceit. A legal avenue of escape no longer existed.

Despite the truth, Malcolm claimed they'd found two. One sample came from a tall well-educated, athletic man, a sure descendant of the Nephilim, he'd said. He kept the man's identity a secret, even from Monique, to "preserve him." Malcolm proclaimed they had a second perfect sample from an influential dark-haired woman of Mediterranean complexion. "We have found the seed of the Nephilim and their Mother," she'd heard him say. "Soon we will join them together in a rebirth of the original Father Race."

If that's so, Monique thought, turning the lies over in her mind, *then I must be that Eve.*

Below, two figures moved into the slushy courtyard on their daily walk. She forgot Malcolm, imagining the feel of the muddy water-ice squishing around their shoes. They walked hand in hand, talking. She longed in that moment to be the teenager in the hand of the woman below.

Suddenly she realized they were peering up at her, hands shading their eyes. Malcolm would slaughter her for this indiscretion if he caught her. Struggling not to run, she forced him out of her mind, extended a hand, and waved.

A woman of medium height looked up and raised her hand in a simple wave, her long braided brown hair falling over her shoulders. The girl enthusiastically jumped up and down, yelling. "Mom! She sees us!"

Monique wept. This was her fault. They'd been there six years, and she'd never even considered them worthy of a gesture. Yet somehow, in this moment, all that changed. She leaned into the cold air and started swinging her arm, her other hand stifling her sobs. The girl waved with both arms, then clutched the woman she called "Mom."

"Look!" Monique heard her exclaim. "She's waving! Will we get to leave?"

Monique fell back from the window, pierced by the words.

Will we get to leave?

Her chest heaved with hard coughs, fits of tears, and anger. Surely she had it in her power to help them. But Malcolm could never know.

7

"THIS ISN'T A DEMOCRACY, Geo. You're on Melanie's team. So you stay." John slammed his fist on the dining table, sending two cups flying, laden with dregs. The four crew all jumped as the cups leapt off the table: Melanie Knox, Sam Readdy, Robert Witt, and Melanie's fourth member, astrophysicist Dr. Ramona Ramirez—flight call sign "R2."

"If anyone has a right to go with us," John continued, "it's Mel. She always gets stuck here."

"We're the safety backup, Geo. You know that," Melanie huffed. "At least we'll lift off if there's an emergency. Beats getting stuck on Mars."

"That's not the issue, Mel, and you know it," Geo said. "I'm a geologist. I *need* to go. You're crossing geography I *must* see." He leaned over the table, waving his hands.

"And you're *not* going, Geo. Get that through your head." John stood and zipped up his jacket against the chill in the room as the Mars temperature plummeted to 220 degrees below zero outside their habitat's skin.

"I'm taking the Blue Team. Gold Team stays here. Sam, you're the backup doc. Melanie, if we need rescue, for whatever reason, you have the Mission 2 rover. Send two crew members, keep two back. If that fails—no more rescues." John surveyed the room: three astronauts who had nothing to say, and another itching to tangle. Then he stalked out, glancing at the sulking forty-five-year-old adolescent, one of his key scientists.

Geo sank into a chair in his usual pouting slump. His droopy, wide-set eyes and big-beaked nose reminded John of a pelican. Had John known about the man's latent tendencies to complain and disrupt, he'd have booted Geo the first day he saw him on the mission list. Geo wasn't the first astronaut to change stripes once he left Earth. There were plenty of horror stories from Shuttle, MIR, and Space Station days to match Geo's. John would be free of him in a few months anyway and would relegate the whiner to arcane science duties during their four-month return trip.

Melanie caught up with John as he entered Hab One. "Got a minute?" she called.

John smiled. Geo had run him off again. *It's easier to walk out than to deal with the twerp. But I need to pray for him, not avoid him.* "Yeah. Sorry, Mel. Let's go to the galley."

A minute later, the two sat across from each other at a small table, packets of cold juice in hand. "Have you thought about the impact if they *do* let you into the colony?" she asked.

He nodded, sipping on the juice in silence.

"Okay. You didn't get that hint, so I'll be more blunt. Have you seen the way Jake looks at May Randall?"

"Rex's mom? No. Why?"

"Come on, John. Open your eyes. You have two single men on your team. You cowboys don't talk about guy stuff?"

"Nope. Just business. Amps and kilometers and space tools. That's about it." He grinned ear to ear. "Girls any different?"

Melanie smirked. "Sure. We sit around here knitting while we wait for you stallions to ride home. You know the drill."

"Good. I need a new horse blanket."

"So, have you noticed? Jake's crazy about her. No idea why . . . but you're headed to a colony where there are single women. Four of them." She looked at him with a weird sort of "finish my story" stare, and then threw her hands up in exasperation. "Don't you understand why Geo is so bent on going?"

John flushed. He understood—but he'd never admit it.

Melanie shook her head, smiling. "You're such a boy scout."

"Nope. Didn't have a Scout troop where I grew up. But I hear what you're saying."

"Good. So don't hold it against Geo. He just wants his fair chance."

"That's a laugh," John said, and regretted that too. He had to learn to curb his tongue, particularly with regard to Dr. Witt. "For the record, I spoke to Jake. Says he's attracted to her. And yes, I've considered the impact of wanderlust setting in when we get over there. I'm most concerned about the impact we'll have on Rex and May after we leave—if they let us visit. Those other women might hold our visit against them. No way we'd ever know."

Melanie sipped on her drink, slurping the last and wadding up the metal foil. "You like the kid, don't you?"

John nodded.

"He'd be what, Alice's age?" she said softly.

John nodded again, lowering his head, blinking rapidly. He didn't try to hide his feelings any more. Especially from Mel. The scar would be tender 'til he died, and he'd decided to be open about it. "Yeah, she'd be almost fifteen," he said. "Know what's weird?"

She shook her head as she watched and listened. Mel had a great ear.

"Sometimes I just want to hug Rex, you know? Like I might connect with my own son." He wiped his jacket sleeve across his face, sniffling.

"The other night, it was like he was reaching out. Told me about his dad, how little they related or spent time together. It's crazy. Rex Sr. had a lifetime to spend with his kid and didn't want to. I lost my kids early and couldn't." John stood and began to pace. "Confession time," he said at last to Melanie, turning toward her. "This stays with you. Got it?"

She nodded again. John knew she'd keep a secret. He'd shared many with his second in command these past years since they'd both been named to the crew.

"Given a chance, Melanie, I'd opt to stay."

"You'd *what*?" she asked, her voice rising. She came out of her chair.

"You asked if I'd thought about the impact of mixing my mustangs with their mares. Well, I have. But I've also pondered something else. What's waiting for me back on Earth, Mel? My family's dead. I've done all the astronautics I can hope to do in a lifetime. My parents probably won't live much longer."

John took a deep breath, trying to hold in a pain that screamed for release. "Other than my parents, there's no one there for me, Mel. So why not just stay here?" He looked away.

Melanie sat down, leaning back in her chair and crossing her arms. "You can't talk like that, Hawk. I might start to believe you."

He looked up, tears visible. "Believe me, Mel. That's how I feel. And there's a boy out there," he said, pointing toward the other hab module, "a boy needing a dad. Maybe—maybe that's where I'm called, you know? To stay on Mars, to mentor him, help him feel like he's got someone to point him in the right direction. After all," John said, with a chuckle and a sniffle mixing together, "can you imagine how difficult it will be for him growing up around four women?"

Melanie tossed her wadded foil pouch at him. He dodged the bullet. "Could be lots worse," she said. "He could grow up without *any* women."

John smiled and wiped his face. "True. You understand what I'm saying, though?"

Her head moved up and down in that soft way she managed when seeing past his "I'm in charge" attitude. "Yes. And given the chance, no strings holding me back, I'd want to do the same thing." She walked across the compartment to pick up the wadded foil. "Did you talk about it with Rex?"

John shrugged. "No. But," he began, "I wanted you to know I was at least considering it. So, if I seem a little short with bozos like Geo, it's because I have a lot on my mind. Staying on Mars is a permanent decision. I don't have much patience for people who are only thinking of themselves."

Melanie stood quietly a long time on the other side of the galley. She sighed, and then spoke in her soft tone.

"Be careful, Hawk. You might need to listen to what you're saying. Life's not over for you on Earth. Don't assume the only future you have is on the fourth rock from the sun. And," she said, moving toward the hatch, "you need to know you're not alone. If I was a betting woman—and I'm not—I'd say half our crew would stay here, given the chance. I hear stuff you never notice. Think about that before you go making any life-changing decisions."

FRIDAY, MARCH 6, 2020:
MARS

"Childbirth isn't trivial, John. They're crazy." Deborah huffed loudly, a sure sign of her exasperation.

The MSR bounced over rocky terrain as John, Oz, Jake, and Deborah followed Rex's rover on the first day of their five-day transit toward the colony. Driving the MSR was like riding in a Range Rover with busted shock absorbers through the headwaters of Grand Canyon National Park. Boulders and plateaus flanked rust-red rivulets that grew into gullies, pouring eventually into deep gorges—all of them dry as a rice cake. Every step of the trek required constant vigilance, ensuring the path wouldn't dead end at a cliff. This was a water-worn maze on a bone-dry planet, yet Rex seemed to have it all figured out up ahead of them.

Oz dodged rocks and navigated in Rex's dusty tracks while the rest of the team talked about the past two weeks—weeks filled with remarkable revelations about the planet and about their unknown neighbors riding in the rover just ahead.

"They brought OBs so they could have babies. Why else?" Jake remarked. "And May's a good one. Went to med school at Georgetown. Residency in southern California. That's where she met the Rex man."

"Yeah. I know," Deborah said. "I checked it out too. May really *was* the surrogate birth mother for two children. She ran a small OB practice until she did the surrogate mom thing. The report I found called it 'a serious breach of professional ethics.' The state medical board jerked her license. She dropped off the radar and probably hooked up with Rex."

"Why can you do nearly anything in California and call it progressive, but you want to have a baby and they kick you out of business?" Jake wondered, his frown deepening. "It's stupid. She's a baby doc, right? Anyway, she told me her side of the story—he paid her to be a surrogate mom, employed her as a nanny for his kids and as a doctor for his staff. The change was for the best. It got her *here*. And she's good."

"What would you know?" Oz asked as he drove. "You've never used an OB. Maybe a gynecologist though," he said with a grin.

"Shut up and drive," Jake said.

"They came here full of resolve," John said, watching his crew. The four would be cooped up in the MSR for the next ten days or more, and he needed everyone to be honest about their concerns. Five hundred kilometers to the colony and another five hundred back, at one hundred clicks a day. It would be a long week and a half. Or more, if Rex and May assented to let them visit. He prayed silently again for that opportunity.

"They intend to have babies, guys. Get it?" Deborah said, her displeasure more apparent by the moment. "But whose?"

"Anyone bother to ask Rex or May?" Oz asked, turning around in the seat. "Pretty important detail."

John shrugged. This was the first time he'd heard the issue verbalized. But it had been on all their minds.

"No," Deborah said, looking out the window. "But I just remembered something."

"What?"

"You know how May was so confident when she talked about their mission, to bring the Father Race to Mars?" Deborah asked. "Like she didn't even miss Rex?"

"Don't keep us in our seats, Doc," Oz chimed in.

"*Edge* of our seats, you idiot." Jake punched the back of Oz's seat.

"Come on, you two." Deborah turned away from the window. "May told me they brought the Seed of the Father Race with them. So, maybe that's just what they did."

John saw the surprise on Jake's face. He felt the same way. Confused.

Deborah laughed. "Okay. I'll spell it out for you. In vitro fertilization and implantation. The same process May used to get pregnant. It's a complex procedure, but it's well understood. Four women and a bank of prescreened embryos. Genetic preselection. Four highly trained surrogate mothers come to Mars to birth a Father Race of children that represent the best and brightest that Rex could bring with him. Maybe," she said, her voice drifting off again, "maybe that colony's not a chicken ranch at all."

Oz spoke up in the silence. "I've seen this movie," he said as he drove. "You have, too."

Deborah shook her head. "And that was?"

"*Alien*. All about a spaceship full of babies just waiting to hatch."

SATURDAY, MARCH 7, 2020: NAZARJE, SLOVENIA

Eight long buses trundled along a two-lane road weaving through the central Slovenian countryside. In her seat at the front of the first bus, Monique plastered her face to the window, treasuring this drive she'd made nearly every weekend for the past six years. She tried not to focus on the plans of the giant beside her. Or his vulgar fascination with the girls behind her.

Slovenia was beautiful, even in the early spring. In a few weeks the hills would be a verdant smash of green. Rolling hills turned to mountains as their buses continued north toward the Alps. Beyond the tall mountains lay Austria.

Hilltop churches, Romanesque chapels, and hidden convents were scattered across every village and town. Christian churches were everywhere, peaceful little buildings that seemed to call out to her more strongly every time she passed.

This was her last trip from Trieste. Eight buses, each with forty or so girls and all their belongings. Hundreds of anxious young women setting out for a new home, chattering about decorating their new apartments. Identical girls with wonderful Mediterranean complexions, high cheekbones, long thin bodies, and waist-long black hair pulled into the ponytail that distinguished the Mother Seed. Each mane bound at the top with a fluffy red elastic band.

Nagging dread overwhelmed Monique. She could no longer deny what she'd willingly ignored during her years of service. She was a witting accomplice to a bitter travesty. The lives of these girls would soon change forever, like the inbred child wives of a polygamist, if Malcolm's plan succeeded. She had to find a solution, and very soon.

She watched yet another white church on a gentle rolling hill pass by, her eyes on the cross topping it. She wiped a tear from the corner of her left eye, a rare display for her. Her heart was breaking for these girls, heading to servitude, like Pinocchio and a boat load of donkey boys.

But unlike in Pinocchio, these weren't strangers. She was sure they were all her sisters.

In the second bus, Sonya and Kristen sat together. As they rounded corners on the narrow Slovenian road, Kristen leaned into Sonya's shoulder, her head resting on a small pillow. Sonya held her friend's hand, squeezing it occasionally to reassure her when they made a particularly tight turn. Sonya was glad she had no motion sickness. Days in a dinghy with her brother, bobbing on the waves of a mad ocean, had cured that malady forever.

Pressing her face against the window, she felt as though she could push through the tall, wide pane of smoky glass and feel the wind in her hair, the sun on her cheeks. Hills rose and fell in the distance, pastures rolling as far as she could see, rising up to the foothills of majestic mountains, capped in snow. The sight of the crosses on hilltops warmed her heart, reminding her of the tiny silver cross that had once dangled from her own neck.

She touched her throat. The cross was long gone, taken by stern matrons in Washington who'd prepared her for Father Raines on that scary night she'd traded her clothes forever for black Lycra. She was sure her skin would turn the color of night if she wore these stretchy suits much longer.

Sonya looked down at Kristen's hand in hers. Her sister's fingers were exactly the length and thickness of her own. Every feature from their faces to their skin coloring was alike, down to the wrinkles on their palms. Twin sisters, in body and spirit. She put an arm around Kristen, pulling her close as she saw a curve coming. A shepherd waved from the roadside, a boy about her age with a small motorcycle, a flock of sheep, and a shaggy dog running circles and barking as the buses sped past.

Sonya craned her neck to watch them as they disappeared into the distance. Short and wiry, the shepherd bore a strong resemblance to her memory of her brother and best friend. It was a distant memory, now six years since she'd been given to Father Raines.

The boy looked just like Rex.

*

An hour later, Monique looked up, her breath quickening. The bus crawled around a steep one-lane curve, revealing the outlines of a monolithic structure that squatted like a great mastodon on a verdant hillside. Two tall towers, like sentries, sprouted from massive stone walls, their gray surfaces absorbing the light of the cloudless day. Narrow windows high above the ramparts reminded her of tiny apertures that archers used to shoot through in times of war.

Her new home. A fitting prison.

8

"SEE THAT?" OZ ASKED, pointing right. "A hundred meters out. Your two o'clock."

"See what?" John drove the MSR in the tracks of Rex's plodding rover near the end of their third day en route to the colony.

The landscape appeared unchanged, barren, and lifeless. Scatterings of black rocks or occasional craters filled to their rims with drift-like piles of Martian dust covered the undulating plains. John saw nothing out of the rusty red norm, except for the vertical drops of two canyons on either horizon. Their options for excursions were severely limited.

"It's silver. Out there!"

John nodded. "Got it now." He lifted a gun-like device from the MSR's console and aimed it at the point of light reflecting the morning sun. Slowing the MSR to a stop, he commanded a laser designator on the rover's roof. As he pulled the trigger, a red dialog box popped up on the MSR command screen. "127 meters."

"Good eyes, Oz," John remarked. "Call Rex. Tell him we're deviating a little right to check out something on the ground."

"Roger that," Oz replied, picking up a headset. "Hope it's not another guy in a space suit."

✳

Two hours later, Rex, Oz, and John knelt in the red soil together as Oz captured the moment on camera.

"We must show respect," Rex said. "The Oracles of the Father Race may have perished here."

John shook his head, hoping Rex wouldn't notice his movement. "It's a *machine*, Rex," John said as patiently as he could. *Get a grip,* he thought. "It's got propulsion systems, electronics. Was probably autonomous. But it was *not* alive."

"The Unknowable God and our Fathers sent this Oracle to proclaim the Gnosis. We should honor its sacrifice." Rex poked reverently in the red dust around edges of a broad clamshell-shaped silver metal object, which, John was sure, was a portion of the upper half of one of the alien spiders. The same spiders that drew America to Mars the first time.

In his Michelin Man-like hard white suit, John watched Rex for a moment, then reached down and picked up a long silver object that looked like a giant snow crab leg. The contraption was almost a meter long, with dents, scratches, and burn marks perhaps suffered during a fiery plunge to the surface. The leg had two joint segments and was tipped with a point. Cables and wires, shredded at a joint, dangled in the cold atmosphere as John turned it over before the others.

"Looks like parts from one of the polar landers," Oz said.

"Nope." John turned the broken leg over, and brushed off the light coating of red dust. "Definitely not Mars Polar Lander. She had jointed legs, but none of that silver clamshell over there."

"How can you be sure, sir?" Rex asked.

"For one thing, this isn't the south pole. Mars Polar Lander made it to the surface, contrary to popular opinion."

"You sure? I thought we lost it," Oz said. "The software mixup, English and metric. Remember?"

"Yeah. I'm sure." John inspected the leg. "But it *did* land. NASA's imagery shows it sitting where we sent it."

"Whatever." Oz examined a small PDA-like device that was imaging the parts on the ground. "Got a perfect match on the pattern recognition, Hawk. This definitely matches our stored images of the alien spiders. To a tee. Leg's a dead ringer, too."

We were right! This is proof!

John wanted to shout for joy. Years of wondering if he'd dreamed up the evidence of the man-made spiders Michelle and Sean had discovered when they came here the first time. These *had to be* the spiders they'd confronted—the confirmation he'd known must exist, but that he could never produce.

They're no more alien than I am.

"This is your Oracle, Rex," Oz said. He patted the boy on his backpack. "Sorry, kiddo."

Elated, unable to find words, John grunted. Yet he also felt terrible. For Rex and May. "If these are the spiders that met Sean and Michelle eight years ago, the skin will type out as OT-4-1 titanium. Russian grade."

"That's not possible, sir. They aren't from Earth!" Rex protested.

John nodded, sure they were about to find out more than Rex wanted to know.

Oz snapped away with the miniature camera, imaging John

holding the leg, its upper end as thick as his biceps. Noticing Rex's rapt attention, John held it up to stare at the dangle of wires. He knocked some dust free, wishing he could blow off all of the thick covering of red talcum. His heart began to race—suddenly he was sure of what he'd noticed at first. Struggling with bulky gloves, he grabbed a shredded wire between two fingers' rubber-tipped ends.

"Hey, Oz. Get this. Close up."

"Moving in," Oz said as he approached with the camera. Rex stepped aside.

"What is it, sir?" Rex asked as Oz whistled and moved back, looking toward John.

"Get the picture, Oz. I need to show this to Rex."

"Check." Oz moved in again, clicked off a shot, then waved to John. "All yours."

"Look at this wire, Rex," John said. "Tell me what you see."

Rex approached, and John saw the boy's eyes through the clear visor of his silver helmet. Rex withdrew quickly, horrified. "That's not possible, sir. It's a mistake."

"No, Rex. I'm afraid not. This confirms what we learned years ago but NASA wouldn't talk about."

"Say what?" he heard Deborah ask over the radio.

"He's got a tip of one of the spider legs, Deb," Oz said. "Drive closer, and we'll hold it up to the window. You need to see this."

Rex staggered away, collapsing into a soft patch of soil. His gloved hands shook. John handed the discovery to Oz who examined it as the rover approached.

"Rex?" May asked over their comm system as she watched from her own vehicle. "What is it?"

John lifted a palm, letting her know he'd help Rex. "Son? I know it's a shock. Let's talk about it."

"You knew? All these years?" Rex asked, his face blanched.

"I suspected, yes, but I couldn't prove it, Rex. Our samples and data were destroyed on the way home when the meteorite hit the ship. NASA hated losing the proof and all—but what could they do? Without the physical proof those spiders were made on Earth, the public would've said NASA made it up to discredit Malcolm Raines and his believers." John sighed. "My friends died to come here the first time. And our biggest discovery—that the aliens were fake—stayed under wraps."

Not any more.

"Would somebody please tell me what's going on?" Jake asked, trundling up.

"Yes. Please," May added, her voice alarmed.

John extended a hand to Rex. "We found one of the spider's legs. Presuming it *is* from one of the aliens. There's a shredded wire bundle coming out one end."

"And?" May asked.

"It's got a label on it, Mom," Rex replied, his voice quivering. He took John's hand and stood up with some difficulty.

"A label? In the language of the Father Race?" she asked, excitedly.

"A label, yes. But it's in English."

"This can't be!" May exclaimed inside the rover an hour later as she examined the shredded electric cable protruding from the leg's end.

Tears rolled down her light-brown cheeks, and she looked at the men gathered around her. Deborah held her hand. Her grip was firm, but May couldn't concentrate on anything except the horror of Oz's discovery. The walls seemed to be closing in. Her eyes darted about the fancy rover compartment, looking for a way out.

Rex removed his suit as John and Oz clambered about the crowded space, still in their hard Mars expedition suits.

"All of these broken parts came from the Oracles? From this one site?" May asked as she released Deborah's consoling hand and sorted through the cache of silver parts.

"I'm afraid so," John replied as she turned a circuit board over in her hands. The label "Japan" was prominent on one of the microelectronic chips. Deep sobs wracked May's small frame as she held a fragment of another circuit board.

A terrible deception . . . my life wasted.

She gripped the shredded part with trembling hands as the awful realization broke over her soul.

How long since they first met us? Eight years?

The Oracles had appeared on Mars near the Viking lander, in pursuit of the latest robotic rover sent by NASA in 2012. They'd crawled out of swamps at the Cape Canaveral space complex, landed in Ivory Coast, and scaled Mont Saint Michel to speak in French to tens of thousands of faithful adherents of Saint Michael's Remnant. They'd flown in from the sky to land in RFK stadium in Washington. They had greeted mankind's first manned mission to Mars.

Rex had encouraged her, even pushed her, to consider the possibility of intelligent alien life. "Stretch your mind," he'd said dozens of times, to her and the children. At first she was sure there could be no life beyond Earth. "Get outside that Bible and use your eyes," he'd said once, in a gentle tone unlike him. Inspired by his sudden tenderness, she had.

Like a blinding flash of the obvious, there she was, in Rex's employ when news of alien visitors on Mars took the world by storm. She was swept up in the excitement and challenge. He'd made her a key member of his team. And the proof of intelligent alien life grew more ironclad every day. His consuming joy—his business and interest in life on

Mars—carried her along in its wake.

They were real! Alien life had come to Earth! The Father Race reached across the galaxies and touched us!

Now, like shiny metal tumblers in a bank vault door falling into place, the word "Japan" set in motion a cascade of agonizing memories: her gradual acceptance of the Father Race's existence, then mind-numbing grief over the loss of her daughter, sent by Rex to serve the Priest of the Heavenlies and to seek the Unknowable God.

I gave them my little girl!

She'd set aside her Bible and her fears, studying the Nephilim, probing her inner being for the god within her. She was sure that, if Rex committed his own daughter to their service, Saint Michael's Remnant must be right and Malcolm Raines a modern prophet. Raines was now her daughter's Guardian. She felt herself careening toward a yawning chasm in her soul.

The last tumbler fell into place, a padlock cinching the mammoth chains that bound her, an unbearable weight dragging her toward the abyss.

They took my daughter. I worshipped them! I abandoned God for the Father Race.

She screamed as she fell, but no words came from her mouth.

A bright light exploded in her eyes, and life went dark.

SUNDAY, MARCH 8, 2020: NAZARJE, SLOVENIA

Sonya awoke to bright light streaming in tall windows trimmed in delicate lace and swags of heavy cloth.

Where am I?

She lay still, wondering, then turned over, looking for Kristen. A carpeted floor stared at her. She rolled on her back and pulled the covers over her head, laughing and kicking with glee.

"My own room!"

Sonya bounded from bed and ran to the window, pulling back lace sheers. Sunbeams sliced into the room. In the distance, left of a rising sun that peeked through low hills, she saw snow-capped mountaintops. *The Alps! A corner room!*

Below her and left and right, windows stretched for what must be a hundred meters. Dozens and dozens—hundreds—of windows. Deep windows, surrounded by stone, with high sills, their tops at least three meters high. Red clay tile roofs, white painted stone walls, blue trim, and beautiful gardens. *Green!*

Massive stone ramparts sloped up from below, defending the tall facility that surrounded her. She was ten, perhaps fifteen, meters above the ground. Firs waved from the distance, down the hill toward the little town where morning sounds of cars and an occasional horn said "peace." No bustle of Trieste or dark buildings stained with age and industry.

Nazarje. *That's it.* She remembered now, her friend Pina telling her in broken English as they moved in late last night. This had once been a monastery, built by the Franciscans after they escaped the Turks in Bosnia four hundred years ago. She could see the white steeples of the original buildings, the Church of the Holy Mother of God, and the monastery of the Poor Clare Sisters. All perched up here on a grassy hill, far above the tiny town. She'd read about it when they lived in Trieste. It all belonged to Father Raines now. Her new home!

A clock bonged, then another, and bells suddenly erupted in the valley below. Deep slow bells and fast, high tinkling sounds. Bells tolling the time; others ringing a minute or more, calling the town to join them. Sonya's heart swelled, at once free of the oppressive tar pit that had again sucked her deep in black dreams last night—she'd woken to light!

She pushed up the window sash, lifting the heavy glass with ease. Breezes of a cold March morning swept her nightgown back; her long black tresses flapped in the frigid wind. Air scented with the fragrance of fir and pine, of baking bread and wood smoke, blew into her spacious room.

Sonya closed her eyes and breathed in her new life. Leaning against the window frame, with closed eyes, she sensed mountains and fresh air and dark green. She raised her arms high like wings and bent out the window.

Her head hit iron. Sonya opened her eyes. Decorative gray bars, twisted in sharp spirals, rose from the window's base to its peak. She lowered her hands to the rods, her skin chilling on cold steel. In the rush to grab her new world, she'd never seen them.

Sonya sank to her knees, her face barely reaching the sill as she hit the floor, the air and mountain views forgotten. She wiped her eyes, wishing Kristen were here.

Suddenly she was very alone.

MARS

"Cracked her head but good," Oz said, placing clean gauze under May's head while Deborah lifted her gently.

John moved to give him room. Six people now crowded into Rex's rover, half of them dressed in EVA suits. It was the second time they'd treated May on this vehicle's floor.

"Good thing I came along, huh?" Deborah examined the bloody bandage. "Probably sustained a concussion when she fainted. Bleeding should stop now that I've got the gash sutured." She caressed May's face. "How's the pain, sister? Need another jolt of happy juice?"

May whispered, "No."

John picked up the circuit board where May had let it fall. Rex knelt at his mother's side. John knew the boy was taking this hard, so convinced the Father Race was real. But John also felt enormously relieved. He'd devoted an entire mission to reach Mars and meet these alien spiders the first time.

Six years ago, he and Michelle had proven the spiders were a hoax—programmed in English and constructed of Russian titanium. But without the proof, NASA kept quiet and let the lie gain a foothold.

"We should get going," John said. "Home or colony, it's up to you, Deborah."

She bent over May, reviewing digital notes on her medical tablet. "I don't have the diagnostics to see more than a skull crack, and we're halfway to the colony. I vote we keep going. It's the same distance either way. " She smirked. "And the colony has three more docs."

"Good enough," John said. "To the colony. Stay here with her, Deborah. Oz and I'll drive the MSR." He turned to Jake. "You stay and help. Okay?" He patted Jake on the shoulder. "Take good care of her."

Jake nodded, whispering, "Thank you."

An hour later, the crew was headed east again, no chatter on the communication circuit. Behind John, Oz plowed through the stash of alien detritus recovered from the Martian plain. "Take good pictures, buddy," John said.

"Another development," Oz said, with a rare serious tone. "Not good, Hawk."

"What's up?" John asked, turning in his seat.

"Chinese," Oz responded quietly. "From the markings on these circuits, I'd say there was quite a bit of assembly work done there."

"So we've got Russian titanium, English labels, Japanese circuits, and Chinese manufacturing. Right?" John asked as he followed Rex and Jake. They could drive another three hours tonight before the sun set. They had plenty of methane and oxygen to drive all night. But John didn't want to press forward in the dark with deep ravines flanking both sides of their path.

"That's about it, Hawk. What now?"

"We call Melanie. She needs to know. Send her the images you took, Oz. Soon as you can. Get close-up details of the markings."

"Got it. You know, it's kind of a shame."

"How?" John asked.

"The Father Race, Rex and May's reason for coming. It's all a bunch of hooey. They came all this way for nothin'."

John glanced back and shook his head. "No, Oz. Not for nothin'. Rex Sr. and his crew colonized Mars." He took a deep breath, focusing on the rover ahead. "That was a first. An important first."

"True." Oz stood and leaned over the back of John's seat as the MSR bumped along. "But old man Rex, he missed all the fun."

9

JOHN FOLLOWED REX'S TRACKS, amazed at the boy's instincts. The amazing youth had navigated a dizzying labyrinth of serpentine canyons in the southeast extent of Nirgal Vallis, a complex web of river valley geography that reminded John of an English hedge maze. He'd found his way through this complex web of gullies and escarpments all by himself, determined to save his mom's life.

There was no doubt that water had once run here. Rugged erosions and small lakebeds revealed its ancient violent force.

Where'd it all go? John wondered. If you froze all the water from today's atmosphere, it wouldn't cover Mars with more than a hundredth of a millimeter of ice.

"Jake seems to enjoy her company," Deborah said, breaking his daydream.

"Probably good medicine for her," he replied. "Between her cracked noggin and that recovery from the lithium poisoning—she's had a tough road."

"Jake's the best medicine now. Along with her son."

"Any idea why she fainted?"

"Imagine how you'd feel, Hawk. That fake alien stuff tore her world apart."

John drove in silence, Oz on the floor behind them snoring. Deborah stared ahead. They were almost to the colony.

"Is there any chance," Deborah asked after a long quiet period, "any at all, that someone planted that crash evidence for us to find? To discredit this Father Race thing? And use us as the scapegoats to pull it off?"

"You mean someone like NASA? Fly a mission here, salt the Martian plains with some spider guts made in China, and hope we'd find them?"

"Yeah. And maybe not just NASA. The Russians? Chinese? Or some enemy of Malcolm Raines? Lots of potential culprits—although not many with the capacity to pull it off."

"Done nothing but think about that since we found the site. It's almost *too* perfect, Deborah. I mean, why does Rex Edwards just happen to plant a colony on a path that runs from our place right through that debris field?"

"My question exactly." She leaned forward.

"I researched the charts again," John said. "The route he took through Nirgal Vallis—the one we're on now between two huge canyon systems—was the only way to reach our base." John shrugged. "Who knows? Maybe Rex put that stuff there."

Deborah sucked in her breath. "How weird is that?"

John watched branching tributaries on either side of the rover wind like dry, rocky snakes through the hilly region as he followed Rex, a hundred meters ahead.

Finally Deborah spoke again. "Yeah. And why, on this entire stinking planet, is the debris within MSR range of our own habitat? Why'd we find it just now, and not on the previous manned mission? I'll bet the first mission crew drove out that way, too."

"They did. I checked it out. Went there twice, in fact."

"This thing makes me dizzy, John—too many directions it could go."

"There's one option we haven't discussed." John smiled and winked at her.

"That is?"

"They really *are* fake. The spiders crashed right where we found 'em. And God opened our eyes so we'd see them." John raised an eyebrow. "Wouldn't be the first time for you and me, now would it?"

Deborah shook her head, then looked out the window. "No, John. It certainly wouldn't be." She let out a long breath. "Maybe we've answered your first question."

"Refresh my memory."

"Why'd she faint? Remember?"

"Go on."

"Maybe that evidence lit some fire that caused her to question. May's a doctor, after all. Hardwired to ask diagnostic questions. All of a sudden, she realizes things don't stack up. Maybe it confirmed her worst fears, that she'd put her life, and her children's lives, at risk for a lie."

"You have my word," John said over the radio later that day. "No one will tour your complex without an escort. There'll be no press conferences and no unchaperoned contact between male and female. Not a problem, May. And thanks, by the way. We're honored the five of you trust us."

John's crew of four sat in the MSR at the colony's edge, awed by the array of habitat and laboratory modules, greenhouses and brick vaults. John was sure his people itched to look around.

"John, if it weren't for the crash evidence you found Sunday," May said, "I'd never have agreed to this. We came here committed to remain separate, to succeed on our own. But in light of the developments—including Rex's talk with his dad—and what you said you'd discovered about the Oracles on your last trip, I think we need to have our crew meet yours. And hear your side of the story. But expect some pushback."

Rex's talk with his dad? "We understand," John replied. "You came to Mars for a noble cause, May. No reason that it can't still be as noble, even if the focus has changed."

"Thanks, John. I know you're trying to be nice. I appreciate that. You'll be docking to the hab module. It's identical to yours, in the middle of the four domes. We call that the quad. See you soon." May clicked off the net.

"What was that all about?" Deborah asked later. "His dad's dead." She rolled her eyes. "This is creepy."

"Guess we'll find out soon enough," John said. He and the crew squeezed into the front of the MSR to watch as Oz drove the last few hundred meters. In the fading sunset, they saw the four greenery domes, nearly ten meters tall, each topped with a pulsing red strobe light. In their midst John made out two structures like their own at Mars Base.

Squat cans suspended inside cage-like structures sat on four legs, with wheels identical to those at the NASA base. Connecting tubes—like gerbil tunnels above the ground—ran from the Hab and Lab to each dome, feeding out in four spokes from the center of the quad. A smaller gold tunnel ran from dome to dome, in a circumference about the square of the four greeneries.

The more he focused on the domes, the more John thought about fresh vegetables instead of the engineering feat of transporting and inflating these semi-rigid transparent structures. He was famished.

"Some camouflage, huh?" Oz said as they approached the Hab dock seal. He waved at the structures that had marvelously appeared out of thin air when they were a hundred meters back. They were completely invisible to any high-flying craft or space system. "Adaptive camo. Old Rex was pretty tricky. We only use that stuff in the military."

"Explains why we never saw this place with our satellite camera," John answered.

"No," Jake interrupted. "You can't see something this size with a weather bird. Unless it's reflective or lights up the sensor some other way. Like his rover did."

"Would you like us to turn it off?" someone asked at the colony through the radio.

John flinched. *How'd they hear us? The radio's off.* The more he saw and experienced of this group of six colonists, the less he understood.

Oz drove the MSR to a soft bump with the Hab. Everyone remained glued to the windows, trying to make out the colony in the fading light of a sun that set long ago.

"Okay. Who's ready to meet the parents? Everyone on your best behavior?" Oz joked.

"Chill, Oz," Deborah said. "This is weird enough without you making fun of it. We didn't know they existed a few weeks ago."

"Ten-four, doc. I think it's gonna be fun. Meet some new faces."

"Shhh!" Deborah hushed as a call came in.

"Admiral Wells," Rex said on the radio as Oz began shutting down the drive systems. "I know you'll enjoy this part. Did you see the gold tubes connecting the domes around the periphery?"

"I did. That the access way?" John asked.

"Yes, and air ducts," Rex responded. "We pump air from habitat to greenery, letting the plants scrub the carbon dioxide and add oxygen. Same for our water supply. Wastewater goes through a grinder, then to the tilapia fish tanks. We cycle the water all around the circle, from one dome to the next. When it's through the fourth dome, we use it to hydrate the plants. It's great fertilizer. And nothing's ever wasted."

As Rex described their home, and Oz tested the airlock's pressure integrity, John imagined their marvelous atmosphere and water treatment systems, a far cry from the mechanical scrubbers and purifiers NASA engineers used . . . and less likely to break. Rex did it the natural way. John couldn't wait to breathe fresh air.

"I copy, Rex. Any words of wisdom when we meet your crewmates?"

"No. They aren't exactly looking forward to having guests. Let's eat before you tell them your news. That all right?"

"It is," John replied on the radio. "Russians used to say you have to eat a bag of salt with a man before you really know him."

"Nicci and Kate have dinner ready, sir. No salt, but lots of fresh beans and a special Mars squash. You hungry?"

John's mouth watered. This arrival felt like a real homecoming, like a return to Sistersville, West Virginia, and the family farm. Mom's in the kitchen whipping up a meal, and Dad's bragging about the new hog waste pond he's installed in the back pasture. Pies are cooling on the window sill, and his brother's complaining about picky pigs that won't eat table scraps.

John stifled a laugh. Some things never change.

✳

"These are our friends," May said five minutes later as the four emerged from the MSR and stepped into the hab module to meet the Edwards colony. Now there were nine English-speaking, two-legged Martians here. Five of them women. John realized he'd never, in his entire NASA career, been in a space exploration environment where the women out-numbered the men.

Three women comprised the icy greeting committee. Like May and Rex, they wore desert khaki flight suits rather than the NASA stan-dard polo top and kangaroo cargo pants. The group of five had a mili-tary air, too. Even May seemed official when she stood near her fellow "mothers," as Rex called them.

The place reeked of iron-fisted discipline, a curious characteristic for history's first commercial space enterprise. It reminded John of a championship grudge match, each intending to dominate and destroy the other, but willing to shake hands and say "good luck."

"John Wells," he said. "Thanks for meeting with us." John extended his hand first. No one took it.

May stood silently at the end of the line, her arms crossed, nibbling a fingernail. She nudged the woman to her left with an elbow and said something under her breath. The woman stepped forward, her hand extended.

"Dr. Nicci Tabor, chief scientist," she volunteered. Of medium build, she looked like an adult version of the heroine in *Little Orphan Annie,* with her curly red hair and pale freckled skin. "My background's obstetrics and biomedical engineering."

Dr. Tabor nodded to Deborah, then pointed to her left at an Asian woman, even smaller, also of medium build. There were no skinny women here; Sergei Nickolaeiv, his first Space Station commander, would say they were "strong."

"Dr. Sachiko Tamaguchi," Nicci said. "Our lead obstetrician and botanist." The Asian woman bowed but didn't extend her hand. John bowed in return.

Nicci continued. "And this is Dr. Kate Westin, our resident geologist and biochemist. She was a friend of your late crewmate, Michelle Caskey."

Kate took John's hand in a long grip. "Hi. I know you and Mich were great friends. I miss her."

"Me too. Thanks. Good to meet you, Kate." He pointed to a patch on her flight suit, a number one inside a crude circle, like a numeral chiseled in stone. "I heard about that from May."

Kate blushed as she looked down at the faded cotton logo. She pushed curly brown hair back over her ear. "That? May told you?"

"Yep," John said. "You're the world's expert in paleo-obstetrics, I'm told."

"Pay Leo what?" Oz asked.

Finally, someone's waking up back there, John thought.

"Paleo-obstetrics," Kate said, moving toward Oz, her hand extended again. "The study of ancient childbirth methods. Pretty handy stuff when you don't have a hospital around and a baby's coming. And who are you, Scarecrow?"

Deborah let out a long cackle. That set the entire crew giggling like a bunch of nervous school kids. "Scarecrow" it was.

"We call him 'Oz,'" Jake said, choking on laughter. Oz stood next to him speechless, his face beet-red. "Don't mind the scarecrow," Jake said with a chuckle. "He's mute. But only around women." Jake punched his tall friend in the back. "Say hello, stupid."

"These cutups work for me . . . I think," John said with a laugh as he pointed to his right. "Dr. Deborah Readdy, our flight surgeon and physician. Jake Cook, call sign 'Ice Buster,' our hydrologist. Since we haven't found any water yet, we just call him Jake. And you've met Martin Oswald, our tongue-tied flight engineer. We're honored to be here." John waved toward the hatch. "There's four more where we came from. They wanted to come, but—"

Kate held Oz's grip a long time, then stepped back into line. "And what do they call you, Admiral Wells?" she said with a gentle smile.

"Hawk," Oz volunteered, speaking at last. "He *used* to have great eyesight."

Nicci and Kate laughed, and then shared something in Japanese with Sachiko that John couldn't understand. "We've got a big dinner ready," Nicci said. "I imagine you're sick of rover rations."

"Rex told us," John said. "Made it sound like dinner on the farm."

Sachiko smiled and spoke in heavily accented English. "I have vegetable you find very tasty, Mr. Hawk. You please to come." She turned and walked toward the dining area, waving to follow her.

John looked at his crew with an expression of wonder, then shrugged and smiled. After its initial coldness, this was quickly shaping up like a meeting of old friends.

"May?" John asked as everyone started to file out, headed for what smelled like a great meal.

"Yes?"

"I don't want to complain. Not a bit. But I'm a little confused."

"Yes?"

"We were warned to expect a tough crowd, but . . . I felt like family."

May smiled and pointed off in a direction beyond the dining area. "That's true, John. We asked Rex how to approach this. Your coming here to meet us, since you cared for me and all. He told us it was all right. To forget about The Covenant. That was a huge relief."

"Rex?" John asked. He nodded toward the teenage boy.

"Oh, no! Sorry. I meant his dad." She waved to him as she left the compartment. "Come on, John. Rex. Supper's getting cold."

His dad? She said it like the old man was standing in the next room.

John glanced at young Rex as he turned to follow May toward the meal. The boy stood silent, watching them as they walked out.

Everyone was smiling. Except Rex.

NAZARJE, SLOVENIA

Monique stole through the halls of the ancient monastery while Malcolm was distracted with a video teleconference, or so he'd said. He'd told her that coordinating business at his offices in Phoenix and New York often kept him up late at night. She knew it was a lie, a chance for him to curl up with his hidden cameras and illicit images. She took advantage of the lull in his control over her. Monique crept along the cool stone curved stairway, circling up the walls of the stone tower, listening.

When she and Malcolm bought the old monastery from Franciscan monks, a curator told her the building was haunted. He'd claimed, and she'd snickered, that strange songs of long-dead monks drifted through the hallways at night. She wasn't laughing any more.

After her first five days, she'd heard the distant singing every night. Always around eight or nine p.m. It was strongest when she walked the circular staircase of this tower headed up to their bedroom. She'd heard it again tonight, a brief few minutes. Now the sound was gone.

She shivered, wondering just how accurate the wrinkled old monk had been six years ago. She began descending the stone steps, then heard it again. A woman's voice, clear. And another, higher. Monique put her ear to the inside wall of the circular stairway. At a junction between two stones, she felt air blowing on her face, a gentle breeze, fresh, not the dank atmosphere of a basement or crypt. If this place had ghosts, they lived inside the stones.

Monique followed the tune, descending, listening, and descending more.

There! Through the cracks. But where's the breeze coming from?

Where she heard it the loudest, the stones were set apart a bit, and wind blew between them, as though the center of the broad sweeping circular staircase was a hollow shaft.

It must be three or four meters across. But if it's hollow, where does the wind come in? Where does it go?

Monique followed the stairs down, stopping at the first level. The floor here, like all the old parts of the monastery, consisted of timeworn, rough-hewn planks. She shut the door from the stairway where it emptied into the grand hall, once the sanctuary of the Church of the Mother of God.

At the door's base, hollowed into the floor planks, were a rusty clasp and a hand-forged metal ring. She'd opened that door from the grand hall a hundred times before, stepping into the stairway to climb to her room, but she'd never noticed this. The open door covered the access. Monique reached down, grasped the ring, and pulled. Her muscles tensed, ready to spring if something popped out of that crypt-like hole, unable to dismiss that old monk's prognosis.

Years ago, a young Monique had pinned Malcolm Raines to a wall and kissed him the first time. That strength, cultivated for years through disciplined weight training, paid off again. She lifted a thick oak floor panel, a meter wide on each side and hinged on the edge away from the door.

Probably hasn't been opened for decades.

Dirt and sweepings filling the gap around the access fell away, creating a cloud of dust that blew up into her face. The staircase continued to wind down below this floor panel, plummeting into the dark. Her skin crawled as the dirt swirled around her face, clouding her view of the dense black below.

Monique tilted the panel back against the wall on its hinge and descended into the dark, slowly letting her eyes adjust to the dim light.

"When we've been there ten thousand—" Two female voices wafted up from the darkness below.

The prisoners! Somewhere below.

Monique's heart leapt—then she realized that, if Malcolm opened the door from the grand hall, he'd fall into the hole. Or worse, find her out. The Priest of the Heavenlies had expressly forbidden her any contact with the prisoners.

The singing stopped. Monique listened a moment longer, then retraced her steps. She'd return, perhaps later tonight, with light. As she walked up the dank steps of the long-hidden compartment, ascending to the lighted stairway, she hesitated at the heavy oak plank. Its raw mass was comforting in her strong grip.

He'd never find me down here. Monique smiled as she lowered the door into place behind her.

For the first time in days, her heart warmed to a sense of hope.

10

A SUMPTUOUS DINNER OF fresh fish, steamed vegetables, potato bread, home-brewed tea, fruit compote, and a sampling of their first strawberry wine made this the meal to remember on Mars. Nothing cooked and sealed two years ago by NASA was as delicious as this feast prepared by the four female colonists.

Now, food and fellowship aside, John continued to share the news of the crash site as they sat in the dining area of Rex's hab module. The room was painted a light blue with colorful accents. Nothing was white, and he liked that. The colonists sat in silence, digesting the news.

He watched the body language of the women and Rex. Many thoughts, unspoken, were passing between them in knowing glances, rolling eyes, and shifts in their posture.

How do I talk to these people, Lord? he asked in silent prayer. John was slogging into uncharted territory, presenting to these colonists information that might undermine their faith—a faith completely opposed to his.

"You all came here to create a new life in a new world. Your mission hasn't changed," John said.

Across a long table, Dr. Kate Westin gripped the tip of the spider appendage, examining the wire bundles in silence. A fat tear began to drain from her left eye, then another. She lowered the leg to her lap, bending over in pain.

Is she sick? John wondered.

"Kate?" Dr. Tabor asked, leaning toward her and placing a hand on her shoulder. Kate shrugged her off and stood, then cocked her arm back and flung the spider's severed leg against the blue bulkhead. Everyone jumped as the leg spun out of her hand, whirling across the room, her scream in synch with the crash of metal against metal. Tears coursed down her face.

"I've given eight years of my life to this mission! You can't waltz in here and exterminate my faith in the Father Race with . . . with *that!*" She spun around, waving a hand at the other women in her crew. "Maybe you'll scare *them*. But not me."

Dr. Westin glared at Rex Jr. "*You* set this up. Some son you turned out to be." She stomped out of the galley.

May took a deep breath after a long silence, wiping her eyes. She stood and retrieved the spider appendage, touching the deep gash in the otherwise flawless aluminum wall. "This hits us hard, John. We came convinced that we were led to Mars by the Oracles of the Father Race." She waved the leg. "This could have been faked, right? To discourage us?"

"It could have," John responded. "Not likely, but it's always possible."

Dr. Tamaguchi chimed in. "Conspiracy theory is most logical,

Admiral. Improbable that the crash happened where we would find it. Could have been anywhere, right? Big planet." She looked around the room at her audience. "Saint Michael's Remnant says Father Race placed humans on Earth. Thirteen hundred years ago they promise to come back when we had technology to reproduce ourselves and could reach planets. Cloning and spaceflight. We have both. Father Race *has* returned. We have proof. So crash evidence must be false."

"And even if they were made on Earth, they could still be the Oracles, you know?" Rex interjected, his first comment all evening. "The Guardian has prophesied that the Father Race lives among us. He says they're on Earth, even now. The Father Race could've built the landers on Earth and sent them to Mars. To get us moving. Right?" He looked to his mom for affirmation.

May shrugged, nodding toward John. "Rex has a point. No one said that the Oracles had to come from another planet. We just assumed it."

John shook his head. Part of him wanted to scream "wake up!" to these deluded people. Another part of him said "patience." He tried to change the subject.

"I understand your position," John said, not sure he really did. "We'll leave that up to you." He smiled and pointed at Dr. Tamaguchi. "The dinner was incredible, Sachiko. Best I've had in ages. Please tell Kate, too." He waved at his crew. "Any chance my guys could get a tour?"

Rex looked dejected, but motioned to John and the crew. "I'll show 'em around."

John's crew stood in the middle of the third dome on the tour, each dome connected to an automatic airlock at the hab module. If the thick inflatable dome failed, the locks would seal the Hab off from the dome.

John tossed a cracker crust Rex gave him onto the fishpond circling the dome's outer edge like a little river. Several fish rushed the crumb, then the surface stilled again.

The water reminded him of the lazy artificial rivers he, Amy, and the kids used to float in at Texas water parks, touring the entire park in a large inner tube. Here, its imperceptibly slow cycling was the natural way of cleaning the colony's wastewater on its way to irrigate the field of plants before him.

"Californians grow tilapia in irrigation canals," Rex said, tossing another crumb. "They're hardy."

Verdant green assaulted John's eyes, a color he'd missed more than he realized. Under the dimmed lights, John saw a circular field of vegetables and root crops laid out like pie wedges. Above, the dome's thick skin shed drops of water as the moist, musty air condensed on the cold roof and fell. John, accustomed to dry rock and cold metal, Mars red and NASA white, felt like he'd been transported to another world.

"How do you maintain temperature?" Deborah asked. "It's two hundred below zero out there."

"The electrically conductive dome material becomes reflective at night." Rex pointed at the dome's wet surface beyond the lazy river. "It reflects the heat back in. The dome surface gets cold and condenses out water. But heat from hot groundwater keeps each dome around eighty-five degrees. In the daytime, we cut the heat back and let the sun in."

"Fascinating," Oz exclaimed as he strolled, gazing upward to the roof. Suddenly he tripped into a moist bed of red soil and new tomato plants, sinking up to his wrists in rust-colored gunk. The crew got a good laugh.

"Never thought I'd see mud on Mars." Oz wiped his hands on his pants.

"Martian soil isn't that great for most of our plants," Rex said to

John. "Too acidic. Sometimes we use mulch and artificial soil. In another two years, we'll have enough mulch for an entire dome of plantings." He led the group down a path toward a tall bin in the facility's center where all the pie wedges met. "Everything we can't eat or plant goes in here, except for metal and plastic."

Rex dug a short spade into a pit of dirt and garbage, pulling out a decomposing mass of food scraps and wriggling creatures. "It's full of worms. Life on Mars. They love it."

MONDAY, MARCH 16, 2020: NAZARJE, SLOVENIA

Malcolm snored. Monique checked her watch. After two a.m. She slipped out from under his long thick arm and headed to the bathroom. Malcolm never stirred.

Fifteen minutes later, Monique stood atop the heavy plank that opened to the hidden staircase. She'd carefully removed the last four bulbs from light sconces on the stairway wall, hit the bulbs against her leg to break the filaments but not the bulbs, and replaced them. The stairway was dark now for the last turn and a half of its steep descent. If someone followed her without a flashlight, day or night, they'd have to move slowly. Darkness covered her tracks.

She pulled the heavy door up with ease and felt a rush of cool air. As though entering a cave with two exits, wind blew through the big opening, cold and damp. She stepped down the continuation of the steps and then lowered the heavy panel behind her, sealing herself into the dark pit as she turned on her light. She imagined she felt something crawl on her neck, swatting with her hand at the phantom insect. She steeled her resolve to penetrate this crypt—and find the prisoners.

A long arc, the descending stair circled about the three-meter-wide central core. She went down a full spiral until the stairs ended at a dusty stone floor. Decades of undisturbed dirt had fallen through the cracks around the hatch, sifting down. Her footprints shone in the small flashlight's glow.

Monique's light revealed a large opening cut in the wall of the circular staircase's central core. She shone it into the dark space, the beam showing a second stair winding up the inside wall, spiraling high into darkness. There was no handrail, probably for thirty meters or more, and a sure plummet to the bottom if she lost her footing on what looked like rough stones poking out of the wall. She hesitated to call them steps. Cold air rushed down toward her—night air, blowing her dark hair back with that damp evening smell of fir and mountain, an aroma she recognized from many weekend nights at her open tower window.

Where's the air going?

Monique explored the stone floor until her light penetrated a hole near the floor spacious enough for her to crawl through. Kneeling on the damp stone, she peered in. A tunnel three or four meters in length stretched out beyond her, ending in a metal grate.

A ventilation shaft! She crawled into the hole, ever mindful of the time. Malcolm could wake at any moment.

The access was damp but not wet, and formed of fitted stones that tore into her elbows as she wiggled forward. Her only retreat would be to reverse this process. Claustrophobia, a sensation she'd never experienced, began to grip Monique halfway through the long tunnel. Her entire body was crammed in the access, with the exit grate still a meter or two ahead of her.

Sweat formed on her face, yet she could barely wipe it on her shoulder, her arms stretched out before her. Monique closed her eyes, willing her thumping heart to slow. Cold air rustled her long tresses, blowing the loose hair forward as it cooled her face. Again, she began to crawl, switching off her light. The phantom spider plopped itself on her shoulder again, crawling slowly up the nape of her neck. She willed it away.

Monique's eyes quickly adapted to the dark, and she could see a dim glow beyond the grate. Like a tiny bulb, or a night light. Perhaps a reflection of something more distant. Her eyes struggled to interpret the scene through the small holes in the rusty iron.

A room!

The moon's last quarter, shining strong in a clear March night, made gentle beams on the floor and on a bed across the room. Monique's heart leapt, all thoughts of the restrictive access forgotten as she wriggled for a better view. It was a small bed, with two occupants. She could only see a portion of the room beyond it, including a table and a pair of chests against the far wall.

The prisoners.

Monique lay on the stone, her heart hammering in her ears. She propped her head up with her hands while she watched the bed's motionless occupants for a long time, measuring her breaths, fearful she'd be heard. They must be asleep. Her watch's glow alerted her at last.

An hour. He might miss me.

Monique struggled with the decision to stay or to back away. If she *could* back out. She forced her thoughts away from the claustrophobic rock shaft to memories of vanquished foes. Men who'd tried to take advantage of her as a young girl, her unusual strength overcoming their age and mass advantage. She recalled challenges to Malcolm's security, autograph seekers and hecklers trying to approach him, and again, her physical dominance like a brawny bodyguard, protecting this powerful man who, for years, she'd been sure had loved her.

But we know better now, don't we? she thought as she squirmed, pulled with her feet, and pushed backward with her hands. Soon Monique's feet emerged from the end of the shaft, and she wrapped them around the edge of the access to extract herself. Free of the opening at last, she shined the light back in the direction of the sleepers.

She'd return tomorrow. There was much to do. And much to learn. About them.

TUESDAY, MARCH 17, 2020: MARS

Standing in the lab module by the rover airlock access, John gave May a strong squeeze and released her, then turned to Rex and grasped his hand. "You're one amazing young man. I'm proud of you."

Rex held his grip for a long time. "I haven't . . . haven't ever heard that. Except from Mom. Thanks," he said, glancing at the floor. "Thanks for everything." Rex sighed then looked up. "See you again?" he asked, releasing John's hand.

"I imagine so. Let me know you're coming next time. Okay?" John said, a hand on Rex's shoulder. "Take care of your mom—*all* your mothers," he said grinning. "You've got your hands full here."

John waved at the other three women, standing back while May and Rex said their final good-byes. Kate Westin wouldn't look him in the eye, fidgeting as if she wished she were somewhere else. She hadn't shared a word with him since she'd blown up at dinner last week.

Rex moved forward, his hands in his pockets. He looked at the floor of the Hab, then up at John, his jaw clenched. "There's something I need to say," he began. "I'd have come here, to Mars, in any event."

"What's that?" John asked.

"Dad brought us here for a reason, sir. The Father Race. Maybe that stuff we found was planted, you know? It could be a hoax. But, still, it doesn't matter. Father Race or not, I always wanted to come here." He looked down again, then straightened up and stood tall before John. "I came to Mars because Dad believed in this mission."

"Know what?" John smiled. "Me, too. I'd have jumped at the chance to be here, spiders or no spiders." He extended his hand, taking Rex's grip a second time. "And I'm glad I came back to Mars, Rex. To meet *you*."

Rex brightened. "Glad to hear that. Me, too. You were right, by the way."

"About what?" John asked.

"We were talking about The Covenant. You said I used all the resources at my disposal. I kind of pushed back. Didn't want you to come to the colony, you know? But guess what? Dad said the same thing. He said it was a good thing I did what I did. And a good thing that you came here, too."

"You're losing me, Rex. When did your dad say this?"

"Oh, yeah. You haven't seen him yet, have you? Too hard to explain right now. But I'm serious. Without your help . . ." Rex motioned toward Deborah, "Mom might have died. We might have all died if you hadn't solved our water problem." He laughed. "I'll introduce you to Dad next time you come visit, okay?"

John shrugged. "Sure. Next time." He grasped Rex's shoulder. "I hope there *is* a next time. Soon."

Rex took a deep breath, his eyes searching John's as his own sons' had when they were seeking affirmation, or when they said thanks but really wanted a hug.

"And about your mom," John said. "You're welcome. Maybe one day you can return the favor." With that, John gave Rex's hand an extra squeeze, released him, and turned to the MSR. Any longer, and he might not be able to leave. Rex reminded him so much of Albert, his third son. He ached to hug the boy. But this was not the time.

Once seated at the controls, John looked back, checking on his crew's final good-byes. Jake held May in a close embrace. Even from several meters away, John could see the man blushing from the attention of this public and intimate good-bye. Oz and Deborah delayed at the door, waving and shaking hands.

"Time to go," John announced over the loud speaker. The three came through the hatch at last, with Oz pulling the metal door into place.

John engaged the methane-oxygen engine, and they began their five-day trip home. Minutes after they began bumping across Mars, Deborah tapped him on the shoulder.

"Who'd have thought?" She gazed out the window as she spoke. Jake and Oz stood in silence behind the two of them, watching dry streambeds grow into gullies, then steep-walled river valleys, as they drove. Nirgal Vallis beckoned them home.

"A penny for your thoughts." Deborah turned to face him.

John sighed, looking back at the hatch, and saw part of the colony through the portal, disappearing in the distance. "I have this feeling," he said as he turned back to watch Mars's first road, worn by the passage of three rovers in the past four weeks. "Got this strange little feeling," he repeated, "that we'll be coming back. I *want to* come back."

And I want to find out more about Rex's dad. Something strange about all that.

Deborah raised an eyebrow, then cocked her head and hummed out loud. "Better make your return reservations, gentlemen," she said with a quick chortle as she turned to Oz and Jake behind her. "'Cause when that little voice starts talking to John, it's never wrong."

11

SHE DREAMED OF TEXAS. A scalding place. A bright, white-hot, sweltering hell. Miles of concrete highways and scorching parking lots and vacant concrete drives that fed yawning garages on the fronts of identical stucco houses. A concrete madness baking in stifling muggy heat. A vivid nightmare that replayed itself less often each passing year.

A dream. Yet it suffocated her as though the heat blistered her face, choking off her air. She fought to breathe, to break free of its smothering hot fingers. Her heart pounded as she sweated her way through the raw fear. Then she screamed, jerking upright in a small bed. Perspiration soaked her chest and arms in the chill of the night.

A cold breeze blew out of the wall as it did every evening. The consolation was that this tiny room, now her home, smelled fresh, and the air was cool during the warm summers. She pulled thin covers over her daughter, the tall blonde to her right, who snored lightly in her sleep. Amy Wells moved to the edge of the bed, letting her feet dangle above a damp stone floor, listening.

Nights were her freedom. A canopy of stars on clear evenings often beckoned her outside. The peace of the nighttime quiet made her feel far away and free. In that quiet blanket she often imagined herself bathed in calm, reunited with her family, and living a tranquil existence someplace familiar — free from the mind-numbing monotony of a tiny room and its small garden.

Amy opened the door of their stone cottage, an ancient annex at the base of a tall stone tower that soared above. She stared out at the cold night, shivering in her sweat-dampened gray shift. A biting cold wind wiped away the oppressive heat of her dreams.

Her sons were asleep, she was sure. She marveled daily at how tall they'd grown, so much like their lanky father. They grew and matured despite the bad diet and the endless imprisonment that was their lot. Amy stooped in the door, her shoulders bending as she lowered her head in prayer. She poured out quiet thanks — thanks that at last she'd been allowed contact with her three boys.

For five years she'd lived without them. Then, mercifully and without explanation, she'd finally been allowed to see them, to talk with them each day through the window in the garden wall. They labored in a garden of their own; their home was in a similar cottage, at the base of the same tower, on the other side of the wall — young men on one side, the woman and her daughter on the other.

Alice's gentle rattling snore soothed Amy. She had her father's nose; her face was a beautifully softened replica of her husband's strong features. Amy's precious daughter had grown through the toughest years of her life in this garden and cottage, locked away from the rest of the world. From little girl to young woman, Alice had been Amy's constant companion.

Together, they'd helped each other over the hurdles their changing bodies posed, teenaged Alice and Amy in her early fifties, each wrought with emotional highs and lows, tears and pointless arguments. Somehow, they'd conquered their challenges, leaning on each other and depending on God.

"Thank you, Father, for waking me up," Amy prayed, standing in the doorway. "For the cool air. Be alive in my kids' hearts and help them see you. Give me more time with them. Thank you for Alice and my sons. And for John, wherever he might be, out there somewhere. And thank you for life, Jesus. I don't know why we're here, but I know that none of this took you by surprise. Put your Spirit into the hearts of my kids, Lord. And in me. Give us hope. Every day." She sniffled, her heart beating faster. "Help us bear up under this trial. And please bring us back to John."

Amy bent lower, taking a deep breath and knowing she needed to say the next words, yet fighting them. Every night she waged an ever tougher battle not to give in to hate. "Please help me to forgive, Lord. Whoever it is that's keeping us here. Work in their hearts. For their sakes—and for ours."

Amy opened her eyes and straightened, knowing that on the other side of her dream and her prayers, was blessed rest. She lingered in the door, looking up.

Jupiter shone brightly above her in the midnight sky. Somewhere out there—she had no idea where—a fuzzy red Mars dotted the sky.

It all started with that. Mars . . . the planet that took John away.

When they'd finally been reunited, the Red Planet had somehow torn her away from him again and brought her here. She loved the night sky, yet its cold lights seemed hostile, too, a bitter reminder that space had driven a wedge into her family in a way few women had ever experienced.

Imprisonment with sensory deprivation was her lot, never able to face her oppressors. Nameless, faceless people on the other side of a revolving door who supplied her food and insulin. Never a face except those of her own children. That is, until days ago, when she saw a woman at the window above, waving. A long-awaited answer to prayer. And then, she too, had disappeared.

Is John alive?

He had slipped out early one morning, kissing her as she'd hugged the bed, taking yet another early flight to Washington for important liaisons with people she'd never met. That night, not long after midnight, she and the children left for what they'd thought would be a joyous trip to join him.

Where's my John?

An endless series of questions pelted her, a repetition of uncertainty that had dogged her for seventy-three months.

Why doesn't he find us?

Was he a prisoner in some faraway place? Or locked up just across the wall, unable to respond? Since she'd heard nothing from him or about him for six years, perhaps he was dead. No one would search for them then. Amy longed to hold her husband, to rub her hand across his short stubby haircut. She longed to be held.

Is he with someone else?

Amy turned, determined not to let her questions, and the wondering and tears that always followed, stay her from the sleep she wanted —even needed. Slumber was her only escape. She closed the door and padded barefoot across the frigid stone toward Alice. At the edge of the bed, she stopped, listening.

Rats.

She shivered, not from cold, but from the impending emergence of another creature from a hole in the wall. The scratching grew louder, unlike any rodent she'd shooed away in the past six years. Amy sat on the bed, her legs pulled up, heart racing. Her eyes focused on the old iron ventilation grate.

The scuffling became even louder just as Amy noticed a light. A tiny beam seemed to bounce inside the grate, occasionally piercing through the orange-sized square openings. The rat holes.

The light beam's jiggle matched the scraping, sliding sound, growing louder by the moment. Shivering, Amy slid off the bed, moving to the wall adjacent the grill. She could see distinct lightbeams now, dancing on the opposite wall. Standing beside the grate, she listened and watched the beams on the wall.

The sound grew close—labored breathing. Amy squatted on the floor, out of view. She watched the voyeur reach the grate and point the beam through the holes, illuminating their bed.

Alice!

The beam sliced erratically around the room—her absence from the bed discovered! It whipped across the closed door, moved to the chests holding their simple clothes. Then sliced back toward the bed. She heard muttering but couldn't make it out.

Plastered against the wall, fearful of exposure, Amy held her breath, her heart slamming against her chest. Four fingers reached through a hole, trying to probe the room. Amy had tried to plumb the depths of that air source more than once. It had never budged.

The light disappeared. Amy tried to will her heart to slow, to silence the pounding in her ears. The breathing was still there. In the stillness, she thought she heard a sniffle and a cough. Then a voice, English, but with a hint of a French accent.

"Mrs. Wells? Are you there?"

✴

"Mom?" Alice asked. Monique saw her sit upright in the bed in the dim moonlight. "Mom?"

Monique watched Alice rub her eyes. "Why're you standing over there?" the girl asked. "What's wrong?" Alice froze as though someone had hushed her. She pulled back, jerking her covers about her, her eyes locked on the grate. Monique checked her light. It was off.

What's she see? Surely not me?

Her racing heart refused to calm. She'd taken the ultimate risk contacting these people, and Malcolm wouldn't hesitate to crush her for it. She hoped against all odds he was still asleep above.

She'd once heard prayer described as wishful thinking. Monique doubted, in this moment of desperation, that the walking woman's prayers she'd heard from her window were empty wishes. She wanted to pray—to pray for contact with them, and for safety—but had no idea how. Her life depended on the next few moments going her way.

"Are you Alice?" she asked, her voice cracking at her words to these forbidden people.

The girl nodded, pulling the covers higher. She didn't answer.

"Mrs. Wells? Are you there? Please, don't be afraid." She gulped, her eyes riveted on the girl and her reaction. "I want to help."

"Who are you?" a timid voice asked, immediately to Monique's right.

She's hiding! She heard me!

"I—I can't say. Not just yet," Monique said, trembling. "Where are you?"

"Here," the voice said, a face moving in front of the grill.

Mrs. Wells!

It was like coming face to face with the ghost of Nazarje. The woman in the garden, close enough to touch.

"I thought you were another rat," Amy said. "They live in there."

Monique's flesh began to crawl, imagining a large castle rodent creeping up behind her, gnawing at her shoe or her ankle. Her hands shook.

"Are you Mrs. Wells?" Monique whispered, forcing her thoughts to this opportunity. "Amy Wells?"

"Yes. How'd you know? Have you come to free us?" The woman's voice sounded excited, and Alice jumped off the bed, running to her side.

"Please," Monique said, pushing her fingers through the square openings to touch Amy's hand. "I want to help. But it's not yet time."

She and Amy connected, two women bound together, she realized, by Malcolm Raines. Both captive, in different ways. Amy squeezed back.

"What's your name?" the girl asked, her face up to the iron grate.

"I—I can't . . . I . . . it's Monique."

"Can't see you very well."

Monique flipped on the flashlight, a black cylindrical military model that would make an excellent weapon, if the moment demanded it. The bright diode bulbs blinded her for a moment; then her eyes adjusted. She shone the light under her own face so the two women could see. "Here. Take this." Monique clicked it off and pushed the light through the grate. "You might need it. But keep it hidden. The guards have cameras."

Amy jerked her head back, searching the room.

"Not now. I reassigned them. It's safe. But only for a little while."

"Thank you," Amy said, looking back at Monique, her voice cracking. "Why'd you come?"

"I had to. That's all I can say right now."

"Are you the woman in the window?" Alice asked, her voice lilting.

"Yes."

"In the tower?" Amy asked. "You leaned out to wave? I've seen you, watching us on weekends. And on Sunday mornings."

"Do you listen to the bells?" Alice asked, rapid fire.

Monique nodded. In that moment, she felt the warm spot that emerged every Sunday, watching these two below while Malcolm slept into the day. It was a warm place deep inside her that wanted to understand those bells the way Amy and Alice knew them. The warmth gave her strength. Her hands calmed.

"Why do you listen? What do you hear?" Monique asked. "And why do you always sit in the far corner of the garden?"

"That's where we can see the cross," Amy said. "On the steeple. We give thanks, and pray." Amy's voice was strong. Monique was accustomed to the patronizing syrup of conniving women who sought to seduce Malcolm, or those blathering "yes men," his business partners. Amy's voice was unique. It had a ring of truth, of conviction.

"Give thanks?" Monique blurted. "For what? You're a prisoner here."

Has she lost her mind? Who could be thankful for this?

"We give thanks for life, Monique. Whoever bottled us up here hasn't taken that away. And we give thanks for Jesus."

Those last words stopped Monique's heart. It was true. These were Christ followers. Memories of a thousand talks with Malcolm flooded her, talks about the error of Christians' ways, the lies and half truths they spun. She remembered Amy debating Malcolm on television several years ago, when the world thought John had been lost on his ship's return from Mars. Amy had been strong and resolute then, tackling Malcolm verbally in a way Monique never saw another person accomplish.

That same woman faced her now, but the voice was not one of anger or debate. Instead, it was as if this woman's voice sang to Monique's heart. She squeezed Amy's extended fingers. The connection energized her.

"For Jesus . . ." Monique repeated, her thoughts drifting to the questions that pulled at her every Sunday as she watched them. Now she knew.

Alice turned the flashlight on. "Can you tell us why we're here?" she asked. Monique saw Amy nod, her eyes locked with hers.

"I . . . can't tell you. Not yet." She released Amy's clasp. "But I will soon. I need to go."

Monique began to push back in the tunnel, fearing she'd already said too much. "The guards will be back soon. Please. It's not safe much longer." She glanced at her watch and wiggled back down the tunnel faster. "I'll be back," she said. "Late at night. I promise."

Amy's voice stopped her. "Thank you, Monique. For coming to us. We'll pray for you."

The vigor in Amy's voice stung her. A burning desire to ask the nagging question "what is prayer?" stopped Monique as she watched the flashlight. Two faces were hidden behind the glare. She felt tears well up in her eyes and quickly lowered her face to her shoulder to smudge the dampness away.

"You'll pray for me?" Monique asked, her heart racing again, yearning to push through the grate and spirit them away to safety. "How can I pray?" she asked with a sniffle. "Please tell me."

"Talk to God," Alice said slowly, as if coaching her. "Thank Him. Then tell Him what's on your heart."

✳

Amy saw one glistening drop fall from the young woman's cheek as she pushed backward in the narrow tunnel. She put a hand on Alice's shoulder and nodded in Monique's direction.

With the flashlight, Amy could see the length of the short passage, twice as long as the woman who'd come to their aid. Monique crawled out of the tunnel, waved quickly, then stood and ran up what sounded like stone steps. She kept the flashlight focused down the tunnel as Monique had asked, the beam illuminating a room and a wall at the end. She was gone.

Familiar silence consumed the tiny cottage room, a jarring reminder that, moments ago, someone had reached out to them, and that now she was gone. The voice was still. Too brief, only minutes of contact after years of solitude.

"Will she come back?" Alice asked, her voice breaking. Her daughter worked so hard to be brave.

Another world lay just beyond her reach. *Escape.* Amy watched down the lighted tunnel aching to be with their visitor, to break free of this prison of gray clothes and tiny rooms and years of toil in a walled, miniature garden. A world devoid of music except for the bells, an existence without visitors or friends. Her only stimulation her children. And books. Blessed books that somehow kept coming. Someone on the other side of that rotating door still cared.

Everything here was tiny, like the damp narrow passage through which Monique had appeared. As a door somewhere distant slammed shut, and the last sounds of her steps died away, Amy turned out the light and pulled it from the grate. She turned and settled onto the floor, wrapping her arm around Alice.

"She came for *us*, Alice. God's answering our prayers. In His time."

12

"THE FRIEND OF MY ENEMY is my enemy," Shawnda Kerry muttered. "And my enemy's friend shows up over and over." The sharp odor of an uncapped blue dry-erase marker stung her nose as she stared at the wall, arms crossed.

Shawnda capped the smelly marker and pushed long black bangs out of her eyes. She paced the tiny office, pondering the whiteboard on her wall, its slick surface covered with colored boxes and lines. Two hundred hours of work stared back at her, a month's worth of ideas, hundreds of thoughts about relationships emerging from her classified research.

Thick red letters said "Iran" at the top. Six lines fanned out from that word to six columns below, with at least a dozen names and locations penned below each column title. A week of modifications, with the brilliant colors rubbed through and replaced, gave this presentation the look of genius hard at work.

She stood back, pulling straightened hair back over her shoulders, and took a deep breath. At the bottom of every column she'd circled an acronym common to each grouping: FMI. She crossed her arms again and squinted at the board.

The door opened. An older man stepped into the room, his belly rolling over the top of expensive suit trousers that stayed in place only thanks to leather suspenders. Walter McClannahan, deputy director for Middle East operations at the Central Intelligence Agency, wiped sweat from his brow with a yellowed handkerchief. He waddled toward a chair on the room's far side. "You ready?"

Shawnda smiled. Her light-chocolate skin, narrow waist, and sharp business dress made her the antithesis of this morbidly obese white man with yellow armpit stains spreading like an oil slick across a rumpled white short-sleeved shirt. But for all his largeness, he was her boss. And a good friend, too. His only fault: he didn't know when to say "no" to food.

"Thanks for coming down, Walter," she said. "This is important."

"Better be. You've been holed up here for a month. I'm paying you for breakthroughs," he said with a smile. Shawnda cringed as he shifted in a small straight-back chair. The black wingback Windsor had been a doctoral present from her parents; the University of Virginia's crest was now hidden behind Walter's sweating frame and rolls of flesh.

"Remember that 'friend of my enemy' thing you quote all the time? I think I found that friend." She pointed to the whiteboard. His eyes ran over it like a scanner. She was sure he'd see every nuance, and perhaps some she missed.

"FMI again?" he asked, pointing an aluminum walking cane at the board. "You're sure?"

"Positive. Federated Mining Industries. Seventy-five thousand public and federal documents and four hundred thousand news reports, give or take ten thousand, all digitized, analyzed, and catalogued by the software tool. I tuned it to search Farsi and English materials." She tapped the board. "There's no doubt, Walter. Wherever you look—at any major industry or military activity in Iran—you'll find them. Nuclear power or suspected nuclear weapons, FMI is there. Oil exports, chemical weapon precursors, technology transfer—they're up to their ears in Iran. Always under the cover of a subsidiary, a subcontractor, or a front company. But they're there."

"Did you check to see if FMI shows up in Syria, Yemen, or Saudi?"

"I did. And they don't. I found tight relationships in Iran, Indonesia, and a few Eastern European nations—old Soviet bloc locations. All of them date before the first Iranian nuclear weapon test. FMI covered their tracks well."

Shawnda could hear the lithe chair squeak as Walter began pushing up out of the Windsor. "Good. I'm convinced. I want your report on my desk by tomorrow morning. Hope you planned to work Saturday," he said with a grin, shuffling out the door.

He left a sour smell—a scent she'd come to associate with Walter. He also had a remarkable understanding of the Islamic caliphate, rivaling the insights of any other man or woman alive. Walter McClannahan lived the Middle East.

Shawnda could prove now, beyond question, that an American corporation had siphoned millions of dollars from Iran, the newest member of the nuclear club, using a complex but definable network of business interests. Iranian terror connections tied directly to friends of friends of friends of FMI.

At the end of every string she pulled, she always found the same connection: FMI—the common denominator to Iranian industrial support, spread across half a million documents. And every FMI trail led her to the one politician she'd hoped to forget: Lance Ryan. That's why Walter was here.

He stopped just outside the room, turning back to lean on the door jamb. "FMI's no friend of ours, Shawnda—but that connection you found might explain why Ulrich killed the Veep six years ago. I'll place the call. The director will know within the hour." Walter shifted positions, using the cane as a third leg. "I'll be sending some very senior fellows to see you soon, Shawnda. Don't ask them who they work for."

"The big man sent us. What you got?" one of three suited senior government servants piling into Shawnda's meager office asked an hour later. Unlike his wooden partners, one agent smiled at her colorful cycling posters. They made eye contact at once.

She watched the three sit down, unbuttoning suit jackets and mentally scanning her board full of theories and links. She was sure none of her ideas would survive the day; like human computer drives, these men were soaking her up, along with her theories. They'd probably memorized the board by now. No worry. She had, too.

There were no introductions, just an arrogant flip of badges Shawnda assumed meant they were from the White House. The men sat shoulder to shoulder in her cramped office, trying not to touch each other.

"I can prove a connection between FMI Corporation and Iran," she began, looking the trio over. One of them, a short Hispanic, had a Secret Service Bluetooth transceiver wedged in his ear like a hearing aid. "And I can prove a connection between FMI and Washington."

The oldest of the three, a pot-bellied man with a comb-over haircut, waved dismissively. "Start from the beginning, Mrs. Kerry. Like you did for Director McClannahan."

Shawnda nodded, no stranger to presenting executive briefings to mysterious, unnamed guests. She turned to the board. "I was on an Indonesia assignment. Tagged to identify what I could of Muslim terror activity on the far eastern end of the caliphate."

"Caliphate?" asked the Hispanic agent.

"The Muslim crescent. Runs from West Africa through the Pacific Islands. Indonesia has the largest Muslim population of any country."

"Yeah. Okay. I knew that."

The older man shrugged. "Go on."

Shawnda continued. "We kept losing track of terror cells in Indonesia. Tracking some old intelligence summaries, we found key Indonesian authorities consistently turned their heads to the existence of terror camps right under their noses. That's where we dug in."

Shawnda produced a map of Indonesia rolled up in a corner. She loved paper presentations in this digital world. "We found terror cells in these provinces. Including the Aceh region. Leftist leaning politicos there will accept money from any source. Most of their money, as you might imagine, runs to Iran. Oil's over a hundred dollars a barrel—so the Persians have a lot of money to give away."

"How's FMI tied in?" the senior man asked.

"Aceh—primarily Muslim—is oil rich. They've been fighting for autonomy for decades. It's the next Balkans." She pointed at a column on the board labeled "mining and oil." "Irian Jaya, their sister region, also has huge natural resources. The Ertsberg and Grasberg copper and gold mines bring the region major revenue. FMI wants some of those mining leases for itself. Their dollars line the same pockets Iranian terror cells do, and the Iranian terror cells train in that locale, away from prying eyes, preparing for worldwide operations."

"Your connection between FMI and Washington isn't clear," said pot belly.

"FMI mines uranium. In Indonesia. They sold about six thousand metric tonnes last year—compared to five hundred tonnes mined last year in Iran. The Iranians have been courting the Indonesians for more of that uranium since the middle of the last decade. And most of the FMI uranium gets bought by the Iranian government, through a third-party vendor. Guess who?"

"And Washington?" the older man repeated. "The connection to Vice President Ryan?"

"FMI's gotten congressional and White House favors in the past, including mining legislation affecting West Virginia and Kentucky, preferential treatment for mining permits in the Pacific Islands, and special-interest exceptions from environmental regulations. I can show every benefit tied in some way to FMI's Political Action Committee and congressional contributions."

"And?"

"And, in every case we find a common political thread. The West Virginia legislation, the Kentucky environmental exceptions, the Pacific Island mining leases from the federal government—every one of their federal favors had a common name. Lance Ryan."

"The Veep?" the Hispanic asked, brow furrowing.

"The same," she said. *This isn't so hard to understand.* "You look at Iran, you'll find FMI. You look at FMI, you'll find money or decisions running to Vice President Ryan. It's a six-year-old trail, but something stinks. I picked through half a million documents, and the link finds its way, over and over, straight back to the White House. Always through Iran and FMI."

The older man sat stiffly in his seat, but the others fidgeted. The young one, the Hispanic who Shawnda assumed to be Secret Service, shook his head slowly.

"Erase the board, please," pot belly said. He motioned toward the agent who liked her bicycle art. Shawnda protested, but the young agent moved past her and wiped an eraser across the colors. In a moment, her months of work were gone.

"Surely you don't think I'm so stupid that I didn't write this down," she said defiantly.

"Perhaps not," the older man replied, standing and turning toward the door, "which is why I got advance permission from Walter McClannahan to commandeer your computer. I'm sure he'll get you a new one soon."

Shawnda gasped as the agent reached across her desk, unplugged the micro-tower, and slipped it under his arm. He pushed past Shawnda without speaking.

"This is nuts," Shawnda said as the three left. The older man faced her as he adjusted his pants below an ample stomach.

"Mrs. Kerry, as a contractor analyst with SAIC you serve the needs of the Central Intelligence Agency. You did your job well. Now I suggest you move on to another task. Mr. McClannahan will have one for you shortly. The vice president's dead, killed six years ago in a terrorist-inspired shoot down of his helicopter over the Lincoln Memorial. We know who did it, and he did *not* work for Iran. Your husband caught him, in fact. You should know."

He buttoned his coat slowly as he talked, watching his buttons instead of her. "Considering the state of affairs—Iranian nuclear weapons, an Iranian Shahaba missile that can attack with impunity anywhere in the Middle East, and incredibly tense relations between our two countries—the last thing the president wants to do right now is broadcast the wrong message. Construed the wrong way, your material is explosive."

The senior agent turned to the shorter agent. "Please escort Mrs. Kerry to Mr. McClannahan's office for an immediate debriefing." He extended a hand toward Shawnda, who ignored it. He withdrew his hand and headed down the hall, speaking over his shoulder.

"I'll make sure you have network access by Monday morning, Mrs. Kerry. Good night."

LONDON, UNITED KINGDOM

Hot lights glared from all angles as a makeup technician put the final touches on Malcolm's forehead. Foster Williams shuffled through papers and conferred on his lip mike with a producer somewhere. The studio, a remote location created just for this interview, was a jumble of cords, lamps, and cameras. Yet no one spoke to Father Malcolm Raines.

Until the show starts, they don't care what I have to say. One day, they will.

Foster Williams nodded toward someone offstage, then in an instant was all smiles—"America's favorite talk show host," a voice announced.

"Live from London!" said another voice in his earpiece. Someone smelling like jasmine squeezed his shoulder lightly.

"Thank you, Father. For what you do." Jasmine swirled about him. He turned to face the gentle voice as a short woman, in jeans and a sweatshirt, disappeared offstage. Malcolm turned back to Foster as a red light came on to his right. Foster stared into the camera.

"Welcome to *Foster's World*, live from London. And welcome to our special Friday edition with Father Malcolm Raines. A prophet for our time."

At last.

Malcolm nodded, determined to capture the lead early and keep it. Foster had always been putty in his hands.

"You've come a long way, Father Raines. Tell us where home is these days."

"Our new home is in Slovenia, Foster. And thank you for bringing the show to us so we might continue our mission—an important mission rapidly coming into its greatest hour."

"Slovenia?"

"South of Austria, northeast of the top of Italy, at the top of the Adriatic Sea. We have recently moved our headquarters from Trieste to Nazarje, Slovenia, south of the Alps. A new home where we retreat to prepare."

"Prepare?" Foster asked.

Time to go off script, Malcolm thought, a small smile emerging. *Do it early, before the first commercial break.*

"We are preparing for the Harvest, Foster. Our most important mission is at hand."

Foster tried to sort through his notes without appearing to look down, but Malcolm had dropped the bombshell early. Foster would never catch up.

"The Father Race sent Oracles six years ago to herald their coming, portents of our original fathers who seeded life on Earth thousands of years ago. Those Oracles, the blessed visitors who met me on Mont Saint Michel and in Washington, and met others in Florida, Africa, and on Mars, have now left us. But we have their instructions, to prepare the way for the Father Race."

"But—"

"Now the Father Race calls us to complete our blessed mission. First, we were to show our ability to reach another planet, as they did bringing the seed of man to Earth. Then, we were to master the sacred genetic arts, which we have done so well. In fact, I can report our global search is now complete. We have found the perfect seed of the Nephilim and our mother, Eve."

"And—"

"Yes, Foster, and we're ready to rekindle the perfected human form, reproducing the seed of each—Nephilim and Eve. Once we accomplish that, we will be ready to pick the fruit of the future of mankind. Fruit that will pave the way for us to reshape this world—a new world—in our image."

Foster was speechless, his frustration at being upstaged so great he'd reddened from the neck up. Malcolm knew the producer. She wasn't about to shut off his camera.

"Slovenia is essential to our mission, Foster," Malcolm said after a pause in which Foster was obviously taking instructions from his production team. "There, in our expansive new facility, the Mother Seed is preparing for their future mission as vessels of our Harvest and as students of enlightenment. They are our beacons of the Gnosis. Daughters of Eve, every one."

"Father!" Foster blurted.

Malcolm leaned back, nodded once, his hands folded.

"Yes, Foster?"

Foster sucked in a deep breath as the camera cut to him. "Fascinating! It's remarkable what you've done in such a short time. Tell us more about this 'harvest.' And how it affects our viewers." He smiled his broad, toothy grin. Foster had gotten in a few words and would be content for a moment.

"We will bring forth a selective generation of perfected humanity, Foster. No more genetic flaws, no more inbred disease, weakness, and failures. No more grit in the smooth gears of humanity's gene pool. With our global DNA bank, and samples from hundreds of millions of your viewers, we can prune the bad branches to maximize the yield. Mankind will live longer, better, and more productively. Disease, inadequacies, every human frailty created by the brutish random breeding of four hundred generations, will be behind us."

Malcolm put his hands together in a steeple-like gesture and leaned toward Foster.

"The genes of the Father Race are in our hands now, Foster. I intend to bring them into the world, harvesting the best and the brightest among us, for the betterment of all mankind."

13

"HOW'S YOUR GIRL?" Oz joked as Jake removed his headset. It was Jake's third call to the colony that day. Privacy, in this small bouncing rover, was nonexistent.

John watched Jake blush, then smack Oz with a playful punch to the belly. "She's fine." Jake slapped Oz hard on the back. "Thanks for asking."

John was sure the MSR would become a tinderbox if they stayed in it much longer. His team was used to traveling for a *day*, not living in the rover for a week and a half. John would comment on that design problem later. It needed bunks and privacy—especially for women. All they had was a cramped bathroom to hide in. Otherwise, life here was an open book.

"Oz," John called. "What's our status on methane? Can't afford to break down out here."

Oz was still rubbing his stomach, feigning pain with a long face. "It's fine, Hawk. Just like it was last night when you asked. Gassed up at Rex's place, remember? We'll get home with a 62 percent reserve."

Deborah was taking her turn driving back across five hundred kilometers of parched Martian desert and the rugged Nirgal Vallis region of canyons and deep, dry river beds. She looked straight ahead as she drove. "It's time we talked about this."

"'Bout what?" John asked. He sat in the copilot seat, his feet up on a console, watching for boulders and other hazards.

"Pioneer spirit. Relationships. And our future. That's what."

John shook his head, certain he could sense a lecture coming.

"Go ahead, Deborah. Spit it out," Oz said, leaning on the back of John's seat. "What're you talkin' about?"

"The spark. At the colony. You felt it. You *had to*. You guys are running around this rover like three caged boys. You've been bitten. You just don't realize it."

John smiled. Definitely a sermon. Deborah style.

"You lost me somewhere around the first word," Jake said, moving up from the back. "Be more precise."

"Yeah. We sure don't have any time to waste," Oz said, getting a guffaw from the team.

"Okay," she said. "Pioneer spirit. Spark. Did it grab you back there? Greenhouse domes, fresh sweet air, brick-making machines, fish ponds. Even nurseries and plans for babies, for crying out loud. They intend to stay here — for good."

"And?" asked Jake.

"And who wouldn't want to join 'em? Right?" She turned her head a moment and John could see her expression. Her eyes were wide, alive with discovery and joy, like she was looking ahead to a time when she too might be one of Rex's mothers.

"Planning on having some Martian babies, are we?" Oz joked, poking her in the back. Everyone knew she wanted children, but not as much as she and Sam wanted to be in the space business together. That her biological clock was ticking loudly was no secret. She shared that fact all the time.

Poor Sam, John thought. *He's in for a big surprise.*

"No," Deborah replied. "I wasn't talking about kids—although the thought had occurred to me. I'm talking about a vision, you idiots! Vision for exploration that says 'grab it with both hands and hang on!'" She punched the air with a fist. "Pioneer spirit, in the face of adversity."

John saw in her the same gleam he'd noticed in Jake, and that he suspected had taken root in Oz the first time he saw Kate Westin wearing shorts. Like summer camp love, Jake and Oz were smitten, but they weren't about to admit it. And Deborah saw a fulfillment of her dream. Space *and* family—together. John let out a long sigh, wondering at their radical transformation in so few days.

"Would you?" John asked, turning toward Deborah as she navigated around some sharp rock outcroppings.

"Would I what, Hawk?"

"Would you stay? If I offered you that option?"

She was quiet a long moment. Oz and Jake hung on the back of the seats, watching her. Oz started popping his knuckles, his absentminded stress relief. John cringed.

Deborah slowed the MSR to a stop, and John heard her click it into neutral in the silence. The soft spot on her throat was thumping away like a hummingbird's heart.

"Okay. Since you asked," she said, her voice shaking. "I talked to Sam last night. A long time. It's hard, you know, with you gorillas snoring right under my feet. But we had a good heart-to-heart." She looked down at the floor, then wrung her hands together. Very unlike Dr. Deborah Readdy.

"Yes, Hawk. We'd stay. In fact, if having us on the flight home wasn't such a firm requirement — to keep you morons healthy for four months — we'd petition NASA right now to let us stay behind." She looked at the two men, then back to John. "This is what we've always dreamed of." She shrugged. "So there." She silently turned, put the vehicle in drive, and began to move ahead.

Jake clapped. "Go, girl! My sentiments exactly. This is the next frontier, Hawk. We can't live in space without a lifeline. And the Space Station wasn't really living. But we *can* make it here. And yes, I've talked to May about it. Sure, we're an unlikely pair. A white man with a black woman on Mars. But you know what? I'd have a very hard time turning down an opportunity to stay. I can always go home and sign books and do talks at high schools. But I can only be a *Martian* if I stay here."

"Ditto," Oz said, looking into the distance.

"Ditto? Man of many words, eh?" John said, turning around to face his lead engineer.

"'Ditto's' a good word, Hawk. That colony of theirs fires me up in a way NASA never did. I vote we stay." He turned to John. "What about you, Hawk?"

John grinned. "Well, it sounds like it'd be a lonely trip back to Earth if everyone feels the same way you three do. I flew home from Mars alone once. That eight-month trip was enough to last a lifetime." He scanned their faces. "Since we've all been on the radio to somebody, it seems, what does the rest of our crew have to say? Any other secrets I should know about?"

Deborah shrugged. "I can only tell you what I hear from Sam. Geo wouldn't stay here for love or money. He can't wait to prance around green Earth and show off his rocks. Melanie's got a family. She's ready to go back."

"What about R2?" John did a mental tally for the minimum crew needed to head home.

"Ramona's on the fence," Deborah replied. "Hasn't seen the colony. Has a family back home. She probably wants to go home." She slowed the vehicle to a stop and put it in park again. "Why do you ask, John? I see that look. You have a plan—don't you?" A smile grew across her usually straight-lipped face. "You agree with us, right?" She prodded him. "Out with it, Hawk. Now."

John frowned, afraid to show his true feelings. Like a contagious virus, the colonists' vision had infected his entire team, including him. He couldn't blame these guys for wanting to stay. But the decision to remain or to go—and who got that chance—would ultimately be his. And the colonists'.

NASA will blow a gasket. But it'll be fun to watch.

"One of us isn't being honest," Jake said with a sort of chortle in his voice. "What about you?" He pointed at John.

John's heart raced as he weighed the options. A giant door would slam shut if he said "stay"; perhaps he'd never see Earth again. And on the other side of that door, if he returned, there was no imaginable way to ever return to this planet he'd helped explore more than anyone else. Stay or go? He was sure he could hear a clock ticking, as the three awaited his answer.

John took a deep breath. NASA would never forgive him.

"I'd stay."

The rover was a rolling echo chamber, its white metal walls reflecting the four chattering voices.

It reminded John of flying home from a seven-month Navy deployment, a ten-hour Atlantic crossing with his crew of thirteen crammed into the cockpit of his P-3C Orion submarine hunter. Everyone wanted to talk at once as the coast of Maine came into sight. This felt good.

Oz was chatting about the engineering improvements he'd make to the water and air regeneration systems in the greenery domes. Jake mostly listened, a dreamy look in his eyes. John had known Jake the longest, and they'd often shared Jake's desire to meet someone special. Like John, Jake was a widower, but with no children.

Deborah did an about-face, wondering out loud to John about how many children the colony could support, asking him how difficult it would be to outfit a special mission to the planet with extra supplies for neonatal care.

"I expect they came prepared for that," John replied. "But more baby wipes couldn't hurt." He smiled. No one's mind was on returning to base. They lived in their daydreams now, every one fantasizing about the colony. Including John. A new life on Mars was on his mind every minute.

The communication channel barked with an incoming request for an encrypted comm circuit, and Oz entered the daily encryption key. This had become a common occurrence recently, with the revelation that the colony listened to all their unencrypted calls. Soon, a decoded voice transmission played on John's head set. He selected it for everyone to hear.

"... and we've gotten the best possible support from the

intelligence community. We think we have an answer to the source of the crash site material you found ten days ago."

With a one-way communication delay of more than ten minutes, no one expected a two-way conversation. Mission Director Dodd Marsh's voice shifted to Greg Church, Johnson Space Center director. "John. Share this material with the others at your discretion. It's serious but fact. We need to be blunt, as I'm sure you'd want us to be.

"Those parts you found were definitely made on Earth. We ran extensive evaluations of the markings on the wire bundles and the microchip markings in those pictures Oz made. Each marking refers to a common manufacturer in China—who, we've learned, has ties to subcontractors all over the world. CIA helped us to determine where some of the parts were assembled. Asia, Middle East, some in the US. That investigation is ongoing. But we know for sure companies on Earth made the alien spider parts you found. That entire alien spider mess was a ruse. Unless—"

Everyone held their breath. Greg Church had as hard a time saying what they all feared as they would have. "Unless Raines is *right*. The Father Race lives among us. In that case—well—who knows what we call that crash evidence. Human? Alien? Life is getting very confused; I'm sure you'd agree."

John felt conflicting emotions. Though he'd been convinced the evidence pointed to a hoax, he'd half hoped for Rex and May's sake—for all the colonists—that his new friends could save face. This revelation would strike at the core of their beliefs, and roughen up old wounds.

Church continued. "John, we've got a list of companies; the FBI's working through it to find out who knew what and when they knew it. If we can locate even one supplier that had an idea what the parts were for, or who the master buyer was, we can get a handle on this thing. For now—" He paused. "We intend to keep a lid on this.

"We can't afford to pit Malcolm Raines's machine and millions of his followers against our manned space program. They'd think we set this up. I mean, look what we've got here. Crash evidence on a direct path between the two Mars camps. No one would believe us, particularly now with the news about the Edwards colony."

"This is stupid!" Oz shouted, away from the mike. He slammed his fist into the bulkhead. "They're gonna sit on this? *Again?* What if we found green men poking around the Hab? Would they cover that up too to keep Raines happy?"

"Shhh!" Deborah put a finger to her lips.

"We need your input," Church continued. "What does the colony think about this? Of course, they could end up breaking the news, and we'd have no control. That worries me. The way this is shaping up, we could look bad, real bad. So that's the extent of it. Over to you, John. We need your recommendation. Houston out."

John switched off the speaker and removed his headset. "It's up to us now."

"They don't trust the colonists!" Jake blurted. "And Church doesn't even know 'em! All he cares about is looking good. You heard him!"

Deborah shrugged. "No surprise there. NASA's always been about image. Problem is, this time—"

"This time they can't *control* the image," Oz said. "Dollars to donuts, they're trying to spin this to make the colonists look like kooks."

John slowed the MSR to a stop and turned around. "Hold on, guys. We're making some tough accusations, and we've only just heard from Church."

"Don't take his side. Not now." Oz's face was red with rage. "We all know what you think of the backroom politics back home. You should be the first to protest."

John held up his hand. "Agree with you there, Oz. Most of the leadership's more concerned about their hide than science. Or colonies. That's not what I meant, though."

"Let him speak," Deborah said, laying a hand on Oz's arm.

"What I'm getting at is this," John said. "You wouldn't have had a problem with that call from Houston ten days ago, when we found the spiders." He gestured at the plastic-encased material in back of the rover. "But now that you've tasted what the colony has to offer, and you're excited about it, this news feels like an attack on people you've come to like — even trust. So let's think this over for a minute. I mean, Church has a point. If NASA comes out hard against spiders the world has thought for years were aliens, and says they have evidence they're manmade, NASA will be up against a hail of protests."

He looked around the compartment; his friends were nodding. "We confronted this problem ourselves," he said. "Back at the colony."

"It's like the fiasco with fossilized life found in Antarctic meteors," Deborah said.

"Exactly. They'll say, 'NASA, you got it wrong thirty years ago with those rocks you found on the South Pole.' No one — change that — *none* of the general public, except those looking to discredit Saint Michael's Remnant, will ever believe NASA. Or us."

"What about you, Hawk?" Oz asked. His red subsided.

"Me? The spiders are fake. This just confirms what I tried to get them to publicize before."

"Which they didn't," Jake added.

"Right."

"So," Deborah said as she scratched her chin. "What if NASA *didn't* expose this? What if *someone else* broke the news?"

"Who?" Oz asked. He cracked his knuckles like castanets.

"You don't mean . . ." Jake began, making eye contact with her, then John.

"Yep. Let the colony spill the beans. Keep us and NASA out of it. They'd have no reason to expose this data. But if they did, the findings would have more credibility."

"And how do we do that?" Oz laughed. "They didn't buy the story the first time."

"They might over time," Deborah said. "Let them hear what we just heard. Except, don't hear it from us." She winked at John. "Get my drift?"

He nodded. *Smart lady, that doctor.* John keyed the mike, catching the befuddled looks on Oz and Jake's faces before he turned around to the control panel.

"Houston, this is MSR2, Gold Crew, transmitting on K-A band secure. We copy your last. We've talked this over and agree the best approach is to let the colony know everything you found. Request no more secure comms. Repeat, no secure. No NASA press announcement. In the meantime, keep us informed daily, and go out of your way to tell us everything in the clear. Let the colony hear everything we do, and let them draw their own conclusions. If the colony announces the hoax, that news has more credibility coming from them than it does from us."

John turned around and saw all three astronauts nod, then continued. "Request you repeat your entire last transmission, in the clear. Just the way you said it, with the concerns." He paused, as he considered the ramifications on manned spaceflight and their mission if this strategy backfired.

"We trust the Edwards Colony to make the right decision. That's our unanimous recommendation. MSR2, out."

14

"**THEY CAN'T BE THAT STUPID.**" *Then again, maybe they can,* Shawnda thought. The implication sickened her.

She wagged her finger as she said it. Across the small dinner table, her trim African-American husband of six years, FBI Special Agent Terrance Kerry, smiled as he rested his head on his hands, elbows on the table. They were enjoying a brief time together in their Georgetown home. "Don't give me that schoolboy 'dreamy eyes' look, Terrance. I'm talking business."

Kerry chuckled. "Sorry. I love watching you when you get mad."

"Not mad. I'm *torched.* So — *can* they be that stupid? Think that by erasing my whiteboard and stealing my computer, then trying to get McClannahan to erase my memory by giving me another assignment, I'll just walk away? Forget everything I learned?"

"They might."

"Might?"

"You're a hired gun, Shawnda. You work for the CIA's major support contractor. They probably figure you're a good company woman, and that you'll follow the party line. So, are you?"

"What?"

"A company woman. Are you willing to do whatever the customer asks and not question it, to make sure you win the next contract?"

"You know me well enough, Terrance Kerry. I am *not*."

"Good. So what're we gonna do about this?"

"Inside the system? Nothing. McClannahan's shut me down. I touched a nerve somewhere inside the Agency or Secret Service. If past experience is any gauge, I'll be transferred to a different directorate, as far from Middle East operations as possible. But close enough for McClannahan to make an occasional sweaty waddle by my office to have a chat." She shook her head, running her fingers through black locks. "I thought he was my friend."

"He might still be. Did those Secret Service guys say anything about me—that we're married?"

"Yeah. Said you knew who killed Vice President Ryan." She looked out the bay window, watching a loud truck labor up the hill, then turned back to Terrance. "I didn't think much about it. Figured they were just minimizing the value of my research."

"Good. Anything else?"

"Good? What's good about it?"

"No one told you to keep this stuff to yourself? To keep your mouth shut? Specifically, you weren't told to avoid discussing this with me?"

"No. Just a standard Middle East operations debrief, telling me to cease work on the case and I'd be reassigned to a new theater of operations Monday. Told me to leave this alone. For good."

"For good . . ." Terrance repeated, his face screwed into that strange "I don't know" look he got when he didn't accept a conclusion and was trying to cipher his way out of it. She'd seen this look many times, the first time when he was chasing Elias Ulrich. "Yeah. They're either stupid, or cunning. But not likely both."

"Why?" Shawnda asked, leaning closer to him over the table. She could see his mental gears at work.

"If they really wanted to shut you down, they'd find a way to prevent you from talking to me. Don't know how, but they'd try. We have to assume they think we'll talk. Right?"

"So," she said, starting to see where this was headed, "they're either too stupid to figure out our connection and its implication, or . . ."

"Or they *want* me on the case but can't ask for it outright. Or won't. I'm betting they're no dummies. Which means—"

Terrance stood up and walked to a kitchen cabinet for some paper and two pens. He returned and sat next to her. She loved his inquisitive fix-a-problem nature. He was coming to her aid. Her venting had worked.

"Draw it out, Shawnda. Before you forget it." He put his hand on hers. "Presume they need me to know."

She took a pen, then gave him a light kiss on the cheek. "Already drew it out, Special Agent man. Multiple copies."

"That's my girl. Thought you would. Now show me this magic relationship."

Shawnda went to a loose corner of the carpet in their den, lifted it, and pulled out a thin file. "What?" she asked as she caught his eye when she laid her papers on the table.

"Nothing," Terrance said with a smile and a shake of the head. "Good hiding spot."

"Thanks. So. Here it is." Shawnda spread her material on the table.

The pencil drawing laid out the six columns of relationships and the common thread running across all six columns—Federated Mining Industries. She spent the next ten minutes describing what the agents had heard.

"And there's more," she said at last. "FMI's been diversifying their portfolio. Getting into a new kind of mining. Remember I told you that every time I put the relationships together, they kept leading me back to the late Vice President Ryan?"

He nodded, making some notes as she spoke.

"FMI began to invest in biotech back in 2005. DNA mining, so to speak. Laboratories in China and Eastern Europe that specialize in DNA typing, genomics, and cloning of bacterial genes. The new tech business wave."

Kerry looked up at her. "Go on."

"Guess who owned the DNA laboratory that identified Vice President Ryan's remains? And those of the Wells family, when the helicopter was shot down? FMI's wholly owned subsidiary, General Research and Performance Studies—GRPS.

"Vice President Ryan was up to his ears in favors and FMI mine legislation when he was Speaker of the House. He cosponsored the bill to open up the Pacific Islands in the US Territories for mining and exploration. And when he gets killed, the same folks he supported with legislation are standing there ready to label his body parts. Thanks to a sole-source contract with the Secret Service. It's too perfect."

She pushed her ladderback chair away from the table. Leaning on the rear legs, she watched her husband. He was the veteran of dozens of investigations, and architect of the major breakthroughs that caught the 2011 terrorists, Elias Ulrich and his team of nineteen domestic terrorists, who had attacked Washington and Colorado Springs.

"Why does the firm that funds pro-terror groups in 2020," Terrance began, drawing a timeline on the paper, "and funds the election of a pro-mining vice president in 2008, also own the DNA lab that types his unidentifiable body parts when he's killed in 2014? Accidental? Not likely." He made some doodles on the timeline Shawnda couldn't decipher, and then leaned back in his own chair, raising the pen to chew on the cap. She hated that habit.

"I've got an idea. You follow McClannahan's guidance. Go where he sends you. Pretend you moved on to a new assignment like the good company woman. Since they didn't specifically tell you to lock me out, I'll take this over to the FBI on Monday and run it on my side of the house. We'll see if anyone at CIA complains."

Shawnda rested her chair on four legs again and took Terrance's left hand in her own. "Be careful." She smiled. "And you'd better tell me what you find. I want to help."

"*You* be careful. Help me, but only from a distance." He stroked her hair. "Just in case. In case we misread their intentions. Secret Service, I mean. Like you said, they might just be stupid. But I don't want to take that chance."

MONDAY, MARCH 23, 2020: NAZARJE, SLOVENIA

"Your room's bugged, Amy. He can monitor everything you say and do. I got the guards pulled off last time. But I can't do it every night. I should've told you."

Amy knelt by the stone wall, a flashlight in her hand. The cold night wind blew around their visitor behind the grate.

"Turn off the light. Only use it in an emergency," Monique said.

Amy saw her point through the iron slats across the room. "A microphone's hidden in each bed post, and there's another in the table.

Two cameras. There," she said, pointing toward the cottage door, "and another directly above us right now. Pretend you're praying while you sit here."

Amy pulled Alice closer, and the two of them knelt in front of the grate, their backs to the door. She whispered, "Why?"

"Why what?" Monique asked. "Why are *we* here? Or why are *you*?"

Amy prayed for the right words, fearing the worst—that this woman was setting them up in some way. Or trying to find out more about them to harm them somehow.

"I'm asking you," Amy repeated. "Why *us*? For six years?" The memories of two thousand nights in this place merged into one interminable darkness.

"I don't know. He hasn't told me everything. But the Father Race told him—"

"Father Race!?" Amy blurted, her pulse starting to race. "Who is 'him'?" Somehow, she already knew.

"Father Raines, the Guardian of the Mother Seed."

The dark room swirled around her, and Amy crumpled, her head thudding against the stone wall. She smelled something damp; cold stone touched her cheek. She vaguely felt Alice trying to catch her before she hit the floor and lay there.

Her heart skipped erratically, like those stressful days waiting for John's return from Mars, the wild pulse slamming against her temple. Images whirled in her mind, tall, dark Malcolm Raines in his purple robes, spouting lies about the Father Race and mankind's future. Amy's hands clenched into fists.

Suddenly she was back on the television interview where the two faced off years ago—the day he'd told a world of viewers her husband was dead somewhere in interplanetary space. The day she'd verbally pummeled him. *It all makes sense now.* This was some demented version of vengeance on Raines's part, covered in the thin veil of Father Race prophecy. Struggling to sit up, she grabbed the grate and stared directly into Monique's face. "Where are we?" she growled. "Tell me, Monique. *Now.*"

Monique hesitated, then looked down at the tunnel floor, unable to face Amy. "Nazarje. In Slovenia. South of the Alps."

"Why?"

"I'm sorry. I don't know. He said the Father—"

"There is no Father Race! It's a lie."

"You can't say that! We've seen their Oracles."

"Oracles? You mean the spiders? That's a hoax." Amy tugged at the rusty slats and cried out loudly. "Why? Why are we here?"

Monique looked up; her eyes locked with Amy's. "Please!" she whispered. "You'll get us both killed! Be quiet!"

Amy jerked her hands free, turning to Alice and pulling her daughter to her chest. She bent her head over Alice's blonde curls and began to sob.

"Take this," Monique said, forcing a gray bandana through a hole in the grate. "I can help."

Amy looked up through wet eyes, her daughter cradled in her arms. "How?"

"I have a plan. But I can't share it. If he finds out, if he hurts you to learn more . . . We're both in terrible danger."

"What are his plans, Monique? Why are we here?"

While Monique was silent, Amy sensed the Holy Spirit reminding her of the bondage that imprisoned them all. Including this woman.

"The Mother Seed," Monique whispered at last. "They're here."

Amy gasped. "The identical ones?"

"Yes. Three hundred twenty-one sisters." She paused, clearing her throat. "*My* sisters."

Amy gasped. "Are they safe?"

Monique shook her head. "We have to get you—and *them*—free of this place." She extended her fingers through the grate, and Amy clasped them.

"What's he planning to do?"

"The Mother Seed has a great mission. . . ." Monique choked on her own words. Amy saw her look down again, in shame. "A providence promised to them from the beginning of time . . ." Her voice drifted off as if she relived some memory or replayed a prophecy she'd heard a million times. Then her eyes fixed on Amy, and her fingers clutched Amy's in a tight, sweaty embrace.

"They're destined to carry the seed of the Father Race. As am I."

MARS

"John. Come here a sec'." Melanie was sitting with her legs curled under her, reviewing system diagnostics at the habitation module's console. The MSR was back at home base, in its usual docking bay, just before sunset. Their five-day transit completed, the crew of four had rushed to the kitchen for some warm chow. No more rover rations tonight.

John set down his fork, pushing aside the plate of warmed lasagna —cooked the first time more than eighteen months ago. He longed for Sachiko's fresh vegetables.

"What's up?" He wiped some tomato sauce off his mouth and rose slowly, preoccupied with thoughts of the alien hoax and his life-changing decision to stay on Mars . . . given the chance. It was hard to get excited about yet another mechanical fault.

Normally effervescent, his deputy commander was suddenly

serious, shaking her head with a finger to her lips as if to say "shut up and hurry up." She glanced toward the rest of the crew gathered around the communal table and put a finger to her lips.

"Trouble?" he whispered, drawing close. Leaning over Melanie's shoulder was like burying his face in a bouquet of fresh flowers. He hadn't smelled something this nice in two weeks. Deborah didn't use perfume; neither did any of the women at the colony. Her fragrance reminded him of roses—and his wife.

He pushed the thoughts of women—of Melanie and of Amy—deep down as he focused on the telemetry screen in front of her. Something was amiss. He didn't believe it at first.

John leaned forward, adjusting his reading glasses, and put a finger on the soft plasma screen as if the touch would confirm he'd misread the data. Perhaps he'd read the decimal point in the wrong place, or the system reported the data in the wrong units.

But there was no mistake. The hair on his forearms stood up. A sweat chilled his forehead and neck in the cool cabin. Like a statue, he stood transfixed, feeling dizzy.

"Here!" Melanie said, grabbing a chair behind him and sliding it into place as he half settled, half fell, from stooping over her terminal. He plopped into it so hard the diners behind him became silent.

"Hawk. You okay?" Deborah asked. He heard her but couldn't look up. His eyes were glued to the floor. Just as he felt he was glued to Mars. His legs were rubber, and he couldn't catch his breath.

"Hawk?" Deborah repeated. He heard her chair slide across the floor. His overly protective doctor would be at his side in moments. But he didn't care.

I must be dreaming. It's happened—again!

"Mel! What's going on?" Oz asked, walking over to John's side to see the screen that had just brought John down. He stopped in his tracks and whistled. "It's gone! D'you check backup telemetry, Mel? Confirm it?"

"I did," she said, selecting some alternate views of their data. Each showed the same result. A graph on a side pane of the monitor showed a precipitous drop in a pressure reading, plummeting from a green threshold, through yellow, into red, over the course of half an hour. It had now reached a value near zero. She turned to John. "We should call Houston." Melanie's words reverberated in the tiny room.

John nodded, then turned to face the silent team at the dinner table. He pointed up, trying to find the words.

"It's the Earth Return Vehicle, guys. Our ride home, waiting up in orbit. Its methane and oxygen fuel loads have suddenly disappeared. In the last half hour. There's . . ." John choked, his voice stuck in his throat. "There's no propellant to take us home."

Oz had squeezed himself between John and Melanie, commanding a variety of control screens, and pounding the control panel with each frustrating result. "It's been hit!" Oz blurted. "Just like Epsilon was. Probably Swiss cheese by now. Lost all tank pressurization, along with the oxidizer and propellant. Unresponsive diagnostics mean the data cables might have been severed."

Oz shook his head and swore. "ERV's shot, guys. Whether you wanted to leave or not, we can't get off Mars now." He threw his napkin down in disgust. "There's no ride home."

15

"I DON'T NEED A SEDATIVE!" John yelled. "That's an order!"

"You need *something*, John. You're on a rampage." Deborah wagged her finger at him like an old school marm, her hand loaded with a hypodermic full of some happy juice. John steamed, facing her on his stool in the laboratory. No matter what she said, he craved to punch Geo—to draw blood.

Reluctant to take his eyes off the armed doctor, John fidgeted on the stool. But a soft hand touching his, and the smell of Melanie's fresh-washed hair—like a sachet of dried rose petals—snapped his rage.

Amy. Snuggling up close to him at night after a long soak in her claw-foot tub.

He looked up into Melanie's eyes, brown saucers brimming with pain.

"He'll be okay, Deborah," Melanie said. "Isn't that right, John?"

In his shock at Melanie's gentle contact, he never felt the doctor take his forearm; now she was ready to plunge the needle. He jerked back as Melanie's deep wet eyes pleaded with his.

"John, *please*. We all understand why you're upset. But we've gotta work through this, okay?" She squeezed his hand, soft skin and a firm grip that sent tingles up his spine. "You with me, John boy? Let's show Deborah she can put that sedative away. Okay?"

He nodded, broken. Geo might live to see another day.

"You scared me back there, John." She held onto him with both hands. Her voice was as soothing as gentle rain on a metal farmhouse roof. "You gonna be all right?"

He nodded, locked on her eyes, a well of peace.

"You're too defensive, John. You need to hear that. We know the meteoroid impact on *Epsilon* wasn't your fault. Even if Geo says it was. He's an idiot. Right? And whatever creamed the ERV wasn't your fault either. We know that." She held him with one hand and caressed the back of his hand with the other. "Breathe deep. Show me you understand."

John nodded in silence.

"What happened on *Epsilon* was a statistical improbability, and we don't blame you. Ignore what Geo said for a minute if you can."

"Their deaths weren't improbable," John said, his voice shaking. "It was a *colossal impossibility*. Tiny little people in a universe of space, and the rocks hit *them*." He shook as he let out a long breath.

"Right. I agree. So Geo's a jerk, and he deserves to have his face rearranged for implying you could have done something to save Sean and Michelle, or prevent the ERV's damage today. But if you'd taken his head off back there—if Oz hadn't pulled you down—would it have solved anything?"

John smiled. "Geo would have ceased to exist as a life form."

Melanie gasped.

"Just kidding. He'd probably start breathing eventually. Doc would have made sure of that."

"Not funny."

John spoke more softly. "I'm prepared to stay, Melanie. To die here, if that's what it calls for. But you—and the rest of Blue Team—I've got to get you home, if that's where you want to go." He released her hand and pounded his thigh. "I must."

Melanie stroked his forearm. A tingle coursed down his spine as her delicate fingers ran across thick hair, lingering at his wristwatch, and took his hand again in hers. Melanie was the best friend he had on this mission, but something inside him whispered "too close."

"John, you're so focused on getting us home you're not thinking straight. You say it all the time. 'Use all the resources at your disposal.' You told Rex that, too, remember?"

John cocked his head, trying to shake the tingles. The little voice inside him was getting louder: *Move away.*

"I've tried, Mel. I'm so focused on a conspiracy at this point I can't think straight."

"Here's a hint." Melanie gathered his hands together, their four sets of fingers and palms wrapped together. "Think, John. You're the Space MacGyver. Bring back that part of the Hawk that we love . . . and need."

John lost himself in what she'd said—there was an idea there, something just beyond his consciousness. . . .

"Yes!" he yelled. Melanie flinched as he broke their connection and leapt from his seat. "You're a genius, Mel! The colony's Earth Return Vehicle! It's sitting five hundred clicks from here. We can still get home!"

Then, heart pounding, he realized the desperate consequence. "But if *we* do? How do *they* leave?"

"That's not the main question, I think, John." Her voice cracked for the first time that afternoon. "The real question, you know, is—is who stays behind? There are eight of us here, John. But their ship only holds five."

GEORGETOWN, DISTRICT OF COLUMBIA

Shawnda pushed open the unlatched door to the dark apartment and paused in the entryway as their antique Navy brass clock bonged six bells. She was certain she'd locked the door when they'd headed their separate ways that morning, she to the CIA, Terrance downtown to the Bureau.

She froze, her heart beating erratically at memories of the three secretive men erasing her notes, confiscating her computer, and her boss reassigning her to a dead-end analyst job. She nudged the door open and stepped to one side. The door squeaked on its hinges, the clock ticking loudly in the silent room.

"Shawnda?" a voice asked.

She gasped, then giggled and stepped inside, holding her hand to her wildly thumping chest. "Terrance? What're you doing home so early? You scared me to death!"

"It's seven. That's early?"

"For you, yes," she said, dropping her bag on the couch and hugging her husband.

"Did you run up the stairs?" Terrance pulled her tight. "Your ticker's going nuts."

"No. My imagination ran away with me. It's just that . . . well . . .

after all I've been through the past two days at work, I thought . . ."

He held her at arm's length, his gaze meeting hers. "You thought some hit squad from the White House was rifling through your personal effects to find out what else you knew about FMI, right?"

She nodded and gulped a deep breath.

"If it'll make you feel better, there's no bugs here. I swept the place today. It's clean. Okay?"

Shawnda nodded. "McClannahan assigned me to work the Balkan operations today. The pits. Worst place an analyst can end up these days."

"Didn't waste any time, did he?" Terrance said, leading her by the hand to the kitchen. "He's getting you out of the way, honey. Maybe to protect you. Him, too, if I don't miss my guess."

"Maybe," Shawnda said, narrowing her eyes at her husband. "So, *did you* come home early to search my things?"

"No." Terrance laughed. "But I do bring news." He handed her a glass of red wine, pulling her along to the couch. Shawnda's heart raced again, sensing a revelation in his unusually early return and his voice.

"Tell all." She sat on the edge of the deep sofa pit, hanging on his next words. The red wine calmed her, and she took another long sip.

Terrance swirled his wine, looking at it for a minute. "Your concerns—about the open door? They're valid." He looked up. Her FBI Special Agent husband had on his work face.

"You—and I—have stepped into the middle of a *very* difficult situation, Shawnda."

She breathed at last. "How?"

"I went to Quantico today."

"The FBI Academy?"

"Yes, but first, I paid a visit to the Marine Corps. The presidential helicopter squadron's based there. They gave me access to the crash evidence from six years ago. Seats, cushions, and other material where I could find blood samples. I called them Friday night after you and I talked. They had the stuff ready when I arrived."

"And?"

"The Academy's FBI lab ran some analyses on the evidence over the weekend. As a special favor for me. Some of it was expected." He handed her a sheet of paper.

At the top, she read "Vice President Ryan. Mrs. Ryan. Lieutenant Colonel Gurley." Shawnda gasped as she read down the list of crew members and passengers. "There's no one from the Wells family on this list! How's that possible?"

"That's what I asked. You'd think the authorities—that's us, by the way—would have figured this out a long time ago. I assumed they made a mistake. But they're adamant. According to our lab analysis, using crash evidence, there's no DNA evidence from any member of the Wells family to prove they were on that flight."

Shawnda felt dizzy. "And?"

"I have no idea why. Except I do know this. We just stuck our noses into a massive cover-up, tied to the vice president's assassination and the murder of a dozen people. So it pays to watch your door. That's why I had our place swept by the counterintelligence team today. Just to be sure."

Shawnda let the paper slide from her hand onto the floor. "The Veep and his wife are dead, but John's family isn't? Why on Earth?"

"'Why on *Mars*?' might be more appropriate," he said. "John Wells is convinced his family's dead. I know him well. He went back to Mars, in part, to escape the pain." Terrance took a deep breath, looking again into his swirling wine. "Imagine how he'll feel when he learns they weren't on that helo."

She looked up at him, her intelligence analyst's sixth sense clicking into action. "We need—"

"—to exhume the bodies." Terrance completed her sentence. "It's being done as we speak. I had to bring the director in on this. Top level stuff. That's the other reason I'm home so early. You opened a huge can of worms, sweetie." He looked back at the door again. Shawnda was glad she'd bolted it on the way in.

"We'll know in a couple of days if the remains match John's family. If not—"

She felt sick, imagining the parts of bodies, shredded by a disintegrating helo, decomposing in a grave for six years. The dizziness got worse, and she set down the wine. "If they're not in those graves, we have to find all five of them, Terrance. For John."

He nodded and looked back at the door.

"You're worried about me. Aren't you?" she asked.

Terrance's mouth was a tight, straight line. "I'm worried about *both* of us. The people who did this, if my hunch is correct, fooled the Secret Service and the nation for more than six years. Taking the two of us out of the picture would be much simpler than faking the deaths of John's family."

FRIDAY, MARCH 27, 2020: MARS

"NASA's sittin' on this thing, Hawk. We gotta do somethin'," Oz said as the two men labored in their Mars suits under the glow of a distant sun. A steep crater rim rose behind him, covered in soft red dust—Martian sand snow.

"Yeah. You're right. We do," John said with a grunt. On a typical day, working in this desiccated world of fine rufous powder and jagged black boulders, John would be whistling, thrilled to explore the Red Planet.

Today, he never noticed the grandeur, but the hard work felt good.

John was glad to be sweating for a change, even if that meant laboring in a suit that smelled like an overripe gym locker. This short geology excursion to a little-visited crater to search for ice was a good way to create a much-needed diversion for the crew. Everyone—particularly John—was focused on the busted ERV. It wouldn't be so bad if they all wanted to stay on Mars. But they didn't.

John handed the drill motor to Oz as Jake and Melanie rigged another extension on the coring bit to gnaw red rock at the crater's base. Images of Amy and a blue Earth filled his mind as he talked—gurgling streams of cold water, tumbling down a remote wilderness holler in the Pisgah National Forest. For a brief winsome moment he was on the Appalachian Trail with her, surrounded by an arching tunnel of blooming rhododendrons, the aroma of skunk cabbage wafting on cool breezes. He stubbed his toe on a rock and came back to Mars.

"You know, they're probably trying their best, Oz," John said, glad body language didn't show with space suits. He didn't believe his own words. "They'll get an ERV headed our way soon." John pointed at his wrist monitor.

Oz got the hint and changed channels to a private frequency.

"You wanted to stay here, remember?" John asked once he was sure Oz had changed channels.

"I know. Still do." Oz didn't look up. "But we gotta get the other guys home."

"I've got a backup plan. But I'm not ready to hatch it yet. Wanted to pressure Houston first."

"Me, too. Make 'em earn their keep. You gonna rustle us up a spaceship, Hawk? Like one sittin' 'bout five days away?"

John looked up at his tall friend. "Could be. Have to wait and see."

Geo walked up, waving a heat gun used to shrink-wrap plastic around his rock samples. Oz and John switched back on their common frequency.

"What're you complaining about, Oz?" Geo said. "I heard you gushing when you got back from that girly farm. You *want* to stay here. I say, you got your wish."

Oz brandished a meter-long drill bit extension at him. "You know what, meteor mouth? We could save lots of oxygen and food if we just leave you out here."

John grabbed Oz's arm, shaking his head.

"On second thought, though, you're not worth the trouble. He's *your* problem, Hawk." Oz dropped the drill extension and walked away.

Melanie halted her drilling and faced Geo. "Put a lid on it, Witt. We're all on edge, okay?"

John walked to Geo and laid a gloved hand on the man's suit shoulder. Their geologist tried to back up, but John held on.

"I'm sorry I started to hit you the other day, Robert. I was wrong."

Geo tried to back up again. "Yeah. Sure. Like when you whacked that terrorist who killed your wife and kids, huh? You wanted to kill me, too. Admit it . . . you're a menace, Hawk. A powder keg waiting to blow. NASA just doesn't know it." He stalked away.

John fought the urge to pick up a rock and chunk it through Geo's visor, then shook his head and turned back to Melanie. "One more drill sample, over there." He pointed to the last survey stake. "Then we'll call it a day."

"No problem." Melanie touched his suit, then waved him toward the sulking geologist. She was their peacemaker.

Geo picked up his heat gun and wrapped rock samples, stowing them in a special tote cart and transporting them to the storage lockers outside the MSR. John walked over, offering to help. Geo waved him off again.

"Leave me be, Hawk. I don't trust you *or* those weenies in Houston who claim they're doing all they can to get us home. And I don't trust those bimbos who think they're gonna birth a new race of Martians. NASA sent us here on a wild goose chase, and now we're stranded. Funny how that's always a problem when you're around, huh? What's this—the third time in a row you've been marooned?"

Geo shoved John out of the way and starting maneuvering the cart toward the MSR. "Just my luck I hitched my star to your rain cloud. Now leave me alone."

John sat in the quiet white of the MSR, watching his crew working their way up the long slope to the crater rim. Still encased in the dirty white suit, helmet unlatched, he pondered his next move.

Mel was right. "Use all the resources at your disposal." Can't wait on NASA any longer or we'll be at each other's throats.

He reached for the communication panel, selecting a frequency he knew the colony monitored, and keyed the microphone. "Colony, this is John. Trying to reach May." He waited a moment, watching the crew approach, and repeated his call.

In a few seconds Dr. Tabor responded. "This is Nicci. Is this John?"

"Yeah. Thanks for the quick response. Can you get May for me?"

"Hold on." Nicci was short with him. Feelings were still raw there, no doubt.

No wonder. Their entire world's been turned upside down.

The next voice was soothing. John understood why Jake was so drawn to her.

"John? This is May. What can I do for you?"

"Hi, May. Thanks for taking a call. We've got some serious problems. Think you've heard."

"Yes. We've been waiting to hear from you. Rex talked to his dad about this, too. We think we can help."

"His dad?" *There it is again. Talking to a dead man. Are they nuts?*

"Forget it. We'll show you when you come over next time. But we *have* been waiting for your call."

"Really? Why?"

"Food and water, among other things. We've got enough to get you through the six-month delay till the next ERV arrives—if you want it."

"We might. Thanks. But I had something else in mind," John said, trying to sound at ease, his heart a jackhammer under his ribs.

"What else, John?"

"We need a ride home, May. You've got one. I'd like to talk about a swap."

May didn't answer right away, but he was sure she'd already considered that option. They all had. Oz's last comment was proof of that.

"Let's talk tonight, John. I know what you're getting at. But there's a catch."

"Your ship only carries five people, right? And we're not trained to fly it."

"Partially correct. We can teach you the launch systems. That's not hard. No, the catch is we've also got a problem. We're seriously divided on this hoax issue." She paused, and he heard others in the background arguing. "Rex insists there wasn't a hoax. He wants to return to Earth to counter the lies about what you found. To stand up for his dad and our beliefs. But the rest of us are happy to stay." She stopped, her voice cracking. Jake said she cried herself to sleep most nights.

"I don't understand," John said. Soon the crew would be inside and his conversation public.

Her voice got more introspective. "We girls have been listening to NASA's talk about the manufacturing markings on the crash-site materials. Whether they're alien or not—and we believe they *are*—we want to stay. Rex wants to go home, to carry the banner for his dad." She paused. "But he can't go home alone."

The airlock light cycled, a hiss of rushing air indicating the lock's return to atmospheric pressure. John couldn't believe what he'd just heard. Sweat formed on his palms.

"So, John, it seems we have a mutual opportunity. Rex needs a ride home, and so do you. We'd be willing to make a trade, as you say. Your MAV and ERV later for ours now. But you can only take half your crew with you." Another pause. "I'm sorry."

John felt a sudden rush of elation—*a solution*. Melanie was right!

"We'll talk tonight," John said. "I have to get off now. But the number of seats going home might not be a problem." He paused, watching the airlock door open, Melanie at the front of the soiled group of quibbling astronauts. Geo had them all worked up. Again.

"I have at least four people here who want to stay." He paused. "Five of them, if you count me."

16

TWO AMBULANCES SHOT DOWN Rock Creek Parkway, the forested byway hidden by a steep embankment behind Shawnda's apartment. As she paced in the den, the persistent far-off beat of a drum and cymbals reminded her that it was Friday night. Georgetown was alive.

She was happy to be settled down at home, away from the madness. Glad to be with him. Since her miscarriage a year ago, their time together was even more special. She didn't want to be in public. She just wanted Terrance. Other than her work, he was her only world.

Special Agent Terrance Kerry pored over papers with his reading glasses, his gun still holstered in a black leather underarm package he could reach quickly. Although he never mentioned it, Shawnda noticed he wore his weapon all the time of late.

"You remember that night?" Shawnda asked as Terrance labored over the kitchen table, a mechanical pencil in his teeth and scraps of paper spread before him. She twirled a lock of black hair about her finger, awaiting his answer

"I've never forgotten the day Amy died," he said at last. "I was headed to DC to watch John receive the Congressional Gold Medal of Honor. On behalf of the deceased crew members of the first Mars mission." Terrance leaned back in his chair and stared at the ceiling, pulling ideas off the wallboard.

As he leaned back, his triceps flexed under a tight white T-shirt, short arms bulging under the sleeves. Shawnda's girlfriends reminded her often he was "lots of fun to look at." She agreed, but wished he'd stop leaning back in the chair.

"What I remember—" he began, snapping her muscleman daydream—"and what I actually *saw*. We have to separate those." He wadded a paper ball and tossed it at her, laughing. "That's why I need a CIA puke like you to help me figure it out."

"Here to help." Shawnda laughed and batted the paper away. This was a chance to work together again, like when they'd first met, chasing Elias Ulrich. A thread ran through their marriage, attached to John Wells. This was the third time in her husband's career that John had figured prominently in an investigation.

"When did you arrive?" She sat down, watching his face. He pursed his lips, looked at his watch, and closed his eyes. She imagined little pistons pounding under that close-cropped black and gray hair. He was always thinking, planning, evaluating.

"The Veep's helicopter was shot down at 3:21 p.m. Took me a long time to get there with all the traffic and Secret Service. Arrived just after dark. Probably five-thirty or six."

"Where'd you go first?"

"Sacrifice Monument. At the end of Memorial Bridge."

"Why?"

"Capitol Police told me John was there. At the base of that big horse with the gold rider, near Lincoln Memorial. Shredded helicopter parts were everywhere; jet fuel drenched the place. It was dark, but I remember the site well. Body parts were labeled with flags on the ground, and draped in orange or black plastic." He took a deep breath. "It was gross."

"What was the very first thing you did?"

"Found John. He wasn't at the monument, so I asked an officer. She said John took off in a canoe, of all things. Crossing the Potomac. Couldn't figure why—'til I found him. And Ulrich with him, about to run John through with a dive knife."

"Did John identify the bodies?"

Kerry chewed on the blue mechanical pencil as he leaned back, grasping for more clues on their kitchen ceiling. Then he looked at Shawnda with a puzzled expression, the pencil drooping absentmindedly from his mouth. He cocked his head for a moment, and his eyes went wide. "No!" His arm muscles tensed as he balanced the chair on two legs.

"No *what*, honey?"

"No! He told me he couldn't stand to see them. The body parts. The Secret Service agent told me John had seen Amy's torso strapped in a seat. John threw up when he saw it. The agent sat him down at the monument to recover."

Kerry slapped his thigh. "Yeah! John *never* looked at 'em! And when he and I came back to the site months later, he told me it was too painful to see all the dismembered parts."

Shawnda felt ill; seeing your spouse's severed body would do more than make her vomit. Terrance leaned forward and scribbled on some paper.

"Did anyone identify the parts? Did you interview any of the crash-site workers? Police? Anyone?" She realized she sounded desperate. She was. John and Terrance had both missed huge clues, right under their noses.

Kerry stopped note-taking and locked eyes with her. "No again. I took off after John when I heard he'd left in a rage. You remember. John figured out where Ulrich went after the helicopter went down."

Terrance shook his head, tapping the pencil. "Still amazes me John figured out Ulrich in the midst of all that grief. But he found him, and then I chased him down. Never asked any of the agents for ID at the crash site. You wouldn't do that anyway—not with all those Capitol Police and Secret Service around. You'd just assume . . ."

"Yeah." Shawnda shrugged. "Same guys who ripped off my computer and erased my board? Maybe they had something to hide."

Terrance's eyes narrowed. "That's a dangerous allegation, sweetheart. Better be able to back it up."

"Sorry. Did anyone—I mean *anyone* you worked with after the crash—ever say anything about identifying the bodies? Concerns? Loose threads?"

He shook his head. "No. The helicopter had the Veep; I know that. There was no question. His body parts were independently identified by several officers. Ugly situation. Dead Veep, burning bodies . . . it figured the other bodies were Amy's and the kids'. After all, they were supposed to be on the helo, right? Secret Service found their IDs in the wreckage, and the parts had clothes on them John recognized. We even found Amy's purse. The works . . ."

Shawnda raised an eyebrow, watching Terrance draw the same conclusion she had.

"But they weren't on the flight—were they?" she asked quietly. "Sounds like we need to find out where they went. And when. They took Air Force Two from Ellington Field in Houston headed to Andrews Air Force Base in Maryland. The presidential helicopter picked them up there. Right?"

"If they *were* on Air Force Two, there's no way someone made the switcheroo at Andrews. Too many eyes. Too many escorts. They'd have been whisked with Vice President Ryan and his wife out of one aircraft into another."

"So that puts us back at Houston. Who picked the family up?"

Kerry scribbled on the paper. "Secret Service probably got 'em at their house that morning. The executive thing, black limo, police escort. The works."

"How would Secret Service ID them?"

Terrance made a face. "Likely they wouldn't have had any idea who they were picking up, not without some picture ID. Fake the ID, put the wrong people on the plane, and if they were good actors, you might never know. Especially if the Veep never talked to them."

"Wouldn't the Veep have figured it out? After all," she said, "he was escorting the Wells family to the big DC event."

"Not a chance. Lance Ryan didn't give a flip about anyone but himself. Unless he'd met her before—I mean, really spent time with Amy. And he wouldn't care if he *did* forget her. He was just that kind of guy."

"So where are we?"

"We're in Georgetown, and that's where *you're* going to stay," he said. "I'm going to Houston to poke around. Find out who picked them up, ask what the neighbors remember."

Shawnda stood up and headed to the kitchen. The vestiges of a Chinese takeout dinner waited to be put away, the distinct aroma of ginger and garlic in the air.

"Why?" she said, opening the refrigerator for juice. "Why would a grown woman and four children of precisely the right age and body type fake their way onto a plane headed to Washington with the vice president? Surely they knew they'd be found out."

Terrance joined her in the kitchen, leaning on the tall serving bar. "Maybe they did it because they wanted to. Devoted to the cause. It's a macabre option, but remember Jim Jones and the mass suicide in Guyana?"

Shawnda nodded, seeing where this was going.

"So. Somebody lifts Wells's real family and inserts stand-ins. People who can recite the Wells's history to a tee, able to answer the questions all the right ways on a long flight to Washington. It's a duty . . . an obligation . . . the great last rite culminating whatever sick belief system motivated them."

"Or maybe they never knew what they were flying into," Shawnda countered. "Didn't see it as a sacrifice, but as a test, the ultimate actor prank. Fake their way into the White House for the cause, and somebody would reward them.

"Or they did it because they were convinced it was a matter of national security. You know? Like a stand-in for the president, but in this case, a stand-in for VIPs to allow John's family to move unimpeded. That kind of stuff."

"I'm more inclined to choose the Jim Jones option." Terrance furrowed his eyebrows as he watched her over the counter. "Horrible as it sounds."

"But the *kids*, Terrance! Their daughter was what, elementary-school age? How could someone pull that off?"

"Happens all the time. The kids could've been actors, or the adults could've brainwashed them to believe they are who they say they are. Eventually they start believing it. It's not impossible—or improbable." Terrance began closing the takeout boxes.

"We're not talking about an amateur operation here," he said. "Someone wanted the world to believe the Wells family was dead. They penetrated the Secret Service, or pulled the wool over all our eyes with a fake DNA report, something like that. And for six years we've believed it. Only you, the amazing Shawnda, broke the code."

Shawnda stood in silence next to Terrance, a cold glass of red cranberry juice in her hand, and a few blood-like drips on the white counter. She set down the glass, the idea of food or drink revolting. In her mind's eye, she saw a little blonde girl holding the hand of some warped woman who looked like Amy Wells as they climbed into a big black limo at John's house. A trusting little girl, believing this was what she was supposed to do. To pretend.

There was nothing pretend about it. That little girl never saw the president—the FBI had exhumed what remained of her body a few days ago. And somewhere, perhaps, the real Wells daughter was out there waiting for someone—like Shawnda—to figure this out and find her.

NAZARJE, SLOVENIA

Malcolm Raines's voice boomed within the mammoth meeting hall at their new home in Nazarje. He didn't need the amplification, but he loved the booming bass, and insisted on it.

Towering video screens on either side of the stage carried ancient painted images of the Nephilim, medieval representations of tall dark winged men, holding plump naked Romanesque women swooning in their arms as they swept upward in the sky.

As the Nephilim climbed heavenward with their consorts, images flashed of Earth disappearing in the distance and the outer planets passing at dizzying speed. Saturn's rings and blue Uranus flashed by, fading into the distance with the Sun. Ever faster, the Nephilim flew until the galaxy was only a speck of dust. Somewhere out there, the Unknowable God received them, the Father Race, our blessed progenitors. The images faded to black and were replaced by a single giant infinity symbol, a gold figure eight lying on its side against a field of violet.

Three hundred twenty-one fresh faces smiled his way, hanging on his every word as Father Malcolm Raines brought his daily instruction to the Mother Seed. He lifted his hands high, then lowered his left arm, keeping his right hand elevated, palm facing out. Three hundred twenty-one hands followed suit. In silence. Malcolm's sign for the Mother Seed. Monique thought it looked like a crossing guard stopping traffic. Three hundred twenty-one crossing guards and their frocked leader.

Malcolm was particularly agitated tonight. He'd been so edgy all week that Monique hadn't been able to visit Amy and Alice at night. He slept poorly, rolling over on her, snoring, and waking at odd intervals. He mumbled in his sleep, as though fighting some unseen war within. No wonder. The Father Race spoke to him in ways no one else could understand—if you believed that. She'd begun to wonder.

Malcolm dropped his elevated palm and so did the three hundred twenty-one.

"Blessed One," they responded as a single eerie voice. Monique's strong suspicion, that these girls truly were her sisters with her exact DNA, unnerved her. The differences, between her and these developing young women, were minute, almost imperceptible.

Following her hunch, she'd found more proof today. Not just the hair color and eyes, the first clues she'd finally admitted a month ago. But super-elevated levels of high-density lipoprotein. And their rare blood type, AB negative. Hundreds of girls, and her, a wealth of blood donors for desperate recipients. So many identical rare blood types was too remarkable a coincidence to be accidental.

Monique watched his eyes as he scanned the crowd of adoring Mother Seed, chanting in unison with his trademark mantra, "Venture Forth." Malcolm strolled the dais, his gaze feasting on the bouncing nubile teenagers. It sickened her. He wanted them all, her sisters, half her age. Three hundred twenty-one Moniques. She wasn't enough woman for him.

Malcolm signed for silence. The evening training was completed, and they sat down as one. The girls did everything as one, in fact, like black-jumpsuited, ponytail-wagging automatons. Their mindless compliance with Malcolm's commands would make them difficult to save. She hoped they'd understand when and if the day came for her to free them of his control. At this point, that opportunity seemed hopelessly remote.

"I bring good news!" he began with a lilting smile and the voice Monique recognized as his "in distress" mode. "Very good news! I have heard from the Father Race. Their words were clear: 'It will soon be time to plant the Mother Seed.'"

Liar! Monique gasped in amazement that he could say this in her hearing. *You told me you hadn't heard from the Father Race—for months!*

"Your time has come, Seed of Eve, far earlier than we could have hoped!" Malcolm strained to raise a fever pitch as his warm, adoring audience suddenly chilled. A few girls clapped. Others sat ramrod straight, unflinching, as if their lot in life was to be used. More looked down, or glanced around for comfort.

They know what's coming. Monique was sure. She'd trained them herself for six years, in preparation for this time. There were no secrets. These were all mature young women, wise in the world's ways. She'd made sure of that, before she'd realized how he was using her. And them.

"Soon the Mother Seed will be ripe, and we will issue in the new era of the Father Race, the direct descendants of the virgin Sophia . . . of the lineage of Nephilim and Raksasa . . . to again inherit the Earth. A line of seed preserved until this day. You will carry the germ of perfected mankind into the next generation!"

You're using them! And me.

Monique's stomach turned, her mind serving up images of the girls exploited as she had been in the years before Rex Edwards adopted her and her sisters out of the orphanage into his home. Three hundred plus girls, surely her sisters from the data she'd uncovered in the past days, turned into human warehouses for the freakish genetic games her boss was about to unleash.

Spring rain pummeled the tile roof of the great hall, and wind blew hard against the soaring new structure. Somewhere, near the back of cavernous room, a half-open window whistled in the tempest. Their lofty stone temple stood atop a mount whipped by night storms. Malcolm waved to the audio technician to boost the amplification, then renewed his nauseating chant to overpower the gale.

"Venture Forth," he bellowed.

She'd watched hundreds of thousands scream themselves silly with these words. And now Malcolm's mind-numbing bass overwhelmed these adoring girls, too, seeming to erase any memory of his pronouncement.

If he succeeded, huge financial gains waited, groundbreaking research into the psychological and physiological aspects of a burgeoning clone industry. Hundreds of human copies, exact duplicates down to the cell. He would analyze these identical girls, born of hundreds of surrogate mothers, raised by him for just this day. He'd compare them, their behaviors, personalities, and growth, and make a fortune from his studies. Three hundred twenty-one women with the same DNA.

Her DNA.

It was the ideal biotech study, every one alike in body, spirit, character, and—or so Raines thought—personality. She knew better. They were 321 distinct individuals. Girls he'd never taken the time to know.

They were proof, he'd say, that genetic diversity wasn't essential to human refinement, and was, in fact, counterproductive. "Diversity leads to disease and death," he'd repeated over and over. Monique's heart sank as she watched them applaud him, her own body perhaps the source of the cells that must have spawned them. Perfect replicas of herself, yet none of them were her.

These were his Mother Seed, reproductive pawns devoid of liberty. Father Malcolm Raines's collective womb for a perfected Father Race.

Gooseflesh rose on Sonya's arms and legs under her tight black skin. Miss Monique, executive assistant to the Priest of the Heavenlies, stood before her and her sisters, occasionally glancing at the Guardian. Her head pivoted from her charges to her boss; her frown deepened by the minute.

Their dour taskmistress had not smiled since they'd arrived at the gray fortress, as if some black cloud hung over her. Sonya shuddered, wondering how such a beautiful and intelligent woman could dedicate her life to a man who had just claimed all their bodies for his personal gain.

Judith and Celeste cheered loudly to her right, chanting "Venture Forth" and bouncing on their toes, like they were celebrating some wonderful news. To her left, quiet Kristen reached out and squeezed Sonya's hand.

"No," Kristen murmured, shaking her head. The velvet maniac exhorting her sisters into frenzy had stolen her voice.

Sonya could feel her friend's pulse pounding in her own sweaty palm. She pulled Kristen closer. "Stay with me," Sonya said. "It'll be a madhouse. Then we get our chance."

Kristen's face went white, fear transforming her olive Mediterranean complexion. "A chance for what?"

"A chance to escape," Sonya said, looking back to the stage, Miss Monique, and the Guardian. "That's all it will be, Kristen. Just a chance."

17

AMY'S KNEES WERE SORE from kneeling on the hard stone floor in front of the ventilation duct. The cold air blowing past Monique numbed Amy's cheeks. It smelled of fir and mountains, mixed with something like moss, a damp odor of wind coursing through a slimy old stone shaft. It was the odor of her room, of the castle, and of this primitive rock tunnel where Monique lay, shaking, black hair dancing in the breeze that originated somewhere behind her.

Pointing the light at her, Amy saw Monique better this time. High cheeks and thin eyebrows framed brown eyes. Red, black, and olive dominated: long black hair, a red elastic hair band, olive skin like a Spanish or Italian girl's, the shiny black outfit, and deep red lipstick.

She must be freezing in that thing! Amy thought, watching Monique crawl into place.

"He intends to use them all," Monique blurted out, panting. "He's desperate." Her voice cracked as she whispered to Amy and Alice in the dark. "I have to find a way! To get you out. And to free my sisters."

Amy saw the distraught woman's panicked look, her long taut fingers gripping the cold iron grate unsteadily. "The Mother Seed's just a tool to him."

Amy touched Monique's quivering hands, trying to calm her. She'd begun to wonder if they'd ever see her again; it had been so long since her first visit. Now Amy understood the delay. Malcolm was raving and paranoid with some kind of bad news, something Monique had tried to explain but couldn't force through her choked attempts to talk. She bound some pain deep inside, unable to let it go. Amy patted the white knuckles.

"Try again, Monique. Tell us what's happening."

She nodded, working her shoulder back a bit to wipe damp eyes in the tunnel's tight confines. The tight clothing revealed what looked like a hard body, not soft, but sinewy and athletic—the defined shoulders of a runner or a rock climber.

"Thank you," Monique said. A quivering lip and shaky voice highlighted her struggle to contain her emotions. "There's so much you need to know. But first, get a cover, drape it over you. Bring two chairs. Set them in front of the wall facing the grate. Bend over and pray out loud a while. We have to do this, or we'll all be caught."

Amy did as instructed, rising to pull the gray wool blanket from their bed as Alice moved chairs toward the wall in the dark. Amy threw the blanket around the two of them as they sat down and bent over. Then she prayed silently for Monique: *Lord, give her strength. Calm her in the midst of her fear. Show her that you will provide our every need.*

Alice began praying out loud first, her voice strong as Amy hugged her tall daughter. Alice shook a little in the cold of the room, and Amy tugged her closer.

"Jesus. We sure do need you right now. Please help us find our way home. Please take care of my brothers and my dad. Help them with whatever they need to make it through the day. I want my special friend to know you the way that I do. Thanks for what we have, Jesus. Thanks for the sacrifice you made for us on the cross."

Amy's heart swelled, and she muttered an "Amen," too moved to say more.

Monique's next whisper was barely audible. "Thank you. Were you praying for *me*, Alice?"

"Yes," her daughter said in a quiet tone, the gray blanket covering her head.

"No one's ever done that."

"*We have.* Since the first day you came," Amy said. She could no longer see Monique's face, only a few fingers poking through the grate, visible in the dim light.

She heard Monique sniffle and clear her throat. "Can I ask you something?"

"Yes?" Amy bent further to see Monique's face behind the grate.

"How do you do it? I mean, survive this, and still smile? How can you pray for someone . . . like me?" She wiped her face and nose again on the shiny black of her upper arm, wet glistening on the slick material.

Amy sighed. *How?* She'd wondered that herself, many times. Dark times. "Were you here when they brought us to this place, Monique?" she asked.

"No. Not here. I had the girls in Trieste then. But I saw you a couple of years after you arrived." She looked up. "I watched you from the tower room, once it was prepared for Malcolm and me."

Amy felt her stomach roiling, the memories of her early days here flooding back. Memories she desperately wanted to forget. Memories made worse by Monique's confession that she was Raines's consort. They were one flesh, and of until late, it appeared, one mind. Amy prayed for the ability to forgive. And to forget.

"I didn't always smile, Monique. Alice was nine when we were kidnapped. They took the boys from me right away. I cried for weeks."

Amy took a deep breath, grateful for her daughter's embrace. The child had become a young woman, her girlfriend. They depended on each other so. "You know I'm a diabetic, right?"

Monique gasped. "No! He never told me. How? I mean, how do you—?"

"They bring insulin, but I have to inject myself. I try to control my diet . . . what diet there is. Raines doesn't overfeed us. I sank into a deep depression after we'd been here for several weeks. My diseases—the diabetes and my problem with anxiety—they overwhelmed me. Stress makes the diabetes worse, and I've gone into insulin shock several times. We've run out of insulin, too. Bouncing between stress and diabetes, those first two years all but killed me. And Alice."

"Alice?" Monique asked.

"She got sick. A year after we arrived, in the late winter. She almost died of bronchitis and asthma. This place is so damp, moldy, and drafty." Amy took a deep breath of the air blowing past Monique, shivering as she recalled those bleak days.

"That broke me," Amy said. "Alice was slipping away, her coughs and wheezing so horrible that you could almost see her spine under her tummy when she tried to get a breath. I had nowhere to turn, not enough medicine, no doctor, no one that cared. It was just us."

Monique sniffled, then spoke with a gurgle, her broken voice echoing in the damp tunnel. "I didn't know. I'm . . . so sorry." She coughed as she tried to talk. "What did . . . what did you do?"

"I prayed. I stopped my crying and screaming, stopped tearing at my hair and sulking in the corner. I put my heart into prayer. I was broken, completely at my wit's end before God, with a little girl, unable to get a single good breath, dying in my arms. There was nothing left I could do, and tears wouldn't bring her back. I gave up and let God take control." Amy took a deep breath. "Once I was broken, God could put me back together the way He wanted me."

"Did it—well—did it work? I mean, Alice is healed, right?"

"Yes, Monique. But faith is about more than just whether our prayers work. Jesus says, 'I'll never leave you or forsake you.' I'd simply forgotten His promise. No, not forgotten. I'd never taken it to heart, never really lived that. I'd been a praying woman, a believer, but I was never broken before the Lord the way I was here. It made me totally depend on Him."

Amy patted Alice on the leg. "I quit focusing on myself and my problems and gave all my attention to God, and to Alice."

"We got well together," Alice said. "I learned to breathe, and Mom learned to depend on God. We're good for each other."

"That's right. We're a team. And we've had lots of trials. My depression, Alice's loneliness. Life's been hard on both of us. We only had each other to lean on."

"And complain at," Alice said with a hint of a chuckle. "She's a good teacher. Did she tell you? I'm a sophomore. 'Jail schooled,' we call it."

"Thank goodness they give us books," Amy said. "But no Bibles. I miss that so much."

Monique looked away, as if she were trying to avoid something touchy.

"There's so much you need to know," she began. "You must keep what I tell you between yourselves, in whispers."

"We will," Amy replied, pulling the gray covers farther over her head.

"Malcolm hears from the Father Race. Somehow. Their prophecies are silent to us, but he hears commands and words of knowledge. They told him to bring you here." She looked straight at Amy. "I do believe he heard that. How he hears them, I don't know."

"He's a liar," Amy said out loud, moving under the cover.

Alice put a finger over her lips with a "shhh!"

"Mrs. Wells. Please!"

"I'm sorry. Go on."

"He says the Father Race told him to preserve you."

"Preserve us? Alice nearly died," Amy said angrily. "What are we? Meat? We've been rotting away in this room half of Alice's life."

"I know. I mean, I understand. I'm so sorry. You're right. He's a liar. Something in me, like a voice of my own calling me in a different direction, kept saying to watch him, to listen. I mean, really listen to his words." She sighed. "The truth I'd ignored for a very long time was hard to accept."

Amy dared not speak. Perhaps in Monique's story she could find the reason for their imprisonment. The real reason, not some excuse tied to talk of the Father Race.

"He's always been a liar. And now, the NASA Mars mission claims they have evidence the Oracles of the Father Race were a hoax."

"Hoax?" Amy asked, puzzled. "You mean John's proof that the spiders were faked?"

"Admiral Wells learned this?"

"Admiral? You know something about him?" Amy asked, in that moment overwhelmed with the pain of this separation. Monique knew something about her John.

Where is he? What's he doing?

"Dad's an admiral?" Alice asked, her voice high and squeaky.

Amy had sudden visions of his promotion, a wonderful day they could have celebrated as a family. She began crying, unable to contain it any longer. Six years of their life together, lost. "Please," she sobbed. "Where is John? Is he all right?"

"I'm sorry. There's so much to tell you."

"Is he all right?" Amy asked again, too loudly.

"Please," Monique pleaded. "I must know first. What did Admiral Wells tell you? About the Oracles? A hoax?"

Amy tried calming herself with a deep breath. "John took a secret sensor to Mars. They proved the spiders were robots programmed in English. They even got metal samples of the spiders, proof they were made of Russian titanium." She paused, sure this news was as painful to Monique as news of John was for her. "The spiders were built on Earth. They don't come from another planet."

Monique's fingers trembled as they gripped the vent. Amy prayed for the woman, asking again for strength. She desperately wanted to know about her husband. Where he was. If he'd waited for her.

"Why didn't they share this?" Monique asked. "About the Oracles? We've been misled for years."

"NASA was afraid to challenge Raines without physical proof. The titanium sample and the remains of the sensor were lost when *Epsilon* was hit by meteoroids on their way home from Mars. It stressed John so; he'd come all that way, survived a deadly mission, yet had no proof of their discovery. No one would act without it."

The three women were quiet, each processing the years of lies that brought them to this place. Together. Amy felt faint and held Alice close as her daughter struggled to control her own shakes. Amy wanted to reach through the vent and pull word of John from Monique's throat.

He's an admiral? Surely he's still looking for us.

"NASA returned to Mars four years ago," Monique began. "They established an initial base. A second mission of eight astronauts returned to Mars two years ago. They're supposed to return soon." Amy could hear panting.

"Monique? Do you know where John is? Has he tried to find us?"

"Yes . . . yes, I know where he is. Admiral Wells is the commander of the latest exploration mission. Your husband is on Mars."

The wind blew and a long chilling note whistled through the grate. Time hung in a void.

"Mars?" Amy whispered weakly. She slipped to her knees in a heap of gray blanket, head spinning.

Alice's shaking hands pulled Amy upright. They sat on the floor and looked into the grate. Amy no longer cared who saw them. She ached to know if she'd heard wrong.

"Yes. He's on Mars. Admiral Wells is the commander of the third manned mission. My adoptive father, Rex Edwards, also took a mission there to establish a permanent colony. He and his crew landed near John's base. Father died shortly after they arrived, but the colony is still strong."

Monique paused. "I must go soon." She pushed her fingers through the grate, trying to touch Amy. The two connected again. "I'm sorry I was part of this, Amy. Sorry for keeping you all here. Please . . . forgive me."

Amy's heart felt like it was bursting. John had abandoned her and returned to Mars. He cared more for spaceflight than he did for her. That very fear had always gnawed at her, but she'd forced it down for decades. Now the rotting demon erupted inside her, consuming Amy with the realization that, with her and the family out of the way, he'd pursued his great dream. John had left them behind.

"Mrs. Wells, John doesn't know you're alive."

Amy bent further, releasing Monique's touch. Nausea overwhelmed her.

Alice cradled her mother, and spoke the words that Amy couldn't voice. "Why?"

"He believes—the rest of the world believes—that you're dead. You were replaced by loyal adherents of Saint Michael's Remnant on the vice president's helicopter, the one headed to the White House."

"But Dad would've noticed when we didn't get off!" Alice protested. "He had to!"

"You never—*they* never got off, Alice." Monique's words spread like ice across Amy's body. "The helicopter was shot down. The vice president and his wife—and the Wells family—were all killed that day. Someone in the leadership of the Remnant set that up to convince your father that you were lost on the flight. I wish I knew more. Malcolm hasn't told me."

Monique's voice was distant in Amy's ears, but something in her felt the pain in the young woman's voice, as if she were begging forgiveness with every word. Amy forced herself to listen, to hear the pain and the words, to embrace Monique's emotion.

Alice bent over in Amy's arms, wheezing and trying to form her own words. "Breathe. Be calm. Trust Him," Amy said as she stroked her daughter's blonde head, the two of them again hidden under the gray cover, their faces to the wall. Amy had comforted Alice through many spells just like this one in the past two thousand days.

"But we're not dead!" Alice gasped between sobs. Her tears ran like little rivers onto Amy's arms.

"I'm sorry, Alice," Monique said, her voice shaky. "No one knows you're alive. Not even your dad."

18

THE PALE SUN HAD SET long ago on the lonely Martian desert, and the Hab module's four portals were dark. Inside, the warm dining area smelled homey, fragrant with Deborah Readdy's favorite dessert, banana pudding made with dehydrated egg whites, pudding mix, and dried bananas. She scooped up the last spoonful while John stood talking to the seven astronauts from his place at the head of their communal table.

"It's time to take matters into our own hands," John said. Six nodded. Only Geo scowled, arms crossed, refusing to make eye contact with John. Deborah wasn't surprised.

"What'd Houston say when you called them after our little drilling excursion?" Oz asked, keeping one eye on Geo.

"Said they're working on it. Same thing they said yesterday. And the day before. That's reasonable, I mean, considering there're so many contractors to coordinate with, schedules to modify, congressional funding to request . . . you name it. Giving us a quick solution when we aren't scheduled to leave for three months isn't realistic. At least, not from their perspective."

"You're pushing them too hard. You've got a bad case of 'get-home-itis,'" Geo said in a nasal tone, looking away from John.

"Is that a new disease, Geo? 'Cause it doesn't show up in any of my medical texts." Frustrated with the whining, Deborah ran her fingers through the coarse red stalks her mom once called hair.

Talk about latent tendencies. Robert Witt had transformed almost overnight from a brilliant introspective geologist famous for "getting along" to an insufferably rude gripe. She couldn't imagine why.

One thing's for sure. Meds won't fix his problem.

"It's okay, Deborah," John said. "Geo's right. I *do* want to get the crew home. But I don't intend to endanger us while we wait for some NASA bureaucrat halfway across the solar system to figure out how to fix our problem. It's time for a little Space MacGyver action on Mars. Don't you agree?" He waved to the group, who all nodded. Except Geo.

"Fine. Here's my proposal. I've already contacted May and Nicci. Talked to them about our situation. They said they'd been waiting on our call."

"That's freaky. Is there anything about us they *don't* know?" asked Ramona, their quietest crew member. Deborah watched Ramona carefully, mentally tallying her patient's antidepressant dosage, one of the many secrets Deborah kept. Everyone had their issues. Sam dealt with some, and she owned the rest. When you were gone from Earth for years, she'd found, there were very few perfectly balanced people in the universe. Even among hyper-achiever astronauts.

"I'm pretty sure they know just about everything we've heard on the radio since we arrived—except our encrypted calls. That *includes* all the information about the alien hoax. Which was our plan. And," he said with a shrug, "they know we're marooned."

John pointed at the next compartment's communication suite. "Nicci's expecting our call. I want to propose something to the colonists that'll go against NASA's grain in a huge way, but might be the best for exploring Mars." He looked at every astronaut. "And I wanted to ask you all one last time. As a group. Some of you have already talked to me about your desires. But we need to decide on this as a team."

Geo faced his crewmates. "Your plan's probably best for you. So why bother to ask us? You're gonna do it anyway. You always do."

"What I'm proposing might help get people *home*."

"Go on, John," Jake said. He gave Geo, sitting next to him, a look Deborah was sure was meant to shut the loudmouth's trap.

"Here's my proposal." John pointed to a digital map on their video screens. "Trade our Mars Ascent Vehicle for their Earth Return Vehicle. Theirs is fueled and ready to fly . . . single stage . . . Mars to Earth. It's parked a few kilometers away from their compound. Here," he said, pointing to a map of Nirgal Vallis.

"That's stupid!" Geo blurted. "How're we gonna get our MAV across five hundred clicks of Martian desert and canyons?"

Jake stood over the geologist, his big frame filling his NASA jumpsuit, a small middle-age paunch right at Geo's nose level. Geo quieted.

Oz answered, using his hands like he was changing a tire. "We take the transport wheels and transmission hubs off Hab One. Put it on the MAV and drive it to the colony."

"Why?" Ramona asked. "I mean, why give them our MAV? It won't do them any good. They can't fly to our ERV in orbit. It's full of holes."

Oz responded. "MAV could do 'em some good later on. They

could use our new ERV when it arrives in orbit, in return for theirs now. And we know they don't *plan* to leave Mars at all. Pretty fair trade—if we can move MAV that far."

"Will they accept it? The MAV?" Sam Readdy asked. "They'd be crazy to leave it here unattended and then drive five hundred clicks back here when they're ready to get off the planet."

John shrugged. "Don't know. That's why we're gonna call. I researched what we need to get home, but I'm not making this decision alone. We're all in this together."

"Aren't you leaving out the good part, Hawk?" Geo asked, throwing off Jake's big hand on his shoulder. "There's only five seats on that ship, and you know it. Which three of us do you plan to kick off the return flight?"

John raised his eyebrows and nodded slightly, a sort of assent, Deborah thought, that Geo had a point.

"He's not stranding anybody, you weasel. Some of us *want* to stay." Jake kicked Geo's chair with a big boot. "Let John talk."

"You've got this all worked out nice and tidy, don't you, Hawk?" Geo stood up in Jake's face as Oz moved beside him.

"John never discussed it with us," Oz said, his fist grabbing Geo's shirt at the neck and lifting him slightly. Jake touched Oz to hold him back. Deborah was sure someone was about to rearrange Geo's face. As much as she hated ego and violence, the man deserved a good spanking.

"Geo," John continued, "that's why we're talking this over. Together. You're right; the ship only holds five people. May told me Rex wants to return to Earth, to work with his dad's firm and Malcolm Raines. To support Father Race stuff. So only four of us can go home. Question is—which four?" He waved his hand about the room.

"You're not leaving me!" Geo screamed, kicking and trying to pull away from Oz. "I'm *not* staying an extra day!"

Oz lifted Geo further off the floor, the geologist's shirt ripping as the tall lanky engineer reached an emotional boiling point. Jake was at the ready to save him, but let Oz dangle the whiner for a long moment. When Geo tried to kick back in defense, Oz tightened his grip on the collar, choking him. He went limp.

"Rocks for brains," Oz said, nose to nose with Geo. "You'd be the *last* person in the solar system we'd let stay here."

Their geologist's rage fizzled as several of the crew wagged their heads, no one standing up in his defense. Deborah felt for the man. He dropped his head as Oz lowered him to his feet. Geo walked out in silence. Oz pretended to dust his hands and sat back down, his face flushed.

"The two of us have talked about this," Sam said, pointing at his wife. Deborah's rock-stable husband would calm things down. "Deb and I want to stay."

Ramona sucked in her breath. In the momentary silence, Deborah could hear the "tick" of their Navy ship's clock on the dining room bulkhead. It would dong eight bells soon.

"We have a house and friends back home," Sam said after a lengthy uncomfortable delay. "But no kids. Been too busy, I guess." He winked at Deborah, who felt the color rush to her face. "This is the opportunity of a lifetime. We'll stay. That's two of your four, Hawk. Anyone else?" He waved at Jake.

"I'm in. Talked with May about it more than once. She probably heard about the ERV problem from me, by the way. Sorry, guys."

"No apologies necessary, Jake," John replied. "She was going to find out anyway."

"I got a hankering to stay, too," Oz said. "Can't get those greeneries out of my mind—what I could do with 'em—and that brick-making machine. Not saying I want to stay here 'til they plant me, but a few more years would be just fine. You've got four volunteers, Hawk."

John smiled. Those four really did *want* to remain behind. Deborah was relieved; she couldn't imagine how they'd have handled this if no one wanted to stay. She'd have been prescribing all sorts of mood-altering drugs. And she didn't have many left.

"Ramona?" John asked. "We've got all the people we need, but we haven't asked you yet."

Ramona lowered her head, avoiding eye contact and twirling a finger in her straight black hair. *At times, Ramona's antidepressant dosage didn't seem strong enough,* Deborah thought, *or this decision was weighing down the shy Hispanic PhD.* At last she spoke.

"I'd like to stay, John."

Deborah's mouth fell open as she gasped.

Ramona pushed hair back over her ear and sighed. "I mean, I want to. But I can't." She looked up, her brown eyes damp with some emotion she probably wouldn't discuss. With anyone. "You understand?"

John looked at Melanie, the lone person who'd not spoken. Deborah wiped a tear before anyone could see her, but Melanie caught her eye. Saying good-bye to her best friend after years together, training, flying, and working on Mars, would hurt so much.

Melanie responded to John's glance. No words were needed on his part. "I like it here, Hawk, but my family's waiting back home. Sounds like I'll have to leave my best friends here," she said, looking at Deborah and around the room, "but I need to go."

John nodded again, then gestured toward the communication suite. "Then it's settled. We call May and Nicci and formalize the offer."

Oz clapped. "Hey? What about you, Hawk?"

"Me?" John asked. "My personal vote is to stay—but I have a

mission to complete. I'll go home."

"Duty calls, huh?" Oz said. "You want to stay? I say go for it."

John shook his head and looked at the floor. Deborah knew only John's loyalty to NASA and his crew could pull him away from Mars. Certainly not a four-month trip bottled up with Robert Witt. Staying here was the chance of a lifetime—and he was about to give it up for them.

"You realize, of course," Melanie began, leaning back in her chair, "that you're going to change the profile for all future missions if we do this. Right?" She was staring straight at him. Deborah hadn't any idea what she meant. Neither, it appeared, did John.

"Follow me on this, people," Melanie said, looking around the room. "If we move the MAV to their site, and move four of our crew to live with them . . . and if they've got a thriving colony with water and food—maybe even a reproducing colony . . ." she said, looking at Jake for a moment. "Then why should NASA send the next mission *here*, to this rocky dry place where we've tapped out every crater and potential drilling site inside ten thousand square kilometers?" Melanie pointed at a digital map of the Nirgal Vallis terrain, overlaid with dozens of MSR tracks from the past two manned missions.

"They'd be crazy to send a fourth manned mission here. It's a dry hole. If we move now, they'll probably send the next mission to join the colony. You've heard the rumors. The president's fighting an uphill battle preserving funding for the manned exploration program. Joining the colony may be just the solution to keep NASA's Mars program alive. And this proposal could force their hand."

Deborah spoke up for the first time that evening. "Or even better, Mel. We could move it *all*. The MAV, the Habs, the Lab, the power systems. Move it *all* to their site. NASA can't stop us, right? If the next crew comes on time, and I'm sure they will, they'll come to the base. Wherever it is." She looked at John. "Hey, I know it sounds crazy, Hawk, but you say it all the time: Be part of the solution, not part of the problem. This puts the solution to NASA's problem and ours solidly in our grasp."

John scratched his chin, a smile playing at the corner of his mouth. "I like it!" He looked at Oz, who nodded and gave him a thumbs up.

Sam piped up, ever the pragmatist. "We're the ones staying behind, you know? No one should lose their jobs over this. We're simply taking advantage of all the resources at our disposal. Because . . ." he began, looking about the table as if searching for someone to complete his thought.

"Because we're shipwrecked!" Deborah grinned, her heart pounding at the implications.

"Exactly. Thank you, dear." Sam smiled. "Do what you've got to do, Skipper. Our lives are on the line here, a hundred and fifty million kilometers from home. There's no grocery store around the corner, so we're on our own." He looked directly at John. "What are they gonna do, anyway? Take away your birthday?"

CLEAR LAKE CITY, TEXAS

"They left at night?" Kerry stood in the doorway of a neighbor in John's old subdivision. Tall oaks and gnarled camphor trees lined the street of what must have been one of Clear Lake's first neighborhoods just beyond the entrance to the space center. Every house in the subdivision was surrounded with white and pink azaleas.

I'm definitely overdressed, Kerry thought, pulling at his tie and the collar of a tight dress shirt. South Texas was already warm, and it wasn't even April yet.

"No doubt about it," the heavyset man said, still dressed in paja-

mas around ten on a Saturday morning and rubbing away the sleep in
his eyes. "They left about two a.m. In a big black Suburban, the kind
with emergency lights like the Secret Service drives in the movies. I
work the second shift at a Baytown refinery. Walked my dog a little
before two. Saw all five of 'em pile into a limo. Figure that's when they
were leaving for Ellington Field." He yawned, day-old stubble dotting
his face like salt and pepper.

"You didn't report that? After they were killed?" Kerry asked,
dumbfounded by the revelation.

The groggy man took a moment to process the question. Kerry
looked at his watch.

"Report it? Why? The Wells family went to DC. You know who
shot down the helo. So what's to report?" He picked at his nose, looking
Kerry up and down. "By the way, did I ask you for a badge?"

"You did," Kerry said, flipping open his credentials a second time.
"And you've got a point . . . about what we knew and when we knew it.
Did you see any of their faces—the Wells family? Enough to identify
them?"

"Yeah, no doubt about it. That was Amy Wells. I knew her from
TV. Never met the kids before, but they seemed pretty excited to be
leaving." He paused, wiping a sticky index finger on the back of his
pajama bottoms. "Yeah. And she waved at me."

"At two in the morning?"

The man shrugged. "Hey. They were headed to see the prez.
Wouldn't you be excited?" He picked at a scab on the corner of his
mouth, shoots of unshaven hair sprouting up through it. "Anything
else? Or can I crawl back in the rack?"

"No. That's all. Thanks," Kerry replied, closing his digital notepad.
He was reluctant to shake the man's hand. "Here's a card. Call me if you
think of anything else."

"See ya." The door closed hard.

Kerry walked to his car, determined to sort out this dilemma. Every other neighbor he'd talked to who'd seen the family leave in the daylight said they'd departed around seven a.m. Amy had seemed rushed, they'd said, dashing into a big black car with the kids. One woman said she'd waved to Amy while out for an early stroll, but Amy never waved back. In fact, the 'seven o'clock Amy' never said good-bye to *anyone*, which several neighbors thought odd.

Kerry sat behind the steering wheel of his car. If you believed everyone in this neighborhood with a story to tell, it was clear the Wells family left their home twice that fateful day. Both times with bags packed and where they could be seen. Going to the same place.

But why would someone kidnapping them let the family be seen? To promote the illusion?

His phone rang. Shawnda's cellular.

"You at home?" Kerry said, answering.

"No. I went into Langley. To get ahead on some work. I'm immersed in the fascinating world of Eastern Europe. But I've also been working some of the DNA stuff. Calling in some favors." She whispered. "McClannahan doesn't know."

"Watch your back, Shawnda. They'll be on to you."

"I promise. How about you? Anything new?"

"Uh-huh. Found several neighbors who saw the family leave, but different witnesses place their departure at two different times, five hours apart. No question—two families left from John's house. One left happily about two in the morning and waved to a stranger, another left in a rush in broad daylight trying to avoid her closest friends. The first Amy was positively ID'd by a neighbor. No one talked to the second group, though many tried."

"No wonder," Shawnda replied. "The fake Amy was pulling the

switch of the decade. Wanna hear a good one? I got a name on her. Used that DNA file you sent me. Get this—the fake Amy was employed at FMI. Can you believe it? I got a DNA match on the kids, too."

"I thought we couldn't type 'em?"

"Yeah. But I'm good." She laughed. "And I know people you don't. You and I make a good team."

"No doubt about that."

"We got a perfect DNA match. All four children. You'll never believe this."

"Try me."

"Found the two oldest children in the missing persons database. They disappeared as infants almost a decade earlier. The two youngest also have identities, but here's the catch. Each of them is still alive."

Kerry heard her take a deep breath.

"They share the exact same DNA with the dead kids, Terrance. No question. And the living ones aren't twins of the deceased. These people with the DNA match are in their *fifties*." She paused. "They also work for FMI. In clone research."

19

"WHAT WILL NASA SAY? I don't know," John said to May. "We haven't told them yet."

John, May, Nicci, Rex, and Oz teleconferenced from separate terminals in their two Habs, discussing "the plan." Five hundred kilometers separated them, but they spoke as comfortably as if together.

"When you do talk to them, you might have to answer a key question," May said. She looked much healthier now, her black locks draped over her shoulder. Sitting next to her, Rex was almost as tall as May.

"What question?" John asked.

"Why would Rex Sr. bring a return vehicle—an ERV of his own—if he never planned to leave Mars? And why a five-seat ERV when he brought six colonists?"

"Gotta admit," Oz said, "it makes no sense."

"Our ERV wasn't for escape or even medical evacuation. Rex knew if he grew the colony he'd reach a point where he couldn't keep enough ships to get everyone off the planet. So we adopted a 'no rescue, no escape' philosophy. The ERV was his way to get something important back to Earth—if it was key to his strategy. Maybe a science break-through or more evidence of the Father Race. That sort of thing. But escape equated to failure, and with Rex Edwards, failure was never an option."

"So, using the ERV to take my crew home—a crew that your son discovered—would be an acceptable use of the ship?"

"It would," Rex replied. "I confirmed that last night."

"Confirmed?" Oz asked.

"I asked Dad," Rex stated, as if Rex Sr. were in the next compartment.

"You *what*?" Oz blurted.

"You'll get to ask Rex Sr., too, John. When you come visit," May said with a sly smile. "We talk to him every day. On video."

Rex interrupted. "It's a query-based video database, sir. One of my pop's many inventions. You ask a question, the system does a search and addresses your question—as long as it concerns the colony. I queried him last night and sure enough, Dad had an opinion about this."

"He *always* had an opinion." May chuckled. "When you get here, I want you to watch the entire series of his talks. It will help you under-stand our mission better." She paused, serious. "That's part of the deal, John. Those who stay have to at least hear our side of the story, which includes the video training." She smiled again. "Small price to pay for a rocket ship, don't you agree?"

"Small price, indeed," Oz said. "I'm looking forward to it. You can tell Kate for me."

"Tell her yourself," Dr. Westin chimed in, poking her face in front of the camera. "I heard that, Martin Oswald. We'll watch Rex together."

She raised an eyebrow. "Would you like that?"

Oz blushed, speechless.

"I think that was a 'yes,' Kate," May said. "So how do we accomplish this move?"

Oz perked up. "I'll transport all the Habs at once. Gonna take a while, but we can do it."

"How?" Rex asked, wonder in his eyes.

That's promising, John thought as he watched Rex's body language. *He's interested.*

"We'll use the wheel assemblies, Rex. NASA built the Habs and Lab to move."

"Not five hundred kilometers!" countered the teenager.

"We didn't spec how *far* they had to go. Just that they needed to move at two kilometers an hour. It'll take us about thirty days, moving in daylight only. But when we do it, you'll eventually have three Habs and two Labs at your site. Talk about a colony!"

Maybe Rex'll catch the bug. John wondered what NASA would say when he broke the news to Houston. *They'll probably like it a lot less than Rex.*

"We'll leave the MAV in place until a second trip," John said. "Two crew will drive each of the two Habs and the Lab. Oz and I'll each drive an MSR."

John let his mind wander as Oz, Rex, and May hashed out the schedule and technical details. The magnitude of the proposed relocation was daunting. Should he go against NASA, defy them, and move his entire base, navigating across the rugged canyon trail he and Rex had forged?

Do I have any choice?

The point had been made more than once: "We're shipwrecked!" NASA couldn't help them. His crew had to fend for themselves, modern-day Robinson Crusoes that Daniel Defoe never could have imagined.

"We gonna tell Houston tomorrow?" Oz asked, jarring John back to the present. He was exuberant about the idea of leading a space-age wagon train, the most dramatic resettlement in history.

"Yes. Tomorrow," John replied. "You came to colonize Mars, Dr. Randall. And we came to explore. Together, we can do both much better."

"And," she added, "NASA can't afford to say 'no.'"

TUESDAY, MARCH 31, 2020: WASHINGTON, DC

Terrance Kerry's office looked out on busy Twelfth Street in downtown Washington, DC, six floors above streets clogged with commuters making their daily escape from the District. Off-white scuffed walls, too many coats of paint, and 1980s-style metal trim gave the building a distinct "last millennium" kind of feel.

Kerry focused on a picture of Shawnda on his desk, and a treasure on the wall . . . a framed picture of Astronaut John Wells shaking his hand and presenting a sliver of Mars rock. Kerry fondled the Mars chip, encased in epoxy, while he waited for the phone connection with FBI's newest and most unusual director. He checked his watch; 6:35.

"This is Carlene," a soft voice answered. A female boss. That was a dynamic he wasn't yet used to. "What did you find?" She sounded almost happy to hear from him . . . strange, considering that, if the ruse he'd uncovered were true, it would touch them all.

"Good afternoon, Director Whatley. You opened the door just like I needed. And it's as we thought."

"Secret Service talked to you?"

"They did. You set it up nicely. They were sure I was investigating one of their agents. Secret Service confirmed what my witnesses said in Clear Lake City. They picked the Wells family up at seven a.m. The Wells family ID was perfect. They headed straight to Ellington Field and put the family on Air Force Two about ten that morning."

"Anything else?"

"Yes. I confirmed the report from the shift worker living down the street. Another neighbor said the same—saw the limo outside John's house around two a.m."

"But Secret Service says they picked up the family at seven, right?"

"Yes. And I'm inclined to believe them."

"Me, too." Her voice drifted away a moment. "So, Kerry. What now?"

"If they're still alive after six years, Amy and the kids could be anywhere. I'm focusing on likely candidates who might've taken them."

"I'd start with motive first," she said. "Why fake their deaths? It's an enormously complex way to kidnap someone. And what's the gain?"

"Maybe they didn't want Amy and the kids dead," Kerry replied. "Some strange sense of honor. To protect them from the Veep's fate."

"Or," she countered, "it's possible someone knew Ulrich planned to kill the Veep, and they got Amy out just in time. A complex way to preserve her for some future barter, maybe."

"Some queer code of honor? Save Amy and her kids, but let the vice president die?"

"Politics breeds strange bedfellows, Kerry."

"And then there's the nasty option. They made it look like a death to hurt John, and then years later, might reveal they weren't dead. It's a sword that cuts twice." Kerry paused. "Which brings us back to your first question. Who would've taken them?"

"Any ideas?" she asked.

"Don't know yet. I have to ask John."

"Maybe it's time we did that. He know anything yet?"

Kerry sat in silence, holding the phone away as if distance could remove the task before him. Finally he answered. "No. I'll have to start with NASA. They'll need to know—to prepare for his reaction."

WEDNESDAY, APRIL 1, 2020: HOUSTON, TEXAS

Greg Church had the political tenacity of a pit bull. He'd been director at NASA's Johnson Space Center for fifteen years with no end in sight to his reign. Special Agent Kerry had heard that Church ruled the political landscape of manned space with an iron fist, a well-connected autocrat micromanaging every aspect of NASA's manned space flight center. Others said he was just plain good at his job. Kerry suspected the correct answer was some mixture of the two. One thing was certain. Greg Church hated surprises. And Kerry was bringing a bombshell.

Kerry sat in the lobby outside Church's office, waiting for the director. The "I love me" display covered all four walls, frame upon frame with little red, white, and blue cotton flags and colorful mission patches, every one flown in space during his years as center director, or his tenure as director of manned flight operations. He was Clear Lake City's "King of the Hill."

"Kerry!" the director exclaimed, walking out half an hour later dressed in a crisply tailored suit. "It's been what? Six years?"

"Seven, sir. How's your game?" Kerry asked, pointing at the numerous golf photos on the wall. Greg Church in golf apparel with dozens of personalities and political figures, but remarkably few astronauts.

"I'm a hacker," Church said, wiping his brow with a

monogrammed handkerchief. Still hitting in the nineties. But this is your nickel. What's up?"

"John Wells. I need to talk to him."

"That's easy. We have a video-con with him in about an hour. I'll need to prep you on it. What's the rush?"

Kerry looked for a quiet spot in the old lobby and pointed Church to a corner. This place reminded Kerry of his own office, sporting the odor of ancient federal office buildings. "I need privacy. This is very sensitive."

"This is my domain, Kerry. Your secret's safe."

The director's confidence was unflappable, Kerry realized. His moxie could be an asset or a hindrance, depending on how this sorted out.

"John's wife and kids might be alive." Kerry watched the news affect the director as it had him and Shawnda.

Church collapsed into a deep chair behind him, his hand to his forehead. "How? I mean, where?"

"We got some lucky breaks working with the CIA. The bodies in the Veep's helo weren't Amy and the kids. I need to find out from John who might've wanted his wife and kids kidnapped." He settled into a chair before the director. "Our investigation depends on John's insights. We've got to reach him."

The director whistled low, scratched his chin, and leaned back, covering his face with both hands. He moaned and shook his head. "This can't be!"

"Afraid it is, sir."

Church dropped his hands, glaring at Kerry. "You only know half the story. Don't presume to understand what's at stake here. We can't tell John about this. Not today." He swore and kicked at a chair.

"We have to, sir. To find his family."

"They'll just have to chill a little longer, Kerry. There's something you don't know yet—big news that goes public today."

"Sir?"

"John's stuck on Mars. Don't know any easier way to say it. His return ship's busted . . . up in orbit. And I need him running on all cylinders to get us through this crisis. The future of manned exploration depends on solving this problem. Fast."

Church stood and began pacing, kicking a trash can over halfway around the first loop.

Stuck on Mars?

"You wanna be the one who tells him?" Church exclaimed. "Tell him that his family might be alive?" He stomped to his office door, throwing it open and slamming it into the wall.

He waved Kerry inside. "Come here a minute. There's something you need to see." He closed the door behind Kerry as he entered, then picked up a folder labeled "CLASSIFIED" and pitched it to Kerry.

"This is why I can't let you talk to John today. Only five people have seen this. You make six. Keep it that way. "

Kerry's eyes scanned down the single page inside the red folder, topped with a presidential seal. He gasped.

MARS

"I'm proposing alternatives, Greg. That's more than you're giving *me*." John struggled to contain his anger with Director Church at NASA's Johnson Space Center. This was a one-way conversation, thanks to the speed of light and the eleven minutes it took his signal to reach Earth.

John intended to take matters into his own hands, no matter the personal cost. He couldn't see the director but could imagine what would be going through his boss's head when he heard John's words in a few minutes. *Greg will have a stroke.*

He had to make this plan work. John swore he'd go into business for himself if he ever got home.

No more idiot orders from cover-your-backside NASA bureaucrats. No more accommodation and appeasement. No more politics. No more politicians.

"Our ERV's shot," John said, steadying his voice. "So we're staying here, on the surface." He took a deep breath. "Presuming we stay at the base, we have just enough food, oxygen, and water to survive a six-month delay. If you don't launch the next ERV and cargo missions on time, or if one of those missions fails to reach us—and those are all realistic probabilities—or if the MAV fails and we couldn't launch to reach the ERV in orbit, we'd starve or asphyxiate. Any perturbation, any shift at all in your schedule or a failure of one of those components, will kill us all."

John prayed as he talked, asking for the strength and the peace to get through this call without conflict. "I respect your authority, Greg, but in this life-and-death situation, I'm not taking 'no' for an answer."

John looked around the room for support. Every head nodded, except Geo's.

"I've uploaded a complete plan for you. We've coordinated with the colonists and intend to move the entire base—the Habs, the Laboratory, both MSRs, and our nuclear power—in a single wagon train. We'll leave in two days. Oz estimates a thirty-day crossing, and another thirty to reestablish our infrastructure at the colony.

"Their shipment of four inflatable domes will arrive in May, and we'll build their next greenery quad around our Habs. That has us up and running again as an effective exploration mission inside two months. Three months from now, when our launch window opens to return to

Earth, off we go in their rocket."

John looked at his friends. Melanie smiled and nodded. "The ERV can only take four of our crew; we're bringing Rex Jr. back with us. Sam, Deborah, Oz, and Jake have volunteered to stay. The colonists agreed to have our guys join them, and we're looking forward to staking a new claim on Mars. It's a good plan, and we all expect it to work. Stand by for our data upload. Mars Base, out."

John set down the headset with a loud exhalation, relieved they were much too far from Houston to feel the blistering fury of their choleric director.

"That oughta stir up their beehive," Oz said with a snicker.

Deborah winked and shook her head.

"You don't agree?" he asked.

"Nope," she said as she clipped her hair back. "I think you've misread them. We've got about half an hour 'til we hear back from Houston. I say we start a pool. Three options. They love it, they grudgingly accept it since they can't touch us anyway, or they hate it and try to stop us. I'm putting a hundred bucks and my last five Belgian chocolates on the first option. It's a brilliant plan, and they'll see that."

"You're nuts!" Oz replied. "I'll take that bet. My money says they fire John and make me the new mission commander. Whad'ya say, Hawk?" He tossed a cracker on the table as his imaginary chip.

"I'm with Oz," Geo said, his first words that day.

"He speaks!" Oz joked.

"You agree with Oz?" Jake asked. "Man, we're busting mathematical improbabilities every day."

"They ought to fire him," Geo said. "That's what I'm saying. This is ludicrous. We're like the crew of the *HMS Bounty*, and this call is our mutiny." Geo crossed his arms, striking a defiant pose. "That colony's your island full of topless natives, and John is Mr. Christian."

"Well, thank you for your vote of confidence, Robert," John said. "Maybe those natives are cannibals, and we ought to offer you up as dessert."

"Good idea! And who's that make you, Geo?" Oz asked. "Cap'n Bligh?"

The crew laughed until John dragged his hand across his throat, out of Geo's sight. "Enough," he said. "But the pool's a good idea. I'll vote the middle. I want that chocolate."

And so it went, IOUs, chocolate bars, a precious six pack of Coke, and Jake's complete collection of ancient *Alien* movie discs, all wagered. By the time Director Church's voice crackled over the speakers eleven minutes later, the mood was festive.

"Mars Base, Houston. This is Director Church." He paused, and John's heart felt like it skipped a beat. This was the ultimate test of his planning, his leadership, and perhaps their survival. It didn't matter what Greg said, of course, but his boss's support would make all the difference. They were going to move, with or without the director's endorsement. Their lives depended on it.

"What can I say, John?" Director Church began, sitting before a video terminal at Mars Mission Control. "You don't give me many options. You're on Mars. I'm not. And you're only giving me, what—two days to respond? I'd need a year to get this approved by leadership. Maybe more.

"You're proposing to dismantle a base three hundred million tax payers own, and fifty thousand contractors and NASA workers helped build. You want to tear it down and move it—a hugely dangerous undertaking considering local geography—to a site we've never approved.

"You might call this a slap in my face, John. Of course, you're the admiral. You're supposed to know something about leadership, after all.

So . . ." Director Church paused again. "I want you to look at the attached image that conveys my complete answer. This is my final word, Hawk. Don't screw it up."

John's heart sank. He'd gambled—and been spanked publicly.

"Told ya you had it coming," Geo cackled. "We stay!"

John felt like breaking the weasel's beak.

Oz moved for Geo, but John grabbed his arm, holding him back. "No. Split the chocolate with him," he said, motioning to the cache on the table. "I don't care what Church says. We're going anyway."

"That's the spirit!" Oz exclaimed, swiping three chocolates off the table.

"You can't!" Geo yelled at John, his nose level with John's Adam's apple. "You heard the director!"

"Yeah. And so did I," Jake said, pulling Geo back. The geologist raised his fists, but Jake outweighed him by twenty kilos and quickly pinned the hands behind the smaller man's back.

"The director said upload the file, boys," Melanie shouted over the squabble. "So I did. Look at this!"

Jake spun Geo around to face a large screen on the wall of the Hab. No one had watched Melanie while Oz and Geo tangled. The screen displayed a still image of the entire Mission Control team, standing shoulder to shoulder, with Greg Church and the NASA administrator at the front. They kneeled and held a long white banner with giant red and blue letters: "Ask forgiveness, not permission." Each of the Mission Control team displayed an upraised thumb.

Geo's arms slackened, and Jake released him. The still image began playing as a video file, with a raucous audio background. The upraised thumbs changed to clapping hands, cheers and whistles filling the soundtrack.

Director Church turned to silence the team, then faced the camera.

"Desperate circumstances demand desperate measures, Admiral Wells. You always do manage to find a way out of a bind. You've got my complete support, along with all of NASA. Your crew and your mission will be in the thoughts and prayers of all Americans. God speed."

With that, the Mission Control crew waved good-bye and held up the banner. Some joker in the audience lifted a large poster with a caricature of John's face on it. Oz doubled over in laughter, and even shy Ramona joined in the revelry, jumping up and down, her brown eyes alive with joy.

"You win, Deborah," Oz said, tossing the candy back on the table. "Keep your chocolate."

The crew, including a red-faced Geo, faced John and began to clap.

In that moment, John felt he'd been here before—years ago alone on the farm, feeding calves, when he'd first felt that tug on his spirit to go to space. In a flash he relived that magical West Virginia spring morning when he'd heard the words in his heart: *you will make a difference.*

God's hand was on this day.

20

"MALCOLM'S FURIOUS. He heard from his NASA contact," Monique whispered, squirming in the tiny stone tunnel. "He said John's crew claims to have found evidence the Father Race's Oracles were a hoax. Malcolm's convinced NASA wants to discredit him."

She stopped, unsure how fully to bare her true feelings to these patient women fast becoming her friends. "John found some parts from one of the Oracles that crashed on Mars. NASA says the parts were all made on Earth." It was hard to put a good face on this news. If it was true, it condemned her. "If he's right, the faith of tens of millions was misplaced."

"We already know that," Amy said. "Any news about John?" The prisoners huddled by the grate, a gray blanket their only disguise. Fortunately, no one was watching the video sensors at night anymore because Monique had invented new assignments for the guards. But if

Malcolm ever woke when she was gone, it would be her undoing. She knew she was living on borrowed time.

"How do you find out these things?" Amy asked.

"He has a NASA source. Dr. Bondurant, the director of the Jet Propulsion Labs."

"Felicia Bondurant?" Amy exclaimed.

"Yes. You know her?"

"I did, but never liked her. What have you heard from John?"

Monique hesitated. "Your sons are fine, Amy. I watched them on the video this morning. I check on them once or twice a day now. They're strong young men."

"Thank you. I know they're lonely. We can speak to them through the wall, but I want to hold them. To be free." She paused. "Any news from John?"

Monique stuttered, then blurted it out. "Malcolm said they're planning to move the NASA base. From the original landing site, five hundred kilometers east, to join the Edwards colony."

"What on Earth for?" Amy asked, moving her face closer to the grate.

"To expand the colony. And for other reasons."

"What other reasons, Monique? I want to know."

Monique hated this. This news would break their hearts, but no news at all was worse. Her last message, that John thought them dead, wasn't as troubling as this.

"Monique?"

She had to be honest. They had no hope of escape unless she led them out. And John was in danger. But she couldn't tell it all. It was too much.

"What is it, Monique? It's about John, right? Please, we need to know. If he can't know about us, I at least want to know about him. To pray for his needs."

Monique sucked in a deep breath. "I—I don't know if this information is correct. I heard it from Malcolm. I have no other access to news."

"Then tell us what he told you!"

"Their return craft is damaged, Amy. It's lost all its fuel." At times like these, she so desperately wanted to know more about this thing called prayer, and why Amy and Alice felt so comfortable talking to their God. It was a strength she needed. Right now.

"Lost their fuel? Can they get home?"

Monique shook her head. "No," she squeaked, a dry swallow barely relieving her emotion-parched throat. "Not on their own. They'll have to return using the colonists' craft. It will be months before NASA can help."

Amy was silent. Monique was thankful the questions had ended, if for a moment. How did Amy do it? Imprisoned. Separated from her sons. Six years behind these walls. Presumed dead. Isolated from her husband. And he, with no idea she was alive, unable to return to Earth to find her even if he did know.

She heard faint sobs. "Amy?" Monique screwed up her courage. "Amy? There *is* hope. But we have to act quickly."

Amy wiped at her eyes. "Act? Yes, I'm ready. Soon?"

"I'll tell you as we go. I have a plan. When I come, you must be *ready*."

She felt a squeeze and a tear drip on the fingers she'd extended through the grate. Soft words emerged from under the cover of muffled pain. Words that spoke to Monique's heart.

"God! Please hurry to my rescue! God, come quickly to my side! Those who are out to get me, let them fall all over themselves. Quick to my side, Lord. Quick to my rescue! Please God, don't lose a minute!"

Monique waited until the soft words stopped, then forged ahead, determined to speak her heart. She hungered for this strength, this peace—the spark she'd just felt as the prayer rolled off Amy's tongue. "Amy? Alice? Would you pray for *me*?"

FRIDAY, APRIL 3, 2020:
NAZARJE, SLOVENIA

"Do you have a mirror?" Amy asked Monique the next night. "Like a compact you could slip through the grate?" She squatted back against the stone wall. Alice snored lightly in their small bed.

"I can get one. You don't have a mirror?"

"No. We can only see our reflection in our basin's water. Alice would love to have a mirror. And a new brush."

"I'll try," Monique said with hesitation. Amy hoped she didn't ask any more questions. She didn't want to lie.

"There's more news about John. Malcolm heard it from the Master of the Remnant, late tonight, before we went to bed."

Amy's heart jumped at every mention of John's name. Her pain had intensified once she knew he was alive, and then turned to grief when she realized he thought her dead.

As Monique had recounted what she'd heard over the years from Malcolm, Amy imagined the horror of that evening her husband thought she'd died. Monique explained that when John had confronted Raines trying to enter the crash site to pray over her remains, it had infuriated him; he'd pummeled the preacher and broken Raines's jaw in two places. Amy gained a little satisfaction in that story, knowing that, although she had already been abducted and on her way to Slovenia by then, her husband had unknowingly defended her honor.

Amy wondered how John had endured such a loss. Every time she imagined the funeral—with five caskets, her own and the children's—she cried for him.

"John has proposed moving their Mars Base. They'll move *everything* . . . the Habitats, the Laboratory, the Rovers . . . five hundred kilometers to join the colony."

Amy saw John in her mind, directing seven fellow astronauts who, over the past nights, she'd come to know through Monique's stories about the mission. Amy knew many of them from her days in Houston, particularly Jake Cook, an old family friend.

She pictured John embarking on the most significant planetary exploration feat of all time. He was taking action. He intended to survive, to find a way back. That was her John—always solving problems. He never gave up.

Amy prayed God would work a miracle in her new friend's heart with her next words. *Please, Jesus.*

"Is there any way," she breathed, "any at all, that you can get word to John? Let him know we're alive?"

"I've tried," Monique said at last, her words interrupted by a series of coughs—a sure sign, Amy had learned, that Monique was trying hard to cover her pain. "I have no access to the outside world. No phones, outside networks, or television. Not even mail. We only know what Malcolm shares with us." She sighed. "My detainment is different from yours, Amy. But we're both prisoners."

"I hadn't thought about it that way," Amy said softly. "Thank you for trying."

Amy pulled her knees closer to her chest, wrapping the coarse wool blanket tighter around her shoulders. She imagined the opportunity: Monique able to find a computer terminal somewhere, locating John's electronic address at NASA. It couldn't have changed that much in six years. A quick e-mail: "Slovenia to Mars. I'm alive! Love, Amy." She wanted him to know, to encourage him, to spur him a little more to do everything he could to make it home.

So far from Earth, so many hurdles for them both. Burying her head on her knees, she prayed softly, yet loud enough so Monique could hear. "Give us encouragement, Jesus. Help John find answers. Make his heart glad. And somehow, through your Spirit or someone you can touch, let John know we're alive."

MARS

"Wagons ho!" Oz yelled over his suit radio as he stood in front of his train of Martian prairie schooners. John laughed, imagining he was the trail boss on an old episode of his favorite childhood television western, galloping along the line of wagons, exhorting the drivers to action.

Head 'em up! Move 'em out!

The newest rover, MSR2, waiting for John to climb aboard, would lead the way, their scout to plot a course through five hundred kilometers of rocky terrain filled with canyons, desert plains, washes, and gullies. Moving the NASA base through Nirgal Vallis was like towing a street full of houses through the Grand Canyon, while wearing biohazard suits and scuba gear.

Hab One, Hab Two, and the Lab module lined up like strange rolling tuna cans, their squat structures suspended inside four legs tipped with large silver wheels. Behind the line of giant structures, the older MSR1 took up the rear, driven robotically by Geo in the last Hab. It towed one of the wheeled nuclear power generators, their electrical cables snaking from the plant to the MSR and then to each of the structures like a low-hanging electric service wire. Which is exactly what it was.

They were moving their entire base—less the Mars Ascent Vehicle—fully powered and livable every step of the way. With one exception. Once in a Hab or the MSR, you stayed there all day. The connecting tubes had been withdrawn. For the next month, you could get from one to another only by transferring in one of the rovers.

"Wagons ho?" John asked. "Bet you've been dying to say that for a week." He rested a gloved hand on his friend's shoulder.

"You kidding?" Oz laughed. "They'll make a movie about me. This is famous."

"He's right," Sam Readdy said, the third suited astronaut. "We pull this off and we'll have Hollywood knocking on our door." Sam extended a hand to John. "You took a gamble, Hawk. Thanks for doing that. Whether or not this works, it was worth the attempt."

John gripped Sam's gloved hand. "Thanks, Sam. It *will* work."

"Darn tootin'," Oz said, waving as Sam returned to Deborah in the lab module. Two drivers drove the Lab and each of the Habs, and John and Oz took the newest rover.

Jake and Ramona waved from Hab One's window, and Melanie waved from Hab Two.

Poor Mel, John thought. *Cooped up with crazy Geo for a month.* It wasn't fair. But that was Mel, always taking the dirty assignments. The unsung hero of this mission. A true servant-leader.

John and Oz climbed into their rovers. At the top of the ladder, John looked back down the line of their Mars craft, remembering eight years ago when he and Amy watched the first televised images of supposed alien spiders walking on Mars—and the words God had placed on his heart that day as he sat there spellbound, Amy cradled in his arms:

I have called you for a time such as this.

Those words now echoed in his heart. As hard as it would be for

Amy to deal with her anxieties right now at his being stranded on Mars, John wished she were alive. Alive and praying for him, united with him in spirit as she had been so often in his earlier days in space. He needed her. All their lives depended on what he and his crew were about to do. He missed her prayers and her missives, encouraging and sustaining him.

John waved at the crew behind him, then turned inside and shut the door. For better or worse, the door on NASA's first permanent Mars Base was now closed. There was no turning back.

"Let's go, Oz," John said, pointing southeast. "Follow that yellow brick road."

MONDAY, APRIL 6, 2020: MARS

John checked the seal on the MSR door. He was by himself in the scuffed white rover, and the atmosphere was holding. He turned to the control panel and the communications display. The e-mail message from Houston had said to take this call alone. To be sure of it.

They were four days into their transit across the eastern reaches of Nirgal Vallis. John parked the rover far ahead of the slow-moving line of modules and waited for Houston's next transmission.

This mysterious emergency call had his heart pounding. He'd never seen such secrecy since his first mission to Mars years ago, when he'd communicated with NASA about a possible hoax involving the alleged alien spiders. Even more amazing was that the colony crew had intercepted the first call today from Houston to inform him a message was waiting. He'd missed NASA's notification as he'd worked with Oz to find a path through the rocks for Hab One.

A minute later, John had a secure connection ready. He waited eleven minutes for his signal to reach Houston, and another eleven or more to hear back. Twenty-three minutes after he entered and sealed the MSR, Director Church's unscrambled voice emerged from the speaker. It was an audio conference only. John wondered what was transpiring on the other end that would lead them to speak . . . and not want to be seen.

"John, this is Greg Church. What I'm about to share is being said in private. No fanfare, no Mission Control team. I'm here with Special Agent Terrance Kerry. You remember him, no doubt. Kerry brought us some disturbing news. No, let's call it hopeful news, but distressingly incomplete. We need to share it with you. And we have to ask some very pointed questions. So sit down."

A maddening pause followed in the transmission. Church's voice crackled again in the speaker.

"John. Special Agent Kerry has unearthed some new information about the attack on the helicopter that killed the vice president and your family. I'm putting him on the line. Stand by."

John's heart raced as he remembered that horrible day. He'd relived that night of six years ago a thousand times, both waking and dreaming. A dead wife and four children, a dead vice president, and John's haunting blind-rage attack on Elias Ulrich. Nearly slashing the terrorist's head off with a canoe paddle, then reviving him only to have Ulrich knife him deep in his thigh. In the final moments Kerry had saved him with a single bullet to his assailant's forehead.

Kerry came on the line. "Hi, John. Terrance Kerry here. I don't know whether to be happy with this news, or apologetic, so I'm just going to tell you what I know. My wife Shawnda, at CIA—you've met her—uncovered some important information about a terror cell that led us to some data about a DNA typing lab. One with ties to dirty political money, and the same one, it turns out, that typed the evidence from the crash site the night that Amy . . . that the vice president . . . was killed."

Why'd he correct himself? John wondered.

"We've determined beyond question that Amy and your kids were not on the helicopter that afternoon." Kerry paused.

John slid down in the driver's seat, suddenly unable to hold himself up. He felt a plug of food begin working up his throat and grabbed a cup, too small to hold what was fighting to escape his stomach. "What?" he croaked, forgetting they couldn't hear him. Not for eleven minutes.

"We exhumed your family's bodies, John. I take full responsibility. We had to be sure."

John coughed, almost ready to puke and not caring where it landed.

"The bodies in those graves are not—repeat, not—those of your family. They had your family's clothes and ID, but none of the DNA matches. We know who the woman and children were, but we can't imagine why they were on the helicopter. I'm leading this investigation, and we know for sure Amy and the kids left your home in a black limo around two a.m. on the morning of the attack."

"No!" John cried.

"We have two witnesses. Your family left in the night; a woman and four children were seen repeating the entire process five hours later. You mentioned to me, or maybe Dr. Pestorius told me, that Amy didn't sound like herself when you talked to her that day.

"We need some clues, John. When did Amy say she left the house? Was there any reason for her to depart at two in the morning, eight hours before the flight for Washington? And if she was . . . well, if they were . . . abducted . . . who would possibly want to do that?"

John felt faint, unable to believe what he was hearing. His family might be alive! And they'd been alive, perhaps, during the six years he'd been grieving over their loss. The console seemed to waver, like he was losing consciousness or his sense of balance was collapsing from too many stimuli. He grabbed at a handhold and steadied himself.

"I need help. I need to know: Was there an enemy—someone you offended or someone who threatened you both—anyone who might've done this? I know it's gonna hurt, that you're on Mars and can't be here to figure this out. But we've solved some tough problems together in the past over the radio, you and I. So tell me what you know, buddy. I promise I'll move heaven and Earth to find them." Another pause.

"There's hope, John. Amy and the kids might still be alive."

21

"HAWK? YOU COMIN'?" Oz asked, transmitting from the Hab One module as it crawled along, finally clear of the rocks. "Yo, Hawk! Answer up, man, or we're gonna turn these yurts around and come get you."

John heard, but it didn't register. Something said it should, but he was oblivious to all but one thing.

Amy's alive.

Actually, Kerry hadn't said that. *Your family* might *be alive!* That was it.

He stared at the MSR control panel, a voice inside saying "react, take charge, find a way home instantly." Yet part of him felt moored to a giant anchor hopelessly dug into a mucky ocean bottom, never to break free.

Stuck.

Oz called again. "I'm serious, Hawk. Either you answer right now, or someone's headed to get you. Speak now, buddy. I need to know you're okay."

The little voice in John snapped him to attention. He keyed the headset. "I'm here, Oz. Sorry."

"What is it, Hawk? Something's not right. You're the most talkative pilot on this mission." He chuckled, and John heard Deborah laughing in the background.

"Second most talkative. You win that one," John said, desperate for some humor. He should be rejoicing but felt like screaming instead.

Marooned. And Amy possibly alive, waiting on him to find her.

"So I asked you, Hawk. You okay?"

John didn't answer, staring at the control panel, only dimly aware someone spoke his name. He began working the computer, calling up the navigation utility and accessing orbital mechanics profiles. He worked through the orbital trajectories and software tools with the skill born of two decades of practice. No one could solve a trajectory problem on the fly like John Wells, and, heart racing, he dove into the problem.

How soon can we leave? How much faster can we get home on the ERV's limited fuel load?

"I see what you're up to, Hawk. I'm monitoring the MSR data utility. Please, talk to us." Something soft and melodic tugged at John. It was Melanie, pleading from her station on Hab Two. Geo would be railing at her right now for slowing their advance. John looked up at the line of rolling metal yurts, all of them stopped.

For me?

Hab One was headed his way. *How'd he turn that big thing around?* Oz wasn't taking any chances, and that thought warmed John.

If he's already coming this direction, I'll just work. Nothing mattered now, except finding a way to get home. Fast.

John had plugged the numbers three times and rechecked them before Hab One docked to his airlock with a gentle bump. The airlock door hissed open, and Deborah ran through, Oz behind her. John looked up. He had the answers he'd been searching for. But none offered any hope.

Option one, not good enough. Drive an MSR as fast as possible to the colony, arrive in four days. Maximum effort might get a launch off in a week using the colonists' ERV, with a lot of help from Nicci and Rex. It was an unlikely scenario, probably too hard, and he'd have to leave half his crew in the wilderness to finish moving the base. The space transit would take six months because the planets wouldn't be aligned. Total: six and a half months to Earth, starting today.

Option two, no better. Crawl to the colony at their current speed and arrive in no less than three weeks. Take a ponderous month to prep the ERV and learn its systems—a more likely ground scenario. Leaving later, with better planetary alignment, the space transit would take five months. Total: six months, three weeks.

Option three, let God work. Wait for the planets to move into place and launch at the proper window: June 22, eleven weeks away, followed by a fast four-month transit to Earth. Total: six months, three weeks. Leave in two weeks, or leave in two and a half months, and get there at the same time using the limited load of methane on Rex's ERV. John pounded the armrest of the driver's seat as Oz came through the airlock.

"Hawk?" Deborah asked, stopping mid-rover. John didn't acknowledge her. He was leaning over the control panel, his insides racked by dry sobs. Like a case of the heaves, but without the nausea, John's guts were being jerked out his throat. The red dusty plain and deep gorges on either side of the rover, once a sight of interplanetary beauty to him, were now an anathema. Mars mocked him. He couldn't get home, when he most needed to be there.

When the tears finally came, John felt Deborah's soft hands on his neck, gently stroking him. He heard Oz whispering to her about the meaning of the computer profiles on the command screen.

"Why?" John heard Deborah murmur to Oz over his choked sobs. He no longer cared if they saw him break down. He'd been valiant too long. Six years too long. Years of pain at the loss of his family poured out now, his heart broken at last.

Someone had warned him. Who was it? Mel?

She'd told him once, training for this mission, that he'd never properly grieved the loss of his family. He was compartmentalizing, like Michelle used to accuse him of doing. Mel said that one day immense grief would steamroll him, like being run over by a train. He could outrun it for a time, but eventually he'd succumb. Today he was paying the price.

"Looks like he wants to get home, Deborah. And *fast*," Oz said quietly, scanning the screen over John's shoulder. "Trouble is, you can't beat physics, Doc. Limited by fuel. Can't get there 'til just shy of seven months from today, no matter how soon you leave."

Deborah patted his neck some more, the two of them silent as John tried to get hold of his emotions. "What is it, John?" she said, her voice soothing. "We want to help." She passed a cloth to him.

John blew his nose on something that smelled like baby wipes, then looked up, his vision blurred by tired, wet eyes. He tried to smile but couldn't. His two dear friends stared at him like he was some sort of freak, so unlike their usual in-control admiral.

"You got a call. From the Big Man," Oz said. "Wanna tell us about it?"

John nodded, trying to form the words, but the raw, parched Mars he saw out the front window eviscerated his lungs. He was shipwrecked, stuck here on this barren planet. He'd even relished the opportunity to stay here, as recently as an hour ago.

What if I'd stayed—then found out about Amy after the crew left? He shivered.

John took a deep breath and patted Deborah's hand. She let him go and stepped back. He exhaled loudly. His answer, whatever it sounded like, would have to do.

"Yeah. Greg Church. He said . . . Amy's alive. Might be." He choked on the last words. "And my kids," he said, another sob choking him. "I need help. We have to get home."

TUESDAY, APRIL 7, 2020: WASHINGTON, DC

"No!" Kerry yelled as he jumped up from his desk in his FBI office, the day after his difficult call to John. "Don't spook him!"

He expanded the news view running continuously in the lower right corner of his computer screen. An image labeled "Dr. May Randall" overlaid another image of the now-famous Martian colony. Since Rex Jr.'s trek across Mars, he and the Mars colony were household words in America and worldwide. Particularly in the Kerry home.

The headline screamed: "Alien hoax!" Kerry watched in silence as the interview played out, a suited correspondent with a comb-over interviewing a khaki flight suit–clad African-American woman with dark curly locks.

Interviewing? It takes hours to converse with someone on Mars.

"Dr. Randall. The information your colonists provided today is remarkable—on two counts. First, your goal in establishing the beachhead on Mars, as Rex Edwards said often, was to continue the

Father Race's mission—to extend mankind to another planet, same as on Earth. Now, you're negating the underpinnings of the Father Race movement, Dr. Raines, and Saint Michael's Remnant. You've also undercut the very reason for your mission."

He rustled through some papers. "Your evidence points to one conclusion, that the spider visitors on Mars were a hoax. And by extension, so were those visitations of the Oracles on Earth." The reporter shook his head, as if he too were a Remnant believer. "This will dash the faith of tens of millions of adherents."

"Is this an interview, Walter? Or is it a news analysis? I can't tell, with you drawing conclusions about our motivations. I should tell you, to keep this news fair and balanced, that we colonists don't agree about the veracity of this evidence. Some of us wonder if these remains really were from the Oracles of the Father Race."

"It's mathematically improbable," she said, "that such an advanced race of beings, one that seeded life on Earth tens of thousands of years ago, would crash a Martian landing craft after coming so far to this planet. It's also hard to believe that, of all the places here, such evidence would fall on the *only* direct line between the *only* two human habitations on Mars. Some of us believe NASA or another entity has planted false evidence to discourage us, to suggest the Oracles were fake."

"I'm not taking a position on the authenticity of the crash site data, Walter. And I won't speak to our motivation, except to say we're reporting the facts. You must draw your own conclusions." She shrugged. "As you apparently have already done."

The reporter's face was a mixture of surprise and wonder. Like Kerry's.

Gutsy lady. But how could she do this? And why her? Why not NASA? They've been sitting on this information for weeks. He remembered his classified discussion with Greg Church and the red folder marked with a presidential seal. There was so much the world had yet to learn.

"This is an interview, I assure you, Dr. Randall. Not a news analysis. As I said, this information is remarkable on two counts. The second is this. Why hasn't NASA been forthcoming about this information? Their astronauts recovered the crash materials with your son—along with four witnesses, I might add. Our calls to Johnson Space Center to interview Director Greg Church, and our queries of the administrator's office in Washington, have all gone unanswered. Why?"

"I'm unqualified to answer that, Walter. Ask NASA yourself. I can assure you, however, from what we know here, the astronauts reported the information to their superiors as soon as they told us. There's been no effort by anyone here to withhold it."

"Yet you yourself are just now revealing it, Dr. Randall. You said this evidence, as you call it, was discovered some weeks ago."

Dr. Randall smiled and tilted her head. "True. Perhaps you can understand, with our mission resting entirely on our belief in the Father Race, how difficult it was for us to share this with you. Doing so, in some sense, might legitimize the find. Do you understand?"

"Maybe," the reporter countered, "unless you believe NASA set it up. And you're letting us know about it just now to take the advantage. Why anyone would sit on this news makes no sense to me."

Dr. Randall's face shifted to a frown. "You're a reporter, so no, I'm sure you can't understand our motivation and devotion to a single cause, Walter. We aren't trying to force anyone's hand or take an advantage. We're simply reporting information that's remained hidden too long. Draw your own conclusions."

She pushed back from her seat before the camera. "Now, if you'll excuse me, I have pressing duties here at the colony." With that, May's image disappeared.

"This interview, with Dr. May Randall, commander of the Mars colony, was recorded earlier today and time compressed to remove the radio delays. Again, if you are just selecting this broadcast, we've been—"

Kerry muted it and leaned back in his chair, thinking.

"If Raines was behind the spiders, he'll bolt," Kerry said out loud a moment later. "If not, he'll fight this tooth and nail." He leaned into the dented aluminum windowsill, gazing at rush-hour traffic crawling by six stories below.

"Maybe you're right, Dr. Randall. Maybe NASA *did* do it."

Someone's lying, that's for sure.

Someone on Earth sent the spiders to Mars. Either the Martian plains were salted with artificial crash evidence, or the spiders were truly the fake aliens he and John had always thought them to be. After all, the busted spiders were definitely built on Earth. The wires and circuits were definitive on that count.

"Perhaps it's a test," Kerry mused. "Like crazy Raines said. A test from the Father Race to put our belief to the trial." He laughed as he said it, remembering a year of chasing Elias Ulrich around the globe while the terrorist transported six "alien spiders" in his special submarine. Somehow Ulrich was always a step ahead, planting the spiders at each international site of "alien landings" for the Father Race. If he had that prize, Ulrich's sub and load of mechanical spiders, he could bust this controversy wide open.

"This is nuts," Kerry said, shutting down his computer for the night. He'd go home to Shawnda, and dinner, and together maybe they could sort this out. "Someone big's behind it," he said, flipping off the room lights.

A line of purple-white headlights stretched down Twelfth Street in one direction, and a sea of red glowing taillights in the other. *Thank goodness for the Metro,* Kerry thought, grabbing his overcoat and umbrella.

He pulled the door closed, speaking to an empty hall. "Somebody big is pulling all the strings. And we're dancing to every one. That somebody won't be happy when we expose this."

"Question is," he said to a surprised elevator guard, "who are we looking for?"

WEDNESDAY, APRIL 8, 2020: NAZARJE, SLOVENIA

Distant stars twinkled through the thick wavy glass of Monique's tower window. Their freedom drew her like a distant harbor beacon in a storm. Focusing on them, she imagined she could fly out of here. She heard rustling behind her, then tired bare feet scuffling across the stone floor.

"Did I disturb you, Father?" Her voice quivered as she turned. Malcolm stood behind her, his immense frame looming larger in the dark than in the day. She sucked in her breath, laboring to appear calm.

"Yes, you did. Like last night. Where are you going?" His gruff voice in the inky darkness sounded formidable.

"For a walk, Guardian. Would you like to join me?" Monique acted like his company was a planned part of her excursion. She lifted his night coat from an antique prayer stand under the window. "I love the dark, Father. Come. Join me."

Raines stared at her, as though peering into her heart. With a steely resolve she'd learned from the Master himself, she pasted on a smile, pushing the pajama coat into his chest. "The exercise will be good for you. It'll help you sleep." With that, she maneuvered around Malcolm and headed toward the door.

"Come, Raksasa. Please. Be part of my nightly walk just this once."

She smiled, raising her eyebrows, trying to look inviting. Mysterious.

Raines shook his head, probably wondering, she hoped, at this fickle female. He turned, rubbing his face, and headed back to the bed.

"No. Please! Come along. Just once. You'll be refreshed."

Raines hung by the bedside, then shrugged, picked up the light cotton coat he'd dropped to the floor, and joined her at the door.

"You do this often?" he asked, as though he found it hard to believe.

"When I can't sleep. A few times a week."

They headed into the hall, then down the winding circular staircase to the first floor. She stepped across the plank opening to her secret tunnel, stealing a glance at Malcolm to make sure he didn't notice it.

As they crossed the great hall, he asked her, his voice aggravated, "Why can't you sleep, Monique?"

She slowed, turned, and took his hands in hers, mustering all her courage and wiles. "I cannot wait, my Priest. My body will soon be prepared for you. I'm anxious to be put to your test." She squeezed his hands. "I want to be a living vessel for the Father Seed."

Raines smiled; it was a broad smile, not some artificial television grin. He was genuinely pleased. He returned her grip, with a power that would've crushed most women's hands. Monique met it with a strong force of her own.

"You shall indeed be my vessel. You, and the Mother Seed. In just a few weeks you shall knit the flesh of Eve into your own."

Malcolm slept soundly. The walk had indeed done him good. But more valuable was the conversation about Monique's enduring loyalty, her flawless preparation of 321 young women, and her joyful expectation of the planting of the Mother Seed in her womb. Malcolm was at peace, his own anxieties—about the widening rift between him and his flock over the news of an alien hoax—forgotten. By three a.m. he was asleep again.

Monique stood at the window, opening it to the cool April night breeze. Cold gusts rushed down from the mountains to the north, and warmer currents tumbled up from the tower base. She dared not attempt to visit her friends tonight. Pulling a small package from her nightgown, she tossed the dainty clamshell device out. It impacted silently in the middle of the dormant garden below.

The stars were clearly visible now. Somewhere out there, she imagined, Amy's invisible God heard their prayers. She wondered what He looked like, this Jesus whom Amy and Alice loved so much.

Does He love me? If I talk to Him—in my thoughts—can He hear me?

Malcolm woke as she closed the double panes. "Come to bed," he commanded gruffly. "The night is short. Your ripe body needs rest."

Monique looked again at the stars, now distorted by the glass. She turned, swallowing her fears, and pretended to smile.

"Yes, Father. As you desire."

22

"**I TOLD YOU IT WAS STUPID.** You just wouldn't listen. *No one* listens to me. And now, we're stuck."

"Shut up, Geo," Melanie shot back, watching the habitats crawling slowly away from her. "Or go climb in the airlock and shout at the walls. But leave me alone. We're not stuck." Frustrated, she pulled at her thick brown hair.

"You can't make me," Geo yelled, leaving the control compartment. "I can go wherever I want on this . . ."

Melanie tuned him out, expert after a week of his relentless ranting about John, his leadership, and the danger of moving the Mars Base. Yet he'd never complained about John's recent news regarding Amy. It was as if Geo relished John's pain—John, her closest of friends.

Let him scream.

"Problems?" Melanie heard on the comm circuit as she tried

rocking the Hab backward to start forward motion again. She'd get one chance. After that, the slack in the power cord would play out. They'd all have to stop, like a line of elephants, trunk to tail.

"Yeah. You guys better stop. I think I'm jammed on a rock."

"Lemme look," Oz said. She saw the MSR make an immediate right and spin back around. At their frustrating progress of two kilometers an hour, Oz would enjoy policing the problem. He could easily outrun the giant lumbering habitats and laboratory.

"Yup. You're pinned, little lady. We'll need to give you a tug. Stand by."

Melanie pictured the rock outcropping, the tall boulders either side of the tracks of the Hab and the Lab ahead of her. It shouldn't have been a problem, but then, she was driving a house on wheels. It was amazing they'd come this far without a problem.

Melanie ached for a tractor. Something big and red with a throaty engine to jerk her back into business again.

"Headed your way, Mel," John radioed a moment later, like he was reading her mind. The Lab and the Hab ahead stopped, and in the viewer window she saw the robotically controlled MSR and its tow package of nuclear reactors stop behind them. At least Geo was doing his job. All eyes were probably on her.

Half an hour later, the line remained stationary. Oz was somewhere under the Hab in his Mars suit. She'd seen him exit the rover. The longer it took him under there, the worse the problem must be.

His voice finally crackled on the communication link, confirming her worst fears. "Gonna be here awhile, Hawk. She's not on a rock. The wheel's crushed. We need a spare."

"Do we have one?" Jake asked from Hab One at the front of the line.

"Not unless you give up one of yours," Oz said, his voice

overflowing with frustration. If he said it couldn't be rebuilt—it couldn't.

"Hawk," Oz said, "it's time to call for that help you and I were talkin' about."

"Rex?" John responded.

"The same. We need to see if we can steal one of his wheels. Probably ought to pull a couple of 'em, along with the axle, and bring 'em all back. Just in case. I have a feeling we'll need 'em. Still got a long way to go."

Now she had to deal with Geo. He'd be in her face within a minute, telling her how he'd predicted just this problem.

"How do you do it?" John had asked her once over a private cup of cocoa, the night he nearly decked Geo for the remark about Amy.

"Remember Legion?" she'd replied with a laugh. "That guy in the Bible who lived in the tombs and ran around yelling at people and cutting himself?"

"Yeah." John had the strangest look when he'd answered. "You think Geo's demon possessed?" He'd moaned. "I can see why."

"No, John. But Legion turned out to be a nice guy once he got free of what bound him, right? Something snapped in Robert Witt. Before it did, he was a hard-working, quiet scientist. But when we went a year without finding water, well . . . Now, he's competing with a colony full of nongeologists who doused their first drill with a gusher. Can you blame him?"

Melanie stared out the window at the immobile line of habitats. She thought of John, a friend since her early days as an Air Force major and Shuttle pilot, and he a mission specialist during his fourth mission, his first to the Space Station. Since then, he'd been her mentor and friend, her closest confidant in the many years away from her husband. She knew some people wondered about their relationship. She didn't care. Hawk was the big brother in her life . . . and her absent father, restored.

But he wasn't the same now, distracted since NASA's call about his family. It was like a clock was counting down in his head — counting down to Earth. *At least*, she thought, *we'll get to fly home together.*

"Melanie!" someone yelled. She spun. Geo stood a few meters behind her, huffing like he'd been running wind sprints. "I heard Oz. We *cannot* sit here for days waiting on a new wheel!"

Melanie pictured the geologist layered in dirt and blood, just crawling out of his cave in the Gerasenes region of the Holy Land. Chuckling, she didn't even hear his ranting as she imagined him disgorging a thousand water demons into a herd of Martian pigs. When he finally got her attention, she just said, "Shut up, Geo," before he could scream again. "Pull on your bubble suit and go help them, why don't you?"

He didn't move, and she shook her head. "Well? What about it, Legion? I'm sick to death of your snotty-nosed whining. We've got a flat, you bonehead. The wheel's shot. So leave me alone and do something useful. Like buzz off." She pulled at her hair and shrieked, doing her best to make her eyes bulge.

Geo stood speechless for a moment, head cocked, mouth open. "My name's not Legion." He spun around and left.

Melanie thrust a fist into the air. *Yes! No more Miss Sweetie Pie. I told him!*

She chuckled again and looked out at the row of vehicles. Rock-speckled, rusty-red gullies stretched in every direction from their place on a mesa-like plateau. It looked like their last base location, just different rocks and craters, plus a few more ditches. And with Geo grousing in the Hab's bowels, nothing had changed.

They were no worse off — better even — than the place they'd left a week and a half ago. But until they reached the colony's food, water, and rocket ship, they were still marooned.

In the middle of nowhere.

✦

"I'm asking for *your* help this time," John said. The rest of the crew gathered around him at the Lab's communal table as they teleconferenced with Rex, May, and Nicci. "We'd like to ask for your donation of some wheels and an axle. Like we'd discussed when we started this odyssey."

He paced, imagining Amy and the kids. The crew had to get going. Somewhere out there, she waited for him.

"I have a surprise for you, Admiral," Rex said.

"You usually do." John forced a smile.

"I have *four* wheels and *two* axles loaded on the rover. Strapped to the cab, two wheels and an axle on each side. I can be out of here tomorrow morning, and arrive in about three days. A day to replace the equipment, and to lash down the rest, and another three days back. I'd be gone for a week. You'll have three spares—and no need to send someone later for more parts."

"You amaze me," John said. Rex's preparation had saved them two valuable days, perhaps more. A little voice inside reminded him that this provision wasn't his doing. In fact, John couldn't have done anything. God was moving in the lives of others.

John's stomach settled, the way it often did lately when he saw vivid reminders to put his trust in the right place. He smiled, for real. The grin felt good.

"He amazes *me,* too," May said, beaming at Rex. "I'll send Nicci with him along with some ripe veggies. So sit tight. We're on the way."

"Good. We'll celebrate," John said.

"Celebrate?" Melanie asked.

John turned to his crew, aware of some of their sensitivities to his occasional expressions of faith, but determined to remember God's hand in everything. He watched Geo, sitting with a scowl on his face at the end of the table, and Jake, watching May on the screen. The eight of them were each distinctly different people, stuck in more than one way, on Mars.

"Well?" Melanie said, poking at him as though trying to dislodge John from a daydream.

"Huh? Oh, yeah. Tomorrow's Easter, guys. We're stuck here. Might as well relax and celebrate."

"What on Earth for?" Geo asked, a huge scowl creasing his face.

"You mean *on Mars*," Oz said. "What on Mars for? Get it right, Geo, if you're gonna speak in clichés all the time."

"You're one to talk," Geo snarled. "Why the sudden interest in relaxation, Hawk? You've driven us nuts with your 'we've gotta get home right away' line. You don't even know if Amy's alive. Now you want to party out here in the middle of nowhere."

John resisted the urge to snap off Geo's long nose and stuff it down his scrawny throat. Melanie was right—Legion was a great nickname. Then that strange calming peace returned, reminding him he wasn't in control. He never had been. John smiled. "We're gonna celebrate, Geo. It's resurrection time. Rex is on the way to give new life to our Hab."

"And ultimately," Melanie said with a wink, "he's going to help deliver us to a new and glorious home."

WASHINGTON, DC

"Who else?" Kerry asked, pushing his food around his plate at dinner late on a Saturday night. His mind wasn't on the meal. "I mean, who else but Raines? At this point, he's as good a candidate as anyone."

Shawnda touched his forearm with the tine of her fork.

He looked up. "Raines has the most to gain if the Father Race thing prospers. And the most to lose with a hoax."

"I said, 'I agree.' Did you hear me?" she asked.

Tiny dark freckles blended into the creases on her cheeks when she smiled. Kerry shook his head, embarrassed he'd been too preoccupied to notice she'd spoken. Sometimes he wondered how many details he missed in his personal life by focusing so intently on his work.

She's beautiful.

"I said I agree about Raines. Definitely our best suspect for now," she said. "I put in a standing order today with the Collection Committee. The next Balkans satellite overflight will be early tomorrow morning their time. They'll take some happy snaps of his Slovenia compound and the Trieste headquarters. They might also send a reconnaissance aircraft."

Kerry nodded, spearing a slice of beef. He suddenly realized he was pushing around food she'd worked hard to cook for him. Dinner together was a rare treat. They often didn't see each other until well after nine on weeknights, stressed by their schedules and late evening tasks at the Agency and the Bureau. "I'm sorry," he said, setting the fork down. "I've been ignoring you."

Shawnda reached across the table and took his hand. He loved her constant forgiving of his near-total immersion in this case. A case he'd been on in various stages the past nine years, since the first terror attacks on Washington and Colorado. When he'd met John. Before Shawnda.

"I understand. Just don't give up, Terrance. We'll find them. I can feel it."

"It takes me away from you. How much longer are you willing to make that sacrifice?"

"What about John? What was taken from him? It's the least we can do."

"Yeah. You're right." Kerry stood and wandered to the window, a hand on the sill as he stared out at nothing in particular. "D'you ever wonder? About how people could do that?"

"What?"

"Clone themselves. Then sentence their clone to death? Like the people did who put those kids on Air Force Two?"

"I try not to think about it. But you never know . . ."

"Know what?" He turned from the window.

"Just because they donated a cell to make the clone doesn't mean they know what happened to the child. Might not even know they've been cloned. Just takes a few cells' worth of genetic material. Any trip to the doctor could be a fishing expedition for a geneticist."

"It's sick any way you look at it. Someone sent four kids to their deaths. You run anything to ground with FMI yet? Their biotech labs?"

"We're working on it."

He walked to Shawnda and took her hand. "That's the spirit. So. I've got a surprise. It'll make your day."

"About us?" Her face brightened.

Kerry's smile faded. "Uh—about them. John and Amy and Raines. All that stuff."

She looked down. Kerry joined her at the table.

"I'm sorry, honey. It's just—well—the Bureau got a signal on Raines today. That tooth transmitter thing."

Shawnda looked up. "The cell phone in his molar? The one John knocked out of him when he slugged Raines?"

"Same idea. Different molar, maybe. He can hear a call, but he can't phone out with it. We developed them years ago at Quantico, and he's been on the Bureau's radar ever since John whacked him. We figured whoever put that in his mouth the first time would replace it somehow, if they wanted access to him. All we could hope was the new insert kept the same frequency and phone number."

Kerry broke into a grin, his face wrinkling from ear to ear as he balanced a pea on his knife, flipped it into the air, and caught it again on the knife. "Bingo. Today someone called that number, honey. And it connected." He pulled his shoulders back and stood again, strutting. "It routed to Slovenia. *His* number."

"Why didn't you tell me earlier?" Shawnda squealed and jumped up to tickle Terrance. "You're holding out on me!"

"It's more fun that way," Terrance said with a big grin. "It was a short call. We ran an origin ID, but it traced to Belize."

"What'd they say?"

"More of that crazy alien stuff. 'Do not lose faith. The Father Race is here. Venture Forth.' But it could be some kind of code."

"I wouldn't give Big Purple that much credit. You know that's his nickname, right? He actually likes it. The Spanish version, at least. I'll bet someone's been playing him for a patsy with that talking molar for years. Think about it. It's the perfect scam. Feed his ego and let Raines do your dirty work for you."

Kerry watched Shawnda busy herself with the dishes, connecting her logic with what he'd observed the past few weeks, and what he'd learned today.

"You're right!"

"About what?"

"Raines. He's clueless. A fall guy. He does the dirty work, thinks it's in support of a real Father Race, and off we go to Mars, chasing a new god. He gets rich in the process. With no trail to the source."

"Where's that leave us?" she asked, facing the sink of their small brownstone. Another ambulance roared down Rock Creek Parkway, its siren wailing.

Kerry stood and moved in behind her, wrapping his arms around a slender waist. He nestled his face in the crook between her neck and shoulder, pulling his arms about her.

"It leaves us right here, Mrs. Kerry. Now put down those dishes," he said, pulling her into the den and turning off the light.

EASTER SUNDAY, APRIL 12, 2020: WASHINGTON, DC

"Let's go. Please?" Shawnda pleaded, nudging Terrance in bed. Georgetown wasn't yet awake in the early morning hours of mid-April. The city had been hopping last night in the warming spring evening and now was sleeping off its late-hour revelry.

"Are you serious, girl? *Church?* Like bells and communion and stuff?"

"Yes, I'm serious. It's Easter Sunday. A new start for us." Shawnda bounded from the bed and threw open the curtains. She looked down on the postage-stamp lawn she could cut with a pair of scissors. Her micro-lawn in front of their micro-home, she liked to call it, one of hundreds of identical brownstones lining the treed Georgetown streets.

Home.

Outside the window, a dogwood bloomed. She lingered at the windowsill, watching the light pinkish-white blossoms, their four petals like a cross.

Everything's being born again. I want that.

The last time dogwoods bloomed and the grass was new, she'd been expecting. No more. The emptiness inside fought to consume her. She fought back.

"How fortunate we are, Terrance. We can get up, make our own decisions. But if you're right—if the analysts are right—Amy Wells is probably alive out there somewhere with no idea what today is, no way to get up when she wants, or make breakfast, or get to church. We owe it to her."

"To find her?"

"That, yes. And for her sake, we should go. To church. For them. John's stuck on Mars. Neither one's free to leave or to move. But we're free. So what's there to lose?" She turned and ran to the bed, launching herself on top of him.

Go with me. For us. Please.

"Hey!" he yelled as she dug her fingers under his armpits, raising him out of bed reflexively.

"Come on, sleepy head. The sun's up." She lay next to him as he settled into the bed, pulling a pillow across his head.

Shawnda kept thinking about Malcolm Raines. He hated the cross. And if he hated it, that made her want to know about it all the more.

"That was actually kind of cool," Terrance said as they exited Washington's imposing National Cathedral with a throng of pastel-hued women and children, and men in spring jackets and ties. "Kind of festive."

"Thanks for coming, Terrance." Feeling like a little girl, fresh and clean, she skipped across a small patch of green lawn, then back to him. "This is a special day. We needed to be here." She closed her eyes and breathed in the cool air.

Thank you.

She took his hand as they walked around the back of the cathedral, its spires casting late-morning shadows. Blossoms blew about them on the sidewalk, and the odor of newly mown grass reminded Shawnda of attending services as a child at the A.M.E. church in downtown Montgomery, Alabama, all dolled up in pink with her grandmother.

Those days, and her grammy, seemed very far away. Yet, here she was dressed in pink on Sunday, three decades later, questions about faith tugging at her once again as she and Terrance tried to unravel Amy's mystery.

A warbling phone jarred her into the present. "Shawnda," she answered, recognizing the number immediately. She stopped, suddenly oblivious to the spring air.

"Thought you'd want to know," the voice said. "Your priority request for overhead surveillance turned up some interesting results today. Go secure."

Shawnda punched the code to encrypt her cellular, confirmed by a beep. The display read "CIA. Langley. Top Secret." "Go ahead," she said.

"We put an airborne asset on a flight plan through Slovenia. Over the Raines compound you've been watching the last month. Three overflights crossed around ten o'clock their time, with some good sun angles, and we got some excellent images of the compound. There's someone working the gardens there. Two women. They bear a strong resemblance to the women you're looking for, but we couldn't be sure. We only got three passes, and they were only outside part of one photo pass."

Shawnda felt her pulse go wild. She was almost unable to speak. "Get . . . get a . . . priority request! Priority for additional overheads. Run it up to the Balkans division director. I'm headed in. Now!"

"Already done, girl. We're on this. Something to warm up a dull day, huh?"

"It's Easter!" Shawnda pulled Terrance toward the car with one hand. "Nothing dull about that."

"Sorry," the voice responded. "Got a little extra tidbit just for you, since you filed the request. Guess what else we saw?"

"I'm all ears. If my heart'll slow down so I can hear."

"The aircraft flew its usual collection mission up high. But during the one photo pass when we saw the women, we got flashes. Bright light from the garden, like from right in front of her. Couldn't figure it out at first. There was an airliner going over Nazarje, situated between the collector and the target. Our guys got it all on video. You hearing this?" He cleared his throat. "We got a close-up shot of the woman. She's got a mirror in her hand — Mrs. Wells or whoever's in that compound. She's trying to flash an airliner, you know? Like signaling for help."

Shawnda was silent, imagining Amy Wells so desperate that she found a way to attempt to signal a passing airliner, flashing it like you might during a wilderness expedition. Shawnda looked back at the steep National Cathedral, its roofline stark against the rising mid-morning sun. A bright shaft of light was just starting to break over the roof. Just like Amy's reflected light, hitting the camera lens of a plane she couldn't have possibly known was sent there to take pictures of her.

"That's the confirmation we needed," she said, her mind racing through the myriad responses they could make, using special forces, or negotiating through diplomatic channels, or confronting Raines directly, with Slovenian police. She had to get to the Agency and tell McClannahan. She finally had some proof, and this time she wouldn't lose her computer and assignment for finding it.

"I'll be there in half an hour." She snapped the phone shut and stood, statue-like, staring at the sun rising over the church roof.

"They found something!" She grabbed Terrance's hands. "At Raines's compound in Slovenia. It might be Amy!" Shawnda bounced on her toes. "Balkan operations confirmed it just now.

"If it was her," Shawnda said as they reached Terrance's old Chrysler sedan, "then she never gave up hope." At that moment the sun cleared the peak of the cathedral roof, its radiance enveloping them.

"She never ever gave up. And neither can we."

23

| MONDAY, APRIL 20, 2020:
| WASHINGTON, DC

SHAWNDA QUIT WORRYING about the size of her tiny cubicle in the CIA's Balkan Operations Center. Today she felt like she owned the entire floor. This case was the biggest thing to hit the Balkans since peace broke out. If only Terrance would settle down and listen!

"We've got some great pictures! This is no joke," Shawnda said again over a secure connection, raising her voice to overcome Terrance's hilarity. He was too jovial in the morning, laughing at his own joke. It wasn't human to be so happy this early in the day—one of her husband's very few faults.

"The satellite pass over Slovenia—remember? The weather cleared, and we finally got some more shots."

Terrance quieted. "You've got images?"

"Yes! Great pictures. We got a sweet satellite pass just after dawn. I swear you could see footprints with that new bird. Know what we found?" She was dying to tell someone outside her circle of intelligence spooks.

"Amy?"

"One better. But first you need the background. Raines has a huge compound. Bought it from some Franciscan monks and renovated it to house three hundred girls."

"Three hundred twenty-one, honey. Every one of them fifteen years old. What did you find?"

"Hang on! Patience is a virtue, Terrance. The compound has an old side and a renovated side. The girls are in the big new section. Huge imposing place, high walls, top of a hill. Gothic architecture, with modern apartments inside. The old half was originally a castle with two walled gardens. One garden," she said, staring at the glossy image, "is planted in the shape of a cross."

"Nothing unusual there," Terrance said. "It's a monastery. What about the other garden?"

"Freaky. That's the one we're most interested in. Something green there, too. Three rows, the first with three distinct green circles, the second with three green rectangles, and the third with three circles again. Unmistakable."

He was silent a long moment. Then he whispered, "Morse code. SOS."

"The same. John's eldest son had a ham radio license, according to my research. John's a ham nut, too. Remember? No one else would ever guess that Morse code stuff these days. It's archaic."

"Any chance of a fluke? Analyst's misinterpretation?"

"None," Shawnda said. "I ran it past three of them. They all agree it's too coincidental to ignore. Someone down there's stating their faith and calling for help."

"Maybe," Kerry said, "but we can't tell John yet. Not until we're sure. Can't afford a false alarm or else Raines might bail on us."

"CIA's working on a rescue plan." She paused, unsure if moving ahead with agency rescue options would offend her husband who'd helped to break this case. "We're talking to the Pentagon, Terrance. I wanted you to know. You're one of the very few."

NAZARJE, SLOVENIA

"John's about a week away from the colony." Monique recited the latest news from Malcolm. "And Malcolm's livid. He says the astronauts will ruin the colony's purity." She paused. "You must be proud of your husband."

"I am," Amy replied quietly. "But I try not to think about it. He's so far away."

"He never gave up on you, Amy. He loved you . . . *loves* you. He said that many, many times on the news, and spoke of you often before he left."

Amy sniffled and squeezed Monique's hand. "Thanks."

Monique sighed, remembering John's launch day and one particular news interview. She'd never forgotten his words. She'd thought they were supremely stupid at the time. But now she understood.

"Is this the culmination of your life's dreams?" a reporter had asked. "Could you hope for any greater honor than to explore Mars?"

John hadn't answered right away, and she'd thought he must be some kind of dolt to stand there, deaf and dumb. There was only one logical answer, after all—"yes." Instead he only looked at the reporter with strangely sad eyes.

"I'd trade it all," John had said unexpectedly, "just to get my family back."

Monique wondered if Malcolm would trade his kingdom to keep her. She coughed. *I doubt it.*

"What about us?" Amy asked. "How much longer?"

"Be strong and be ready," Monique said, uncertain her plan would work. "Our opportunity will come soon. In thirty-two days. When he takes the Mother Seed."

"What?" Amy stared. "You mean the girls?"

"The Harvest will begin soon."

"The *harvest?*" she said with a gasp.

"The Mother Seed will be harvested, Amy. And, ultimately, become the vessels of the Father Race, carrying embryo daughters, exact copies of themselves. That's their destiny." She swallowed hard, trying to bury her conscience, her role in her sisters' doom. "They'll be mothers very soon."

"They're teenagers! How can he?" Amy's voice cracked as she shook the grate. Alice sat transfixed at her side.

Monique tried to hush Amy. The guards were supposed to be busy, but she could never be certain. "Yes. They're fifteen. But this has been planned for years, Amy. I can't stop it." She hung her head. "I want to. But I can't."

When Monique looked up, Amy was watching her, speaking under her breath. At Monique's glance, Amy closed her eyes and whispered "Amen." Then she said, "Monique. Please. Tell me exactly what's about to happen."

Monique took a deep breath and began reciting from memory without looking at Amy. "Today is April 20. It will be a new moon in two days. At the next new moon, thirty-two days from now, the Mother Seed will be ready for harvest. Months of hyper-stimulating oral hormones have timed our cycles perfectly. We will all ripen on the same day."

"*Our* cycles?" Amy touched Monique's fingers where they grasped the grate. "Ripen? You're a woman, not a piece of fruit."

"Yes. Our cycles. I am also a vessel for my Master. He will harvest us to create more Eve vessels for the future of our faith." She shrugged in the tunnel's tight confines. "I must."

"Oh, Monique. I—I want to help. What can we do?"

"I'm his servant, Amy. And his companion. The new moon will be our time." She paused, hating herself for being part of Malcolm's strange mix of religious ceremony, lunar worship, and celebration of female fertility rites, wondering what she thought she'd gain years ago when she gave herself over to him. *At what price?*

"We've been carefully medicated, Amy. Our bodies' production of multiple ova are timed exactly with the darkest day of the new moon. On May 22, the ova of the Mother Seed will be harvested and prepared for the insertion of our own donor DNA. Viable clone embryos—exact duplicates of ourselves—will be frozen, then implanted in us a month later. At the next new moon. June 22."

"Implanted? You will—*they* will carry these children?"

"It's the culmination of Malcolm's dream—his supreme mission from the Father Race. The story of our faith . . . and his."

"That faith is a lie, Monique. You understand that, right?"

Ignoring the question, Monique closed her eyes and began reciting as if Malcolm were testing her. She couldn't speak this in Amy's presence and still look at her. "In the beginning, the Supreme Unknowable God issued the Aeons, lesser beings than herself. Among them was the virgin Sophia. Without permission, Sophia birthed the creator of this world. That creator made the giant Nephilim who came to Earth hundreds of generations ago as our predecessors." She heard Amy whispering some kind of prayer but pressed on.

"Through time, humanity's genetic makeup decayed and mankind fell. Our Priest of the Heavenlies heeds the call of the Father Race—a call only he can hear. They've blessed him with a responsibility for the Mother Seed, to bring forth a rebirth of the Father Race." The concept now sounded so foreign and perverse to Monique that she was ashamed to share more. But Amy needed to know.

"He will use our ripe ova to create clone embryos of each of the Mother Seed, producing yet another season of my sisters so that one day those daughters might also bear the future race." She paused and took a deep breath, forcing herself to speak the conclusion she'd determined in the past days. "Another generation will spring from my sisters . . . as they have all sprung from me." She coughed, fighting the knot in her stomach. Amy gasped again.

"He will knit those embryos with my flesh and with the flesh of each of our virgin Mother Seed—every one a modern Sophia. On March 21, 2021, we will bear yet another generation of ourselves. A year later, on April 11, the fourth new moon of 2022, the Mother Seed will be implanted with embryos of the descendant of the Nephilim, the perfect DNA of man. The Father Race will then be completely reborn in the wombs of his Eve. Every year, on April's new moon, the Mother Seed and I will receive another implantation. For as long as we bear strong children."

Monique shuddered. She had spoken it at last: Within a decade, thousands of school-age Mother Seed girls and Nephilim boys would fan out into the homes of Saint Michael's Remnant, their future mentors. The Mother Seed would blossom yearly with alternate bumper crops of precious baby girls, then boys, destined one day, Malcolm claimed, to carry his message to another planet. Fifteen years from now, another season of the Mother Seed would be ready—more ripe wombs for his bidding, when other wombs were nearing their end.

It was like the Christ seeker's story of Adam and Eve—but

hundreds fold—humans without genetic flaw spawning a new origin of humanity. And Malcolm would reign as the modern Yahweh, bringing forth thousands of perfect and identical genetic replications of one man and one woman. Ultimately, she feared, he might take as his wives hundreds of those compliant identical Eves.

Monique shook, her stomach in revolt. Sharing this with Amy—with anyone outside Malcolm's inner circle—was the most foul treason. She wished she could muster prayers for peace and protection like Amy did.

Amy spoke. "Monique. The Father Race, Sophia, the Nephilim—they're all lies. Do you understand that?" She squeezed Monique's fingers again. "Monique?"

"Count the days and watch the moon," Monique said, desperate to escape. "And watch for me. When harvest time comes, they'll remove the girls to the medical suites and anesthetize them for the procedure. The guards will be consumed with moving so many through the process. That will be the only time for our escape."

"Monique," Amy said again. Monique looked into her eyes, smothering in shame. "It's a lie. Do you understand that?"

She nodded.

"How will we escape?" Amy asked. "Can we help the girls?"

Monique hesitated. *Would it work?* They had to try. "I expect at least two of the Mother Seed—perhaps more—will resist the Harvest and the implantation. When they do—and guards come to aid the doctors—I'll come for you. It's the only way."

Alice was crying and Amy breathing hard. It would be upon them all in only a matter of weeks.

"You'd sacrifice them—to save us?" Amy asked. "Can't we save them, too?"

"I'll try," Monique said, her heart heavy. "But most of my sisters see this as a great honor—it's the culmination of their dreams and their life effort. To serve the Father Race."

"It's wrong!" Alice cried.

Monique winced. "Yes. Yes it is, Alice. I know that now—but I can't stop it." She sighed.

Then Amy spoke. Her words had power, a certainty Monique had never heard before. She wanted to soak in that balm.

"With men," Amy said, "this is impossible, but with God all things are possible."

TUESDAY, APRIL 28, 2020: MARS

The crew vibrated with anticipation as the line of two squat habitation modules, a laboratory, and two rovers crawled toward the Edwards colony. There was more chattering on the radio and over the inter-module communication link today than any day previous. The end was finally in sight.

The past week had seen a desert plain pockmarked with dusty craters slowly fade into a gouged topography of rivulets yielding to gullies, then gorges, and finally the canyons of Mars's most rugged regions—the "foothills" of Valles Marineris, the solar system's largest canyon. It was as long as the United States was wide, and as deep as Mount Everest.

Beyond the canyons, Mars transformed before their eyes into a land of escarpments, plateaus, and mesas, the erosion detritus of ancient rivers. At the base of a ridge running through the region, a tiny city of domes and squat habitats snuggled up to red rock like a little town in the hollow of a creek back home in West Virginia. This was their new home.

The painfully slow progress across Nirgal Vallis had consumed

John for the past weeks. He'd stopped asking forgiveness for his short temper and constant pacing. Everyone knew, he was sure, of his incessant focus on the only thing that mattered now: Getting them off Mars and headed home. No matter what.

Two kilometers and an hour from their destination, John saw Rex's brick-making rover dozing the area where the colony would receive the new settlement. The surface preparation was a nice touch. No more rocks scattered about the area where they walked and worked. The colonists were rolling out the Martian version of a red carpet.

The domes of the Edwards colony rose like clear inverted bowls arrayed about their habitation and laboratory modules. In the distance, John made out the second of two Roman vault structures Rex and the women were erecting with homemade brick. Far left, more than five kilometers north, the Earth Return Vehicle stood, barely visible with its Mars camouflage. A cloak it no longer needed. All of humanity knew they were here. They were a team now, colonists and astronauts.

John marveled at the tall ERV, a self-contained rocket and interplanetary return vehicle, fueled and ready to go. Another of Rex Edwards's wise decisions. Twenty-five years ago, a prophetic Robert Zubrin had warned NASA that ERVs left in orbit were a huge liability and an unnecessary expense. But NASA wouldn't listen, opting for a system twice as risky, with a MAV to lift a crew to orbit, and an orbiting ERV to return them to Earth.

Zubrin—and Rex Sr. after him—argued for the safer approach. Bring your return rocket to the surface of Mars with you, where you can work on it and protect it—and live in it if you have to. Zubrin and Edwards had it right. But NASA said no.

John's gaze lingered on the ERV while Oz drove. He imagined meeting Amy and his children at the landing on Earth. Of course, that wasn't possible. He had no idea where they were, or if they even knew he'd gone to Mars. He ignored the demon of doubt screaming *"they're dead!"* John shut his eyes, praying silently for his family's protection. The radio chatter brought him back.

"Jake, this is May. Park your Habs and the Lab in a straight line where Rex leaves the markers. We should have you all hooked up to our transit tubes by dark. You'll have to walk through two or more domes to reach us—but you can come over *any* time."

John noticed May's added emphasis of "any time." He knew she and Jake anxiously awaited this reunion. And he was happy for them both. That is, after all, what they were doing here: building a new life on Mars, whether relationships or colonies. Five habitation and laboratory modules, four domes, three rovers, two power sources set five kilometers away, and one launch vehicle. A marriage of two bases—and two cultures. They could survive here together, and NASA would be proud.

"I propose a toast," John said, hoisting a glass of the colony's special strawberry wine. "To fellowship. And the solar system's largest extraterrestrial colony."

"To fellowship, the colony . . . to progress!" Jake said, raising his glass. "And to extraterrestrials!"

"To us!" Oz howled, his cup raised high. The tall skinny man liked wine too much.

Glasses were refilled, and the din rose as the evening wore on. The only person left out of the fun seemed to be Rex. Their young recluse.

"You have a great deal to be proud of here, Rex," John said, pulling his chair near the boy. He waved in the direction of the noisy astronauts. "This is historic."

Rex hesitated. "My father wouldn't have wanted it. But you saved my mother. And now you need help. It's right to do this." Rex fumbled.

"I . . . I'm sorry . . . I mean I'm glad . . . or whatever. About your family, you know? I hope you can . . . I mean, do find them. Know what I mean?"

"Yes, Rex. I do," John said. "Thank you. And this consolidation wasn't right just to save some lives. It's right for us to *make a life*." He nudged Rex in the arm, pointing toward Kate Westin in a corner where Oz was spinning some tall tale, amplified with his long hands and yet another gulp of strawberry wine. Jake and May talked quietly, leaning into each other to be heard. Deborah, Sam, Ramona, Melanie, and Nicci were in a spirited conversation about the origin of the universe. Geo sat nearby, listening like he didn't care.

"That's living, Rex. Conversation, friends, fellowship. It's healthy. It helps us grow."

"I know that, sir. But Dad said we should remain pure. We've lost that now." He turned to John, embarrassed. "I'm sorry. I didn't mean that the way it came out. It's just . . ."

"Hey. I understand, Rex. Sort of like Captain Cook's men meeting those Pacific Islanders, eh? We're bringing a new look at life, and that might damage your culture. I see your point."

"It couldn't be helped, right, sir? You're marooned. For now, at least."

John nodded, sipping their new lithium-free water. It tasted much better than the two-year-old stuff from Earth.

Marooned.

Despite the revelry, the word gnawed at him. An image of Amy crying out to him flashed before his eyes. He pushed it away, trying to ignore his anxiety demons.

Get through it a minute at a time.

"I'm glad we'll be together for the trip back to Earth, Rex. There's lots I want to know. About your dad. The colony. About you."

"Would you like to see him? Dad, I mean?" Rex asked with a slight smile.

"Your dad?" John exclaimed.

"On video." Rex waved at the revelry. "Let's skip this and hear what he has to say. Wanna go?"

John smiled. "I'd be honored, Rex. Let's go meet your pop."

24

"HOW'S THIS THING WORK?" John asked, running a finger over the large screen and its shiny silver side panels. Holes of different sizes at various levels penetrated the mirror-like panels that ran from the floor to the ceiling of the compartment.

Rex stood back, watching. "It's complicated," he said with a chuckle.

"I can keep up," John said with a smile. "Show me."

"Good!" Rex rushed forward, like a boy anxious to show off his new toy. "This'll blow your mind. I mean, I still can't completely comprehend it myself." He walked up beside John and touched the mirrored surfaces, tracing the large and small silver holes with his index finger. "These," he said, tapping a hole, "are sensors. Video, temperature, infrared, motion, you name it. They're Dad's eyes and ears."

"I hope you're kidding."

"Actually, I'm not. Like I said, this'll throw you for a loop. Hang with me, okay?"

"Hangin'."

"As long as you stand in the room to talk to Dad, he can sense your temperature, your heart rate, tell if you're slouching or notice when you make a gesture, even read your facial expressions. The entire thing. An infrared scanner, an ultraviolet laser, and several other sensors tell him every move you make. Remember that."

"Him?'" John asked, his brow furrowed.

"Well, not technically 'him.' It's known as the Decision Assistance Device—DAD. But I call it Dad for short. It's saved us many times. Like having a talking encyclopedia. Computer-assisted decision making."

John smiled. "Go on."

"These," Rex said, tapping other holes, "pick up all the audio. Every word, every expression, even the way you speak—they're all digitized, catalogued, and become part of him once you speak—even when you exhale. Whatever. Remember that, too. Because this—I mean, Dad's like an elephant. He never forgets, even though you might."

"There you go again with the 'him' thing. Scary."

"I used to think so. Now I really depend on him. But I wonder sometimes . . ."

"What?"

"If this is a good thing, you know? To depend on a digital father? He hardly ever talked to me when I was a kid, and now I can visit with him any time I want. So what's missing?"

"Flesh and blood, Rex. A handshake, a hug. Emotion."

"Right. But he's still one smart guy. Watch this."

As Rex touched a plasma panel, the screen lit up and lights illuminated some of the panel holes. "Stand here, sir. You can move around, just don't leave the room if you want the full effect." Rex's grin stretched from ear to ear.

"Hello, John. Welcome to the colony."

The deep bass voice rumbled in John's gut. His skin crawled. He knew that voice. Rex Edwards Sr. The man stood before him, all one point eight meters of him on a life-size plasma screen—bulldog jaw, muscle-bound neck, a stiff gray flattop, and the ubiquitous red bow tie. John coughed.

"I've surprised you, John. I'm sorry. It's been what, nearly two years since we last spoke?"

John's heart raced, and he wiped his forehead. Sweat was beading fast.

It's talking to me. A virtual Edwards.

"Uh, yeah. I saw you about a week before launch." He looked back at Rex Jr., whose Cheshire-cat grin overpowered his face. Their resemblance to each other was uncanny. John's heart felt like it skipped another beat. He'd never been afraid of the boy—before this.

"Ask him a question, Admiral Wells. He won't bite."

"No, I won't, son," Rex Sr. said with an eerie chuckle. "I certainly can't bite."

John screwed up his courage and spoke, his voice cracking. "How are you, Mr. Edwards? I mean, you're looking good."

That sounded stupid.

"Thanks, John. You can call me Rex."

"Gets kind of confusing, doesn't it? Two people named Rex?"

"Very well. 'Mr. Edwards' will do. How would you like me to address you? 'Admiral Wells,' or 'John'?"

"You always called me 'John' on Earth."

"Very well. I'm fine. My son told you about my heart attack?"

John shook his head. *This is too weird.* "Yes. He told me."

"Unfortunate. I'm sorry I couldn't greet you in person when you arrived today."

"Greet me?" John asked. "My impression was you wanted us to stay away."

"I did. Until your ERV failed. Then, well, it was the humane thing to help you out. I'm glad you're here."

"I don't believe I'm hearing this."

"Believe it, sir. It's my dad." Rex Jr. sighed. "He can sense your nervousness, your heart rate, even your fatigue. What's his heart rate, Pops?"

"Elevated, son. I think he's a bit concerned, you know? Shocked might be a better description. At this moment, one hundred eight beats per minute."

Rex Jr. watched with a self-assured look while John touched his wrist, counting on his watch for ten seconds. Eighteen beats. *He's right!*

"He's good," John said, taking a deep breath. "But that's not what I meant. That I couldn't believe it. I can ask him any question?"

"You can, John. I'm a query-based system. Ask away."

John shivered in the presence of what could best be described as a digital ghost.

"Your Covenant. Rex Jr. saved his mom by bringing her to us, and all the way he wondered if he'd broken your cardinal rule. Your women—all four of them—lived in mortal fear of our coming here. Then, all of a sudden, it's okay. That's a long way of asking, Mr. Edwards—Dad—why? I mean, why were we trouble one day and friends the next? I like being on good terms, but I'd like to understand the sudden transition."

"That was not a long question, John. And I have an answer. Simply put, I was wrong."

John exhaled something like a half laugh, half cough, in surprise. "What?"

"I was wrong. I advised my son that contact was the incorrect approach based on all the data I had at my disposal. He disobeyed my explicit directions yet saved the life of his surrogate mother as a result. That proved that The Covenant was subject to error. Therefore I reevaluated my decision. I have rescinded The Covenant, and have informed the Mothers of this fact. From his recent questions, I sense that my son does not understand my recent change of heart."

John whistled.

"I heard that whistle, but I don't understand, John."

"Nothing, Mr. Edwards. I mean, Dad. It's just I've never seen this happen before. Glad you reconsidered, just never thought it was possible."

"What is that, Admiral?" the video image asked.

John clapped, amazed every day at what he was finding in these new friends on Mars. "Never thought I'd meet a computer with . . . what did you call it? A change of heart?"

He extended his hand to shake Rex Jr.'s. "But I'm really glad computers can change their minds, 'cause you've saved us, son. You and your dad."

"My father was a genius, sir," Rex said, motioning Admiral Wells to follow him out of the room. "But, you know, when you break this system down to its essential components, it's remarkably simple."

John followed him out of the compartment, wide-eyed, into the adjacent conference area.

"He comes on by himself now, without any warning. I haven't been able to override that feature. It can freak you out pretty bad if he pops on and starts asking you why you're sad or something."

Rex grabbed a digital marker and went to an electronic drawing board. He selected a blue streak and began to sketch a book. "Imagine, Admiral Wells, a document. We'll just look at one page. Nine paragraphs. About thirty sentences. Three hundred words. I want you to pretend that each paragraph is an Internet website, each sentence is a page on that website, and all the words in that sentence are the content of that web page. With me?"

Admiral Wells had taken a chair, wiping at his forehead again. His hand looked like it was shaking. "With you." He took a deep breath and let it out long and slow.

It's a good thing I got him out of there before Dad woke up again. "All right. Now imagine someone built a Web-crawler—a search engine like Google—to crawl every web page . . . every paragraph . . . every document ever written. Hundreds and hundreds of billions of paragraphs. Maybe multiple trillions. We've lost count, to tell you the truth. We're pretty close to finishing that data load now."

"Where?" Admiral Wells asked. "On this ship?"

"No, sir. We're just a thin client hooked to a massive parallel processor and server on Baker Island. We query it daily and upload the stuff we need. I call the Dad back home *The Wizard of Oz*. My dad—the real one—built the system on Baker Island. It's essentially a larger-than-life version of the one you just saw, with curtains and smoke and a big throne . . . the whole works. Just for fun. It has all the data. 'The whole enchilada,' he used to say. Dad's talking to it right now. Getting his daily updates."

"Absolutely amazing."

"No, sir. Remarkably simple. The crawler analyzes each paragraph, all the Web content—then it grabs the content that matches your query. Get it? Your question—whatever you say to it, in any context—is nothing but an Internet search. Fifteen years ago you could query a Google crawler that hit forty billion pages, and get an answer in five hundredths of a second. Easy. This is the same thing. Just a million times bigger and faster."

"But he talks to us! Understands me!"

"He does. Inflection, dialect, sarcasm, innuendo. You name it. He's been studying you, Admiral Wells. For years. Every news file, even all the video files that my real dad saved from your first flight to Mars—eight months of them—and all of your communications since we arrived here. They've all been stored back on Baker Island. Of course, he can't really understand anything. He's just super smart, from a data point of view. But he's catalogued you quite well."

Rex watched for Admiral Wells's reaction. His mouth fell open. No words emerged.

"Human emotion is expressed in relatively few ways, sir. My father's expressions were all digitized, and the program reacts to your comments, your meaning, your words. That's why he shows facial expressions. It's an easy video program. Actually, I built the emotion feature. He used to just stand there like a politician—a talking head—and lecture at me. I got tired of that and wanted to have some fun."

"He understood me, though, right?"

"Absolutely. The technology's been around nearly twenty years. Used to be called Latent Semantic Indexing. You use the machine to look for relationships between words, for repetitions, and patterns. You can scan an entire book—or with my system, an entire movie—and use that to look for all other writings or movies with the same theme, plot, or words. It's pattern recognition, nothing more."

"Complex and brilliant."

"Thank you, sir. It's not only fun, but it's helped me to understand my father a lot better. He kept meticulous audio notes his entire life, dreaming this capability up long before we had the processing speed to make it work. He recorded his entire thought life, his dreams and aspirations, his emotions, what made him mad, what he did, who he met—he kept audio notes on all of it. He's inside that system."

Admiral Wells stood and wrote some numbers on the white electronic surface. "Have you ever stumped him? It?" he asked, still writing.

"No. I've tried." *Where's he going with this?* "Why do you ask, sir?"

"I was wondering. You say it's digitized all of his information all these years, and it catalogues news reports, scientific observations—all that stuff. Right?"

"Yes, sir. That and more."

"Then I want to talk to your dad again. We'll get his answer to my stumper." He penned some last numbers on the board, then put down the marker. "I want to ask Dad my question of the day."

"Sir?"

"How fast can we get home? Rex built that ERV. He knows everything regarding orbital mechanics, fuel load, and reliability. You name it. I want to ask the designer himself, Dad Edwards Sr.—how soon can I get out of here to go find my wife and kids?"

MONDAY, MAY 4, 2020: MARS

"Spring veggies," Nicci said, placing a steaming plate of pasta primavera on the dining table. "Served in a mouth-watering mixture of tomatoes, basil, oregano, and cheese. And our special! Steamed tilapia!" Thirteen astronaut colonists surrounded the table of bounty.

Dinner on their sixth night at the colony was heartier, and more congenial, than any of the nights they'd shared together in the past week. The crews were bonding, that was sure. Even Geo was on good behavior, proof that the way to a man's heart was through his stomach. John watched them, twelve astronauts, well on their way to a future together — and strong bonds for those who would stay behind.

After a dessert of sugar-coated strawberries, Jake tapped a knife handle against his plastic cup, mimicking a "ding" sound with his mouth. "We have an announcement," he said. May sat at his side, where she'd been at every meal since John's crew arrived a week ago. "We have a request," Jake continued, looking directly at Rex. The table of astronauts quieted slowly, all eyes on Jake.

"Deborah, you said once that there was more pioneer spirit here than you'd ever seen in NASA." He waved at Nicci, Sachiko, Kate, and Rex. "You were right."

Jake turned to face John. "There's not enough room on Rex's Red Rocket to get all of us home. But I'm just fine by that. *This* is where I want to be." His hand went to May's, then he turned to face Rex.

"Your mom and I want to face this pioneer thing together, Rex. I'd be honored if you'd give us your blessing. I've asked your mom to marry me."

A collective gasp and something that sounded like a cooing "ooohhh!" arose from the women in both crews. Oz laughed. Geo groaned, his face in his hands.

"And . . ." Jake said, "I'd like to ask my best friend, John Wells, to do the honors."

All eyes were on Rex. He turned beet red from the attention, looked down at his plate, then nodded in silence, eyes wet but a big smile on his face. He looked at his mother, tears of joy flowing down her dark freckled cheeks. She nodded at her son, communicating heart to heart, without words.

"I want you to be happy, Mom. Captain Cook's a good man. So yes, you have my blessing." Rex looked around the table of smiling colonists and raised his water glass. "A toast," he said, a tear forming at the corner of his eye. "To the first couple on Mars!"

"No! The *second!*" Sam and Deborah sang out together. "To Jake and May," Sam continued. "And to Mars's *first* wedding!"

Not to be outdone, Oz stood and hoisted his glass once again, brimming with Nicci's special Martian blend of sweetened iced tea. He'd already downed the last of his wine. "To Captain Cook, who sailed across the uncharted void to a tropical paradise, deep in the midst of a barren galactic wilderness, and swept a Martian maiden off her feet." He clinked his cup with others, then hoisted it high before he drank.

"Live long and prosper!"

25

SHAWNDA FACED SIX MEN, she the lone woman in the small, well-appointed briefing area on the Pentagon's E-ring. The brass plaque beside the door read "Assistant Secretary of Defense, Special Operations and Low Intensity Conflict. ASD-SOLIC."

This was the Pentagon's funding source for the super-secret activity she hoped to one day take part in — the heartbeat of Special Forces. The crest of the Secretary of Defense emblazoned a deep blue carpet in the ornate, walnut-paneled room. Everyone, except for a decorated military officer standing by the video screen, sat in expensive black Windsors like her own doctoral chair just up the Potomac at Langley. She recognized one of the attendees immediately. Director of the National Security Council, Dr. Norman Hackerman. He'd be here at the president's direction. The White House had already given the Pentagon a green light for the operation; this meeting would only rehash information she'd passed a week ago to Joint Special Operations Command, or JSOC, at Fort Bragg.

Dr. Hackerman nodded ever so slightly as she smiled his direction. *Does he know me?* She fought to control her wild pulse. She took a deep breath, focusing on her charts.

"Sir," Shawnda began, addressing a suited man seated at the head of the table, "the mirror flashes continue coming from Nazarje, no later than mid-morning each day. Every airliner in the area gets flashed if it's visible before ten. None of the commercial pilots have located the flashes; they all say the light is coming from the general area of town."

She paused, selecting a series of images that focused on a white spot in the middle of a woman's torso. It looked like she was holding the mirror at waist level, perhaps trying to disguise it. "We got these with our latest satellite and aircraft coverage. She's in Raines's garden compound."

Walter McClannahan spoke, dressed for the first time she could remember in something clean and pressed, with a tie. "It's Amy Wells, sir. There's no doubt."

"What about overhead recon?" the man at the head asked. "Any more intel on what we should expect when they drop in?" Assistant Secretary Dunovan rolled an old yellow eraser-tipped pencil between his fingers, doodled some thoughts on a pad, then looked up at her for the answer.

"Daily recon, sir," Shawnda said. "Multiple passes. We have air breathers and space assets working it full time. We're siphoning electronic intelligence and all of their phone traffic—which is pitifully little, by the way. There's no landline telephone, satellite, or Internet connectivity we can determine. The steeples may disguise satellite dishes, but no signals give those away. And there's no cell phone use."

"Like a real monastery, huh?" Dunovan said. "Disconnected from the world?"

"Not exactly, sir," Shawnda said. "There are lots of internal wireless communications. And internal video. The place is a maze of thousands of special cameras and audio sensors."

"Why so much video?" the head of SOLIC asked. "What're they protecting?"

"You'll find this hard to believe, sir," she said. "It's voyeurism in the extreme."

"Excuse me?" He leaned forward. "Be more specific, Mrs. Kerry."

"Sir . . ." A military aide at Dunovan's right interrupted her. "There are 321 young women in that compound. Along with quite a number of servants, Dr. Raines, and his staff. The imagery is—"

"The imagery, sir," Shawnda said, cutting the major off, "is of those girls. Every aspect of their lives. More than two thousand separate signals, all wireless on separate frequencies, scattered throughout the compound. There's no Internet, but they've got a hundred gigabits per second of imagery moving through those walls."

Shawnda pointed to the screen. "There are five imagery feeds in each apartment," she said, as an example flashed of a girl cooking, "including two in each bathroom." She took the last image down quickly.

"I get the picture. But those were just of one girl's suite. What about the others?"

"Those *were* the others, sir," the major interjected. "The girls are identical."

"Clones?" Dunovan asked. "For real? I thought that was just Father Race hype."

"Yes, sir," Shawnda said. "It's for real. Clones are the only explanation. As to security, we've siphoned every room, and also scoped out his entire—we hope—voyeur imaging system."

"Stupid." The director dropped the pencil, shaking his head. "Where are your people, Colonel Scales?" He pointed to a tall Army officer standing to the screen's far left. Only three ribbons adorned the colonel's breast pocket. The one on her left, she knew, was the Medal of Honor.

"They're on the edge of the compound, sir. Here," he said, pointing to a map Shawnda cued up on the screen. "Trees a hundred meters down grade from the compound, surrounding three quarters of the facility. We have permanent sensors in place in the treetops and remotes inside on the roof here . . . here . . . and here." He pointed to the top of the ancient monastery and the new compound that housed the young women's rooms.

"I've had men on the ground for two days, sir. We also dropped a bug and a camera inside each garden area and have daily imagery on the woman and her kids."

Shawnda's jaw dropped as he passed out a series of glossy photographs of Amy Wells and her daughter working a garden, and another of three young men, standing at their hoes, taking a drink. "They have no idea we're in there. But we can tell 'em anytime you're ready."

"How long have you had these?" Shawnda asked, picking up an image.

"Since CIA cued us, ma'am. We set up our joint headquarters at Aviano four days ago. We put one of our men inside the garden two days later. He placed the bug—high-fidelity acoustic. You might be interested in what we learned."

"I might!" Shawnda said, restraining herself from screaming. Her boss, fat man McClannahan, put a finger to his pursed lips, trying to calm her. His passivity only infuriated her more. So much for interagency cooperation and a proactive boss.

"Mrs. Wells has some kind of support inside the building. We have no idea who it is. Calls her Monique—"

"His executive assistant?" Shawnda asked, her eyes wide.

"I have no idea, ma'am. 'Monique' is the only other name we have to go on right now. We heard them talk once. Around two in the morning. Couldn't hear the Monique person, but Mrs. Wells is clearly worried about something scheduled for May 22. She said it three times. That day will be a new moon. Gonna be a very dark night."

Shawnda forced herself to calm down. "Sir, Raines is a stickler for this Father Race stuff. With a new moon on May 22, and his emphasis on lunar phases and fertility rites, it makes sense he could have something big planned that day. If she has an inside source, particularly if it's Raines's closest aide, and she's worried, then—"

"I get the picture, Mrs. Kerry. Thank you." Assistant Secretary Dunovan addressed the colonel. "Joe, can you extract them—without Raines's knowledge?"

"No, sir. Not likely. We have no idea, as Mrs. Kerry has stated, what locations his wired security system might be watching. There're no wireless signals with images of the Wells's cell compound. We have to assume we don't have full situational awareness yet, and that we'll encounter some level of resistance." He paused. "The fact that Mrs. Wells might be talking to Raines's exec doesn't make me feel any better about this."

Dunovan looked at Shawnda. "How about you, Mrs. Kerry? Anything on potential resistance?"

"No, sir, except that a public show of an armed force would be out of character for someone like Raines who's so publicly dedicated to peace and tranquility. However," she began, "we know he'd defend his girls to the death—his own. If we ingress anywhere near them, we should anticipate trouble." She shuffled through her papers, infuriated that the colonel had backdoored her. There was nothing in her notes about Monique. She hated being upstaged.

"The girls are on the other side of the building, sir," Colonel Scales said. "We'll go over the wall at the cell compound. Much easier. It's only ten meters."

"How will you—" she began.

"That's our turf, Mrs. Kerry." The colonel waved his hand. "Not a problem."

"The Slovenian government has been officially mute on the Raines issue for years," said a dark-suited man at Dunovan's left who Shawnda didn't know. "State Department can't get anything out of them, and they won't answer questions from amnesty and human rights groups about the girls. Raines picked the right place to hide. No one there gives a flip."

Dunovan nodded again, rolling the pencil with his fingers and thinking. He tapped the perfectly sharpened tip on the table, then pointed at the colonel. "What's the plan, Joe? Gray has joint command at Aviano, right?"

"Yes, sir," Colonel Scales replied. "Rear Admiral Gray and executing headquarters directed us to pull them out no later than the twentieth. Earlier if we can."

Dunovan shook his head slowly, pondering the yellow pencil. "We can't afford to let whatever's bothering her come to pass, Joe. She's been gone for six years—maybe stuck in that hole the entire time. We need to get them home." He turned to Shawnda. "Does Rear Admiral Wells know anything about this?"

Shawnda shook her head. "No, sir. Only that the bodies in the graves weren't his family, and that we're hunting for them."

"Then keep it that way, please." He looked about the room. "This is Special Access Program material. Treat it like SAP. I'll crucify anyone who leaks it. If this gets out, Raines will run, and she'll end up dead, her children with her."

All heads nodded. Dunovan started to rise, placing his pencil behind his ear. "I appreciate your initiative, Colonel Scales, but be sure to keep Mr. McClannahan and Mrs. Kerry informed from now on. Remember, the Agency found her." He nodded in silence toward the colonel and walked to the door. "Tell Gray hello for me. Good luck."

Shawnda rolled her eyes when the colonel smiled her way. "Absolutely, sir. We'll have JSOC's final plans to you tomorrow morning. I'll pass your message to the admiral."

Scales dropped the glossy photos on Shawnda's laptop as he walked out, pausing to stare her directly in the eye. "Don't dare breathe a word to John, Ms. Kerry—or Amy's dead."

THURSDAY, MAY 14, 2020: MARS

"Five weeks, Rex. Why don't we just hit the button and go? Right now. What d'ya say?" John laughed as he and the boy lay in the cockpit seats of the colonists' Earth Return Vehicle. Their backs to the ground, they worked through the switches of their elegant-yet-simple ride home.

"Hope you're joking, Admiral. If we left today, it'd take ten days longer to get there. It's a tight launch window with this minimal fuel load."

"Yeah. I know," John sighed, wishing it were June 22. "You know, your dad never offered NASA something like this." He gazed with admiration at the ERV's commercial flair and simplicity.

"They wouldn't touch it, sir. NASA wanted the return vehicle sitting in orbit where you couldn't fuel it or repair it. I'm sorry, but that was a really dumb idea." Rex caressed one of the clear plasma screens. "Dad offered them this design, but NASA HQ said it wouldn't fly. Even though the engineers at NASA Marshall loved it.

"It won't take five weeks for you to learn this system, sir. A week—if that. Dad built it so anybody here could fly this thing. Always our last-ditch option." He sighed audibly. "Still should be."

"Rex? You need to let go of this guilt thing, okay? You're not giving up on your dad's mission. You're going back to Earth to leverage your dad's company to fight a battle to support the Father Race. A battle you believe in. You know I disagree with what you're fighting for, but I admire your zeal. Don't think of returning to Earth as losing or quitting. You're in the fight more than ever." John patted the switches above him. "Show me one other teenager who's not old enough to get a driver's license but can pilot a spaceship, eh?"

Rex looked at John. "I'm not piloting it, sir. You are."

John knew Rex wasn't sold yet . . . about the integration of the settlements, about the trip home, or about his mother endorsing the impure astronaut society that had invaded his space. That, despite what they'd all heard from the digital Dad that now welcomed the colony's new members and the enhanced infrastructure.

Rex has been talking to that computer way too much.

They'd heard the endorsement from Dad what, six or seven times? Like he was going overboard to eradicate the memory of The Covenant. Maybe because Rex asked him about it so often. Why the women and Rex consulted that freaky program for guidance every day still baffled him. It reminded John of people running to the horoscope in the morning paper to see what their day was going to be like. Now they couldn't make a move without consulting the Wizard of Mars.

John touched Rex's shoulder a moment. "Chin up, bucko. You *are* piloting this thing. It's *your* ship, and you're the one who knows how to fly it." He shut down the panel lights and closed a checklist. "You're the skipper, son. I'm just hitchin' a ride home."

SATURDAY, MAY 16, 2020:
NAZARJE, SLOVENIA

"Where'd you get this?" Amy asked, her face wet with joy. She forced her body back into a pose of prayer under the blanket.

"It was confiscated from one of our girls recently. She'd hidden it in her room. Malcolm told me to burn it . . . but I thought of you."

Amy turned the red miniature New Testament over in her hands. The gold Gideon imprint on the faded front cover confirmed what she'd believed when she first saw the small red book.

"Whoever this girl was, Monique, she's probably a believer. She brought this from the States." Amy's heart felt like it would break for this gift of God's Word after existing so many years on her memory of Scripture, like American POWs had done. Her heart was burdened for the young girl, who'd undoubtedly kept this precious book close for years, never daring to reveal it. Monique spoke before Amy could refuse the gift.

"I can't give it back to her, Amy. He'll punish us both."

"Then get a message to her. Please?"

"I'll try."

"I know you can. You're a leader here. Tell her other believers know she's here and we're praying for her." She gripped Monique's hand through the grate. "Do you know her name?"

"I—I can't—" Monique's voice broke. "I have to go. Amy, I might not return before the Harvest. Malcolm doesn't sleep well. Be ready! When I come for you on the day of the new moon, act like you're afraid of me. I'll mistreat you if I must to preserve my cover, but don't be alarmed. Tell your sons to be ready, too. Take an opportunity if you see it. That's all I can tell you now."

Monique sniffled, and Amy shone the light for perhaps a last glance at this woman who'd risked her life delivering a light in the darkness, the Word in a little New Testament, and hope in a rescue plan.

"Thank you, Monique. We can never repay your kindness."

"Yes, you can," she whispered, her voice cracking again.

"What?" Amy said, tears burning her eyes. "Please, tell me."

Monique coughed, then began to cry openly for the first time Amy could remember. She let Monique take her time.

"I need what you spoke of once. I need it so much."

"What, Monique?"

"You're here—you've *been* here for six years because of me. I didn't try to make your life better. You were the enemy of my faith, of the man I loved—and I hated you. I kept you here, even if it wasn't my decision, because I didn't try to stop it." Her tears flowed freely, pooling on the tunnel's stone floor. "I'm so sorry."

"Monique," Alice whispered. She grasped their fingers, uniting the three women at the grate. "We *forgive* you."

Monique's cries stormed in a torrent of pain. Amy and Alice hung onto her fingers while she suffered on the other side of the rusty bars. Finally Monique caught her breath and wiped her face on her Lycra shoulder.

"You shouldn't forgive me. But you did. Whatever happens, I'll always remember you." Her voice diminished. "Pray for me, please?"

"We will. And when we're separated, you pray, too. Okay?"

"How, Amy?"

"Talk to God in your heart, or out loud—it doesn't matter. Remember that Jesus suffered for our sins. He forgave His tormentors, and He'll forgive you—if you just ask Him. Ask Him to lead you and to make you clean."

Monique squeezed their hands. She began backing away. "I've got to go. Now."

"Monique?"

"Yes?" She continued backing out of the tunnel, her voice gravelly.

"Jesus loves you. We do too."

Monique choked back another sob. "No one . . . no one's ever said that to me. Not even Malcolm, in all these years. Thank you . . . both of you. And I *will* pray. I promise." Soon they heard a heavy door closing beyond the tunnel.

Amy tucked the light under the cover, wondering if they would ever meet again. So much could happen. She shivered and pulled the blanket tighter. Alice took the light.

"Look, Mom." Alice illuminated the open New Testament under the blanket. "There's an inscription in the front. Now we know her name!"

Amy's heart leapt. She pulled the tiny red New Testament, no larger than a deck of cards, closer so that she could see in the failing flashlight's glow. On the flyleaf, an adult had inscribed in flowing cursive: "Keep Him close to your heart. To Sonya, from Mom."

SUNDAY, MAY 17, 2020
NAZARJE, SLOVENIA

Eight hours later, Amy and Alice were wedged into the corner of their tiny, twenty-by-twenty-meter garden, the one spot where they could see the cross. Amy looked up, straining to see whether Monique was watching. She saw nothing.

Ancient stone walls towered ten meters above her; gray, moss-covered stones that had seen perhaps four centuries of sun and dark. Beyond, a cross thrust into the sky, poised at the top of a sharp spire on a gray slate-roofed steeple. The Sunday bells lifted her, pulling her spirit up from this remote corner of nowhere, into the clear blue patch of sky above, free from this isolation and dread.

"Keep your eyes on the cross, Alice," Amy said. "God hasn't forgotten us."

"Shhh!" Alice said, fingers to lips. "The bells!"

The ringing had begun. Amy watched the window a moment longer and then turned her focus to the cross, barely visible through the crenellated ramparts. She prayed for her sons, for Alice, and for Monique. She prayed for the unknown Sonya and her young faith. She asked for some hope of John's return. And as the symphony of bells in the valley below washed over her, she lifted her spirit and sought the Lord.

"Did you hear that one?" Alice asked.

Amy opened her eyes. "No. What?"

"That song! Listen!"

Amy did—and her spirit sang. "It's for us, Alice! They saw it, they saw it! It worked! *Amazing Grace—it's for us!* We've been here two thousand days trying to shine brightly, and they know it!" She hugged Alice joyfully and began singing with the bells through her tears. "When we've been there ten thousand years, bright shining as the sun, we've no less days to sing God's praise than when we'd first begun!"

Alice stared in amazement. "But how can you be sure, Mom?"

Amy couldn't speak, unable to voice the hope burning in her. The bells ended, and she dabbed at her face. All was silent.

Then before Amy could respond, the bells in a lone steeple began to peal. In six years of Sundays, this had never happened. Reverberating off the nearby hills, the solitary church bell rang for nearly a minute before it halted—giving way to two bells working together, one short, one long.

"Ding Ding Ding." Three short, high-pitched rings.

Three long, deep-voiced "Dongs."

Another three "Dings"—then a short pause, and a repeat of the same.

"SOS, Mom! It's SOS!"

"Yes!" Amy sucked in a deep, ecstatic breath. "At last someone knows we're here."

26

THE SKY WAS LEADEN, a solid overcast extending below the tops of the mountains to the north. Wisps of cloud drifted just above the tall fir where Petty Officer First Class Squyres hung in a sling secured near the huge tree's peak. The eyes of his team, he watched with a night-vision scope and long-range imaging optics as the men made their way up a grassy knoll toward the imposing castle. Trading watch every two hours with two other senior petty officers for the past ten days, three Navy SEALs maintained continuous surveillance of the compound. Squyres trained his optics on the window of the closest steep-roofed spire.

"No activity in the window. The girl's down. Proceed."

No light penetrated the dense cloud cover, a blessing for the mission. The Stygian night sucked up the faint light of the town below, creating impenetrable blackness on the castle knoll. The Army's

"Night Stalkers," his clandestine aviator brothers in arms, stood by with their whisper-quiet rotorcraft only twenty kilometers away. They awaited the order to swoop up the entire team within seconds and depart to the safe havens of cloud-shrouded mountaintops and black forests.

Squyres checked his watch, then looked over his shoulder at the town below. One moment a few street lights burned in the Slovenian village, and a handful of homes were lit. The next moment, Nazarje went absolutely black.

"Grid's down," Squyres murmured into his lip mike, training his optics on the compound and searching for any sign the backup power had engaged. "Repeat — grid is down."

If his teammates had done their job, there'd be no more lights. The compound's backup generator would never start. Someone would probably curse lazy installers and wander out with a flashlight. But it was two o'clock in the morning. Only a guard force would care, and from Squyres's observation, they'd probably wait it out, hoping for an early restoration of the region's unstable electric grid. Many of these people still held the old communist mentality of "take no initiative."

"Lights out. No backup. Proceed."

Through his night-vision scope Squyres watched Colonel Scales and his team ascend the knoll, fifteen men in black, all outfitted with the same gear he wore, fingers at the triggers of their weapons. He scanned the building again; no woman in the window.

Squyres selected a new frequency on the audio taps, micro-miniature bugs he'd dropped into key locations over the past week, listening for any activity. Linguists in CIA's Langley facility in Virginia heard what he did a quarter second later by satellite and fed him the interpretations live. A few voices — guards — cursed the darkness.

"One guard's headed to the generator. No alarm. Proceed."

Squyres watched as the team reached the base of a ten-meter wall surrounding the compound. They'd be over in seconds. Another SEAL deployed a light telescoping pole equipped with footrests, shooting it up the wall. In a flash, one man was up the ladder, steadied by his fellow warriors. He leapt over the wall and belayed into the courtyard beyond, his line secured by his brothers in arms. In quick succession, four more were over the top. The remaining ten fanned out at the tower's base, one flashing thumbs up to Squyres, two hundred meters away.

"We're in."

Lieutenant Commander "Mutt" Suttles had met John Wells once, a few years ago, at Panama City, Florida. Suttles was in deep submergence dive training, and Wells was a visiting VIP. It was two years after the Wells's family had died. Or so they'd thought.

As he zipped down the line into the compound, Suttles remembered wondering that day how the admiral managed to carry on with his painful loss. Suttles had long ago resolved that his clandestine job might take his life, and pull him from his wife and kids forever. But until he'd met Admiral Wells, he'd never considered the impact of losing his new bride or, one day, his children.

Now he knew, only too well, that when they'd met, the admiral's wife had probably been right here. He touched the ground and crouched, whispering into his lip mike after a quick reconnoiter of the small garden. "Clear."

Suttles moved across the garden to the far wall, adjacent the wooden door to the women's compartment. In his night-vision goggles, he saw the fake stone he'd placed days ago in the far corner, an imaging and acoustic sensor that monitored this garden through a satellite for dozens of intelligence analysts to pore over. Nothing had moved. He whispered again. "Insert."

Another man was over the wall within seconds and fell into a crouch, gun trained on the door where Suttles waited. Hand signals between the two confirmed what they'd both anticipated. No resistance. The entire compound was darkened and the guards blind.

Suttles lifted the old latch, a throwback to another millennium, and opened the cottage's gray rough-hewn door.

Amy lay awake, unable to sleep. She guessed it was near two or three in the morning and kept an eye on the grate, praying Monique would return. She wanted to share her amazing Sunday revelation.

Alice rolled beside her, slinging her arm across her mother in her usual sleep antics. Amy felt the pulse on the thin arm; her daughter was peaceful.

The bells continued to ring in Amy's head, pealing "Amazing Grace." The song's words of solace washed over her soul with peace—and excitement. God had a plan for her life; she'd always known.

John had lived his commitment to God's plan to such an extent that sometimes the word "plan" grated on her. But not tonight. She sensed closure at hand—for all of them. They weren't alone any more; Monique cared. And beyond the walls, someone knew she was here. Why else an English spiritual tune on a Slovenian carillon, followed by an SOS? It *had* to be a sign.

She lay facing the grate, praying for Monique and hoping for one more glimpse of her friend before the big day, three nights hence. The room was pitch dark, but she knew Monique's light would announce her arrival.

The door squeaked and drifted open. Amy groaned, frustrated with the old latch that unfastened whenever the wind blew. Sometimes she pushed the chest against it at night to hold it shut. But tonight the temperature was pleasant, and she'd let it stand open. Amy closed her eyes and curled up tighter, stroking Alice's arm and praying.

Suddenly she sensed a presence moving by her face, as if Jesus were right there, ready to take her in His arms. She opened her eyes. A gloved hand suddenly clasped the back of her head and another sealed her mouth. She sensed other hands grasping Alice.

They're here! To take her! Terror ripped through her.

Amy launched both hands and a knee toward the engulfing arms. Her fist ricocheted off a light helmet, and her knee connected with a hard plate instead of a chest. She saw only black forms. She felt Alice struggling behind her. She tried to scream, then heard the voice—a hot breath in her ear: "Mrs. Wells! We're Americans!"

She fell limp, transformed from rage into joy, in seconds. Behind her, Alice ceased fighting.

"I'll let you go, but you *must* remain silent. I know John. You ready to leave this hotel? One nod for yes."

Hotel? Ready to leave? Amy stifled a nervous laugh, nodded once, and squeezed his forearm lightly to reassure him. He released her.

The warrior illuminated a tiny LED at the base of his face. The sudden image of the man in black caused her to gasp. He stroked her hair back, then took her hand, whispering in her ear again. "Have to go! *Now!*"

Behind her, another warrior was already lifting Alice off the bed. A sudden twinge of fear gripped Amy. *Are they really here to help?*

She pulled at the arm urging her on and drew him near. "What's my husband's call sign?"

The warrior stopped and once again illuminated the LED under his face. She saw a smile — a genuine concern under the black paint and the Borg-like devices adorning his head. "It's Hawk, ma'am," he whispered as he urged her forward. "Gotta go!"

✦

The next sixty seconds blurred. She was in the garden, the soldier slipping something like water shoes on her feet, perfectly fitted. Then across the garden she'd toiled in for so many years, hooked to a rope, and flying up the wall. She feared she might sail over the top when another man in black appeared out of nothing and caught her at the ramparts, flipping her over the wall, and whispering to close her eyes.

"Don't make a sound!" he cautioned in the few seconds he had her in his grasp.

She plummeted down the wall, a few feet to the right of her daughter dimly visible descending in the dark. The rope jerked taut just before she landed in another man's black-clad arms. He placed her on the ground and whispered, "Lay down!" His breath was hot on her face. Alice fell to the ground beside her, reaching for a hand.

Thirty seconds later, perhaps less, she sensed men standing above her, straining at their ropes, then the sound of sliding. She turned her head, the dim overcast barely sufficient to make out men slipping down poles from the top of the ramparts. They thudded lightly to the ground, ready to run. The warrior who'd surprised her in bed now knelt at her side, whispering between hard breaths. "Can you run?"

"You don't have to carry us," she said. "We're healthy."

"You've got some good shoes. Let's go." He pulled her to her feet, urging her forward.

Amy pulled back, her heart pounding. "The boys?"

"To your right." He squeezed her hand hard. "No talk."

In that second, she made out forms ten or twenty meters away — three — about her sons' sizes. Tears blurred the image as she was pulled into a fast jog downslope toward the treeline.

Amy's heart sang, watching her boys loping along the grassy hill, surrounded by a protective circle of nine black-clad armed men, their weapons ready. Six more urged her on, one hand in hers and another guiding Alice as they raced downhill toward the safety of the forest.

As she passed the first fir tree, she stole a glance back at the hilltop. The firs' tall branches swooped over her just as she'd imagined those many years she'd listened to their sighs in the winds. The peaks of the buildings appeared beyond the limbs, ghostly features against a dark gray sky. For six years, she had wondered what her prison looked like. Now, in the dark, she could see little — but somehow the steeple's cross was visible, her focus for so many years of prayer.

She didn't have to squat to see the cross any more. *I'm free!*

Amy released a branch and dove into the wood, ebony warriors guiding her into the inky depths of perfect dark.

"Guardian? Forgive the intrusion."

Monique started, leaping from the bed at the first knock, and rushed to the door. No one had ever woken them at night. *Trouble? One of the Mother Seed?*

"Father Raines is asleep," she whispered, cracking the door. "What is it?"

A guard stood in the doorway. "Power has failed in the town. Our backups have also failed."

Malcolm mumbled in the bed, and Monique went to her boss's side. "We've lost power, Father. That is all."

"What about the backup?"

"It has failed, Great One," the guard responded for her, peering into the room.

"Then fix it!" Malcolm bellowed, rolling to the edge of the bed and trying to sit up. "Now!"

"Immediately, sir," the guard replied. "I came to alert you that power is also out throughout the town. All of Nazarje."

"I don't care about Nazarje. I care about the Mother Seed. Are they safe?"

"Yes, sir. Sorry to bother you. Good night." The guard shone his light around the room's interior then departed.

Malcolm swore as he searched in the dark for his slippers. Monique retrieved her flashlight. The dark wouldn't bother her friends below. They had no electricity and would never know it was gone.

"Incompetence," Malcolm hissed. "We fund an expensive backup system, and it fails when we need it most." He grabbed the light from Monique and slapped across the stone toward the door. Slamming the door behind him, he headed down the circular staircase, swearing aloud and ranting about shoddy eastern European construction.

Monique was glad for the interlude. Malcolm would be up all night, cursing the staff, insisting that he had some knowledge — perhaps from the Father Race — about why the power had failed. He'd try to tell the workers how to fix the generator and curse the staff for sleeping through the power failure. Finally he'd get hungry and look for food.

Monique opened the door slightly and listened to him descend the stairs and exit into the Great Hall. When she was sure he'd departed, she opened the window to the dark night and a mild breeze.

Monique stood there in the gentle night breeze, staring toward the dark, featureless garden below her. She hoped the power was out for a very long time.

"Woman's at the window now," Petty Officer Squyres radioed to the team. Moments earlier, he'd reported seeing lights darting about the tower room above the women's garden. Something like a flashlight. There one moment and gone the next. His team had safely egressed into the forest below, and they'd left behind no sign of their passage. Squyres continued to monitor as the last of the men withdrew into the forest below him.

"Copy, Big Eyes. Woman at window. We're almost to the road now. Dismount on my mark."

"Roger," Squyres said, then trained his big infrared glasses on the compound, watching for any last sign of a response.

A minute later, he heard the command. "Time to go."

"Outa here," Squyres replied, stuffing the gear into a sack at his side and zipping down a rope from the treetop. He pulled a second line, and the harness and rope slid down to the base, where he gathered it up, stuffed it in his pack, and headed downhill through the dark forest. Only footprints in the dense needles of the forest floor revealed he'd been there.

"I'm Lieutenant Commander Suttles, ma'am. Your sons are in the other vehicle," her warrior guide said as the van that held part of the rescue team began to move. "You can see them when we reach the aircraft." He lifted the night-vision goggles from his eyes, looking like a half-human, half-robotic creature adapted to night war. "Are you okay? And Alice?"

Amy nodded, wiping at her eyes. "What about Monique?"

"Monique?" the officer asked. "She the voice we've heard you talking to?"

"You *heard* me?" she asked, puzzled.

He nodded.

"Yes, that's the voice. Monique sent you, didn't she? Did you get her out, too?"

A tall man with dark brows and deeply recessed eyes bent toward her as they lurched along the rough road. He had a long face, blocklike, with a dimpled chin. Red lights illuminated the vehicle's interior and cast a vermillion glow on the little part of his face not painted black. "Ma'am, I'm Joe Scales. The mission commander. I've known your husband, John, for many years. Glad you found a way to signal us."

"You know John?" She tried to place this man with the prominent jaw and close-cropped hair. Had she entertained him once at their home?

"Yes, ma'am. You know he's on Mars?"

Amy nodded. "Monique told us. Is he all right?"

"Yes, ma'am. Inventive as ever. Moved his entire settlement five hundred clicks to save his crew and find a way home. Do you know about his return ship?"

"Monique said it was damaged. That he's coming home on a colonists' ship."

"Yes, ma'am. Colonies on Mars now. Times change, don't they? Now, who's this Monique?" He offered her a bottle of water and handed another to Alice.

"She told you we were here, right? I mean, Monique said she had a plan. To get us all out." Amy saw the confusion on the senior officer's face as she said it. He looked at the floor then back at her.

"No, ma'am. CIA found you. Don't know why, but FBI exhumed your—the bodies—from the crash. When the DNA didn't match, they figured you might still be alive. Then when John proved the aliens were fakes, and the FBI knew you weren't dead, well, Raines was the first place they went looking. CIA saw your mirror signal, and that confirmed it. My men dropped sensors into the facility, and they thought they heard you talking to that Monique person one night. We didn't know who she was." He shrugged. "CIA said she might be Raines's head assistant. We couldn't be sure."

"She was. Is. You *don't* have her?" Amy said, panic in her voice. She looked around to confirm that what she was hearing was true. "Monique's still inside that place?"

The tall man nodded in silence. Amy felt her chest tighten, like someone had just kicked the air out of her. Alice took her hand. *She risked her life for us—and she's left behind?*

"What day is it?" Her head felt light and she shivered. She needed food. "The date?"

"You're dizzy again, Mom," Alice said. "I can feel it."

Amy vaguely felt Alice release her hand and heard her daughter's take-charge voice. "I need something for Mom to eat. Right now. She's low."

Amy watched the officer in front of her pull some kind of bar from his vest, rip off the wrapper, and hand it to her. She took the dense sweet nutty mass, amazed by the taste of processed food after years of nothing but vegetables, bread, soup, and water. She tried to talk through the mouthful of food and her woozy head. "The date?" she repeated.

"Eighteenth of May, ma'am," Lieutenant Commander Suttles said, putting an arm about her as she began to wobble.

Amy coughed, suddenly sick to her stomach at the thought of Monique in Raines's clutches, or headed to the Harvest under a dark sky. *The new moon.*

"Four days," Alice whispered. "That's all they've got." She leaned into her mother's shoulder, shaking. "Mom, we've got to get her out."

27

THE FAMILIAR SMELLS OF old stone and damp moss embraced Monique as she lowered the huge floor panel back into place over her head. She heard Malcolm cursing the staff somewhere across the Great Hall. As she'd guessed, he was hungry, and normal people were still asleep. His ranting bass with falsetto squeaks hushed and then disappeared as the panel nestled into its ancient slot.

Malcolm would be busy for a while with the generator. She could slip away for half an hour and never be missed. She flicked on her light and descended the winding stairway.

A few minutes later, prone in the tunnel, she glimpsed Amy's secret stash of flashlight and New Testament stuffed into the ventilation duct. An unnecessary precaution, since no one searched the apartment or even visited the two women.

Monique's heart was heavy when she thought back to the day she'd convinced the Guardian to restrict human contact for them, to pass food and bedding, medicine and books, through a rotating access door. She had intended to ensure the purity of the guards as well as to protect her Master. Regret weighed heavily on her heart.

Monique shinnied to the end of the tunnel and whispered for Amy to awaken. Amy was usually waiting at the grate, but tonight, no one responded. She called again, quietly. *No power—and that means no sensors. The guards can't hear us.* She called again, louder. No response.

Where is she? Malcolm would have told her if he'd pulled the prisoners from the room. Yet he'd said nothing. *Perhaps he knows my secret, and this power failure was a trap!*

She tried to look behind her in the tunnel, but couldn't, her panic rising. She was pinned. If Malcolm came looking, she had nowhere to run. She pulled herself forward to the grate and peered through the holes at the bed. It was empty. The door was ajar.

Is she outside? Monique wouldn't be able to get their attention if they were in the garden. Perhaps they'd heard the ruckus, or the guards had rousted them, checking because of the power and video outage. Every possible scenario ran through her head, but she kept returning to the most logical option—*Malcolm set me up.*

She swallowed, the lump of fear growing, and began to withdraw from the tunnel. Halfway back, light beams danced across her face.

"They're not here!" a man yelled, passing near the grate. She heard cursing, then the sound of furniture being turned over. It sounded as if a guard were tearing the room apart. "Gone!"

"It can't be!" said a second voice. "Those walls are ten meters tall. Video showed her in here before the outage. Check again."

The first man swore again at the second, and there was some sort of scuffle. "I told you, they're not here! We should alert the Guardian."

Monique's entire body shook as the light left the room, immersing her in total darkness. She remembered Malcolm's rage when he heard of the power outage. She remembered the girls who'd made mistakes, and his pressure on her to bring them into line. Now Amy and Alice were gone!

Monique's dream—to escape with them—evaporated. Her insides felt empty, void of the spark of their friendship. Her bondage to Malcolm would continue. Escape options she'd once discarded as too risky returned. But you couldn't just walk out the door. She was on her own—unless she had an ally in the Mother Seed. Lots of them.

Monique craved to crawl forward and see for sure if Amy was gone—or, she hoped, escaped. But the guard must've searched thoroughly. She gripped Amy's light and New Testament, unsure why she'd pulled them out. But now they were hers: the light and the Word.

Suddenly she heard Malcolm—*He's coming to Amy's room!* She shinnied backward as fast and silently as possible, images haunting her of his huge hand slapping her down, as he'd done once with a staff member who'd talked back. Just as he entered the room, she exited the tunnel and crouched near the hidden stairway.

"No!" Malcolm bellowed. "The Father Race commanded us to preserve and care for them! We *cannot* lose this prize."

Monique's heart leapt. *Perhaps she* has *escaped!*

"I'm truly sorry, Great One, but they were here before we lost power."

"They had help!" It sounded like Malcolm throwing furniture across the room. "Find Monique!" he screamed. "*Now!*"

Twenty kilometers northeast of Nazarje, a pair of black Special Forces helicopters waited, rotors spinning, on a grassy meadow in the high mountains' thick fog. Amy and Alice exited the nondescript panel van with part of their rescuer escort. The whirring blades sprayed Amy with an angry tempest of mountain mist.

Colonel Scales led the women in a rush toward the helo on their left, his head ducked to avoid the blades. The eerie red glow of the helo's cabin lights reflected off the colonel's goggles and washed over a complex collection of special gear attached to his field vest. He helped her into the black helo.

Amy stopped before climbing in and screamed over the high-pitched engines and spinning rotor, "Thank you! I'll never forget what you did."

"Don't thank me," he yelled. "Thank them!" He pointed to the ten men headed into the second helicopter. "See you in Italy in an hour." He turned as a muscular young man dressed in something resembling gray denim ran up behind her. Abe threw his arms around Amy. A full-grown man, he towered over his mother. His brown curly locks reached down to his shoulders like a young Samson.

Amy yelled with joy as Abe lifted her off the grass and hugged her. Alice jumped out of the helicopter, screaming "Abe!" her long blonde hair thrashed by the helo's mad rotor downwash. Colonel Scales waved them into the aircraft, and Abe lifted both women with ease up to their seats. He turned and helped Albert, the youngest boy, and Arthur, their quiet number two.

Her two youngest sons grabbed seats beside her, their arms stretched over her in a group hug. Airmen rushed to buckle them into their seats. Across from Amy, Alice and Abe settled into red canvas seats like her own as Abe buckled them in. An airman patted her on the shoulder as he cinched her harness, smiling "welcome." The awesome war bird's power made her feel safe.

Colonel Scales slapped the aircraft's side, then, sporting a big smile, saluted Amy. He pulled the door shut and ran to join his team in the second helo.

"It's a miracle, Mom!" Abe yelled across the aisle. "They found us!"

"Praise God!" Amy yelled back. "We're *together* again!"

The sleek helicopter lifted hard, then pointed downslope, gaining speed. Dizziness gripped Amy as the "Night Stalkers" took flight from the mountain into an impenetrable black fog.

"You called for me, Father?" Monique jogged into the prisoner quarters and stopped abruptly, staring at the room's destruction, pretending to be shocked. Despite many trips to the ventilation shaft, this was her first time in the cell.

How could you live here six years and not lose your mind?

Malcolm stood at the far end of the garden with a guard, bent over a rock. He picked it up, turning it over in his hands. When he faced Monique, his expression was unlike any she'd seen him wear in their nearly nine years together: extraordinary rage magnified by abject fear.

His wrath made her want to remain as far from his huge hands as possible. But the fear in his darting eyes and sweating face, illuminated by the guard's flashlight, gave her strength. She walked toward him quickly, head high.

"Where are the prisoners?" she snapped at the guard. Anger from her would go a long way toward convincing Malcolm of her innocence. And she *was* innocent. This disappearance mystified her even more than it did him.

"They were here! Moments ago!" the guard said. "I saw them both asleep."

Malcolm raised his left arm and backhanded the guard, sending him stumbling away. His head thudded against the stone wall, and he sank to the dirt.

"The prisoners cannot fly, so where did they go?" She stood over the fallen guard.

"Monique, come see this," Malcolm said.

Pointing to the prison door, she shouted at the fallen guard. "Leave us!" Turning to Malcolm, she said, "I'm sorry, Raksasa. I should have replaced the night watch."

"No, Monique. You couldn't have anticipated *this*." He handed her the rock. It was lightweight plastic, not stone. The surface felt rubbery. She turned it over, examining a small hole on one end. Her eyes widened as she looked up at Malcolm. "Is this camera ours?"

Malcolm shook his head, his eyes darting to the wall, then up to the tower window, then to the prison door. The look of fear returned. "They were taken. The power outage was their cover. This," he said, taking the rock from her, "is some sort of surveillance system, probably American." He frowned, then threw it over the wall. "It's probably still working."

Malcolm pulled Monique along with him by the arm as he hurried across the dirt to the exit. "Prepare the Mother Seed. We must leave in an hour. Tell them to pack their most essential items, whatever will fit into a backpack. Nothing else." He ducked through the prison door before her — "Tell them the Harvest mission has begun. We must travel a long way and travel light."

Monique's mind raced. She could leave him and this insanity now, suddenly drop out of sight in the confusion. But then there would be no hope of freeing the girls. Freedom dangled just before her, so close. She could dash into her secret place, wait this out, and they'd be gone. *But the girls . . .*

"Monique! Did you hear what I told you? Prepare the Mother

Seed. Now!" Malcolm stopped, glaring at her.

"Yes, Father, I'm sorry. I'll begin at once. What will we use for transportation? And our destination?"

He pulled a small phone from his robe and thrust it at her. "We'll exit through the monk tunnel. Call the Remnant and have buses waiting at the exit, the friary of St. Martin. Arrange for aircraft to move us from Nazarje to Ljubljana."

"And then?" she asked, her own plans spinning as she took the precious phone in her hands.

"To China."

"China?" She cocked her head. "To the Heavenly Home? So soon?"

"Coordinate the flight to Ürümqi. They are ready now for just such a contingency. Make sure the Remnant contacts Xi Wang Mu." Malcolm had lost the look of fear and now appeared determined. "Tell the Mother Seed we'll ship their personal effects. We must leave immediately."

He walked so fast she had to jog to keep up. Malcolm stopped suddenly and turned, pointing across the great hall toward the residences. "Go now! Call the Remnant! Prepare the Mother Seed!"

"At once, Guardian." She bowed stiffly, then turned and ran to her girls, hounded by images of what might be. She dashed through all three floors of the residence hall, calling for the monitors and staff to wake. Nightmares chased her like demons as she ran and yelled out orders. An eternal bondage to Malcolm, sequestered with him in the bowels of China . . . an everlasting Eve vessel for the Father Race. *If I leave with him, I'll never be free.*

The residence hall awoke, hundreds of groggy young women wandering in dark halls under emergency lights, asking: "What's wrong?" "Where are we going?" "Why the rush?" Soon, Monique realized, the pandemonium she'd created would escalate into mayhem, unless she brought it under control. In that bedlam she saw hope.

This was her only chance.

✳

"Kristen!" Sonya shook her friend, trying to rouse her from a deep sleep. "Wake up!"

"What?" Kristen mumbled and rolled over.

"We have to leave. Get up!"

Kristen sat straight up, clutching a fuzzy bear, rubbing her eyes. "Sonya?" She looked around the dark room, lit only by a faint beam from the hall's emergency floodlights. "It's dark. Turn on a light."

Sonya shook her head and touched Kristen's shoulder. "Lights are out. We're leaving." Sonya paused, wondering how to share the next bit of news. She prayed for her sister to be strong, for God to open a door for them. "They're moving us. For the Harvest."

Kristen lowered her head into the bear's fur and began to weep.

Moments later, Pina, their Tuscan matron with the hairy mole, burst into Kristen's bedroom, screaming. "Andiamo bambini! Great Hall. Fifteen minutes. Dress. Bring backpack." Pina had the same panicked look Sonya had seen on Miss Monique's face moments earlier. Pina jerked the covers off Kristen, then dashed out, pulling at her hair and screaming, "Andiamo bambini! Andiamo!"

Kristen stared ahead, teary eyed, as the room went from silence to storm to silence in seconds. In that transition, Sonya saw a chance for freedom. She grabbed her sister's backpack from the floor and thrust it into Kristen's hands. "Pack now Kristen! This is our chance!"

WASHINGTON, DC:
THE PENTAGON

"They've found it, sir," a Navy intelligence specialist said, leaning back in his chair and waving toward his terminal.

"Put it on the main screen, please, Petty Officer Collins," said an officer at the large conference table. Computer displays and terminals ringed the room stuffed with dozens of officers, enlisted personnel, and civilian government workers, all bedecked with a red "NMCC" badge overlain with a personal photo. Shawnda pushed her way across the room, a conference annex off the side of the busy National Military Command Center, the highly classified NMCC deep under five thick concrete rings of the Pentagon.

The intelligence annex and the operations center beyond were a mad beehive tonight. Drones and worker bees buzzed from terminal to terminal, while clusters of military officers talked over the next move. Tonight's queen bee was Assistant Secretary Dunovan, director of SOLIC—Special Operations Low Intensity Conflict—seated at the table's head. His hive was the Pentagon nerve center for tonight's Slovenia rescue operation. Far away in Italy, the joint headquarters fed a constant stream of military intelligence back to Washington. Here in the NMCC they could only watch. And hope.

The petty officer narrated the action on the main screen. "Raines approaches our sensor in the dark, sir. You can see a light beam when it saturates the night-vision sensor. He picks the rock up off the ground and stares into the camera lens. Here's the audio with that action."

"Monique, come see this," a deep voice said. In the background, a higher angry voice yelled, "Leave us!" then something else Shawnda couldn't understand. The deep bass voice returned. "No, Monique. You couldn't have anticipated *this*."

Shawnda stared in disbelief as the sensor appeared to turn, then captured the image of a young woman, long hair and high cheeks her most distinguishing features in the low light. "Is this camera ours?" the woman asked, her lips in synch with the audio.

The petty officer stopped the video and scrolled through the file. "They probably pitched us over the wall, sir. This view," he said as he displayed another image, "is of the forest in the distance. The sensor's outside the wall now."

Monique? Raines's assistant? Is that who Amy was talking to?

"You know Raines," Dunovan said to Special Agent Kerry. "What'll he do now?"

Shawnda caught her husband's eye across the room. This was their first operation together—ever. They'd worked hard not to be seen as a couple together this evening, though she craved to be at his elbow, conferring. The two of them, saving Amy together.

"He's unpredictable, sir," Terrance said. "But now that we have the Wells family, we can push him harder. He'll protect the Mother Seed as his first priority."

The petty officer displayed a map next, showing tracks of the two helicopters that carried Amy, her children, and the fifteen rescuers. The Army's 160th "Night Stalkers" were safely bound for Aviano Air Force Base in Italy at the Adriatic Sea's northern end.

"I've shadowed Raines for months," Terrance continued. "He's incredibly dedicated. I wouldn't put anything past him. I promise you this. If cornered, he'll have a safety valve."

Assistant Secretary Dunovan spun his yellow pencil, watching the Special Forces move across the Italian border on the digital map. The first mission was very nearly complete.

"Kerry's right. We aren't keeping a close eye on Raines," a Navy military aide said. "He could slip through our fingers in an instant. As long as they leave the power down, we won't see what's on his video feeds."

"It doesn't matter," another officer said, hurrying into the briefing room. "He's already on the run. Aviano post-processed the scratchy audio from that bug he *didn't* find. They passed the file. We can understand it now. Listen." Over the speakers, Raines's deep voice spoke rapidly.

"Prepare the Mother Seed. We must leave. . . ."

Assistant Secretary Dunovan slammed his hand into the table, cracking the Staples No. 2 over the knuckle of his middle finger. The two halves fell away as he turned to a senior officer at his right, wearing the braided gold aiguillette of an executive assistant on his shoulder.

"You can't move three hundred girls without being seen. Find out what Rear Admiral Gray plans to do with his second team, Colonel Parker. I want to know where Raines is headed."

I know where he's headed. Right where I want him.

Walter McClannahan, Deputy Director of Middle East Operations, CIA, pushed up from his seat, leaning on the table and his cane to get his balance, then moved slowly out of the conference room toward the Operations Center and the closest available red phone — an encrypted line. His knees screamed every time he walked these days. He fondled a pair of pain pills in his left coat pocket as he stopped at the door and addressed the others at the table.

"Please excuse me, sir. I have an important call I need to place."

Raines is headed east, Dunovan. I'd bet my life on it.

28

"THEY'RE READY, FATHER. As you requested." Monique struggled to appear calm, afraid her panting and her quivering voice would give her away. Little time was left. She had to act now.

Malcolm looked at his watch. "Fifty-nine minutes. You've done well." He stared at her a long moment. "The phone?"

Monique produced the slim cellular, pretending she'd forgotten. He took it and turned, walking to the front of the Great Hall. Before him stood his staff and 321 of the Mother Seed in black. Each girl carried a red backpack and a flashlight. Some carried a pillow, others a large doll or a favorite picture.

Malcolm took the stage, his voice booming in the huge darkened hall, lit only by the lights held by each girl. Hundreds of cylindrical beams pointed skyward into the Gothic rafters. "The time of Harvest has come. Are you ready to serve the Father Race?"

A murmur ran through the sleepy girls. A few exclaimed, "Yes!"

Malcolm raised his arms, urging a response, while aides trained large flashlights on him from below his face, creating an eerie effect. More than three hundred high-pitched voices cried, "YES!" Hands and flashlights waved.

"I am glad," Raines said, lowering his arms. "A beautiful home awaits us, a new home for the Harvest and the planting of the great Seed. Where we can roam and play outside, and be one with mother earth as we're meant to be. A place where there is color in the fall, bright snow in the winter, cool summers, and verdant springs. Tonight, we begin our journey. In four days, your bodies will be ready for the first Harvest. And you will do that in your new place of worship." His voice reached a crescendo, and he raised his arms again. "Are you ready?"

As they screamed a second "YES!" Monique's heart fell. Her sisters were headed to their doom, hundreds of breeding vessels in the hands of a man drunk on his fantasies of a future perfected mankind.

In that moment, watching their bright fawning eyes, Monique saw herself as she had been years ago—craving to be close to his side, willing to trade her soul and body to be part of his mission, to bask in his light. She'd been just like them, caught up in the same blind adoration of the charismatic Dr. Malcolm Raines.

Heartsick, Monique realized that she could no longer turn these girls or dissuade them from their agenda. They were on a path that had been orchestrated for them for years, one she herself, his agent of doom, had set in place. She couldn't imagine anyone more at fault than herself—other than Malcolm. The momentum was now too great to stop. If she were going to help, it had to be from the outside.

Malcolm preached for another five minutes, preparing the girls for travel, then led them, his hand and flashlight raised, to a tiny chapel beside the great hall. Behind its altar, a small wooden door opened to an ancient tunnel, burrowed by monks over the centuries.

The tunnel led four hundred meters down the mountain to a friary near the town's center. She'd already confirmed by radio that six buses were parked near the tiny chapel to carry the Mother Seed to the city airport and a flight to the capital city. There, in Ljubljana, a jet waited to carry them to China—and their final home.

The procession began. Malcolm directed three matrons to lead the line, followed single file by hundreds of black-suited lemmings.

"To the Harvest!" His voice boomed over their excited chatter. "Come, blessed Eve vessels of the Father Race!"

Monique waited at the end of the line where the queue wound back into the Great Hall. Malcolm, per his earlier guidance, would leave with the girls near the front of the line. Matrons would count off the passing girls by room number and sweep up any stragglers. When Monique departed, the compound was to be empty, save the guards. Movers would arrive late that morning to collect all of their belongings.

Monique had arranged buses, aircraft, and shipping in less than an hour, including rousting the matrons to prepare the girls to travel. Her contacts, developed during years in Trieste, were as dependable as ever. And the deep pockets of Saint Michael's Remnant spoke loudly when she called. On faraway Mont Saint Michel, a well-orchestrated team worked behind the scenes, carrying out her detailed instructions. This night would run smoothly because she had prepared her team well—a team she'd had no contact with since leaving Trieste.

Monique stood in shock from the young women's ominous and enthusiastic endorsement of Malcolm. These were girls she knew, had cared for personally—and had indoctrinated for six years about their world-changing mission. They were now little more than automatons. She'd made them that way.

A human stream, they flowed one by one into the dark rough hole in pursuit of a dream. Waves of nausea consumed Monique without warning and she clutched her stomach.

"I—I don't feel well," she said to a matron standing behind the throng with her. "Keep them moving." With that, she turned and slipped through the doorway into the winding steeple staircase, headed up to her room. She'd only made it a few steps before she fell to her knees, stomach roiling, acid rising in her throat. Sweat streamed down her face; her head spun.

Malcolm had them all—every girl—in his hand. And there was nothing she could do. She doubled over, vomited, and collapsed.

At that moment, broken in spirit and body, Monique recalled Amy's words: *Jesus forgives.*

Lying on the worn stairway, Monique pressed her face against the old rock steps, desperate to understand Amy's peace. Her heart had been crying out all night for help. But crying out to whom? Amy had promised that God would hear her, that God could heal her soul.

Another wave of nausea overwhelmed her. Monique curled up on the cold stone, her gut writhing as she heaved.

I'm dirty. Inside and out. Sin, Amy called it.

A pool of yellow bile lay near her head. Images reared of her deceived sisters happily dancing into a dark hole in the ground. Monique wrapped her arms around her middle and moaned.

Her hand touched something firm in the hip pocket of her Lycra skin suit as she bent over again in pain. The New Testament! Monique wiped her mouth on her sleeve and pulled out the little book from her pocket. The flashlight barely worked. She could hear voices calling, looking for someone, beyond the door to the Great Hall. She ignored them, opening the book.

She'd never opened a Bible before. It fell open naturally to the back cover, where someone had printed a series of words. Verses. She could barely read them in the emergency light of the stairway. One said "Romans 10:13." Her heart drank in the words greedily: "For whoso-ever shall call upon the name of the Lord shall be saved."

She curled into a ball, arms about her knees. Warm tears soaked the forearm of her skin suit. She spoke softly, this her first prayer ever. "I'm calling on your name, Jesus. Just like Amy said I could. Please for-give me for what I've done here, and for the pain I've caused. Make me clean and show me what to do."

For ten minutes or more she bent over on the rough stone and poured out her agony. Monique desperately yearned to be free.

Petty Officer Squyres knew it was too good to be true. Team Alpha had been extracted, but he was back in the forest again with no time to set up his viewing post in the firs. Team Bravo slowly scaled the grassy knoll. They'd lost all the element of surprise.

He trained his infrared binoculars on the tower, squinting for the flash he was sure he'd seen. The flash from the tower room was gone, but he could make out a warm infrared target moving behind the glass. There could only be two options. Surveillance . . . someone was watch-ing in that tower. Or the girl was back.

"Bravo lead, Squyres. Possible sniper in the near steeple. I have a target in the window."

"Copy, Murph. Can you make it out? They're looking for a tall woman, long black hair."

"Looking," replied another soldier. Murph, their sniper, huddled next to Petty Officer Squyres. "Where is it, man?" he whispered. "I don't see a thing up there."

Squyres squinted again. "Target's gone, sir. But they're definitely awake inside the castle. Found the bugs in the garden."

"Copy. They might be exiting through some kind of tunnel. Nobody comin' out the gate."

"Blue Team. Move fast," said his commanding officer. "Get inside and get eyes on their escape route. Red Team, proceed to objective. Start your search."

Squyres scanned again, searching the tower and the walls, keeping a frequent eye on his team nearing the compound's wall. His gaze returned to the tower. The warm spot was back.

Someone's in that room. He nudged Murph. "She's in the window."

Monique slapped the dying flashlight against her thigh, hoping a jiggle would revive the battery connection. The light was dead. She felt her way through the tower bedroom.

Monique clicked the light again, and the barest yellow glimmer shone on her jewelry box as she opened it. Holding the small light in her mouth, she pried the velvet backing out of the lid, feeling for the one prize she needed most.

A cross.

Six years ago, while passionately devoted to Malcolm and his cause, she'd confiscated this cross from one of the Mother Seed, from Sonya—the same girl whose New Testament had given her hope in her darkest moment just minutes ago. She'd hidden the cross, fearing in her deep superstition and worship of Sophia that destroying that cross, like desecrating a Christ seeker's Bible, could get her zapped by a lightning bolt.

The cross was always there for me. I ignored it.

She left the box open and rushed out of the room. *I have to find Sonya!*

A minute later, she emerged in the dimly lit Great Hall, the emergency lights in the stairway having nearly exhausted their battery power. The Hall was empty, a ghastly shadow of what it had been only fifteen minutes ago when packed with nearly four hundred people. The banners were draped over an empty throne, the giant gold of Malcolm's infinity symbol speaking to a hollow room. Trash dropped by some of the girls was scattered about the vacant floor. They were gone.

Monique clutched the small silver cross, her heart thudding. She ran toward the chapel tunnel, praying to catch the line of girls, pull Sonya out with some fabricated excuse, and take her into the hiding place. She had to. Sonya had never wanted this. And now, for the comfort this New Testament had afforded, Monique was in Sonya's debt.

Please be there!

The chapel was vacant, but Monique could hear voices far down the tunnel. Shouts and sounds of a struggle. "No! Please don't take me!" a girl shrieked. "Sonya! Tell them! We don't want to go!"

Malcolm looked east, a faint twinge of predawn light backlighting the distant hills. The odor of jet fuel was strong, and the whine of an auxiliary power unit stung his ears. The plane was ready, but they couldn't leave. Not without her. Malcolm held up a hand for the pilot at his side to wait a few more minutes.

She'll come. She has to.

He paced near the bottom of the stairs, trying to control his temper.

"She didn't board, sir. I checked every bus." The matronly woman who addressed him was half a meter shorter than Malcolm, but heavier than he. He despised fat people—but the Head Mother was thorough, so he tolerated her.

"We're done then," Malcolm said to the pilot. "Prepare to take off."

"You checked every bus?" Raines asked her again, looking at the empty vehicles lined up at the small airstrip outside Nazarje. "You sent someone back to check?"

"Yes, sir. I radioed the guards again five minutes ago. She's nowhere to be found. They reviewed every possible location. My count showed we were short two girls, and I sent staff to locate those while we boarded the last bus and waited on Monique. The Edwards girl, and her friend—Kristen, number 217—had hidden in the kitchen. In a food locker."

She lowered her voice. "We had to forcibly remove them, Guardian. They fought us all the way." She pointed to two girls, their hair askew and rips visible on the arms of their Lycra suits. Two matrons held them at the base of the aircraft boarding stair.

Malcolm expected Monique to come careening onto the tarmac with a last-minute correction to some critical problem. Like she always did. His angst flared into anger, and he slammed the side of the stairway. "We're leaving," he growled. "Sedate those two and put them on board. Tell the others those two are ill. Radio the guards. Have one of them get Monique to Ljubljana when she's found." Malcolm fought a welling desire to hit someone but forced a smile.

No anger tonight, he thought, scaling the stairs. *The Mother Seed must feel secure, lest their precious harvest be disturbed.*

"The place is empty, sir. Just the guards left in there. The girls and the big man are gone."

Squyres listened to the calls from Blue Team as he trained his surveillance on the tower. The warm spot had disappeared several minutes ago.

"They say where? Can you hear anything on the sensors?" a voice asked on the radio.

"No, sir. But the guards are hopping mad about some missing woman. The rest of the team took off without her, we know that much. It's somebody important. Name's Monique."

"Good. Maybe we'll find her. Red Team ingress now. Blue Team, find out how those girls got out without us seeing them. Find out where they went. Bravo leader out."

WASHINGTON, DC

"When do we tell John?" Kerry asked, standing before Assistant Secretary Dunovan and a group of thirty watch officers, intelligence analysts, and military brass. The NMCC had become a busy place late on a Sunday night. It was early on a dark Monday morning in Europe.

A Secret Service agent watched in silence from a distance. Even Shawnda's boss, Walter McClannahan, was here. And Kerry's boss, FBI Director Carlene Whatley. The clock in the back of the room read 2300. Eleven p.m. It would be five a.m. in Slovenia, just twenty-six minutes 'til sunup.

"We don't have to go down that road yet," someone said. "John doesn't need to know."

"He *does*," Kerry insisted. "Amy's going to ask to call him as soon as the doc in Aviano sees her. We need a plan."

"Can I talk to you a second?" Director Whatley asked, waving him her direction. Kerry nodded, and they moved into a corner. "Raines," she said. "Are we still tracking his tooth transmitter?"

"It's not a transmitter, Carlene," Kerry said. "It's a receiver. We've recorded a few calls to him over the past year. We know when he gets a call, but we can't follow him."

"Good," she said, touching a manicured finger to her lips in thought. "I want to tell John about this. But more important, I want NASA to know what's happening tonight." She pushed straightened gray and brown hair over her ear, then looked back at the leaders at the conference table.

"Why, Carlene? They're gonna find out soon enough."

"NASA can't keep a secret, Terrance. If they know what we're up to, we don't have to release a press statement. They'll blab it to the world, or whoever's feeding Raines will do it for them. We can deny whatever we want. Raines is airborne, right? Probably headed to Ljubljana. So let's use this occasion to catch the big fish, the person who's calling his tooth phone. Break this case once and for all."

"You assume he—Raines—hasn't checked in with them already."

"You said it yourself. It's a one-way tooth. And you know what? Maybe he really *does* believe all this stuff about the Father Race. He might be on the run to protect those girls just like you said. We figure out who's calling him, pretending to be some alien god, then get that person off the net, and we can use that phone implant to bring him right to us." She raised an eyebrow and pushed her hair back again. "Worth a try, don't you think?"

Kerry nodded. He'd considered that approach himself.

"Shall I ask permission to tell John?" He smirked.

She shook her head. "Ask *forgiveness*, Terrance, not permission. It worked for you and John in the past. Tell NASA right now." She pointed at the crowd of military planners and law enforcement officials. "Let them argue about the next step while we get something done."

29

MONIQUE OPENED HER EYES and stared at her hands, wet with tears and grease-stained from the bolt she'd thrown to seal her secret crypt under the stairway. Despite her fatigue, the aftertaste of nausea, and the grit and the grime, she felt clean, filled with a new peace.

Dear Alice and Amy had shown her the way. A path to forgiveness.

She longed to gather Sonya into her arms, to apologize for the years of mental abuse and repeated lies about the "god within you," about Sophia and the Mother of Eve, and, worst of all, the Father Race.

Monique wept with longing for Sonya's forgiveness—for being too late to pull her from the group leaving for China, and for the cross she'd taken from her as a little girl, when the Remnant had snatched her from her mother. Monique ached to share her own decision to follow Jesus. She longed to be Sonya's big sister, to laugh and share times together. Far from here.

What do I do next? How long do I hide?

She heard voices. Military voices with clipped sentences and hushed tones. Speaking in English.

Monique pushed the cross into her pocket, turned out the flashlight she'd picked up in the Great Hall, and listened.

She felt an inner prodding: *Act now.* She slid into the narrow tunnel, determined to contact the voices, hoping they could be trusted.

A minute later, Monique lay prone behind the grate, watching, as three black-suited men entered Amy's room. In the early morning light, the place was a shambles, furniture tossed and broken, the bed torn apart. It bore no resemblance to the place of peace that Monique had visited so many times to learn about Amy and her God.

"Red Team ingress. Female barracks empty." The first man entered in a crouch, his weapon ready. Dressed entirely in black, with a black vest and a black web harness holding all manner of equipment, he moved catlike, his head down and swiveling. A set of electronic eyes covered the top of his face, basking his skin in a greenish glow. He moved his gun about as if it were a sensor, finger ready at the trigger. He waved to another man, then a third. He pointed to the bed, then to his ear, whispering into a lip mike.

"Acoustic sensor there . . . and there. Video up there. And behind you." He waved his hands in each direction.

They know where every sensor is! How? Are they part of Malcolm's team?

She waited, holding her breath, wanting to confirm she could trust them—with her life.

The men backed out of the space, one covering their exit with a gun trained on the courtyard, the other two retreating, and guns at the ready.

Monique felt her inner prodding again: *Act now!*

"Please help me!" she cried.

The lead man froze, his eyes and rifle scope directed at her.

Monique felt a strange chill; it was the first time anyone had ever pointed a gun at her. "Don't shoot. I'll turn on a light."

"Do *not* move! Turn off the light. We see you." All three men had weapons trained on her. One shone a bright purple-white beam of light into her eyes.

When she regained her night vision, she saw two rifle barrels inserted through the grate.

"State your name. Why are you inside the wall?"

"I'm Monique. Dr. Raines's personal assistant. I hid from him, to escape. I know where he's gone, and I want to help."

She heard the two men whisper something to each other, then into their microphone. "Claims to know where Raines is. Says she can help." A few seconds later, the guns still pointed into the tunnel, she heard "Copy. Bring her out."

"Who can vouch for you?" the first man asked.

"Amy Wells. Did you save her?"

"Maybe. Anyone else?"

"Alice. She knows me. Can you call them?"

"Stand by. Bravo leader, Red leader. Interrogative, comms with Alpha Whiskey, over? Request you confirm target 'Monique' is friendly."

"Copy," he said moments later. "How do we get you out of there?"

Monique sighed. Had she convinced them of her innocence? She knew in her heart she was anything but innocent in this situation. Malcolm's empire, at least part of it, was her doing. But she believed she was forgiven. And she intended to make a difference now.

"I can crawl out and meet you in the Great Hall," Monique said. "Or you can pull this grate out of the wall. Your choice."

In a few seconds, one of the men slipped a thin rope through the grate holes. Two men tugged, and the ironwork popped free.

I could have done that with my feet weeks ago! she thought. Yet they might never have escaped the compound. This was all part of what Amy called "God's plan." She wished she'd known more of it in advance.

"Copy," the man said again into his microphone. He lowered his weapon and reached into the tunnel to give Monique a hand. "It seems, ma'am, that you're one of the team. Glad to have you on our side." She took his hand, and they pulled her out of the tunnel.

The men stood slightly taller than Monique, their weapons lowered. The lead man spoke first. "Who's left here? What resistance?"

Monique shook her head. "Seven guards, all up in the Great Hall or in the residence areas by now. Everyone else left with Malcolm—Dr. Raines. The guards have pistols. Other than that, no resistance or weapons. This was a place of peace."

He waved his hand toward the overturned furniture. "This is *peace*?"

She shook her head again. "We have to stop them. He's headed for the airport, then to China. With all the girls. We have to save them— before he harvests them."

The second man's jaw dropped. "Body parts? He'd do that?"

"Not exactly. It's complicated. But if he gets to China, it all begins. Can you help?"

"No problem, ma'am." He touched his right ear. "Copy. Target en route to Ljubljana, then to China. Clock's ticking, over."

He gave his hand to Monique. "Can you run?"

"Yes."

"Then we're outta here." He spoke into his microphone. "Red Team. Blue Team. Extract now. Hotel Six Zero on deck three mikes." They dashed into the garden, guiding Monique.

The lead man handed her a rope, passed it around her back, and started to create a sling. Monique waved him off, tugged at the rope, and scaled the wall, leaving the man with his mouth agape as she walked up the side of the stone. She looked back moments later, watching the others follow her up the wall. At the ramparts, she paused, grabbed a pole thrust her way, and slid down like a fireman.

Exactly three minutes later, two black helicopters settled on the grassy knoll, their skids touching the ground only a half a minute. In that brief interlude, Monique and the twenty men behind her leapt into the choppers, and they roared away.

As the aircraft climbed, Monique looked back at the stone steeple, the site of her captivity in Malcolm's bed for six years of weekends, and below it, her place of deliverance less than an hour ago in that same tower's stairway. As the dark compound disappeared in the distance, she felt as though a blot in her life disappeared forever.

I'm free.

MARS

"John?" Nicci asked. "You out there? Important call coming in, it says. NASA wants you in person."

Working in his space suit alongside Rex on the dirt machine, John looked like a futuristic version of a West Virginia strip miner, astride a wheeled version of a combination backhoe and rotary shovel. Dust clouds covered the two men as they ripped away red soil that fell into a chute, moved through the complex wheeled contraption, and emerged as a taffy-like slurry into a trailer filled with troughs that looked like bread loaf pans. Oz and Jake walked behind them, unloading wet bricks from the pans and setting them on a drying rack ten meters in length. The apparatus looked like a bakery full of red Martian loaves set outside to cool.

"I'm coming!" John yelled into his microphone. He dropped a brick and rushed toward the access hatch at the closest tube. "Tell 'em I'm on the way."

A stabbing pain hit him behind the eyes, as it did whenever he was severely stressed. He ignored the warning light on his heads-up display, his heart rate jumping out of the norm. *They might know more about Amy!*

"Comms are coming through now, John. We're gonna patch directly to your suit," Nicci said, her voice quavering. She must know. The next words stopped him in his tracks, his knees buckling as he fell into the soft red talcum-like dust at the airlock to a greenery dome. It was the voice of Greg Church.

"John. I don't know how to say this fancy, but your family's alive and in our custody in northern Italy. They've been found! I repeat," Greg said, his voice elated, "we have Amy and the children safely in the custody of Special Forces. They're alive!" John bent at his waist, hands propped on his knees, his heart rate alarm blaring, tears dripping on his visor. He struggled to hear every word over the thrumming of his heart.

"We can't give you any details at this time, John, for national security reasons. But I'm confirming that your family is on the soil of a US military installation and under close guard. They'll be transported to Washington in three hours."

The voice stopped, the soft whine of his internal circulation fan the only sound beside the staccato drumbeat of his heart in his ears. His every fiber strained for more news.

Thank you, Jesus. Thank you!

"Your family's in good health, John. They had a tough time of it, I can say that. Amazing grit on all their parts, particularly Amy. We can't tell you more about where they were or when you can talk to them, but we expect to soon." John shook his head, trying to dislodge the tears from his eyes despite the visor. He stood and rushed toward the airlock.

John heard Greg cough as he yanked open the door. Like the person on the other end of the comm link was clearing a voice choked with emotion. He jerked the door shut and hit the "pressurize" button, counting the seconds 'til he could remove his helmet and suit.

"Forgot to identify myself. Sorry, Hawk. This is Greg Church. This call reminds me of a time almost seven years ago. We thought you were lost in space, but you made it, man. You got home, and you called us one day to let us know you were all right. Well, it's payback time, Hawk. We get to deliver the good news today.

"Hurry back, pal. Your family's alive, and they're coming home."

NAZARJE, SLOVENIA

Malcolm lowered his head, straining to hear. He leaned into the bulkhead of the small jet as it taxied, trying to screen out the din of the sixty or so chattering teenage girls behind him.

Two girls sat to his right, both still and barely awake, one clutching a picture of a family, the other a teddy bear. Malcolm turned away with a grimace. His bone-weary fatigue and the background noise made the distant but certain voice of the Father Race all the more difficult to hear. They were speaking to him. For the first time in weeks.

You are the Guardian of the Mother Seed. We trusted you with another mission, to watch over an enemy of the Remnant. You have failed. Do not fail us with the Mother Seed. The future of mankind, and your future, depends on them. Bring forth the Harvest on time!

The quiet voice with its nearly impossible demands disappeared. He strained to hear more, but the din was too great. Raines settled into his seat as the plane accelerated for takeoff.

The Americans! They'd done this to him.

Who knew what else might have transpired if he hadn't escaped the compound? Malcolm looked at the empty seat next to him, reflecting on the words still echoing in his head. *Where's Monique? They must've taken her.*

She'd been his constant companion, since the first words he'd heard from the Father Race years ago. Now he was alone. Malcolm felt the nervous sweat build up under his robe as he wondered what lay ahead. The Americans had to know he was on the run. Surely they'd decipher where he was headed.

Do not fail . . . your future depends on it.

There were no other options. He had to continue to China.

I must gain favor with the Father Race. Soon I will be one with them.

NATIONAL MILITARY COMMAND CENTER, THE PENTAGON

"Got him!" Kerry snapped his phone closed. He checked a message on his PDD and clipped it back to his hip. "Raines's call just came in!"

Shawnda and her boss, old man McClannahan, stepped over to

hear more. The Secret Service agent, who, Kerry had noticed, hadn't said a word all night, skirted the edge of their group.

"Where?" Shawnda asked. "Did you get a trace?"

"Yep. This time the call initiated with a cellular in the Seattle area. It's always originated from the west coast. We've got agents there now. Tracking it down."

"The Father Race is from Washington State, huh?" Walter McClannahan asked.

"Got the transcript here on e-mail," Kerry said, smiling as he handed his PDD to Mr. McClannahan. "Seems the Father Race is a little perturbed by recent developments." He looked at Shawnda. "Our guess was right, girl. One call to NASA, and Mr. Father Race figured it out." He tapped the PDD's screen. "Either they're listening in on NASA frequencies, or there's a mole in Houston."

"And you can bet it's the latter," Shawnda said. "Now we need to find the caller."

"Or," Kerry said, "NASA's mole."

30

SPECIAL FORCES SOLDIERS in black stood guard every ten meters across the access to the massive hangar as ground crews pulled in two black "Night Stalker" helicopters. More military police in small white trucks, red and blue lights flashing, provided a second layer of defense at the edge of the parking ramp.

All for us, Amy thought as she stood at the back of the hangar.

Nearly thirty people, all of them dressed in black, filled the cavernous room, positioning the two helicopters that had plucked Amy and her children from Nazarje a few hours earlier. Two more black helicopters alighted inside the security perimeter, and more warriors piled out, weapons at the ready. Exiting with them was a woman clad in a black skin suit.

As the helicopter shut down, the woman ran from under the rotor downwash, her long tresses blowing about her, a warrior at each elbow.

They ran into the hangar followed by a line of men. Colonel Scales joined them and headed toward Amy, who stood with her children at the entrance to the "Night Stalker" ready room.

Amy could barely grasp her surroundings. Bright sodium lamps buzzed above her, brilliantly flooding the hangar with an eerie yellow light. White concrete floors, black-clad men, and black aircraft at night—the set for a Rambo movie.

But this was real life. Hers.

Monique? Amy wondered, as the black line ran toward her. She'd seen only Monique's face before. This woman looked like a superhero in black tights, muscles rippling as she strode beside Colonel Scales. Her eyes were locked on Amy's.

The woman approached, then extended her hand toward Amy. "I'm Monique." She stood a head taller than Amy, but the tears on her cheeks softened her otherwise intimidating mien.

"Monique?" Amy exclaimed, recognizing the face at last, but not the body. "You made it!" Eyes glistening with joy, she wrapped her arms about her new friend. "We prayed for you from the moment we realized you weren't with us. We thought you'd arranged this!"

Alice, a few meters away talking with Abe, screamed, "You got away!" and collided with the two of them in a joyous threesome.

Monique nodded, a smile diverting her stream of tears. She pulled them both close and rested her head atop Amy's. "Thank God I found you." Their tall friend held them tight, stammering words of overwhelming relief and joy. Over and over she exclaimed, with a squeeze each time for Amy and Alice, "We're free!"

Amy finally pulled away and took Monique's hand. "Do you remember that compact I asked for?"

"Yes." Monique wiped her eyes with the back of her sleeve. "I dropped it . . . into the garden."

"Did you ever look at our garden? I mean, really pay attention to it?"

"No. It was green. Pretty." She tried to smile; red puffy eyes and swollen cheeks changed her face. She was more vulnerable than Amy had ever seen her.

"I planted mine with cabbages in the shape of a cross. The boys planted theirs with three lines—an SOS signal of three dots, three dashes, and three dots. Raines never noticed, I guess. I used your mirror with the morning sun to signal airplanes. Like John told me he used to do in survival training. Finally the military saw us. Early this morning these men came over the wall and whisked us away. In about a minute. It was amazing!"

"What about you, Monique?" Alice asked again. "What happened when we left?"

Monique's chin and lips quivered, and Amy squeezed her hand. A determined look hardened Monique's features, and she stared beyond Amy. "The power failed late at night, and the guards woke us. They went to check on you, but you were gone. They tore your room apart, then they found a video bug shaped like a rock in the corner of your garden. Malcolm was furious and demanded that we flee from the compound."

Her head drooped. "He took all the girls. He's gone—headed to Ljubljana, and from there to China. He's determined to complete the Harvest." More tears ran down Monique's face, and Amy handed her a napkin. "I couldn't stop them. The girls *want* him. They *want* to be with him and serve him. It's my fault."

Amy took her hand again and held it tight, praying silently for God to give her friend strength.

"How'd you get away?" Alice asked. "What about Raines?"

"We gathered in the Great Hall. I was supposed to follow at the rear. He led them down a secret tunnel to buses headed for the airport. It made me sick to watch them blindly follow him. I ran into the tower stairs and threw up." She took Alice's hand and pulled both of them close. "I prayed!" she whispered.

Amy squeezed her hand again. *Oh, God, thank you!*

"I was so desperate to be free of Malcolm. I wanted the peace I saw in you, Amy. The more I prayed, the more I realized I want what you have. Not just freedom from the compound, but *real* freedom—from my past." A huge smile broke through. "I asked Him to forgive me."

The three women hugged for a long moment.

Monique released Alice and gestured at the room. "Later, I heard these men coming into the compound. I told them who I was. Then they called you to check out my story." She looked into Amy's eyes. "You saved me, Amy. When the soldiers called, you spoke up for me."

"That's the way it is with God," Amy said with a huge smile. "He claims us as His own."

The colonel loomed over Monique, a full head taller. Larger than life and taller than any of his men. He was a black Borg, bristling with electronic equipment and battle paraphernalia. His heavy eyebrows curled over gentle green eyes; a smile curved like a "U" over his blocky chin. He was a paradox—Black Death topped with a caring face. He took Monique's extended hand. Amy well knew the strength in his grip.

"I'm Colonel Scales," he said to Monique. "You're lucky you climbed into that air duct. My men never would have found you otherwise."

"It wasn't an accident." Monique turned and winked at Amy. "It was part of His plan."

"Raines? How?"

Monique shook her head and released the colonel's grip. "That wasn't what I meant. Malcolm's headed to the capital. He has a Boeing 767 waiting for him there. I set it up through our contacts in France. I've got all the flight data. The pilots will take him—and all of the Mother Seed—to China. To Ürümqi. We've got to stop him."

Colonel Scales looked at his watch. "I know about the flight. He's on the tarmac in Ljubljana now. We tracked six regional jets departing the Nazarje strip and followed them by radar to the capital. He'll be in that 767 soon." The colonel waved at another soldier. "Get me a line to Admiral Gray."

"Right away, Colonel."

He turned back to Monique. "Why China? Ürümqi's at the top of the country. Pretty remote place."

"He has another compound there, Colonel. A fully equipped residence like the one they just left. But much bigger." Amy noticed the twitch in Monique's cheek. "He has horrible plans."

"We assumed as much. Amy told us something about it," the colonel said. "Some kind of perfected race thing."

Monique moved forward, her hands clasped together. "Colonel. The Harvest is scheduled in four days. It would be a tragedy to let it proceed."

Colonel Scales nodded. "I'll do what I can. It's in Washington's hands now. But," he said, pointing at his men, "we're ready to nab him, if they'll just give us the word."

He looked back to Monique, sporting a wry grin. "If you want to help, though, there *is* something you can do." He unclipped a radio from his web harness and handed it to her. "We can contact Raines . . . if you're willing."

✦

"I want to call John. Is there any possible way?" Amy asked, minutes after Colonel Scales introduced her to Admiral Gray, the commander of their joint team. He was a short, wiry man with tight skin over a bony face and penetrating eyes.

"I asked about calling John, Mrs. Wells. They said 'yes.'" Admiral Gray smiled, one side of his mouth curling higher than the other. A dimple grew with his grin. She could tell he was glad to deliver that news. "You can use this phone." He handed her a miniature cellular.

"If you'd like some privacy, use that side room." He pointed to the far wall of the "Night Stalker" ready room. "One of my men will stand guard with you. For security purposes." He paused. "You can't say anything about Slovenia, or Raines. Please. Not yet."

He waved to an airman. "Help Mrs. Wells with anything she needs with this call, Shelby. Then get the six of them off to the doc. For their physicals."

Colonel Scales spoke up as he approached them, buckling a package onto his black web belt. "Seems Washington has a new target for us, ma'am," he said, his eyes twinkling. "I think you'll be pleased. We have to leave right away." He nodded to the admiral, then extended his hand. She took it in both of hers.

"Colonel, I owe you my life and the lives of my family."

"This was a night my men won't soon forget, Amy. It was an honor." When she let go, the colonel came to attention, saluting her, Alice, and Monique. "Say hello to John. He'll remember me." Colonel Scales winked at her. "He knows what we do." Without another word, he saluted the admiral, then turned and walked briskly out of the debriefing area, talking into a small radio. Most of his men followed.

"I'm Petty Officer Shelby, ma'am," a young man, Abe's age, said from behind her. "I'll be joining you. This way."

"Just a moment, please." Amy touched the young man's arm. She watched Colonel Scales jog toward a black helicopter, its rotors already spinning. A dozen armed men were rushing from the hangar behind him, and ground crews were frantically pulling away tie downs and tossing black bags into the helo. Moments later, engines whined, and the craft lifted, blades whipping the air. As it headed into the breaking dawn, he saluted them all again from his seat near the open door.

✳

They talk on these things? It's so small! Inside the private room, Amy's hand shook as she tried to dial the number the petty officer gave her. The tiny buttons were hard to control, and she dialed four times before getting the sequence right. The young man said it was a Houston-area number. Probably NASA. After three rings, a familiar voice answered.

"Mars Mission Control. Dodd Marsh speaking."

"Dodd?" Amy's voice cracked. "Dodd Marsh?" It was déjà vu. Just like calling Mars Mission Control during John's first trip to Mars years ago. She'd checked in several times a day to hear if there'd been any word from her husband, lost for more than six months in deep space. How times had changed. John was still gone—but who was lost?

"This is Dodd Marsh. Who's this?"

"Dodd. It's *Amy*. Amy Wells."

"Amy? What? I thought you were . . . oh no—I mean—wow! You *are* alive! I thought that last call from the Pentagon was a prank." She heard him yell at someone in Mission Control, probably telling the world she was on the line. She didn't care. "How can I help? Anything. I mean, I don't even know where you are."

"Dodd!" She fought the sobs crawling up her throat. "I—I want to talk to John."

SOUTH OF LJUBLJANA, SLOVENIA

"Another, sir?" the flight attendant asked. The woman deferred to him in a way no one, not even Monique, had for months. It felt good. She plumped up the pillow behind his head after she'd given him a second glass of wine.

A pilot walked back from the cockpit, four epaulets on his shoulder and a set of gold wings pinned to his chest. "Father Raines?"

"Yes?" Malcolm said. He liked what he saw. The man had chiseled features, like a retired military pilot might. Monique always found the best.

"I have a message for you, sir."

"How? I mean, from whom?"

"The tower, sir. As we were climbing out of Ljubljana." He handed the message to Malcolm, written in plain block letters.

Malcolm unfolded the note.

Went back for medical records of the Mother Seed. Missed you. Have arranged separate transport to Heavenly Home. In your service, blessed Father. Monique.

Malcolm stared in wonder at the message. During the past hours en route from Nazarje, he'd imagined all manner of mistakes and accidents. The more he'd thought about her, the more furious he'd become, presuming her defection from his ranks or her demise at the hands of the Americans. Both options enraged him.

The note was classic Monique—terse, to the point—and worshipful. She was working behind the scenes, completing her assignments, loyal to the Father Race, even when they were both being pursued . . . and she'd been left behind.

Malcolm forgot her imagined failings and folded the note. With a sigh of relief, he reclined in his seat and swirled the fresh glass of wine. The Harvest would occur on time. And she'd be with him again. Soon.

The Father Race will be pleased.

AVIANO AIR FORCE BASE, ITALY

"Mom?" Alice asked, holding a miniature glucometer. "The doctor gave me this. He wants to see you, to check your numbers." She took Amy's shaking hand. "I told him you were about to talk to Dad." Her voice squeaked, her own hand shaking as she tried to test Amy's blood sugar. "Is Dad—is he on yet?"

Amy shook her head, feeling chilled despite the fact that there were three of them in the small space—her, Alice, and Petty Officer Shelby. A shiver ran through her, the anticipation of years coming down to this very moment. *How many times did I pray for this very day?*

"You're low, Mom," Alice said, handing her another of the chewy bars the soldier had offered back in Slovenia. "You need to eat. For all of us, okay?"

Amy nodded. "Where're the boys?"

Alice smiled. "They're not boys any more, Mom. Maybe you noticed."

She's right. It was hard to accept. Abe was a man, Arthur very nearly twenty, and Albert was hot on their heels, all of them tall drinks of water. "Are they outside?"

"Waiting for their turn. They wanted you to have some private time first." She looked at the petty officer. "Is it private?"

"I'm sorry, ma'am." He looked down, then shook his head. "I need to stay with you. To listen and advise."

Amy touched Alice on the arm. "Tell the boys a minute, all right?"

Alice nodded and left, glancing at the young Navy man.

The phone speaker chirped, and Dodd Marsh came back on line. "Amy? You still there?"

She turned off the speaker function and put the phone to her ear, her hand shaking so badly she had difficulty holding the small earpiece in just the right place. "I'm here! John? Are you there?"

"Amy, he can't answer you right away. It's eleven minutes one way transit tonight, and another eleven back. So, you'll need to talk to him for a few minutes, and then we'll wait for his response twenty-two minutes later. Okay?"

Her heart sank. She knew this, but in the rush of the moment, she'd wanted so to hear him say "I love you," right after she did. That couldn't happen. Not tonight. "Okay, Dodd. I understand. When do I start?"

"Any time. The link is live to Mars. He's all yours."

MARS

"He's all yours," John heard over the speaker.

She's alive!

John's heart was thumping like a rabbit's as he sat in the operations control compartment near the Hab Two dining area. Dodd's preparation and Amy's sweet voice were already winging their way past Mars, but she didn't realize he'd heard her.

He waited for the magic moment, her first words to him. Like raising a modern Lazarus, God had restored his wife and kids to him — at least, restored them on Earth, many months and hundreds of millions of kilometers away. But he'd be with them soon. He touched his throat, thinking that if he could concentrate on his wild heart rate, it might slow.

"John? It's Amy. Oh dear God, I wish I could hold you right now and talk to you face to face. But it's me! I'm okay. We all are. Can you hear me?"

Keep talking!

"I hate this one-way conversation, but there's so much to tell you. I can't talk about what happened, I guess. They don't want me to yet. Security and all. But we were found, John. You remember Terrance Kerry and his wife Shawnda? They figured it out, that we weren't in that helicopter. And then when they talked to you, well, they started looking in the right places." She laughed.

Amy, in the midst of all this stress, can be happy? Praise God!

"Remember how you told me you signaled airplanes in—oh, I'm sorry. I understand. Yes. Okay."

What's happening?

"I wish I could tell you all the details, John, but what's really important is that I know somehow we'll be together again. Oh, I'm supposed to tell you hello from Joe Scales. He's a colonel. I can't say what happened, but I guess I can say—I can?—I can say he wanted me to tell you hello and that he found us, John! And that you know what he does. It was so amazing!

"John, I love you. I need to hear your voice. We all do." The transmission ended.

Now it was his turn.

31

MALCOLM FINISHED HIS third glass of wine and reclined in the chartered airliner's first-class accommodations. Flight attendants pulled window shades against the coming day, creating a restful atmosphere for his staff and the girls. He fought to keep his eyes open, fatigue pulling him down into the plush seat like a whirlpool capturing a fish. He was sinking deeper in the soft pillow when his guilt got the better of him.

He rose.

Struggling against the effects of the wine and the lack of sleep, Malcolm strolled the aisle, checking on the girls and conversing with the rare staff member still awake. Virtually all of the passengers, including most of the Mother Seed, had drifted off to sleep.

"They're resting well, sir," a voice said behind him as he reached the rear galley. He turned to face the same pilot who'd delivered Monique's message an hour earlier.

"I have the flight plan and route if you'd like to review it, sir." The pilot offered a glossy folder and package of papers with the annotated, computer-generated flight plan Malcolm was accustomed to.

Malcolm nodded, paging through the material. "Why are we traveling south to go east, captain?" he asked, pointing to the route south from Slovenia, over the Adriatic Sea, then east through the Mediterranean Sea toward Israel.

The pilot shook his head. "We couldn't get clearance over Russia on short notice, sir. We have to follow the Med, then cut up over the Middle East. When we pass Lebanon, we'll deviate northeast into China. Adds about a thousand kilometers to the trip."

Malcolm frowned, dreading thirteen hours in the air. He handed the package back to the pilot with a yawn and pushed around him to head back to his seat. He felt an overwhelming need for sleep; the wine had done its job well.

As Malcolm passed their seats on the way back to his recliner, he checked the cuff restraints on the only two girls in first class, asleep to his right. The sedatives had worked well. Number 217 and the Edwards girl weren't his first problem children, but they'd definitely proven the most troublesome.

As a flight attendant pulled a blanket over him and extinguished the overhead lights in the cabin, Malcolm took one more glance over his shoulder at his flock. Before slipping into slumber, he imagined the internal clocks of the hundreds of young women behind him marching steadily forward to produce the precious genetic material he needed to accomplish his objective.

Soon. Very soon, his mission for the blessed Father Race would reach its consummation.

NATIONAL MILITARY COMMAND CENTER, THE PENTAGON

"We've got a good track on his aircraft," an intelligence analyst said to the assembled crowd at the NMCC. Kerry wondered how they could fit any more people into this concrete complex's crowded basement operations center. More support personnel arrived hourly, and Kerry had been here for hours already. Analysts and intelligence officers seemed to flow in from some endless wellspring of fatigue-clad spooks, each delivering a special surprise or extra bit of intelligence.

He was galled by the track of Raines's aircraft toward China. In twelve or thirteen hours, if they didn't take some action, his quarry would be home free—behind the impenetrable politics of the People's Republic of China.

"You holding together?" Shawnda asked, walking up with a handful of papers. She'd been conferring with other CIA analysts, part of this multi-agency team at the command center deep inside the Pentagon. "I know it's late, sweetheart."

Kerry shrugged. He'd completely forgotten the time. His mind was on the plane with Raines, imagining the sun already up in the Balkans and the preacher rejoicing at his great escape. Amy's call, her personal thank you to him and Shawnda half an hour ago, had so energized him—and filled him with dread for those hundreds of girls—that he couldn't imagine sleeping. Not now. Not until he saw Raines brought to justice.

"Any more on the tooth?" Shawnda held papers to her chest as though she didn't want him to see what she was working on. That's the way it sometimes was in their marriage, but somehow they balanced the odd competition for intelligence supremacy.

"An hour ago. Just before he would've taken off. He got a strong message about guarding the Mother Seed, but nothing else. Did the call we made to NASA set up that tooth transmission to Raines? Maybe. We still don't know where the leak is."

"They could be using code," Shawnda said. "Maybe the calls are someone's way of cueing him."

"Might be. But my gut says 'no.' We called NASA first, right? Told 'em we'd found Amy and she was on the way to safety. Didn't tell 'em where. Right after that, I mean within minutes, the Father Race gets on the party line and starts yakking. Sounded real mad."

She nodded. "Go on."

"Now Amy's talking to John. I'll bet you dinner Raines gets another call. But not 'til after he lands."

"Why? Why not try to reach him now?"

"'Cause he's airborne, over the Adriatic, turning east soon. Probably can't get a cell signal out over the water. If this really was some alien god whispering to Raines, he'd hear from 'em any old time, right? But you watch. Someone knows his schedule even better than we do, and they'll call right after he's on the ground. They'll gush about his success moving those girls, and his success in avoiding us. They'll feed his ego. It fits the model. I've seen it a dozen times before."

"When?"

"When someone's manipulating a patsy."

Shawnda raised an eyebrow. "Makes sense, I guess. You're on, by the way. For that bet. If I win—no call to Raines—you take me to the Peking Gourmet Inn in Bailey's Crossroads next time we're off."

"I won't lose. But when I win, you share some of those CIA papers with me. You're clutching 'em like they might help my case."

Shawnda cocked her head to one side, turning to shield her papers. "No deal, Special Agent man. Gotta go! Love ya." She took a few steps, then turned around to face him.

Kerry watched her. *Why so coy?*

.

"I have an idea," she said with that pixie smile she got when on the trail of some important data. Shawnda set the papers down, selected her PDD's calendar function, and tapped a date on the screen. "May 22 was the date Amy said this 'harvest' thing is supposed to happen, right?"

He nodded again, shuddering at the image of all those young women blindly producing eggs for Raines to make hundreds more clones of themselves. Amy's call minutes ago had provided more detail about Raines and his intentions than Kerry cared to know.

"We need a party," she said. "Something for them to celebrate."

"Are you sick?" he asked.

"No. But *they* are. And we—*you*—can use that to find your mole. Throw a Harvest celebration and invite all the kooks. You might just net the person you're after. Like an FBI sting offering unclaimed tax refunds. That sort of thing."

My wife is nuts.

"Don't look at me that way, Terrance. I mean it. Throw a party. These are people who really get into the fertility rites thing, right? New moon coming up, gonna harvest us some ova from a few hundred girls. We've got them all safe in China. Hoorah! Worthy of a celebration, I think. Hold the party near Johnson Space Center, and another maybe out at the Jet Propulsion Labs in Pasadena. They'll come, and I'll bet one of them is your man—or woman."

"How'll we know we've got our target?"

Shawnda shrugged and flashed her pixie grin again. "Haven't figured that part out yet."

The concept was revolting, celebrating the retrieval of thousands of eggs from the hyper-stimulated ovaries of young girls. But Kerry saw the wisdom of his wife's idea. He smiled and patted her on the shoulder, then headed toward the FBI cell in the NMCC. "Brilliant, Shawnda. Just brilliant."

She smiled as he left. He thought he heard her make a comment but had no time to check. Something sassy like, "I know."

MARS

Melanie walked up beside him as John stood staring out a meter-wide portal in the Lab module toward the colony. Even on the structure's metal grating, she had a delicate and familiar walk, and her perfume's gentle scent also gave her away. She made him feel whole, and he was glad she was there. John turned and smiled. "Thanks for coming up, Mel."

She nodded and gazed out with him at the vast complex they'd helped the colonists establish. The new domes glistened in their array around his Hab modules. "You okay? That must've been an amazing call. With Amy."

He nodded, unable to describe his feelings. Amy alive! His family safe! This day couldn't get any more gloriously shocking.

"Anything I can do?" she asked. She gathered thick hair with both hands and clipped it while she talked. Her eyes reminded him of *The Little Mermaid*, bright and inviting. They dominated her soft features.

He smiled for the hundredth time in the past three hours, his face cramped from grins since his wife spoke to him across a hundred fifty million kilometers and six years, literally returned from the dead. And his children, each telling their stories for a few minutes, then waiting nearly half an hour for his response.

John shook his head. "Nothing I need now except a fast trip off this planet." He put a hand on Melanie's shoulder, at his chest level. She was definitely the shortest person on his crew, yet she stood taller than any of the others in her care and her leadership of this band of egocentric spacefarers. "Thanks for being such a good friend, Mel. I couldn't have gotten through these months on Mars without you. We've had some special times. And conquered some wicked challenges."

John started to pull her into a hug then thought better of it. She moved toward him as he raised his arms, then stopped mid-stride when he backed up, blushing in the awkward moment. They both turned back toward the portal where the dusty red plain stretched beyond the green of the habitat domes under a salmon sky.

"What will you do?" she asked after a long pause. "When you get home?"

"Retire. It's time to move on and spend the rest of my time with Amy. We talked about that. Maybe we'll move to Maine—someplace cool. Amy's always wanted out of Texas. She calls it 'the world's largest vacant lot.'"

"Did she say what happened to her? If it's okay to ask, that is," Melanie said softly.

John shook his head again. "Nothing. She's with the Special Forces, which tells me someone's in a great deal of trouble. Friend of mine, Joe Scales, brought her out—of wherever. You don't want to tangle with Joe or his men. Hope he nails 'em."

"No more paddles, John," she reminded him, an obvious reference to his attempt to kill Elias Ulrich.

Anger rose in John in volcanic spurts, hot waves in his throat as he imagined what he'd do to the person responsible for kidnapping his family and faking their deaths. What Ulrich got—a broken skull, a near drowning from John, then a bullet through the head from the FBI—would be too light a sentence for the person who stole his family. The anger tied his stomach in knots.

"I'm serious. No paddles," Melanie said. "Remember the verses about vengeance?"

He nodded, staring straight ahead. John wished he could ignore her message, but it rooted in his heart. He needed to forgive—to move on—and to be with Amy.

Sachiko was visible inside a distant greenery dome, standing by her strawberries. Elevated stacks of white plastic hydroponics beds rotated before her, six levels of berries as tall as she, with green and red spilling out of each water-fed level. She would be snipping the berries off into a pail using a pair of scissors.

"No revenge. I promise." John turned from the window and sat down at a table. Melanie followed. "It's strange, Mel. No one's talking about this yet. About where she was, or why she was taken. She couldn't even discuss it on a covered comm link."

"She didn't say *anything* about it?"

"Nothing. Someone was coaching her on what she could tell me."

"They're probably trailing the culprit. Maybe they don't want to give anything away. Or don't want NASA to know."

"Well, if they are on his tail, I hope they hang him before I get home." He smiled at Mel across the table as he opened a packet of juice. "Or I might have to swing that paddle again."

"You promised," Melanie said, wagging a finger at him. "Besides, it could be a her. Would you whack a female, too? I mean, you never know," she said, spinning another juice packet on the plastic table. "It could've been a woman that kidnapped your wife. A *jealous* woman."

OVER THE ATLANTIC COAST

"We'll be landing at Andrews Air Force Base in half an hour, ma'am," the Air Force Senior Master Sergeant said, moving down the aisle of the small military jet. Amy, the children, and Monique were racing across the Atlantic to America, safely together in the most luxurious accommodations they'd seen in six years. Damp cells, colossal walls, and Slovenia were seven hours and an entire ocean behind them.

Amy watched out the window as the coast of New Jersey faded into Maryland and the jet screamed south down the eastern seaboard. Green hills and fields were reminiscent of her tiny world at the monastery. She'd never seen Slovenia's hilltop churches and verdant fields, which Monique had described to her . . . only the inside of a gray stone wall, her dirt, and her vegetables.

The fields rolled by like a visual dessert, green upon green, then the dull brown of the bay waters east of Andrews Air Force Base. John would see green soon, too, she hoped. After two years of rust-red dirt, gray and black jagged rocks, and white habitations and space suits, he would soon rejoin Earth's blue, green, and brown. The two were emerging from drab visual prisons to rediscover Earth's beauty together.

White boats dotted the shoreline, glistening in the morning sun, a sun she'd chased all the way from Slovenia. Amy wiped tears from her eyes but kept her gaze locked on the ground. She watched houses and cars, imagining families living out a normal quiet existence as she yearned to recapture that lost part of her life. She tried to hang on to the memory she'd held so long of John cradling and cooing at baby Alice, his flattop haircut and bushy eyebrows dominating a gentle, lanky face.

As they approached Andrews Air Force Base, the image of John and baby Alice faded and vanished. After a panicky moment, it seemed best to Amy to let go of the memory that had sustained her for six years. Alice was no longer an infant. She and John were no longer young. It was time to make new memories.

She would form a new image of John, one of him returning to her, from Mars. Stepping from his capsule into her arms. Forever.

It was an image that would last her the rest of her life.

32

"WELCOME TO THE YIN DU Hotel, Ms. Packard." A perfectly coiffed young Asian woman handed the room key and welcome package to Adrienne. "I trust you will enjoy your stay."

"Can I leave a message for one of your guests?" Adrienne asked. She pulled out a pen and her journalist pad. "For Father Malcolm Raines. I'm covering his press conference."

"I will deliver the message," the clerk said with a courteous smile.

Adrienne tucked her pad away and examined the luxury hotel. Nestled in a city in northwest China said to be farthest from the ocean of any major city, the Yin Du's opulence was breathtaking. The lobby swarmed with activity, all focused on today's big event, and priests of Saint Michael's Remnant scurried everywhere.

There must be a hundred of them.

Gaunt men, every one, with heads shaved smooth except for a long mane erupting from the top of each scalp, bound by a tight purple band.

They look like human mops. Maybe they glue on the wigs.

Purple was the color of the day here, with long crushed velvet banners cascading from the rafters of a cavernous ceiling. Purple roses—a flower she'd never encountered—filled vases on antique Chinese plant stands.

Suspended from the lobby ceiling by hidden wires, a four-meter-diameter model of a galaxy rotated in slow motion. Like a giant pinwheel, brilliant glowing clusters of lights made up a dense core, with glowing wisps of lights flaring out as the vanes. Near the end of one wispy vane shone a distinct point of light, stark purple against the other stars' bright white. Adrienne marveled at the galaxy. It seemed to hang magically in the air.

"Our galaxy," a man said behind her. Adrienne turned to face a mop-head, his body as emaciated as Jews in German prison camps. Cheekbones in a long face poked out under tight skin; his eyes were almost hollow.

Ascetics, she thought. *The extreme of self denial.*

She'd learned more about Saint Michael's Remnant than she cared to know since her visit to Mont Saint Michel with Rex Edwards years ago. Their Gnostic underpinnings of asceticism, to the point of mutilation and near starvation, seeking to achieve spiritual enlightenment, were the stuff of legend. Until now. She was face-to-face with a body-hater—her name for the practice.

Strange, she thought. *Raines doesn't starve himself. He's the Head Cheese.*

"This is the Milky Way, and we're there." He pointed to the purple dot far out on one wisp. "On this tiny scale—a Milky Way galaxy small enough for two men to lift—the limit of our known Universe extends one hundred million kilometers from where we're standing. More than halfway to Mars. Remarkable, isn't it?" The paper thin man stared in awe at the twirling array of brilliant lights.

He worships this. "Fantastic," Adrienne responded, unsure whether to coo or say "aahhh!" "And you are?" She extended a thin hand.

"Servant William." He bowed, but refused to take her hand. "Welcome to Ürümqi."

Before she could probe more, the body-hater disappeared into a mass of other skinny purple mop-heads bustling about on tasks for their master. Adrienne shuddered. Raines held remarkable power over his people, not just with their money, but also their voluntary self-destructive practices.

I'd hardly have believed this without seeing it for myself.

Half an hour later, after browsing the ornate lobby, Adrienne stepped into her room, also lavish. Her veranda looked southeast and the view revealed that her mental image of Ürümqi was incorrect. She was thousands of kilometers from anything she thought of as civilized, yet this was a modern city, a crossroads for Indian, Chinese, European, and other Asian cultures . . . a true Asian melting pot.

To the south, the Heavenly Mountain — Tianshan — soared like a silver cone into a crisp blue sky. The lower slopes were green, even from this distance. Deep in those mountains was Heavenly Lake, the Pearl of Heavenly Mountain. And at the base of that peak, on the shores of the crystal clear, snow-fed lake, Raines's newest compound waited for its famous residents: hundreds of young women and Father Raines. She determined to see it.

Adrienne turned from the view to answer a knock. An elegant Asian girl stood in the open doorway, her black hair in a single long ponytail, held by fluffy red elastic. Her skin-tight bodysuit left no question about her exquisite tone.

"Hello, Ms. Packard. I am Xi Wang Mu, the Guardian's aide. Father Raines wanted me to answer your note. In person."

Adrienne was shocked. The girl's attire was the same as Monique's, but she was distinctly Chinese. Like Monique, this lady was black, red, athletic—and terse.

"Hello Ms. Mu. Thanks for coming by. Is Monique here?"

"No. She remains in Slovenia on business. She is solving problems related to the move, we've been told. Father Raines extends his warmest greetings and thanks you for your trip to China to share in the great day. However—"

"He can't meet. Right?" Adrienne was sure that if Monique were here, she'd get that audience.

"That is correct. Perhaps another time." The Lycra Lady turned to leave.

"Xi Wang. Before you go. I understand about his schedule, but I flew from California across thirteen time zones to reach this place. Surely—"

"I appreciate your sacrifice, Ms. Packard, but our singular focus—from which we cannot swerve—is to accomplish the Harvest. We are on the eve of that great day. He cannot grant you an audience at this time."

With that, the woman left, vanishing like steam. When Adrienne stepped into the hall, she was nowhere to be seen.

Adrienne closed the door and locked it, overcome by a sudden chill—a sense of trouble, like the first time she'd met Rex Edwards in his remarkable glass cupola that hung from the ceiling of his aerospace plant. Also when she'd dined with Rex and Father Raines in the preacher's special suite on Mont Saint Michel the week of the Great Awakening, as he'd called it. Each time she'd felt that same eerie "something's not quite right." She reviewed the girl's words, stopping at the one she'd never heard before.

The "harvest."

It bore no connection to anything she'd ever heard from Raines before. Adrienne searched out her computer; within minutes she tapped into the Web, drilling down into this possible slip of the tongue by Xi Wang Mu.

MARS

John paged through his Bible in the privacy of the MSR. It was the only semi-secure location he could find in their Martian settlement to speak again with Amy—in private.

Each talk with her brought him to tears—for her, for their separation, for the lost years of their lives together. She'd be talking with him again in another hour—words delayed eleven minutes each way. His fingers rubbed the gold-gilded edges of a copy of *The Message*, a Bible Amy had given him years ago, after his first space mission. He opened it to Paul's letter to the Colossians, where the first words he saw tugged at him: "God rescued us from dead-end alleys and dark dungeons. He's set us up in the kingdom of the Son he loves so much, the Son who got us out of the pit we were in, got rid of the sins we were doomed to keep repeating."

Like a siren, the verse spoke to a question in John's spirit—one Amy had not yet answered: "Where have you been?" John had asked her repeatedly, but she always answered that nice men were there advising her about what she could and couldn't say. He had no idea what had happened to Amy and their children, or where they had all been. The information vacuum gnawed at him.

Every call was another opportunity to express their love for each other and for her to share wonderful news of his growing children. But there was no closure, none of the information he so desperately needed about where she'd been—*and why.*

John was wired to repair things. He didn't want to *talk* about the problem. He wanted to *fix* it. And part of him ached to exact revenge on whoever had done this to him—and to his loved ones. Yet the last words of that verse struck him each time he read them. ". . . rid of the sins we were doomed to keep repeating."

His thoughts drifted to that instant of red rage when he'd cracked the skull of a stranger with a vicious blow that had sent Ulrich to the depths of the Pentagon marina.

Because he killed my family.

Sudden panic gripped John. He panted, trying to get a breath. His heart felt first like it was sinking, then ripped out of him—like something sapped everything good about him out of his soul. A banner of searing shame stretched across his mind's eye, followed by deep remorse.

My family was alive when I attacked him!

John had never asked Elias Ulrich, "Did you kill my wife and kids?" He'd assumed it was so. And he took that first deadly swipe at Ulrich—not even sure who his target was as the man emerged in diving gear from the Potomac—a deadly swing of the paddle with every intent to kill.

Now John lusted for the blood of the man—or woman—who'd robbed the last six years of his and his family's life. Hundreds of times he'd allowed himself to fantasize strangling the life out of that person. He'd dreamt these last hours of his hands about that person's throat, watching the life die out in their eyes, like the joy had seeped away in his own life since Amy's death. He'd indulged in mental murder. Over and over.

Kill again?

The words on the page welled up like water to drown the raging fire in him . . . "the Son who got us out of the pit we were in, got rid of the sins we were doomed to keep repeating."

Wet eyes, dripping shame, he searched for more insights in his Bible. He found them, a little further. "Forgive as quickly and completely as the Master forgave you. And regardless of what else you put on, wear love. It's your basic, all-purpose garment. Never be without it."

"Forgive . . . " He laid the Bible down and stared out the rover's cockpit window toward the distant red plains. "I'm in a pit, Lord," he wept. "Everything in me wants revenge. And I'm wrong."

He bowed his head over the console. Tears dripped on the tan plastic surface and ran off onto a Mars-dusted floor at his feet. "You've lifted me from a pit, Lord. I want to have that strength, that glory-strength you talk about. I want to move on. I've got to. Pull me up, Jesus. Don't let me wallow in this sin anymore." He buried his face in his hands. "Please forgive me, Jesus. I took the life . . . of a man because . . . because I thought he killed my family. But they were never dead."

MARS

"We had strawberry pie last night!" John exclaimed an hour later during his one-way dialogue with Amy. Soon he'd get to listen to her sweet voice. He felt clean and at peace. Happy. Even joyful—for the first time in six years. Restored and forgiven.

My family is months away. But they're safe. And it's okay.

John had come to grips with himself at last. He'd given the last thing into God's hands. There was no fast way home, no magic incantation to make Mars line up with Earth so they could fly faster. He couldn't help bring the culprit to justice that had brought such ruin to their lives. He couldn't do anything to care for Amy and the kids now, other than talk to them, pray for them, and share his love for them. Life was out of his control. For the first time in years, maybe his whole life, John understood that. It was in God's hands. The vengeance, too.

"Kate, Nicci, Sachiko, and May are spoiling us. We had a huge fish bake to celebrate your first radio call. They cooked tilapia, zucchini, and yellow-neck squash, with a salad, and fruit for dessert. You wouldn't believe their garden.

"Rex is the man of the colony, for sure. We get a chance to talk every so often, usually about engineering stuff. He's one smart kid. If we modify our fuel load, his dad and I think we can leave a few days earlier. Don't ask me to explain that last comment. It would take me an hour. This place has some quirky elements, but it's a good home. For now.

"Anyway, our return depends on some changes we're making on this end. But I'm counting the days." He pulled up a calendar on his digital kneeboard, and tapped it nervously as he talked. The days couldn't go by fast enough.

"I want to share more time with Rex on the trip home. Learn more about his focus on this Father Race stuff. Speaking of that, we heard Raines is in China now. In Ürümqi, up in the northwest part of the country. Rex says Raines has some big wingding planned. He and the women plan to watch every minute. They don't talk to him, thank goodness, but they absorb every bit of news about the jerk. There's a press conference today. Thought you might've heard about it.

"Well, that's about it for my ten minutes. Gotta go. I love you, sweetheart. Your turn."

ANDREWS AIR FORCE BASE, NEAR WASHINGTON, DC

Amy felt the sweat rising on the back of her neck at his words.

Raines. Somehow, John must know. That's his cue to me! It must be!

Three special agents of the FBI stared at her across the table, like suited Dobermans determined she not say a word about her experience in Slovenia. They'd made that abundantly clear. What she didn't understand was why they sat here, listening.

They could cut out anything they wanted in her conversation and digitally delay it. John was so far away he'd never notice. Yet they kept up the watch. They were nice enough men. But she had no privacy. They promised this was a "temporary measure," while they all lived together for "a few days" in a safe house on the Air Force base in Maryland.

At times, Amy felt like the enemy. Perhaps she'd exposed something with her mirror and SOS's. Perhaps the government had known all along she was with Raines, and she'd been supposed to endure the torment a few more years. Perhaps she was the means for intelligence agents to work their wiles a little deeper into the workings of Saint Michael's Remnant.

She wanted to respond to John's comment about Raines, confirm in some secret way that Raines was her captor, but the image of her little garden and sparse room in Slovenia tore at her as she mulled over his words.

Had I heard about Ürümqi?

It was all she thought about, the girls only thirty-six hours from a painful medical outpatient procedure, some anonymous Chinese doctor piercing them with a long needle, plucking ripe genetic material from their super-ovulated bodies. Each body feeding Malcolm Raines's perfected-race fantasies of human egg factories for his clone embryos.

Amy's thoughts ran to Monique. Their new friend had no family to call and rejoice with, and only Amy and Alice could share her pain and mentor her in her new faith. Monique felt no kinship for Amy's sons—or any man, for that matter. It was no surprise she trusted none of the guards watching over them at their safe house near DC.

Her thoughts returned to Raines's plan. She longed to have John here, holding her, helping her solve this horrible dilemma.

John needs to hear the truth.

Despite these suited men filtering her words with quiet stares, John deserved an answer to his leading question about Ürümqi. If he were here, John would tell her "ask forgiveness, Amy—not permission."

It was that time. She chose her words with care and began.

33

"DR. MALCOLM RAINES. Guardian of the Mother Seed. Priest of the Heavenlies. Father Raines. Oracle of Saint Michael's Remnant."

The titles scrolled across the giant screen in the Yin Du Hotel conference center overlaid on stunning photographs of the exquisite new Home of the Mother Seed. Above the screen, Adrienne noticed a bold new insignia emblazoned on a velvet banner, one she'd never seen associated with Raines—a golden infinity symbol, like a figure eight lying on its side.

As a backdrop to the flashing images of the new facility, the snow-capped Tianshan Mountains, with their soft green slopes, complemented the Chinese architecture. Raines's titles continued moving across the pictures like digital watermarks, a needless aggravation Adrienne resented.

She was first into the conference center, first to sit down, and she intended to be first to ask a question. Adrienne had a front-row seat. Turning around, she watched the procession of media. She wasn't surprised that only a third of the audience was Caucasian. This was an Asian press conference. And no wonder. Ürümqi was as far as you could go into China's interior. But why? To report on a too-tall, ex-basketball star with a PhD in philosophy who was the legal guardian of 321 girls in some obscure cult that worshipped clones and aliens. That's why.

Mop-heads scurried here and there to move chairs, lay out brochures, or tidy a rug. Malcolm ran a tight ship, for sure. Adrienne watched the images on the screen for a while, trying hard to ignore Raines's narcissistic, self-appointed honorifics.

The new facility was wonderfully conceived, based on the Chinese principle of balance and symmetry. The red ceramic tile roof, curved and glazed, swept up to a magnificent point. Tiers of roofs, each slightly smaller, one on top of the other, lifted skyward. Curved roofs, she'd been told, ward off spirits; the Chinese believed demons existed as straight lines.

With concepts like that, she thought, *American architecture must be the epitome of evil.*

She'd learned that the interior layout, a spacious main hall with lofty roofs, reflected Chinese social and ethical values. Raines's offices and residence occupied the main hall. He was at the top of the family hierarchy in this grand palace. Residence wings for women—considered of lesser stature than Raines—spread out either side of the main axis of the giant temple-like building.

Raines had spared no expense. There was room for nearly four hundred residents with, she'd noticed, more residence wings planned. Most important, each apartment had four bedrooms, three of them furnished as nurseries.

Three nurseries for every girl? Why do they even need one? *They're fifteen years old.*

Minutes before the conference commenced, the Lycra Lady strolled in.

Those black suits must be a Raines thing, Adrienne thought. Every one of the Mother Seed she'd seen in the hotel wore the same revealing wrapper. But none of the staff. And, unless she'd missed something, Malcolm Raines was the only male in this entourage of thirty female staff and hundreds of girls. *Wonder how he maintains his concentration?*

Xi Wang Mu addressed the assembled media. "Thank you for coming so far to attend this press opportunity. We appreciate your interest in the events of the coming days." She repeated her speech in Chinese, and all of the little men and women around her began mumbling approval, nodding their heads like dozens of bobbing water dippers. This was an audience of Malcolm worshippers, the priests and the media. *They'll never ask a hard question.*

Xi Wang Mu introduced Raines in English first, then in Chinese. He stood, raising his hands, his right arm at a forty-five degree angle, palm out. *The Malcolm Wave,* Adrienne called it. He waited for his purple-robed robot mops to repeat the wave. When they did, he lowered his arm.

"Greetings, in the name of the Father Race and the blessed Mother Seed—the wellspring of the future of mankind, the ripe vessels of Eve. I welcome you . . . to our Heavenly Home."

She chuckled. He took every opportunity to warm up the locals. Heavenly Mountain loomed above his compound, which he'd built on the shores of Heavenly Pond.

Heavenly Home? Whose heaven?

"Tomorrow is a great day," he began. "A day when the Mother Seed will find their home in the tranquil embrace of Tianshan. We will leave

Yin Du in the early morning. This has been a wonderful, receptive home for us during our relocation to The Residence. Early tomorrow, following five years of hard work on a modern landmark of Chinese architecture, we will occupy our new home." He gestured at the screen behind him, covered in images of his lavish future facility and capped by the garish infinity symbol. "There we will celebrate."

As Raines moved toward a podium, Xi Wang Mu began the interpretation in Chinese.

They all clapped. Adrienne cringed. *Loyal little Remnant Rodents.*

"We celebrate many things." He flexed his massive hands, fingertips together. "We celebrate our recent arrival, and the completion of the grand home of the Mother Seed. We celebrate the health of our charges, precious young women placed under my care by the direct authority of the Father Race. We celebrate a new moon, and a Harvest day in the lives of the Blessed Mother Seed."

There it was again. That word.

She'd not been mistaken. Something was afoot. That would be the basis of her first question.

What is "the Harvest"?

Sonya pulled the plastic shackles binding Kristen's wrists as high as they'd go. Then, as they sat in silence on the heated tile floor, she massaged the red sore areas. The room was barren: undecorated pastel walls and one locked door. Kristen returned the favor, then massaged shackle sores on Sonya's ankles. Sonya wiggled into a standing position and helped Kristen to her feet.

How many days had they been drugged? Sonya wondered.

How many days since she'd bathed, since she or Kristen had had a fresh bodysuit? She'd lost count under the sedatives. She vaguely remembered being pushed into this room. *Hours ago? A day?* The past was a fog.

Kristen's eyes had a distant look, the resigned "I'm going to die" expression Sonya had seen in pictures of prisoners of war. Kristen hadn't spoken for an hour. Sonya led her to a high window, a thick pane of glass with no latches.

Freedom. A land where we can run in the hills and live as God intended. Was that what Father Raines had said? It *was* beautiful. Snow-capped peaks topped green mountains and a crystal blue lake at their base, their front yard. But a Heavenly Home? Sonya shook her head.

Kristen rested her bound hands on Sonya's shoulder, and she finally spoke with a squeaky voice. "We're in China now?"

"Yes."

"Was it earlier today?" Her voice trembled. "The procedure?"

"I don't think so. If they'd put us to sleep and already done it, there'd be some pain." Sonya bit her lip, shivering. "It must be tomorrow."

Both girls sighed, watching the sun's disc soak into the mountains to the west. Rays of red and gold shot through the distant peaks and reflected off the lake's shiny surface before them.

"We tried," Sonya said. She wanted to sound strong.

"I'm glad we did," Kristen responded. "We almost got away."

The sun disappeared ten minutes later in a brilliant red backdrop. Then black night snuffed out the dying ember. The light was gone and the room grew dark.

"Sit with me." Kristen pulled lightly at Sonya's arm, and they sank back onto the bare tiles. She shuddered. "Do you ever wonder . . . if . . . if He's forgotten you?"

"Who?" Sonya asked.

"Jesus."

Forgotten me? Sonya remembered nights in Trieste reading her red Testament under her covers. Compared to now, that life had been good. "No, I don't think so."

"Why?" Kristen asked.

"Mom used to say 'God is there, ready to help.'"

"Then where is He?" Kristen sighed deeply. "I don't think He cares. Why are we suffering like this?"

"I don't know, Kristen. I keep asking for Him—yet here we are." Sonya sank to the floor. She had no strength left, no fight. It hurt too much to pray, to offer up hollow words in her mind to a God she'd never seen. There was no hope.

Kristen lay down beside her and moaned, rocking on her side with her knees curled to her chest. Sonya ignored her, no longer able to act as Kristen's protector, shield, and inspiration. She turned away from her sister, trying to shut out her cries.

I can't be fearless anymore.

THURSDAY, MAY 21, 2020: MARS

John sat astride Rex Edwards's special excavating and brick-making contraption that looked something like a road grinder, slowly chewing up the red soil of Mars. Out the back of the machine, wet, loaf-shaped bricks emerged as fast as Rex could slap the machine's sticky red product on a drying tray.

Clad in his trapezoidal-shaped helmet with two antler-like antennae, Rex looked nothing like John in his white, bubble-helmeted NASA suit. The two of them, one old enough to be the other's father, worked well as a team. But conflict arose when they tried to talk about the Father Race.

"So, Rex," John asked. "What do you think about Raines's take on this Nephilim thing? From the press conference."

"Is this a test?" Rex's voice was tense. Like when they'd first met, and John had quizzed him about The Covenant.

John laughed, trying to put the boy at ease. "No. Not a test. But this Nephilim stuff mystifies me."

"You might not like to hear our perspective."

"Our?"

"Father Raines and I."

"Do you know him?" John asked, wondering how much of an indoctrination his dad had given him. And how truthful his computerized dad would be if quizzed about the Guardian.

"Their genetic line has been conserved in very few human beings, thousands of years after the first Nephilim came. Father Raines found Nephilim's original genetic profile; one man, with perfect uncorrupted genes. He's a direct descendant!"

John bit his lip to withhold his response.

"Your faith demonized the Nephilim as fallen angels or beasts, sir. But Father Raines showed us they still walk the Earth, through their progeny. They were huge men who took Earth's women for wives and were the genesis—literally—of the modern human race. Those early women were the original Daughters of Eve. We call their direct descendants the Mother Seed."

"Sonya—your sister—she's part of that group, right?" John slowed the contraption to spell Rex a bit.

"Yes. Why do you ask?"

John looked back at the boy as he slid bricks off the ramp. He couldn't make out any body language with the *Lost in Space* suit covering Rex. "I ask because I can't fathom it, Rex. Sending Sonya off to join Raines, and then coming here. Seems like your father would have wanted her to be part of the colony on Mars."

He heard Rex sigh twice, a sure sign the teenager was reaching a point of frustration. John pondered how much further to take this.

"The Mother Seed carries an awesome responsibility, sir. It's their mission to bear the clone embryos of a new Father Race. That's how we follow in our Father's footsteps."

John stared at the boy in amazement. "You're telling me that Sonya's DNA—that she's one of these 'incorruptible' women?"

"Not incorruptible, sir. Uncorrupted. Her DNA is pure and without defect. She has no genetic flaw. Were she to join in union with Nephilim, she would bear a perfect child."

John shook his head in wonder, as though Rex, talking about his adopted sister, was describing a champion breeding sow back on the farm. "This is your sister we're talking about, right?" John asked, short of breath from anger.

"It is," Rex said, his voice fast losing its vigor. "And she hopes to one day carry history in her womb."

"She does? You're sure?" John's pulse raced, part of him ready to grab the boy and knock some sense into him.

"Yes." Rex's voice tensed. "She's ready."

"Rex, when's the last time you talked to Sonya? Like on a video conference . . . where you could see her reaction?"

Rex didn't look up even though John had stopped the brick processor. He moved the last of the sticky bricks in silence. John walked around the offload ramp to talk to him face-to-face. He stood in front of Rex in silence a long time before the boy looked up.

"I'm not trying to be critical, although this probably comes out that way. I never had a sister, okay?" John said. "Just me and a brother on the farm. But I had a girlfriend in high school. And I'd be concerned about hooking her up with somebody like Raines."

Rex stood motionless at the offload ramp, a wet brick in his hand. He didn't move for more than half a minute. John counted to ten a few times, waiting on Rex, and trying to calm down. At last, the boy looked up.

Through the clear acrylic of Rex's visor, John could see the boy's face, a contortion of features, his eyebrows pulled down, cheeks yanked up, and lips forming an "S." The quivering chin was the give away. Like he was stuck in some slow-motion, gut-wrenching pain, unable to let out a peep.

John walked up to the other side of the belt, gently taking the red brick from the boy's hands and setting it aside. He laid a gloved hand on Rex's silver arm and changed his tone. Daggers pierced John, realizing he'd ripped scabs off deep wounds in this boy, a devoted son who'd remained loyal to a long dead, and misled, father.

"The Harvest . . . of her DNA . . . begins tomorrow." It took Rex three breaths to get that out.

"Harvest?" John exclaimed, trying not to act too surprised. He'd done enough damage for one day.

"Tomorrow. They will donate their ova as hosts for clone embryos. Another generation of themselves." He hung his head, leaning on the belt. "I haven't talked to her in four years, sir. Since she was eleven." John could hear him sigh loudly. It was almost a moan.

Rex looked up at last, taking some deep breaths. His eyes connected with John's.

"She was my best friend." He lowered his head to the belt, his suit bouncing slightly like he was choking back silent sobs inside it.

"She begged me not to let them take her. When she heard that Dad planned for her . . . to go away to school, she pleaded with Mom . . . and me . . . to change his mind." He looked up with red eyes visible through his clear visor.

"Sonya hates it there. Even when I learned the real reason he sent her, I never tried to convince Dad to bring her home." He coughed. "Neither did Mom." His suit started bobbing again as he choked on silent sobs. "We wanted to believe in what she was doing . . . and in what we stood for . . . to make Dad proud."

34

AMY STARED OUT THE bay window of the safe house, waiting on the sunrise with Monique. They were somewhere on Andrews Air Force Base in Maryland, near Washington, DC. She could see the lights of military jets descending over trees beyond the split-rail fence surrounding her latest home.

Fifty meters past the split-rail, a tall wire-mesh fence rose, topped with concertina wire and bright floodlights that glared in her eyes in the predawn dark. The contrast — an airy weathered railing, and prison palisades — mirrored her spirit. Despite her escape from Malcolm Raines, this was simply a more elegant prison, but on American soil.

"He's on the move," Kerry called out to the women. He entered the living room in a rush. "Just got word Raines moved out of the hotel."

Amy turned from the window to greet him, and Monique rose

from the sofa. Neither woman could sleep, worried for the girls they'd left behind.

Monique's head hung as Kerry spoke, her eyes red. "Are they at Heavenly Home yet?" She and Amy had been in prayer much of the night, both of their hearts breaking for the young women. It was almost sunset in China. This was the last day before the Harvest.

"Is there anything we can do?" Amy asked Kerry as she put her arm around Monique.

Kerry shook his head. "We would . . . if there were any possible way. The Department of State has made some queries. It's in their hands now."

"He kidnapped us!" Amy protested. "Can't you just arrest him and drag him out of there?" Her face went hot at the thought of Raines getting away with this. *Again.*

"State Department's been pressing China to extradite him. They ignored the request." He looked at the floor, chewing his lip. "We're gonna win this battle . . . but not by tomorrow."

"A month, then?" Amy exclaimed. "They'll be implanted at the next new moon."

"It's not too late even then, Amy. We could get them out after the implantation." He hesitated, as if tripping on the next words in his own heart. "The pregnancies could be . . . well, they could be terminated."

Amy grieved for these children, not even sixteen, and the new life they'd carry. Hot tears rolled off her cheek as she looked Special Agent Kerry in the eye, desperate to find words that conveyed what was at stake. "Those are human beings." She pulled Monique closer. "Those embryos—clones or not—are the germ of life. Even Raines, evil as he is, admits that.

"In those young women's wombs, they'll be *babies*. If you 'terminate' them, as you say, you'd be playing god, just as Raines does. You don't have a month, Terrance. We have less than half a day. Once those Chinese doctors start to extract DNA and mix their genetic cocktails, it'll be too late."

"There's nothing I can do, Amy. We've got hundreds of people on this case. It takes time."

Amy released Monique and reached for his hands. "There's one thing we *can* do, Terrance. The most important thing." She looked at Monique, who moved closer to them and laid her hands on theirs.

"We can pray."

Kerry stood at the split-rail fence, staring past the concertina wire. Fresh air was what he needed. To clear his head.

An hour after the tearful confrontation with Amy and Monique, Kerry couldn't get her pain out of his mind. What had been for him a nine-year agonizing chase of terrorists since the bombings of 2011 had taken on a sudden new emotional turn.

Before, he'd have been happy to see any of his quarry perish. Dead, or rotting in prison, he didn't care. Kerry just wanted to bring criminals to justice. And Malcolm Raines was a big one. The word "terminated" had slipped his tongue earlier without thought. After all, that's what girls did with pregnancies they didn't want—they terminated them. Right?

How could he say that? Be so cavalier? The image of his darling Shawnda, weeping in her bed for weeks after the loss of their first child during her sixth month, ripped at his guts. Of course those were children. He didn't have a month to solve this problem. Hundreds of young lives were screaming at him. Right now.

As Amy's tears had soaked his hands during her prayers, something broke inside him. It was like that morning years ago sitting with John at the foot of the Sacrifice Monument in Washington near where his family had died—the family that didn't die after all. While John prayed nearby, he'd felt an incredible urge to grab some of the spiritual strength that held John together despite his devastating loss.

For whatever reason, he'd ignored that flicker of spiritual interest then. The fire to capture John's inner strength had died out, consumed by the great chase, courting Shawnda, and a busy career capped by three promotions. Life had overcome his interest in spiritual things. But John told him, more than once, that there's a perpetual spiritual hunger in every person. That was proving true today.

Amy's tears had fanned that fire again. Her passion amazed him—a passion for girls she'd never met, for babies they might carry in only a month, even for embryos that might be formed within days. She had the same peace he'd seen in John, an empathy unlike any he'd ever encountered. And the same love of young unborn life that poured out of his own wife less than a year ago. A love for life he'd never cultivated or supported. That conviction stung him. Deeply.

Amy's strength and resolve were spreading through him. He saw the faces of the unknown girls, but in a different light. Kerry breathed deeply, leaning over the gray oak rail but not seeing the distant wire. He saw Shawnda.

Easter morning, at National Cathedral. Her face aglow in the same way Amy's was just now. His precious Shawnda displayed that same look in her eyes as she bounced on the bed Easter morning, urging him to get up. Something had changed in her since the loss of their child, a flicker he recognized now but had ignored until he saw it in these women. The same peace.

I want that peace. More than ever.

Kerry yearned for that incredible depth of spirit Amy had, driven to forgive and embrace Monique even after her role in Amy's captivity.

He craved the depth of strength and purpose he'd seen in John these past years as he mourned his wife and children, yet somehow carried on. Catching Raines didn't seem to matter as much as it had an hour ago.

In a lifetime of analyzing crime and becoming a success on his own merit, Terrance Kerry had never seen his own need like he saw it this moment. He knelt in deep fescue grass, the rough splinters of a gray oak rail grabbing at his forearms and palms as he bent his head, no thought to who might be watching.

He'd seen John and Shawnda do it and had now experienced, first-hand with Amy, this thing called prayer. Kerry began to whisper the needs screaming for release inside him, asking for that peace and sense of purpose he now realized he wanted so very much.

| **MARS**

"Back so soon?" May asked as Rex and John entered the colonists' Lab module.

John dusted off his suit and lingered in the suit storage area longer than necessary, mystified, even frustrated, by Rex's explanation of the Father Race, Sonya, and Raines's plans. Rex Edwards Sr. must have held a powerful mental and loyalty grip on everyone around him. The impact of that control was just beginning to show its ugly face.

Count to ten. Several times, he thought to himself. This wasn't something he could fix.

"We're all out of 3-2-1," Rex said to his mother as he came in from the storage area. "Time for lunch, too. We can fill up the brick maker's tanks after we eat. We'll be done by dark."

John's head snapped around, and he walked out of the storage locker toward them. "What'd you say, Rex?"

"We're fresh out of water. 3-2-1, sir. That's why I shut off the equipment."

"3-2-1?" John repeated, his pulse racing. He stumbled as he hurried their direction, forgetting that his rubber-studded space sneakers grabbed at the floor.

"Are you okay?" May asked, reaching out as he tripped and tumbled toward her.

"Yeah. Fine." He faced Rex. "3-2-1 means *water*?"

May laughed. "It's a family code, John. His dad was fascinated with that number." She pointed at a Delta V Corporation patch on her jumpsuit. "3-2-1 was Rex Sr.'s private shorthand for water, and for his company." She pointed at the blue orb in the center of the logo.

Rex and May chanted in unison, like they were repeating some advertising ditty. "Three atoms! Two elements! One molecule! Water!"

"The three-sided Delta symbol," May continued, "overlaid by a two-sided *V*, and a single blue sphere in the center. 3-2-1. He even planned Rex Jr.'s birthday, on November 19. The 321st day of the year. Rex loved numbers." She let out a titter. "That one in particular."

"And it adds up to six," Rex said. "Like Father Raines always says. The number of the Father Race? It's six."

Short of breath, John sagged into a seat at the dressing bench behind him. "And the number of the Mother Seed?" He meant that as a statement, but it came out as a gasping question.

"Yeah!" Rex said, his face lighting up. "The same. Neat, huh?"

John lowered his head into his hands, a frantic pulse pounding in his ears. His face and the back of his neck felt hot and wet, perspiration breaking out as it did when he was violently ill.

"John?" May asked, moving to his side. "Are you all right? You don't look well." She placed a hand on his forehead, but he brushed it off.

"I—I need to go." He stood and turned, his head woozy from a caustic combination of panic and rage. He dared not look them in the eye. He couldn't.

"John? What is it?"

He shook his head, waving his hand, and rushed back to the lock, through the portal, and into the MSR. He heard May's footsteps on the metal grate of the airlock just behind him. John dashed through the rover's portal and closed the door in her face. He secured the hatch and fell into the driver's seat. Images of Edwards and Raines and Ulrich raced through his head. The three men merged into one.

3-2-1 was his favorite number?

Terror attacks. Alien transmissions. Silver spiders, affine ciphers, glowing orbs, girls in Slovenia, birthdays, and Earth return dates. Water and Delta V Corporation. All of them tied to a number with one common denominator.

Rex.

Like escaping the belly of a beast, he switched on the rover and tore away from the dock, looking back only once.

May stood in the portal, her face visible through the window. Her mouth moved like a silent movie actor, pleading.

John was glad the Martian atmosphere separated them. He wanted nothing to do with May or Rex. Or any of their kind.

ANDREWS AIR FORCE BASE

"We've got agents on the ground in China now," the agent on the other end of the phone said to Kerry. "Poor guys are posing as Remnant priests. They hate wearing those purple robes. Had to shave their heads and get wigs, too."

Kerry smiled at the thought of his men in the weird garb. He looked back at the house from the split-rail fence, wishing he could share this news with Amy. The circle was starting to close, and she'd want to know. But Amy and the rest would have to remain sequestered—and unaware—until they had Raines in hand. And until they captured whoever had helped him. Until they knew the extent of Raines's reach, there was no other way.

As Kerry listened to the caller, he touched the rough rail, running his hands over weathered oak in wonder at what had just transpired—and was about to take place. John said once that, "when you give your life to God, you're changed for eternity." How he managed to remember all those John sayings was remarkable in itself. Kerry wasn't a great listener.

I feel different now. A peace. And purpose.

John used to talk all the time about God's plan. Now, nine years after meeting him, Kerry finally understood what he'd meant.

I'm part of that plan, too, he thought. *Right here. Right now.*

"We've got another call." The voice on the phone jerked Kerry back to the present. "To Raines's tooth. Like we'd hoped. You ready for this?"

"Get a trace this time?" Kerry asked, suddenly realizing that the case could come together in the next few moments.

"Yep. Dodd Marsh. The Mars Mission Director."

"Marsh?" Kerry's hand began to shake. "The Mission Director for the Mars program?"

"The same. Got a cellular tap authorized. If he calls again, to anyone, we'll record it." The agent paused. "I'm sure he's the mole, Kerry. We need to move on him."

"Who's on duty in Houston?" Kerry's mind raced ahead to the importance of the next few hours.

Maybe we can save those girls.

"Pulled in a dozen extra agents. We'll shadow every move he makes," the voice said. "But you need to get down here, man. We need you on site."

Kerry hung up and glanced at his watch. It was nearly eight in the morning. He could be at BWI airport in half an hour, in Houston by noon local time. Then in Clear Lake by two, if he was lucky.

Or I could jump a hop from Andrews to Ellington and be there in just over two hours.

Kerry dialed a number he'd been saving for just this occasion. A deep voice answered. "Scales."

"Colonel, Special Agent Kerry. I need help."

"That's what we're here for, Kerry. Life's kinda quiet in the NMCC. Waiting on another move by Raines."

"I need a flight, sir. A fast one. From Andrews to Ellington. The noose is about to close. Can you help?"

He heard the colonel yell to someone in the background. Kerry ran from the back yard, through the house past agents and Amy, and out the front door, phone to ear.

"You with Amy now?" Colonel Scales asked.

"At the safe house. Headed for the flight line," Kerry yelled as he ran across the lawn to his car.

"The ready-alert Gulfstream will spool engines in ten minutes. You're their only passenger. Meet them at the base of the tower at Andrews. You'll be at Ellington before ten."

"Copy that, Colonel. I owe you. Big time." He dove into his car, keys in the ignition with one hand, phone in the other.

"You don't owe me, Kerry. We owe it to Amy and John."

Kerry jammed the car into gear and raced toward the gate. "The girls, Colonel. Can we get them out?"

The tall wire-mesh fence opened, and Kerry sped out of the safe compound.

"That angle's covered, Kerry," the colonel said, suddenly subdued. "Nobody's gonna hurt 'em. You just get down to Houston and do what you gotta do."

35

"ALPHA KILO FOUR WHISKEY Oscar, this is Mars, over."

The universe's background noise randomly clicked and barked over the space radio rig of ham operator Ronnie Williams. He dropped his coffee when he heard the first call, smashing the old stained porcelain mug that had seen thousands of cups of java through years of careful listening to his marvelous assortment of homebuilt satellite communications.

Six years after Ronnie had been the first person to contact John during the hair-raising return from Mars, he still waited for those special days when John called in from the Red Planet, just to chat. *That's him, all right.* And he caught Ronnie just as he was headed to his shift job as a supervisor in a Texas City refinery. It was a little before eight a.m.

"Alpha Kilo Four Whiskey Oscar, this is Mars, over," he heard John repeat on the large speaker he'd wired into a homemade pager system.

The house reverberated with the voice.

"I'm coming, John! Hang on, buddy!"

Why's he calling this time of day?

They usually communicated late in the afternoon if Mars was in view. Today, Mars would set in the morning and rise just before bedtime.

Something's wrong!

Ronnie braked to a stop on ancient harvest gold shag carpet and slid into his old wooden swivel chair. He grabbed the microphone.

"Mars, this is Alpha Kilo Four Whiskey Oscar. I read you loud and clear. Go ahead, over." He waited thirty seconds and repeated the words. Now he had to hang around twenty-two minutes for the next response. That was another reason they didn't talk during work hours. Ronnie checked his watch. Nineteen minutes to be at the plant. He couldn't do both. He reached for the phone. Time to call in late.

Martha was grocery shopping first thing in the morning, and the house was silent except for the crackle of galactic noise. A couple more of John's cueing calls came through, doubtless sent long before Ronnie had responded. Their calls were passing each other somewhere out in the solar system. That always fascinated him. In fact, he and John always talked at once and ceased at a predesignated time, so that when one quit speaking, the other's voice was just arriving. It made conversations much more fun.

With the coffee spill cleaned up, Ronnie waited the final minutes. John's return call was there . . . right on time.

"Ronnie, I'm transmitting from the rover through the synchronous satellite. You should be just getting ready for work, so I hope I'm not messing up your day too much. I need something only you can help with. Set me up another one of those encrypted comm links you used to do for me and Amy. This is very important. And get hold of a friend for me.

"His contact information's in the e-mail I just sent. Decrypt the attachment with that seed you and I agreed to for emergencies. This is hot, Ronnie. I need something up here, and there's only one guy on the planet who can help me find it. Give him a ring for me, please? I want to talk as soon as Mars rises, in about twelve hours. Thanks, pal. Give Martha a big hug for me."

Ronnie called up his mail, and the attachment was there with an empty message body. He opened it. Gibberish, but no matter. They'd agreed to a convenient encryption seed based on the local time in Sydney, Australia. No one would guess it in a few million years, and the number was always changing. Ronnie synched the time hack to the file protocol, and the encryption seed worked its magic. The garbled attachment transformed into a short note.

"Ronnie. Life and death situation—yours and mine. Do not inform NASA or anyone else of this mail. If you do, your life may be in danger. Contact FBI agent Terrance Kerry immediately using the enclosed number. Have him come to your location ASAP and speak to me. Essential we speak today. Move mountains to get him on the line. Our lives on Mars could depend upon it. John."

Ronnie's heart jumped like it did the time Martha fainted on the kitchen floor last year with a heavy thud, lying there immobile for several minutes. He thought he'd lost her as he called 911 and pumped her chest. That same beat-skipping phenomenon consumed him now as he dialed the cellular number.

"Kerry."

"Special Agent Kerry?" Ronnie's voice was shaky.

"Yes? I don't have much time. Who's this?"

"Ronnie Williams, sir. La Marque, Texas. You may remember me. I set up some comms for you and John during his last mission.

Six years ago."

"Yeah!" Kerry replied. "You're the ham radio guy on Shady Lane. How could I forget? Listen, I'm about to board a plane, Mr. Williams. Can I call you back?"

"No, sir. This is extremely important. I got an e-mail from John a moment ago. He needs you here, in my radio room, around eight this evening. Life and death on Mars, he said. And he asked for you. Said to tell no one else." Ronnie gulped. "I've never heard him so insistent, sir. Can you come to Texas? Right away?"

The line was silent, and he wondered if the cellular connection was bad. A moment later, Kerry's voice came through strong. "I will, Ronnie. E-mail a file to my phone with directions to your place. He say anything else? About what's wrong?"

"No, sir. Just that I was supposed to move mountains to get you here."

"You don't have to move them, Ronnie. They're being moved for us. By a force far bigger than we are." He paused, a screaming engine whining in the background. "Send that e-mail, Ronnie. I'm in an airplane headed to Houston right now."

THURSDAY, MAY 21, 2020: ÜRÜMQI, CHINA

Adrienne Packard sat in the hotel lobby watching the arriving guests stream in a few minutes before midnight. Gaunt purple-robed men with hair mops bustled about the lobby, conversing in hushed tones when they passed her. She had half a mind to trip one and see what language he cursed in. She suspected it would be French.

Suddenly she glimpsed someone she'd never expected to see this far from civilization. Dr. Felicia Bondurant—the famously shrill director of the NASA Jet Propulsion Laboratory in Pasadena. The woman responsible for all robotic Martian exploration stood in line at the hotel desk. She waited behind two Spanish-speaking priests. The poor clerk spoke only native Chinese and English, but apparently they didn't.

"Hurry up!" Dr. Bondurant shrieked as the two priests leaned over the granite counter. They started speaking faster in their native tongue trying to make the Chinese clerk understand.

Adrienne rose and walked slowly to the desk. She touched one priest on the arm and welcomed him to China—in Spanish. Then, in English, she asked the clerk, "Can I help?"

"We only have one room, madam. But there are two beds."

Adrienne turned, conveying the message in Spanish. The priests nodded, shook on it, and agreed to share the room. The girl at the desk beamed as Adrienne presented room keys to the happy guests, and Dr. Bondurant moved to the front of the line. She pushed Adrienne out of the way.

Adrienne wanted to slap her. "Dr. Bondurant?" The older woman, her wiry black hair frazzled, turned and frowned. Crow's feet cracked under heavy pancake makeup, like powdered canyons running from her eyes to her ears, and more wrinkles creased her upper lip like a picket fence. *She looks like a powdered prune.*

"What do you want?"

"I'm Adrienne Packard, of *Aerospace News*. We shared a brunch with Father Raines on Mont Saint Michel several years ago. Perhaps you remember?"

The woman's scalp was visible under dyed hair, and a distinct skunk stripe worked its way down the center of her head. She furrowed her brow, cocked her head, and finally recognized Adrienne. "Yes! I remember. You're Rex's bimbo. Reporter or something, right?"

Adrienne felt the red rise in her face. She again fought the urge to slap the prune. But she desperately needed access to this old witch to succeed at her plan.

"Yes," she stammered. "I'm a reporter. The term 'bimbo' is a bit strong."

"I don't think so." Bondurant turned to present her credit card and passport to the clerk.

Adrienne gritted her teeth then continued. "I'm here to interview Dr. Raines. I wondered if you'd also like to be part of my article."

She shook her head without looking back at Adrienne. "No. I'm busy."

"Dinner or lunch perhaps?"

Dr. Bondurant turned, her neck veins bulging as venom rose. She nearly spat on Adrienne. "I'm here for the Harvest. Not for fun. So leave me alone." She turned on a high heel and stomped away.

The clerk called after her, but she never returned. She signaled Adrienne. "Ms. Packard, could you help me again, please? Dr. Bondurant left without these."

Adrienne's heart leapt, and she took a credit card and a card key from the desk girl. She set off in pursuit of the old hag, determined to deliver only one.

MARS

"John?" Melanie stood in the door of his stateroom in Hab Two. "You've been locked up in here since you raced back from the colony. What happened?"

He looked up into the eyes of his dear friend who was, no doubt, completely mystified by his behavior. His anger hadn't subsided, but drawing relationships on slips of paper now posted around the compartment had helped exhaust some of his rage. He saw Melanie's eyes widen at this sudden wild transformation of his private sleeping space, wallpapered with their precious paper. Scribbles and line diagrams raced across each sheet where they hung askew on the bulkhead.

"What's this?" she asked. "A new decorating theme?"

"Can't say just now," John replied, bending back over his work. He tapped his pen on the plastic desk, anxious for Melanie to leave.

"You scared the wits out of May, and Rex thinks he's offended you somehow with Father Race stuff. What happened?"

John shook his head again and bent over further, hoping she'd get the message.

"Don't pull that with me, Hawk. I know you better than your own mother. You're compartmentalizing. Something huge is eating you. Now, you cough up that hairball and let me see it."

John laughed, then started a hacking fit, stretching out his neck as though ready to bark up a huge one on the floor. Then he wiped his mouth on the back of his hand. "Wow. That's so much better!"

"See? Throw that old thing up and we can get on with life. So, what's up?"

John patted the seat near him and pulled a sheet off the wall. "Sit down. I'm working on a project related to probability."

"Probability? This looks more like organizational charts to me."

"Maybe. I'm studying relationships. Getting ready for an important call in about eight hours."

"I don't remember any scheduled calls. Who?"

"Can't say yet. Figure this out first. Look."

He pulled papers off the wall, spreading sheets on the floor. He walked her through issues labeled "Ulrich," "aliens," "Edwards," "space," and "Saint Michael's Remnant." More pages remained on the wall, dozens, every one covered with lines and notes; most included the number 321. He sat down.

Melanie knelt over the papers. After a few moments, she looked up, her eyes wide. "Rex's dad did all this, didn't he?"

John nodded, leaning forward in his chair, elbows on his knees and hands in a fist under his chin. "Same conclusion I keep getting. Every time I look at it." He cleared his throat and took a deep breath. "Bombings, Ulrich, aliens on Mars, even setting up Malcolm Raines. All of that to drive us to Mars—and pull him along with the tide."

"It's sick, John. No, it's megalomania. But how'd Rex Edwards pull it off? The spiders, putting fake stuff on Mars. All that." Melanie sat and pulled her knees up to her chest. "And now he's gone. We can't ask him, much less prosecute him."

John scratched his chin for a moment. "He's gone, yes. But we still have the computerized Dad, right? That's got to be our next stop. We've got eight hours to figure this out." John knelt and started to pick up the papers. "Question is, can a computer confess?"

"I need to talk to Dad, Rex. This is important." John's jaws were clenched, and he fought to keep his voice steady and strong. He didn't want to face the boy, or address any of the colonists for that matter. For the moment, all were his enemy.

Ulrich shot down the helo. Whoever was behind that also kidnapped Amy and my kids. It all points back to Rex.

The boy looked at John a long moment. "I'm sorry, Admiral. Whatever I did today, I certainly didn't mean to offend you."

"Forget it, Rex. I need to talk to the computer. Can you set that up?"

"Sure. I mean, anyone can just step in there and talk to him. There's no switch or anything. I haven't been able to shut his program down the past couple of days. Don't know why." He nodded toward the compartment.

John started away.

"Would you like me to come with you, sir?"

"No, Rex. I need to talk with him alone for a while."

"Okay. I'll be with Mom in the science module. Good night."

"You're nervous, John. Why is that?" The full-size video image stood, hands in his pockets, gazing at him. John felt gooseflesh rising on his arms. This was like a scene from an Alfred Hitchcock movie or *The Twilight Zone*.

"Nervous? Yeah. Probably."

"Your heart rate's ninety-nine now and fluctuating. You're sweating, too. Is it too hot in here, John? I can cool off the compartment."

"Leave it alone. I want some answers."

"That's what I do best."

John pulled some papers out of his pants pocket and unfolded them.

"What are those for?"

"These?" John held up the papers. "They're my notes."

"Can I scan them for you?"

"No. I'd rather use them myself. But thanks."

"No problem. What's on your mind, John?"

"I want to establish some ground rules first. These will be your search parameters. Do you understand?"

"I do. Go ahead."

John took a deep breath, aware that every movement, every breath, even his erratic heart rate, were all under the microscope of the deceased

Rex Edwards through his virtual consciousness. This search could only work if it was structured just right.

"I'd like a detailed latent semantic index search of a series of statements. I want you to run these data elements and word strings against all known documents in your database. You'll need to consult with the Baker Island facility. Do you understand?"

"So far, yes. State your query."

"One more question before we start, Mr. Edwards."

"Yes?"

"How can I—I mean, how do I know, when I ask you something, that you'll tell me the truth?"

"Excuse me, John. Please repeat that question in another way."

"I'm serious. You're a computer, for crying out loud. Not the real Rex Edwards. You could be programmed to say anything that makes a person's heart rate go down. Or up. Whatever." John paused, then blurted out, "Do you lie?"

The reply was instantaneous. "No. I do not. I'm programmed to observe reactions and put them in context, John. My main task is to share the wisdom of the ages with my son, and with the Mothers of Mars. Nothing else. My answers are above reproach. They are perfect."

"All right. Here goes. I want a full search of all documents, news material, law enforcement files where you can get them, and NASA files. I want the common denominator in all of these disparate activities. I want people's names and common numbers. No other relationships. Do you understand?"

"I do. Common denominators. Only human relationships or numbers, nothing else."

"Correct. Are you ready?"

"I'm ready, John. Your heart rate is increasing, and you've begun to sweat."

Nothing gets by this guy!

"Data string follows, Rex. Date of terror bombings in United States, year 2011, expressed as a three-digit number, month and day. Number of octaves and discreet tones used by alien probe in 2011 to communicate with Earth. The number of the Falls Church, Virginia, post office box used by terrorists to deliver their manifesto on the same day as bombings in Washington. The volume of the alien orbs in cubic centimeters. The weight of the alien orbs in grams. The day of the year in a non-leap year expressed numerically, representing the birthdate of your son, my return from Mars, and the arrival of the Mother Seed at RFK stadium. With me so far?"

"Yes, John. Are there more strings?"

"Yes. The alloy formulation of the alien spider skin and legs. The number of girls selected as the Mother Seed. Your personal three-digit number code for the molecule water. Now, compare these data items and express the common denominators. If there's a data item without a common denominator, exclude that and let me know which one you throw out. Begin."

"Thank you, John. I'm going to need some time, okay?" Rex crossed his arms and put a finger to his lips. The next moment he was gone.

John looked at his watch. He felt silly waiting on a computer image to return and talk to him in twenty-two minutes. But this was the only way. Until he could talk to Kerry, all he had were guesses and some limited insights from the colonists. The screen eventually came to life.

"Hello, John. Have you been waiting for me?"

"You know I have, Rex. You watch this room, even when you're not visible. Is that correct?"

"It is. I have your answers, John. This was an interesting search."

"Why, Rex?"

"It took me into some databases I don't normally consult."

"What'd you learn? The number first. What's the common denominator?"

"You're nervous again, John. Very agitated."

"Yeah! So spit it out, Rex. What number's common?"

"There is an exception in your data string, John. One element does not match the number. That is the metal analysis for the skin and legs of the alien spiders. They are constructed of titanium, a Russian formulation known in the United States as OT-4-1. Other than that, the common denominator for all of these data elements is 3-2-1."

John's heart skipped a beat. He knew this already, but somehow hearing it from Rex's own mouth—his digital mouth—made the answer all the more surreal.

How'd he find out about the titanium? From NASA? They were the only ones supposed to know. It has to be Rex.

"Rex—" John's voice was unsteady. "Why are the alien spiders constructed of Russian titanium?"

The image folded its arms when John interrupted. "No! Don't consult the Baker database! I want an educated guess. This is a matter of life and death. Do you understand? I need an immediate answer, a probabilistic estimate."

"I understand. You're quite agitated."

"You have no idea. Now, tell me your best estimate, Rex. Why are the alien spiders made of Russian titanium?"

Rex put his hands in his pockets and looked John in the eye. It unnerved him.

"Because the spiders are not of alien origin, John. My other records, and there are many, clearly indicate these spiders were made on Earth.

Much of that proof came from you, of course."

He does know! He's seen the NASA material from my first mission! And this mission!

John wished for a chair to steady himself. For the second time that day, he felt faint. He took two cleansing breaths, trying to calm himself.

"Rex. Human relationships to this number. Who's the common denominator for all my data strings?"

"I'm surprised, John. I did not expect this answer."

"Why, Rex?"

"Because, John, there are four names." The digital image had a quizzical look. "And one of them is mine."

36

JOHN RECHECKED THE DIGITAL lock to his stateroom. He wanted absolute privacy. Only Melanie could override this code. He paced the small room, waiting on the speed of light. Ronnie, if he'd found Special Agent Kerry, would've already started talking, just as soon as Mars began to rise over his horse pasture in Texas. Somewhere out there, Ronnie's voice, digitized and modulated on a carrier signal, was winging its way to Mars.

He pored over the papers pasted on his walls and thought back on the session with the digital Dad hours ago. The video-Rex had revealed less than John had hoped and confirmed what John had already figured out. The number 321 was a common denominator in all the activities they'd observed these past years, and Rex's fascination with the number made him a prime suspect. Yet three other names fit Rex's analysis, too: Raines, Ulrich, and one John had never expected—Dr. Felicia Bondurant, NASA's director at the Jet Propulsion Labs. Probably because of her link to Raines and her myriad duties with Mars programs.

The radio crackled, and through the computer's special encryption the incoming signal was transformed into the clear voice of his old ham radio friend, Ronnie Williams.

"John. It's Ronnie. Special Agent Kerry's here with me. Just like you asked. We're ready when you are. If you have a good signal, you can start your transmission. We're ready to receive."

John took a deep breath. The distinct veins on his forearm throbbed ninety times a minute. He was in great shape, but the excitement of the past twenty-four hours had been intense. As he began to speak, he prayed for wisdom and for the right words. If he was wrong, his words would ruin reputations and relationships for years to come.

But if I'm right . . .

He arranged his papers before him and pressed the speaker button at his desk console.

"Kerry, it's John. Thank you for coming to Texas on such short notice. I learned yesterday that Rex Edwards Sr. had an obsessive fascination with the number 321. I've been tying threads together the past twelve hours to figure this out, and I've got what seems to be a solid conclusion." He gritted his teeth.

"I think Rex Edwards set this up. He created the alien hoax and enticed America to go to Mars. Probably made a huge profit on the US missions, money he used to get here himself and set up the colony. He intends to populate Mars with the clones Raines is raising in China.

"He left us a trail, Kerry, and we have to run it to ground. The problem is, if Edwards was dirty, his colony might be, too. We've entrusted our lives to them, from habitats and food supplies to a return flight home. If they're part of this hoax, we've hitched our wagon to the wrong tractor.

"We need your help."

LA MARQUE, TEXAS

"Whoever kidnapped your family deposited them in Raines's hands, in Slovenia," Kerry said. "Why? We haven't figured that out yet." He caught Ronnie's gaze of wide-eyed astonishment. It *was* hard to believe, the first time you heard it.

"I know you've been waiting for Amy to tell you what happened. But until now, we felt it best to keep you in the dark. There's a mole in NASA, and we couldn't take a chance with her safety, having NASA listen in on your comms. I'm sorry it took this long to tell you the truth."

Kerry didn't know any other way to say it. This news nearly broke him. He could imagine what John would undergo in eleven minutes when those words had crossed the great void between Earth and Mars.

"You've uncovered a link we didn't know existed, John. If Rex was the big fish I've been searching for, then lots of this alien stuff makes sense. Someone with the funding to support Ulrich moving those metal spiders around the globe, creating alien hysteria. Raines the master dupe, following the lead of a voice in his head from someone's cell phone. It all fits. Except the vice president. Why kill him? And why kidnap your family?"

Kerry hesitated, sure the news about Raines would inflame John. He'd tried to kill Ulrich for his role in Amy's death. Being stranded on Mars and unable to get his hands on the preacher's throat would enrage him. But his friend had to hear it all. Kerry needed John processing ideas for him as he'd always done. John might see more relationships that the FBI had missed.

"Monique, Raines's executive assistant, developed a friendship with Amy while she was in prison. Your wife had a big hand in turning her around. Monique's on our side now and helping to ferret out Raines. It's all pretty complex, I'm sure you'd agree. We're trying to put the pinch on Raines as I speak. For kidnapping and extortion. But he's pretty well protected in China."

Kerry imagined losing Shawnda for six years, then someone finding her—with him being months of travel away from home. John must be crushed—and elated.

"And John, there's a huge hole in NASA. Every secret we tried to pass to you got intercepted. We think we've plugged the leak, though. We'll know for sure tonight. Any insights you have on what I e-mailed would help. We're working on a plan to round up him and all his cohorts tomorrow night."

Ronnie nodded. It was time to let John respond, and make sure their entire message had gone through. Then Kerry could continue.

As they waited the twenty plus minutes for the return comms, Ronnie prepared coffee for the two of them. He showed Kerry his radio room and shared stories of his frequent talks with John these past two years. Finally Ronnie stopped his show-and-tell and indicated that Kerry sit down. It was almost time. He pointed at the speaker. "Could you do it?"

"Do what?"

"Survive. Like these people have. John. Amy. Their kids."

Kerry sighed, again imagining Shawnda taken from him for seventy-plus months. "I don't know how. Unless I depended on God. Like they do."

Ronnie nodded. "It's their faith. Amazing stuff."

GALVESTON ISLAND, TEXAS

Fifteen agents watched from the dunes far out on the west end of Galveston Island. Through their night-vision goggles and night scopes, the agents saw the figures on the beach in green light, their faces eerily glowing. Kerry lay on his stomach in the sand, watching. Along the water's edge, three men and three women stood naked, hands raised to the sky. They were nearly invisible against the dark horizon without the aid of night scopes.

"I'm not believing this," one agent said to Kerry's right, wielding a scope. Kerry chuckled. He was sure the agent had something more crude in mind to share with the group, but he was watching his words in deference to the six female agents prone in the sand to his right.

"Better get an eyeful," one woman said. "'Cause you sure won't see *us* doing that."

Kerry checked his watch. "10:39. Makes it 11:39 in the morning in Ürümqi. Just as John guessed. These guys are celebrating on China time. I wouldn't have believed it if I hadn't seen it with my own eyes."

He looked up at the dark moon, its outline barely visible. "The darkest of nights here and a new moon at noon China time. If we'd done this operation my way, we'd have been out here on the wrong night. May 22."

"Which would have been a day late in China," another said. "Glad you talked to John tonight. He's covering all our backsides. From Mars."

"How'd he know, anyway?" another woman asked. "How's he always seem to know what's gonna happen? Like holding this ceremony a day early."

Kerry smiled. Years of working with John had proven that his friend had a sixth sense about trouble. And how to respond to it. Kerry had stopped wondering about John's prophetic insights. But in days past, he'd been just as mystified as that agent was.

"John told me he figured with all the focus on new moons, babies, and this Father Race stuff, the Saint Michael's Remnant worshippers would probably be into symbolism and fertility rites. Said we ought to follow Dodd Marsh and see where he led us tonight. Here we are. His guess was dead on."

Kerry adjusted the focus on his scope, watching the six walk to the water's edge, foamy waves lapping on their ankles. Even in the light wind, he could hear the group chanting toward the setting moon, completely dark, as it slipped into the west.

"You guys ready?" Kerry heard fourteen whispers of "check" up and down the dune.

"Let's roll. Two agents on each suspect. Three including me take Marsh, the fat guy on the far right. Mark, you guard their clothes. Fritz, stay here and record it all with night video. We might need the evidence in court."

The female agent to his side, Galveston's district agent in charge, came up to her knees as Kerry rose, gun on safe and ready to run.

"Cuff 'em fast, ladies and gentlemen," she said with a coarse laugh. "You won't need to frisk 'em."

FRIDAY, MAY 22, 2020: ÜRÜMQI, CHINA

Adrienne watched as Dr. Bondurant stalked down the hall of the hotel, cursing as she headed to the elevator. It was nearly 11:00 a.m. The new moon would rise at 11:39, the beginning of the Harvest Celebration at Heavenly Home. Dr. Bondurant entered the elevator and disappeared.

A few moments later, Adrienne slipped the extra card key into the door lock. Dr. Bondurant would be on her way to Raines's party—where Adrienne couldn't follow. No one could attend without the Guardian's explicit permission, they'd told her more than once. Adrienne was marooned in the Yin Du.

Dr. Bondurant's room was lavish, much more finely appointed than her own. The four-meter-tall tiered ceiling consisted of sweeping arcs and beautifully exposed beams that reminded her of a temple in a Chinese picture book. The room was spacious, opening onto a broad veranda that overlooked the front of the hotel. The Yin Du entrance was directly below.

Bondurant must be pretty well connected. Or rich.

Adrienne began scanning the room for some indication of what the doctor's connection was with Raines. Something like an invitation. She didn't have to look long. On a low table in the middle of the room, a gold-gilded note sat half opened. A large basket of fruit and toiletries sat next to it. She opened the envelope.

"Our Harvest brings honor to Father Nephilim and Mother Eve who came before. Join us at 11:39 at Heavenly Home." It was signed "To my dearest Felicia. Malcolm."

Adrienne pocketed the invitation and headed toward the door, hoping she could bluff her way into the event as Dr. Bondurant. When she touched the door handle, she heard the shrew herself, bolting down the hall and screaming at the top of her lungs: "In here!" Adrienne heard her yell, as if directing a porter. "No! Turn left. This room!"

As the door hurled open, Adrienne dove behind a folding wood screen that shaded the sliding glass door to the veranda. Tucked behind its solid panels, she peered out through the hinge joints, her heart thumping in her ears.

"Put them down! Here! Now leave!"

A stooped porter bowed deeply, his face toward the floor as he backed out of the room. He left a pair of large suitcases near the bed. As soon as the door closed behind him, Dr. Bondurant tore into the bags with a vengeance. She was checking her watch frequently, cursing as she opened the zippered suitcases.

Swearing under her breath, Felicia tossed clothes with abandon until she found a silver box about the size of a large bar of soap. She turned and pulled a cellular phone from a large black purse, then connected the phone to the silver box with a thin wire. She walked to the sliding glass door that led onto the veranda.

Adrienne held her breath, afraid to inhale as the woman passed. A stream of profanity spewed from the director's mouth, a tirade against airlines and baggage handlers and slow old Chinese porters.

She didn't see or hear me, Adrienne realized with relief. She took a deep, quiet breath.

Dr. Bondurant sank into a chair near the door, on the other side of the panel from Adrienne. She checked her watch again, then cleared her throat repeatedly. She set the silver box on a low Chinese table, holding the phone to her lips, one eye on her wristwatch.

Adrienne checked the time. 11:39. The party would be starting just now. Dr. Bondurant began to speak, in a low deep tone, unlike the shrew she'd heard screaming in the hall. Adrienne felt gooseflesh rise on her arms, realizing in that moment the secret to the Father Race.

"Blessed One, hear my voice!" Dr. Bondurant intoned, an otherworldly voice gurgling deep in her throat. Her eyes were closed as she spoke, her face raised toward the graceful ceiling.

"Guardian of the Mother Seed! Priest of the Heavenlies! Your time has come. Hear our voice!"

She paused, putting the microphone aside and clearing her throat again. She practiced some low tones, then continued to speak.

"The Harvest is upon us! You have brought the Mother Seed to flower. Now is the time. Let the fragrant fruit of the womb be plucked, then its seed replanted to grow and flourish for your future. And for ours."

Once more she put the microphone aside and cleared her throat.

"Harvest the Mother Seed, Great One. Today you shall remove the fruit of their pistil. From them shall spring forth more of our Mother Seed, and from those hundreds, ultimate union with the Nephilim. Bring them to me!"

Felicia put down the microphone, laughing, and then coughing, as she tried to control herself. The laughing fit degenerated into a smoker's hack, gasping for air. In the midst of her racking coughs, Dr. Bondurant didn't hear the door open behind her.

From her vantage, Adrienne watched as the stooped Chinese porter reopened the door, then stood, somehow transforming from an old Chinese man to a well-muscled, middle-aged Asian. Behind him two more men, some of the purple-robed mop-heads she'd seen roving in the lobby, stepped in and closed the door.

Consumed by her hacking fit, Dr. Bondurant never saw them. The porter-turned-bodybuilder slipped a hand and a wad of cloth in front of Dr. Bondurant's mouth as she gasped for air, phlegm gurgling deep in her lungs. His package put her to sleep in one breath, and she slipped comatose to the floor. The phone fell with her, its wire ripping out of the small silver box. The muscled Asian pulled a small hypodermic from a pocket, uncapped it, then knelt at her side and slipped the needle into the unconscious woman's arm. The shot administered, he waved to his compatriots and stood, slipping the needle back into its case and his pocket.

The two priests opened their robes, revealing full body armor. One extracted a hood and a set of handcuffs. He spoke in a southern drawl, like he'd grown up in Georgia. She was sure she'd heard him mumbling in French to another priest in the lobby last night.

Together the priests lifted the woman's body and slipped it into a laundry sack. They pulled the sheets from the bed and wadded them around her. As they forced her in, the Asian cuffed her hands behind her. Adrienne grimaced as they shoved Dr. Bondurant into the bag. Within a minute, the priests headed out of the room and dropped her into a hamper on rollers outside the door.

The porter packed up the phone and silver box and laid them on top of the hamper, throwing bed covers over the entire package. He waved to the priests, who folded their hands, nodded to one another, and began mumbling in French again. As the door closed, Adrienne saw the Chinese man stoop and take on the appearance of someone far more feeble. He closed the door.

Adrienne collapsed to the floor behind the screen, feeling for the invitation in her pocket. After five minutes, she crept from her hiding spot, carefully opened the door to the hallway, and stole away.

Adrienne had no idea why Dr. Bondurant was out of the picture, but she wouldn't let the good doctor's invitation go unused.

37

"YOU WILL GO FIRST," one of four burly matrons said, dressed in starched purple pants and shirts. They bore no resemblance to the bustling Pina in a white shift and apron whom Sonya had come to appreciate so much.

Sonya wiped the tears from Kristen's eyes, wondering if the two of them were any match for the heavy women. *But what good would that do? We don't know our way out of here.*

The two girls huddled together in a corner on the tile floor, Kristen whimpering in Sonya's arms. Sonya's heart ached for her emotionally brittle friend even as her own spirits sank like sand flowing through an hourglass. As time slipped away, so did their chance of freedom.

And if we do get out, what then? Run away in China?

The matron yanked Sonya to her feet, removed her shackles, and handed her a towel and a fresh skin suit. She pointed to the bath next to the barren holding room. "Prepare."

"We go first?" Kristen's voice squeaked. She lay in a fetal position on the floor, shaking. "Will we see our sisters?"

The matron shrugged off her question. Sonya presumed that meant "no." Because of their escape attempt, Raines wouldn't jeopardize the Harvest by allowing them to mix with the others, perhaps not until after the implantation a month from now. If ever.

He'd better not, Sonya thought with fury. *I'm going to turn them against him every chance I get.*

An hour later, four women led Sonya and Kristen out of their temporary cell, bathed and dressed in new black garments, to a massive gathering hall under a vaulted ceiling. It peaked in the center of the room over a throne on a dais. Other than the guards and the Guardian, they were there alone.

Purple gems studded the golden throne, and broad crushed-velvet banners descending from the roof several stories above flanked each side. A gold infinity symbol, probably two meters high, adorned each of the banners. Lights illuminated the ornate seat and reflected from the throne's polished surfaces.

The matrons led Sonya and Kristen across a wide floor that would soon bustle with their sisters, prepared for the big day. Sonya's skin tingled with the thought of what was about to transpire. Under her tight black Lycra skin, goose bumps rose on her arms and legs. Ahead, seated on the gaudy throne, the Guardian waited, hands laced together, index fingers to his lips. At various doors around the huge room, Sonya saw well-muscled Asian men in purple security uniforms, not the guards she remembered who patrolled their homes in Slovenia or Italy. They barred any exit from this place.

Kristen suddenly broke free with a scream and ran. She went only a few meters before two of the male guards collared her and dragged her, kicking and shrieking, back to the matrons. Her cries echoed in the massive hall, but there were only the purple guards and matrons, and the silent Guardian, to hear them.

"No!" Sonya yelled as a beefy matron lifted a thick hand to slap Kristen. She grabbed the woman's arm, straining to hold it back, surprised at her own strength. Then she caught the woman's eye, and the matron released Kristen into Sonya's arms with a snort of contempt.

Sonya stroked her hysterical friend's hair and whispered, "We're in this together, Kristen. I'll go first. Watch for any chance—any chance at all. Understand?"

Kristen nodded and calmed down. Tears streamed from red puffy eyes, and Sonya saw her girlfriend's heartbeat thumping in the veins of her thin neck. She took Kristen's hand and led her toward the Priest of the Heavenlies.

At the base of the dais, Sonya stared up at the imposing figure on his queer throne. It was, Sonya realized, the closest she had been to the man who had engineered all of this—her captor who wanted to people his kingdom using her body. A velvet robe cascaded from muscular shoulders into a pile on the floor around his feet, and dark stony eyes assessed her the way a miser might tally his coins; she felt reduced to a digit.

The matron who'd released Kristen pushed Sonya's back with a rough hand. "Climb," she said. "He has a gift for you."

There's got to be a way out. . . .

She felt the push again, more insistent this time, and reluctantly ascended the stair.

When she reached the twelfth and uppermost step, Malcolm laid his hand on Sonya's shoulder, leaned his face close to hers, and spoke softly. His smell filled the air—an overpowering scent of masculine cologne. Oddly, his soothing voice calmed her.

"You're a leader, Sonya. I depend on you. This is a great honor, what we do today."

Up close, with his hand touching her, he seemed much more human, more sensitive. *Was she wrong?* No! She knew why she was here. And what he wanted.

"What *we* do, Guardian?" she snapped. "What are *you* sacrificing today?"

In an instant, the man's sensitivity transformed to rage, and red rose in his dark face. Bloodshot brown eyes swelled as he gritted his teeth and raised his hand as if to strike her. Then, slowly, he lowered it. "You are here for the Harvest. And you shall be first." Raines waved toward a large white door at her right, then stood, gathered his robes, and stalked off the platform. "Take them."

A guard who had followed her up the stairs grabbed Sonya's arm, squeezing hard. She yanked back, but he forced her down the dozen steps toward the door. The matrons pulled Kristen along behind her, kicking and writhing. A large white metal door opened into a brilliantly lit hallway, with small medical suites and laboratories flanking both sides.

"No!" Kristen yelled as it swished closed behind them.

Sonya spun to see a doctor grab her sister from behind and thrust a hypodermic into her upper arm. The guard jerked Sonya back while Kristen sagged into a brawny matron's embrace. They lifted Kristen and carried her, unconscious, into a suite and drew the drapes.

Two of the matrons strong-armed Sonya into an adjoining suite and locked the door with a digital code. One stood by the door, arms crossed; the other made eye contact with Sonya and shook her head slowly, as if reading Sonya's mind. There was no escape.

God—are you still there? Please help us survive this! Adrenaline racing, Sonya whirled to face a man dressed in a blood-red top and baggy red cotton pants. Like a starched version of surgical scrubs, but the wrong color. "What are you going to do?"

"I'm your doctor, miss. It's a minor surgical procedure," he said, his face hidden behind a mask. He sounded British. "Quite simple, actually. I'll administer a sedative, and you'll feel groggy, then go to sleep. In an hour, you'll wake and experience some mild cramping. Nothing more."

Lord, give me strength.

A nurse handed her a white cotton hospital gown and led her to a draped corner of the suite. Five minutes later, stripped of her black skin, she lay on a soft warm gurney, her legs bound in stirrups. She closed her eyes with helpless resignation as the mask went over her face, and she felt the rush of cold gas in her mouth.

The doctor leaned over her face, forcing the mask down tight. Shadows rushed in, the bright lights of the medical suite faded to black, and Sonya sank slowly into the warm dark tarpit of her nightmares, the doctor's hand lingering on her face.

Six trucks backed up to the loading dock of the Heavenly Home, disgorging equipment and orderlies dressed in crimson scrubs. A procession of white-sheeted gurneys filed into the main hall of the medical facility, red-garbed men and women at the ready, each with a silver rolling table, ready to receive their passengers at the door of each processing suite. A purple-suited guard inspected them closely, walking up and down the long bright hall, checking IDs and correcting slouching posture. It was a military line.

In the trucks at the dockside, other purple-suited guards spoke into wrist microphones, tiny ear implants voicing the conversations of their security brethren located around the compound. Guards lined the halls, protected the loading area, and stood at attention protecting the doors of each suite. The machine was ready, a hundred red and purple men and women at their stations.

The first girl emerged from a suite, pushed by a suited matron. "Number one!" the large woman said, as if she were announcing a dinner order ready for pickup.

An orderly traded her a fresh gurney for the unconscious girl and whisked his charge back down the hall, escorted by the lead guard. "Number one!" he said into his wrist mike. The double doors at the end of the brightly lit hall opened at his voice. Guard and orderly moved swiftly through the portal, headed to the next phase of the operation. It was proceeding according to plan.

Adrienne waited in a long line at the gate to Heavenly Home, still agitated after her adventure in Dr. Bondurant's suite. An hour after the celebration had officially begun, traffic still packed the narrow road leading to Raines's massive temple structure. The views of the facility were stunning, with sweeping tall curved roofs stacked in successively smaller sizes to nearly ten stories height. The famous Heavenly Pond mirrored the beautiful structure, its snow-fed blue waters embraced by mountains.

Adrienne shifted her gaze to the approaching guard, hoping he'd buy her bluff.

"English, please?" she asked him, flashing the gold-gilded invitation. He examined the card.

"Welcome, Dr. Bondurant," he said in perfect English. "You may proceed."

Adrienne let out a long sigh as she navigated up the road to Heavenly Home, her heart rate at its highest, she was sure, in her life.

Except, perhaps, when she'd been behind the screen in Bondurant's room. She had to find out where the old woman was. But first, this.

Fifteen minutes later, Adrienne saw Father Malcolm Raines. He was seated on an ornate chair atop a three-meter-tall platform at the center of a huge hall, surrounded by a milling crowd of hundreds of faithful Remnant followers. The party was well under way. The roof swept up nearly twenty meters above him, and the room stretched out the size of two basketball courts. She was sure Raines could see all from his perch. No doubt he'd eventually see her, too.

A long line of girls stretched before him, each dressed in the same black outfit, skin tight, every curve visible on identical physiques. She'd heard that these girls were clones. Of that, there was no question. Their line ran through the crowd to one of the large doors opening into the massive hall, a serpentine chain of black human links that wound its way up to his great throne.

The girls mounted the platform individually. Raines presented a gift and spoke to each, taking their hands and pulling them close. Each girl knelt and kissed a golden orb Raines lifted from a stand at his right. Then each stood and left the platform, escorted by his black-clad executive assistant, Xi Wang Mu.

Still no sign of Monique.

Adrienne checked her watch. Nearly one in the afternoon. The new moon had begun to rise in the east at 11:39 that morning. For thirteen hours, until the moon set, Raines would celebrate, moving his precious Mother Seed through the line, one at a time. At the rate they were going, it would take hours to see them all.

"Ms. Packard!" someone said behind her. Adrienne jumped, unaware that anyone here besides Malcolm Raines knew her name. "You came!"

She turned, face-to-face with a talkative priest she'd hoped to never see again. She'd bribed him for information the night before with a bottle of cheap Chinese wine.

"Last night was wonderful, Adrienne. It's so good to see you here." He nodded toward the girls exiting the throne. "Would you like to watch what happens next? As my personal guest?"

"We can do that?" she asked, unnerved that Raines's people would so easily compromise the girls' privacy.

"Oh, yes. Remotely, of course. Come!"

The priest, one of a hundred like him, took her hand. He flashed his badge at the access door and led Adrienne down a bright hallway. Through each suite's glass walls, Adrienne saw doctors, nurses, and guards, with sterile white examining tables in the center of each room.

There must be three dozen of these suites.

In most rooms, doctors were working with girls below draped white sheets. In others, sleeping girls were wheeled out of the suites, rushed by orderlies down the long white hall.

Her priest escort entered a six-digit code at one door and led her into a video room. It was stuffy, filled with the heat from processors and monitors. Adrienne watched the medical procedures on an impressive internal video system, remembering her own first trip to see a gynecologist. She saw three dozen images of girls in white medical gowns and doctors with ultrasounds and long hypodermic needles—their weapons to extract the precious genetic material Raines had cultured in their young bodies.

"Are you acquainted with our processes?" a Caucasian doctor asked her, turning from a bank of video monitors.

Adrienne flushed, embarrassed to watch these procedures, even from a distance. She knew what was afoot. She'd done her research. "No. I have no idea," she lied.

"Quite simple. We have it down to a fine art here at Heavenly

Home. With an ultrasound inserted to image her internal organs, the doctor will guide a long hypodermic needle to pierce the vaginal wall, then puncture the swollen follicles of each ovary, suctioning out fertile eggs."

She shuddered. "How many eggs? Per girl?" Adrienne asked, her legs tensing. There could be complications, as generations of coeds selling eggs had already discovered. She ached for these girls, and the long-term health implications of this genetic servitude.

"For a typical girl?" the doctor asked. "The average harvest is fifteen. Depending on their health, their fertility, and their treatment with ovarian hyperstimulating drugs. I've suctioned as many as sixty-six from one particularly productive woman in a single harvest. I paid her generously for that bumper crop!"

Adrienne's stomach turned. He kept talking, pointing to the procedure in progress on one screen. "We film each girl to ensure complete privacy."

"That's privacy?" Adrienne exclaimed.

"Oh, yes. The best protection for our Mother Seed. We're at the cutting edge of the blessed genetic arts in this facility." He pointed to a digital counter above the bank of monitors. "See! We've harvested over a thousand eggs already, and we've only seen fifty girls. Marvelous. Averaging more than twenty per child—far above our goal!"

He faced Adrienne. She felt nauseous and gritted her teeth. She wasn't losing it. Not here. "We need at least ten eggs per girl to assure one viable clone embryo," he said. "We should achieve that goal easily today!"

Adrienne took a pair of deep breaths, wiping at her sweating forehead with the back of a wool jacket sleeve. "Can you show me . . . the lab?" She breathed deeply again. It was helping.

"Certainly!" Her escort chortled. "This way!"

Moments later, she stood in a long air-conditioned laboratory. It felt like a refrigerator. Rows of microscopes and lab equipment lined the room. An Asian doctor approached to explain the process. Like his colleagues, he wasn't in the usual green medical garb, but a strange red tunic and pants. *Weird.*

"Here we complete the somatic cell nuclear transfer. Literally, we take somatic cells—body cells, by another name—and extract the DNA in a nucleus. At this next bench, we extract the nucleus from each egg and insert the somatic nucleus provided by the previous station. We take extraordinary care to match each girl's somatic cell with her own egg. Do you understand why?"

Adrienne understood, but shook her head.

"In a clone, although we remove the DNA from the host egg, the egg's mitochondria still carry short strands of DNA. Those strands, among other things, carry your genetic code for how well you will age. Through the mitochondrial DNA we can trace a woman's lineage all the way back to Eve—but only for a woman. If we harvested your eggs, for example, then removed your nucleus and inserted the somatic DNA of one of the Mother Seed, there would be some small mixing of their makeup with your mitochondrial DNA. Not a perfect reproduction of one of them, but very, very close.

"However," he said, pointing into the air, "our remarkable process in this facility precisely matches the egg and somatic donor DNA—both from the same girl—ensuring a perfect replica of the donor. Never before accomplished in modern science." He clapped. "And we'll do this today with more than three hundred of them!"

He's actually proud of this.

"Once we've inserted the new DNA, we stimulate cell division by shock treatment or drugs. When we have a viable embryo, we freeze it, awaiting implantation in the host uterus after she has been properly ripened at the next new moon. Eventually, every one of the Mother Seed will reproduce an exact copy of herself. A modern virgin birth." He rubbed his hands together and turned back to his station, muttering "Marvelous!"

Her escort pointed her toward the door. "We hope to harvest five thousand eggs today, Adrienne. Which means approximately five hundred viable embryos. A genetic crop beyond our wildest expectations! If we were simply harvesting once every three months or so, instead of implanting new life in the Mother Seed, we might be able to create as many as two thousand viable embryos per year. Remarkable."

He laughed and waved at the apparatus in the room. "Where there are young women, madam, there are ample supplies of eggs. Ironically, our procedure is constrained by the number of surrogate mothers available to carry our creations to term." He frowned. "Nasty limitation, eh? Lots of eggs out there, but the girls can only carry one or two babies at a time. Not terribly efficient."

Adrienne shivered, swallowing to quell her stomach's revolt.

A production line. That's all this is.

She left the laboratory at a fast clip. "I've seen enough. Thanks."

Her priest escort followed. They passed suite upon suite, some with black-suited girls waiting anxiously at the door, others leaving sedated under a sheet. As he droned on about the mission of Saint Michael's Remnant, Adrienne felt sicker with each new revelation. Finally they reentered the bustling arena where she saw a chair and slumped into it.

"You are not well?"

She shook her head. Young women led like heifers to Raines's harvesting suites, and if you believed this mysterious priest, they'd be expectant mothers carrying replicas of themselves at the next new moon.

Adrienne's stomach roiled. She had to escape this place before it sank its sharp tendrils into her soul. Everyone here was scarred—corrupt. They thought this harvest was wondrous. Egg factories and rent-a-wombs bred to feed the genetic visions of Malcolm Raines and his Remnant. Few of his worshippers, she suspected—*few, she hoped*—would endorse what she'd seen today. Someone had to tell this story, to expose the truth.

The wave of nausea overcame her, and she jumped up and ran. Adrienne didn't care if she drew attention, or if she interrupted the great high priest of human harvest. She wanted *out*. Out of this place, out of their clutches. She heard the mop-head running behind her, close on her heels. Adrienne ran faster, dashing through massive tall doors at the front of Heavenly Home and nearly tumbling down a flight of stone stairs.

She no longer cared for the magnificent scenery of a circular blue lake laid out before her like a jewel. This place was nothing but a massive clone factory. She had to get free, to expose it for what it was.

The priest caught up with her at the bottom of the steps. "Adrienne!" he yelled, grabbing her arm. She struggled in his grasp, panicking for fear she too would become an automaton womb for the presiding bishop of ovary worship.

"No!" she screamed, flinging him off.

He stepped back. She recoiled, sliding to her knees on the pavement of the parking lot where she sat bewildered, legs askew.

A hand reached down to lift her up. "Please. Don't run, Adrienne. There's so much to explain. This is holy ground, and you've been privileged to share in our glorious mission."

"I want no part of it," she exclaimed, pulling on his hand to rise. "This is *wrong*. Women aren't some crop you can fertilize to increase egg yield, or dirt that you shove clone embryos into until they sprout. If this is what the Father Race meant by 'blessed genetic arts,' I want no part of it."

She threw off his hand and hurried to her car, pulse racing. Maybe she'd seen too much; maybe they would haul her back in to become part of Raines's egg harem. They could kidnap her, as someone had Dr. Bondurant only hours ago. Or lock her up. Or shoot her. She was deep inside China, and nobody would ever care. She gulped air, trying to calm herself, afraid to look back at the priest. He was much larger and could turn on her; she'd be helpless to fight him off.

Consumed with fear, Adrienne had to look. He was gone. She dashed for her car and five minutes later, she was past the guard shack, hurtling down the mountain road to Ürümqi, a hundred kilometers away.

"The first flight home!" she shrieked at the sky. "The world has to know!"

Monique, dressed in gaudy red scrubs, rushed the next unconscious girl on a gurney down the long white hall while adjusting a surgical mask over her own face. Her sheared hair was stuffed under a red surgical cap. She was glad to be rid of the bouncing mane.

Brushing along the left wall of the hall, she looked up into the eyes of a woman she'd seen before, she was sure of it—a tall blonde scurrying down the corridor toward the arena, one hand over her mouth.

Monique ducked her head, struggling to remember where they'd met, and praying the woman didn't recognize her. She pushed the gurney faster, another of her younger sisters sedated below the white sheet. Time was against her.

Monique's stomach cramped for her sister, images of the doctor and his Harvest needle, suctioning twenty-one eggs from this sister's body. The staff was giddy with the success of the Harvest. That fascination sickened her.

She turned, a moment later, to check on the tall blonde at the far end of the hall, pursued by a jabbering priest. The woman looked nauseous, the way Monique felt. The blonde waved frantically over her shoulder for the priest to leave her alone. Monique turned back to her charge and continued to the end of the hall, waving to a tall purple guard, then passing through a double door.

Mont Saint Michel! That was it. She was the reporter, Ms. Packard, who had escorted Monique's adoptive father, Rex Edwards, to the mount for the arrival of the Oracles six years ago. Her pulse quickened in fear that the blonde might return, perhaps having recognized Monique even under her surgical hat and mask, without her long black hair. She pushed through a double door, sweat pouring down her back and chest.

"One ninety-six," she whispered to a young man robed in medical garb who met her at the door. He was bedecked in a vermillion-colored set of surgical scrubs like her own that would never show blood—the distinctive attire of Father Raines's medical staff.

"Check, 196," the man said. He pulled down a sheet on the gurney beside him, exposing a soft mannequin, a life-size doll the identical twin of the girl Monique had transported—and identical to every other girl in the Harvest suites. Monique reached below the gurney and handed the man her charge's gift from Malcolm, skin suit, and personal identification; then he was off, headed down the next hall toward the residential dorms. Monique knew these corridors all too well. She'd designed the floor plan herself. In five minutes, that mannequin would be fast asleep in the east wing. And her sister would be headed away, to freedom.

Another guard motioned to her and smiled. She diverted through a double door he opened; she wheeled the gurney to a medical supply loading dock, pushing rapidly into a trailer whose walls were lined with white-sheeted bunks. Four men met her, lifting the young girl from Monique's gurney to a soft bed that lowered on a hinge from the wall. One of them patted Monique on the shoulder and pushed her back toward the door.

"One ninety-six."

She nodded, too afraid to talk.

Ten minutes later, she pushed out through the double doors again with another sister and was met by another crimson-suited man in surgical scrubs, who took the girl's personal effects.

"Two hundred and eight," he said.

Pushing her empty gurney back to yet another suite, her mind ran to images of Malcolm, his stranglehold on her, then her harrowing escape. Her heart thrummed in her ears, sweat soaking her undergarments below the thick red scrubs. She prayed he would not come to the Harvest suites.

She'd returned to the dragon's lair. Of her own volition, a member of a covert team, she'd learned, that had penetrated Heavenly Home long ago. Malcolm's Chinese estate was built and run by the CIA. He just didn't know it. And neither, until yesterday, had she.

Lord willing, she would leave this place. Soon. After saving her sisters and robbing her nemesis of everything he valued most.

38

"I'VE DISCUSSED THIS extensively with the FBI. The best course of action is to lay it all out for May and her crew. Right now. On our turf." John leaned against the table, his feet aching after an hour of pacing while sharing with his crew his fears and discoveries about Rex Edwards Sr.

The crew of Mars Mission Three sat around an unfinished lunch at their white dining table, the site of many conferences dealing with challenges from unknown explorers on Mars, broken rocket ships, and moving their base across the rugged planet. Now they faced an even more insidious threat: the colonists themselves. John took stock of the dazed looks around the table. Even Geo was silent. For that, he was grateful.

"You've dealt with this—all this—the past six years?" Ramona asked. Empathy radiated from her expressive face.

He nodded. "I thought Amy was dead. Never dreamed Raines had her. Still don't know why." He pointed at a wall monitor, silently displaying images from the television broadcast of Malcolm Raines's Harvest party in China. He could hardly bear to look at the man, knowing that now he somehow operated beyond the law in China. But not for long. He waved at Oz. "Turn that thing off."

Oz flashed a thumbs-up and grabbed a remote.

"You're sure about Rex?" Melanie asked, taking notes and drawing the same relationships John had on the board. "I've heard this before, but something doesn't connect for me." She raised an eyebrow. "I hate to accuse them of something this serious—that they are aligned with a murderer and deceiver—if we can't be absolutely positive."

"I'm certain, Mel. And we've got a money trail to Raines, remember? They found it a couple of hours ago. But even without that evidence, look at the number code, the 321 stuff. It makes perfect sense—Rex Sr. had motive. He had resources. It's definitive."

"But the 'why'?" Melanie asked. "Why Rex Edwards? Why kill all those people? Including hundreds of his own employees at his Alabama rocket plant? For what purpose?"

"I can see it, Mel," Oz said. "Rex uses the terror attacks to take out the nation's space surveillance system and cover his launches to Mars. Then he uses the fake aliens to draw us to Mars. He makes a boatload of money off that first mission and wins the follow-on contracts for missions two and three. Including this one. That profit funds the launch of the colony. You heard Rex Jr.—he said it himself. His dad built three rockets every time NASA bought two."

Oz jumped up, took John's digital marker, and started drawing lines between boxes on the electronic board. "After he's got the ball rollin', he sets up Raines as the fall guy, leaving him in charge of the long-term stuff—breeding those girls to make future Father Race colonists—while he has all the fun, coming to Mars to develop the infrastructure and start his own family. Even keeps funding Raines to ensure all the pieces are falling into place. The hoax perpetuates the mission, and the missions to Mars, in a sense, validate the hoax. It's a self-licking ice cream cone."

Oz tossed a drink packet to John, who was parched and glad of the refreshment.

"Okay. I get all that," Melanie said. "But wasn't Rex a Father Race believer? How could he be so adamant about this God-within-you baloney and fake it at the same time? The whole alien spider hoax, the phony messages to Raines . . ."

"Maybe he believed his own lie," Deborah said. "He could be schizophrenic."

"Or a compulsive liar," Sam said. "Like people who deny they've done wrong, even in the face of the evidence. Eventually they start to believe their own falsehood. Look, guys. We've got to confront some brutal realities. If the colonists were duped, then that makes us all even. But if they weren't, well then . . . we can't afford to sit here and wait to see what happens. Better to know for sure they're complicit than to wait and find out later."

"But if they're just adamant believers, so what?" Melanie asked. "If they believe in Rex Sr. and the lie he created, even 'til their dying day, what danger is that to us? We knew they were a little fruity when we decided to bargain with them for their rocket ship. Right? It should come as no surprise that they believe in the Father Race."

"I hear your point, Mel," John said, "but if they're in Rex's party, and he was part of a national terror attack and the alien hoax, then we can't just assume we're safe under their roof." He took a deep breath and exhaled loudly. "We need to confront them. Face-to-face."

Others nodded. "Put it all on the table with 'em, Hawk," Oz said, scratching his bony shoulder. "Let's see what they have to say." Even Geo nodded. He was becoming more agreeable by the day.

Jake was silent. He looked up at John, deep pain in his eyes, then nodded once. This showdown might drive a stake in the hearts of many relationships.

John keyed a switch on his comm headset. His crew's safety had to take priority. "We're ready, May. Please. Come on over."

Thirteen silent astronauts crowded the dining area. May and her crew sat on one side of the room, John's crew on the other. He hated that division, but it was to be expected. Surely the colonists could sense it—the incredible tension. Any spark could set off an explosion. Part of him wanted to tear her and her people apart, and the wiser part said to ask questions before shedding blood. The wiser side prevailed.

John saw the looks between Jake and May, like a wall had come up. He prayed in silence for reconciliation—and against the hate that gripped him, hatred for the triple face of Edwards, Raines, and Ulrich. He prayed for God's grace to keep him out of that dark place where he'd languished for six years. *I don't want to sink into that pit again, Jesus. I just climbed out.*

"May. Rex." He nodded to each visitor. "Thanks for coming over. I know things have been a little strained the past day and a half, and I realize we're pulling you away from—" he gulped—"away from Raines's Harvest celebration. But we need to talk to you. I'm sorry I couldn't share any news with you before this. Once you hear me out, you'll understand why."

John went to the drawing board and selected an electronic marker, praying for the right words. "We're all aware of the discussions about the claims that the spider parts we found were part of a hoax," he began. He noticed Rex shift in his seat, but May touched his forearm.

"We're aware," May said. "Is that what this secrecy is all about?"

John shook his head. "Not exactly, but it's related."

Tears welled in his eyes. "You know Amy and the kids have been found. What you don't know—" he coughed, trying to control a surge of rage—"what you don't know is that they were . . . kidnapped by Malcolm Raines."

The women gasped. Rex bowed his head.

Shame? John wondered.

"He held them for six years . . . in prison conditions . . . at his monastery in Slovenia." John leaned into the marker board. Just speaking the news sapped his strength.

"No!" May exclaimed.

Sachiko came off her seat. "Not our Guardian!"

May suddenly bent over, burying her head in her arms on the table. "Sonya . . ." she moaned, her shoulders rising and falling in deep sobs. "What have we done?" Rex moved closer and hugged her.

John looked at the other women, each too shocked to respond. Rex spoke up at last, for all of his mothers. "I'm very sorry, sir. For what has happened. I'm glad they were found."

Nicci looked up with sorrowful eyes. "I'm sorry, too, John. Why didn't you tell us earlier?"

"I just found out." He took another deep breath in the pause between expressions of shock and condolence. "But that's not why we asked you over."

"What then?" Nicci asked.

"This is about Rex." He looked at the boy. "And I mean, your dad. The older one—and the fake one. I'm not always sure which is which."

"What do you mean?" Nicci asked. May remained doubled over,

head buried in wet arms, choking back her pain. Jake stood and went to her.

"Rex Jr.," he said, nodding toward the teenager, "broke the code yesterday . . . on a relationship I've been trying to sort out for years. When he said we were out of water on the brick-making machine." John gritted his teeth. "He called it 3-2-1."

"So?" Kate asked. "His dad always called it that."

John turned to the board, writing a series of statements on the active screen, each with the number "321" at the end of the line. When he finished, he turned to the silent audience, measuring his words carefully.

"The day of the terrorist bombing. 3/21. Post office box with the terrorist manifesto. 321. Alien transmission scheme, three laser spectra, twenty-one seconds each. Three octaves, twenty-one notes. Volume and mass of the alien orbs. 321 cubic centimeters. 321 grams. Number of the mother seed. 321. It goes on and on. I can show you forty occurrences of this number—what you might say is no big deal—and every one ties back to Rex."

He looked at Rex Jr. again. "I even talked to Dad about it. Last night. Your own computer program confirmed my suspicions. It—Rex—or whatever you call it, connected the dots the same way I did. Rex—the computer—accused himself."

"What are you trying to say, John?" Nicci asked.

I've got to say this right. Must stay focused. His fingers hurt, squeezing the marker.

"I'm saying that Rex Edwards Sr. was behind the bombings, the aliens . . . and the kidnapping of my family. He faked the Mars landings and created this global hysteria over the Father Race."

In the tense silence, he added, "Somehow each of you is part of his ruse. Either as a supporter . . . or an unwitting participant." John felt like he was cursing his dearest friends in public. His heart hammered, his hands clenched. "I want to know right now where you stand."

✦

"You're accusing Rex Sr. of killing thousands and misleading tens of millions of people?" Nicci leapt to her feet. "We're saving your skin, and you're accusing us of murder?"

"I'm not accusing you of *anything*, Nicci," John said. "We're confronting you with information Houston gave us, giving you a chance to tell your side of the story."

May's face contorted in a weird sort of half frown, half surprise. She pulled at her long locks, her eyes unfocused.

Rex kept his arm about his mother as Jake moved behind her. She ignored him. "Please, Admiral," the boy said. "Finish what you have to say. I'd like to respond for all of us."

"Speak for *yourself*, Rex. I'm not listening to any more of this." Kate stood, pushing her chair abruptly against a bulkhead.

Oz rose and moved toward her, but she slapped at his hand.

"*No*, Oz. I don't have to listen to this. You don't agree with our mission? Fine. Don't believe in the Father Race? That's your business. But don't think we'll let this slander just slide."

"Kate?" Rex said. All eyes turned to him. He'd never addressed her that way in John's presence. It was always "Mother Two" or "Dr. Westin."

She stopped her progress toward the hatch, her mouth open.

"What Admiral Wells has to say needs to be heard. Please don't leave. For all our sakes—please stay."

Shocked by Rex's sudden transformation, she froze in place, then shrugged and sat down.

May quit pulling on her hair and turned to stare at Rex, her mouth forming a surprised "O."

John raised an eyebrow. He'd never seen Rex take charge like that. And he'd never have expected the women to back down so quickly when he did. A man had replaced the teenager.

"Okay. I'll tell you what I know. You draw your own conclusions." John approached the board with the electronic marker. "In the past two hours the FBI has confirmed this. They pulled computer records from Delta V Corporation and raided the corporate home offices in Palmdale. There are wire transfers, deposits, stock transactions, the works, all of them directed through intermediary accounts to Raines. Going back to 2011, in fact. Before the bombings."

He was there in front of us, all the time, John thought, remembering those days advising Special Agent Kerry on possible motives for the bombings.

"Rex was in league with Raines from the time Raines came on the scene in Phoenix. He subscribed to Raines's newsgroups and funded him in the early years of a crazy new ministry. He was one of the first adherents. The 3-2-1 symbolism weaves its way through all of Rex's business and life. And Raines's cult, too. And the bombings. And the spiders. You name it. 3-2-1 is like a badge of honor for the entire mess."

His voice was rising, his teeth clenched. Melanie's hand touched his, a sure indication that he was about to lose it. She could always tell.

"The FBI's on the way to Baker Island as we speak. It's only a matter of time before this unravels and we have the rest of the proof."

"Enough!" Nicci yelled. "I'm not sitting here while you badmouth Rex. He was an engineering genius! And he's the reason we're here. The rest of you can stick around for Admiral Ego's insults, but I'm leaving." Nicci pushed away from the table and forced herself past Jake and Oz into the hatch.

"Nicci?" Rex's voice was stern, his face red as though at the brink of tears.

"My name is and always has been 'Mother Three' or 'Dr. Tabor' to you, mister." She spat the words out. "Address me properly or shut up. You!" she said, pointing at him. "*You're* the one who broke The Covenant. *You* brought them here."

"Mother Three," Rex said firmly. He stood up. It stopped Nicci in her tracks.

"Yes?"

"Sit down and listen to Admiral Wells." He turned and faced John, his expression wan.

"And why should I do that?" Nicci snapped. She headed toward the rover access tube.

Rex raised his voice as she disappeared. "Because Admiral Wells is half right, Nicci. I already knew that my father did some of those things . . . and many more."

The room was silent except for the soft purr of ventilation fans in various electronics bays. Rex scanned the faces around the table, first those of the NASA astronauts, including Admiral Wells standing at the head of the table. The admiral sank into a chair as if he'd suddenly lost the use of his legs.

Rex had expected shock. Most of their mouths hung open, eyes wide. He looked to his right at his mothers, Kate and Sachiko, astonishment mingled with horror clear in their expressions. He imagined Nicci, dead in her tracks in the connecting tube where he'd interrupted her melodramatic exit. Rex dreaded explaining this to them, especially to his mom. She'd worshipped his father. Once upon a time, he had too. That day had passed.

Pain ran deep in his mother's eyes, but something about her look told him it wasn't anger or shock. It was empathy. And trust. She dropped her hands from her hair and wiped her eyes. She reached up to take his hand and sighed. Jake sat at her side, and she welcomed him.

"Tell them, Rex," she said. "Whatever you know, tell it all. The time for secrets is past."

CHINA

Sonya squinted in the bright white light. The dense black tarpit of her dreams had released her at last. The bindings were gone, and she felt her hands and feet. She could breathe!

Her head hurt, and her throat was dry. She touched her abdomen, wincing at a sharp cramping pain. *I've been harvested!* Tears welled in her eyes. *Jesus! Help me, please.*

"Sonya? Can you hear me?"

She touched her face then rubbed her eyes, willing her body to spring up and run away. She could barely move.

A face hovered above her. A long face, with black hair. And pink. Something soft and pink.

That voice, it was familiar. But not its usual angry self.

No. It can't be her. She'd never wear pink. Her hair's too short.

"Miss Monique?" she rasped, wondering if perhaps she was stuck in her dream.

A smile and a nod. "Yes, it's me, Sonya. You're safe. You were brave."

"Where are we?" Sonya asked, squinting in the light.

"I can't say. But far away from the Guardian. I promise you that."

"Kristen? Where's Kristen?"

"To your left. You were the first. The others are asleep. They're fine."

Sonya rolled painfully to her side. Kristen lay under a blanket on another gurney, like the one she'd been on when this nightmare began. Sonya's bed was warm, the blanket soft. *Cotton!*

Miss Monique grabbed at a handhold, and Sonya realized they were moving. *A train?* "Are we still in China?"

She nodded. "Yes, but not for long. It's over."

"Over?" Sonya struggled to sit up but sank back down, exhausted.

"Yes. By the time the Guardian realizes what's happened, you and I and your sisters will be far away. I want to thank you, by the way."

"Thank me? For what? You barely knew me." She stared at the strange sight, Miss Monique with a short shaggy hairdo. One like Sonya had always wanted.

"For this." She pressed a small silver cross into Sonya's palm. With her other hand, she wiped damp eyes. "I've trusted in Him too, Sonya. Please forgive me for what I did to put you here . . . and for what you endured." She laid a gentle hand on Sonya's belly.

Sonya's heart leapt as she fondled the tiny cross in her hand, touching her throat where it once hung. Then she smiled, sensing sincerity. Miss Monique's words had the sound of truth she used to hear in her mother's melodic words. "My sisters? They're okay?"

Monique nodded. "Yes. Fine. We're all headed home. Not all of them will be as happy about that as you are." Her voice sobered. "They'll come to understand. In time."

"That's what you told me once. About accepting my mission with Father Raines."

Miss Monique nodded, a tear dripping on Sonya's arm.

Sonya's mouth felt like cotton. "I forgive you. And thank you. For whatever you did to save me."

Monique shook her head. "It wasn't me. But they gave me a chance to help last night and I took it. Now, rest." She reached forward with another hand. "Thank you for this." She pressed a small book into Sonya's free hand. The little red New Testament that had made its rounds to so many in the past weeks.

Sonya raised the New Testament and opened it to her mother's inscription in the front. She ran her fingers over the familiar words, breathing in the old pages, a smell that took her back to covers and flashlights, nighttime readings in Italy. And her first prison.

"I'd like to be with my family again, Miss Monique. Do you think I ever will?"

Monique pressed Sonya's hand. "I've learned a lot from your book, Sonya. We can trust God to work out the best solution for all of us."

39

"YOU KNEW?" HER SON asked May.

She nodded. "There were seeds of doubt, Rex. When your dad sent Sonya to be with Raines. When we began planning for this mission. Things happened that didn't make sense. But until now, I couldn't prove anything. I ignored all the evidence, wanting with all my heart to believe." She sighed so deeply it came out like a moan. "I was so wrong."

"May? What are you talking about?" Kate shouted. "John's accusing us of murder! You're on his side?"

She shook her head. Kate hadn't lost a daughter to Malcolm Raines. *Maybe I have more in common with John than I realized*, May thought. "I'm not on his side, Kate, but think about this for a moment. Why'd we bring embryos with us, and volunteer to be vessels of the Father Race on Mars, if the only pure Father Race DNA is with the Guardian? On

Earth? Didn't you ever wonder?

"And Nicci? I know you can hear me down that access tube. You complained about my son breaking The Covenant, but what difference did it make? If Rex wanted us to survive to be mothers to the New Race, why not insist we take every opportunity for help? To survive? For crying out loud, Dad dropped the whole Covenant thing as soon as I got back. It was convenient for Rex to control our access with the outside, but not essential for our success."

She looked at Sachiko. "You love talking to Dad more than any of us. Why does our digital Oracle—a font of perfect wisdom that's supposed to help us make informed decisions—change his mind? Its mind? I know we're talking about a computer program, Sachiko, but Dad should be the most logical of all of us. Yet it isn't. Things don't stack up, people, and you're all smart enough to see that. Right?"

"I don't like your tone," Nicci said, emerging from the access tube. "But I do want to hear Rex's side."

Rex looked at May, who tilted her head with a small smile. "You'll have to speak to that, Rex. I only had my suspicions. I always wondered if you had yours."

He turned toward Nicci. "I believed in my father, Mother Tabor. I never understood him, really, but I . . . you know . . . kinda worshipped him. He invented all this stuff, brought three missions to Mars and then us. He's a modern Magellan. And he died trying. Just like Magellan. So I didn't want to believe anything about him but the best."

"What happened, Rex?" John asked.

"Last night, when you talked to Dad? I saw him after you left."

"This is too weird," Oz said. "You're talking about a computer like it's a person."

"In a sense, it is, sir," Rex responded. "I asked him what your query was, and he told me."

"Should've thought of that," John said. "I was too mad to cover my tracks."

"Be glad you didn't, Admiral. I learned what you'd pieced together. That there are four people who are common denominators in everything tied to 3-2-1. My father, Raines, Elias Ulrich — the bomber — and Dr. Felicia Bondurant. She's the key you ignored."

"What?" John's face turned ashen. "She's just the JPL Director."

"You were right," Rex continued. "My father did fund Malcolm Raines. He told me that once. It was never a secret. My dad believed in this mission with all his heart. And he believed in the Father Race. He lived for the first-ever opportunity to bring the seed of mankind to another planet. He died making sure that happened. But he wasn't an evil man. At least, not at first."

"Rex?" May asked, her eyes wide. "What are you saying?"

"Somewhere along the way, Mom, my father figured it out. That's what Admiral Wells was trying to tell us. When I queried Dad last night . . . and learned about Admiral Wells's questions, I probed deeper. Dad's programmed to consult all available data and always be truthful. He knows everything my father ever recorded. It wasn't hard. A few hours, and he filled in the blanks you missed, sir."

May looked at Rex, amazed at this son of hers and his remarkable resourcefulness.

"My father designed Dad two years ago. He always said he'd built it as a data and decision resource, right? Well, it's that and lots more. When I queried all records relating to Dr. Bondurant, I learned the real reason he built it. He designed Dad to answer his own questions. My father doubted, like Mom just said. The more he watched Dr. Raines, the less all this made sense to him. But he needed help to sort it out.

"He was funding Raines with millions, but no perfect DNA samples were coming forward. Raines never shared that secret with the rest of the world. My father couldn't understand that. So he built Dad to sort through massive volumes of data. When he did, he learned about Dr. Bondurant's connection."

"And?" John asked, his voice hoarse.

"She was in league with the Chinese, sir. You were almost right, but you left her out of the equation. Dr. Bondurant had deep ties with the Chinese through her own father. Dad can tell you the whole story. She had aspirations as a center director and major force in NASA, and the Chinese had needs. She fronted for them, to accomplish their goals. And they helped with hers. Through the late Vice President Ryan, among others. Eventually, Mr. Ryan became a liability. The data supports the conclusion that the Chinese collaborated with Mr. Ulrich, whom they hired, to kill the vice president."

"Goals?" Jake asked weakly, sitting beside May.

"Yes, sir. The Chinese sought a large-scale biotechnology industry related to human cloning and disease-prevention research. They saw a path to that end in Malcolm Raines's early writings. He was a nobody preacher in Arizona, and they propped him up. Given enough of a platform, and some convincing evidence, Chinese leadership believed Raines could lead them into a biotechnology boom. And he did. Over one hundred million DNA samples later, with a thriving therapeutic cloning industry and the Heavenly Home, it almost worked."

"Why the terror attacks?" John asked. "I mean, what was the gain there?"

"Why don't we just ask Dad? He can explain it better than I can."

"You're not serious?" Oz protested.

"He's got a point. It might sort this thing out," John said. "I'm game."

"I *am* serious, Captain Oswald." Rex Jr. looked around the room. "Dad can answer Admiral Wells's questions. And others that some of us might not want answered."

He turned to face May. "I know Dad's an artifice, Mom. Trust me, I'm not freaking out over a computer program. But he listens, you know? He pays attention to my feelings, he hears every word I say and processes them. I can talk to him as long as I want." Rex looked down, then back at May. "My father was never there for me. Dad is."

✳

"Hello, John."

"Rex. I mean, Mr. Edwards. How are you?"

"Fine, John. You're nervous again. Always nervous. Do you get enough rest?"

"Not recently. I've been awake since I saw you last."

"That was seventeen hours twelve minutes ago, John. Not healthy. How can I help you today?"

"Rex talked to you last night?"

"Yes, he did. We talked a long time. Just after you left."

"What about, Rex?"

"He is Rex. I am Dad . . . or Mr. Edwards, if you like. We talked about the same issues you addressed, and more. About Dr. Felicia Bondurant."

"And?"

"'And' is not a valid query, John. State your question, please."

"Was Dr. Felicia Bondurant responsible for an alien hoax and the terror bombings of the United States?"

"No."

"Then for crying out loud, who was?" Oz interjected from the audience.

"Hello, Mr. Oswald. It was the Chinese government. They were responsible for the attacks."

"Why?" John asked.

"The Chinese sought four objectives, John, based on my assessment of all available intelligence. Rex reprogrammed my search parameters last night and expanded the scope of my data retrieval to include Chinese language material. That modification proved quite useful. First, the Chinese sought to disrupt antisatellite weapon development underway at my Huntsville rocket propulsion plant. The facility was a major target of the terror attack. We lost many people from Delta V on that day. That plant was on the verge of a successful antisatellite interceptor technology that could have defended against a broad array of space weaponry, such as was under development in China at the time. Elias Ulrich was their tool to destroy that capability."

"What else?" John asked.

"Second, the Chinese sought to test the limits of the US ballistic missile defense program. They successfully shut down that system for thirty-six hours despite an arrogant administration and military that said it could not be done. All of our country's space-based missile detection was temporarily neutralized, proving the system's vulnerability. Again, Ulrich, in the employ of the Chinese and directed by Dr. Bondurant, dealt a severe blow to our nation's security, in Colorado and in Washington, DC. According to FBI records, John, you were instrumental in that assessment of the Chinese. My data indicates you postulated the Chinese connection early in the investigation while you were on the Space Station. Yet your conclusions were ignored. I could not determine why."

"Go on. What's number three?"

"The Chinese sought to undercut, through a convincing external religious influence, the growth of the Chinese Christian church movement. By seeding doubt on a global scale, and creating a hysteria related to alien life, they sought to undermine activist elements within their own country. Supporting Malcolm Raines successfully accomplished that objective. Dodd Marsh and Dr. Bondurant were valuable sources of NASA intelligence to help cement the hoax, giving Dr. Raines the illusion of knowing more than he did."

"Fourth?"

"Fourth, the Chinese government sought a large-scale biotechnology and therapeutic cloning program, based on various methods of genetic manipulation. They have identified biotechnology as the key industry for the coming century, and sought to establish China as the preeminent power for such work. Furthermore, their own writings suggest a strong interest in genetic selection and disease prevention, supported by DNA mapping and clone research. The funding for such a strategy was a natural outgrowth of goal number three. Malcolm Raines paid the bill, and they reaped the rewards."

"Why didn't you tell us earlier?" Oz quipped from the back of the small room.

"Mr. Oswald, shall I address that answer as Dad or as Rex Edwards?"

"Rex, I guess. Same thing."

"Very well. Dad was developed to sort out difficult inconsistencies I discovered in the underpinnings of the Father Race. Using this tool, without the video enhancement, I learned of the Chinese connection only four months before I left for Mars. At that point, the terror attacks were eight-year-old news, and a limited war had been waged with Iran, the presumed antagonists in the terrorist attacks. America had closure. I believed in my mission to seed new life on Mars and was preparing for launch. I could not back down on my steadfast commitment to the Father Race and still save face. Therefore I proceeded as planned."

"And our daughter? What about her?" May cried. "You gave her to him!"

"I did, May. That was an action I believed in at the time. I wanted to believe. We could do nothing to change that once the die was cast. My investments in Raines, and my leverage in the Mars program, would ruin the company if the news of a hoax circulated. I would be tried in the court of public opinion and found lacking. I had to leave Sonya with Raines, to perpetuate the myth. And we continued to Mars."

"Dad?"

"Yes, Rex?"

"I queried you about the hoax. Who made the spiders? The Oracles?"

"The Chinese. The technology for those machines was mature five years before we saw them on Mars. I suspected early on, wondering why such an established concept appeared as a supposed alien, but could not prove otherwise. And I wanted to believe. The Chinese benefited from the hysteria, with Malcolm Raines's monies, and with the global shift away from traditional religions. They launched several missions to Mars during the missile defense blackout. They used sea-based launchers in the South Pacific. But no one caught them."

"Why didn't information about the manmade spiders come to light earlier?"

"They prevented it, Rex."

"Prevented what?" John blurted.

"The evidence was destroyed, Admiral."

"How, Dad?" Rex asked.

"I have always installed a self-destruct mechanism on every launch vehicle. That is standard industry practice in the event the vehicle endangers others—if it flies out of control, for instance. I was asked, through classified channels, by the vice president's Space Council, to consider providing such a capability in my Mars craft, *Epsilon*. For emergency purposes such as countering possible planetary infection through some deadly Mars contagion. Their argument was that we should sacrifice the few to save the many. Excuse me for a moment. John, your heart rate has increased by twenty-two beats per minute. You are severely distressed."

"What did you do, Dad?" Rex asked again.

"I refused. I felt this solution was unethical. I have learned, through the expansion of my search criteria into Chinese documents, that such a capability was developed, however. Using relatively straightforward explosive techniques, a blast can be created to appear to have been due to micrometeoroid attack. I presume that, with the support of someone in NASA or at my manufacturing plant, such a system was surreptitiously installed. On *Epsilon* as well as the hapless ERV."

"No!" John exclaimed, rushing at the image. Jake grabbed him.

"Thank you, Captain Cook. Please don't harm my display, John."

"Why didn't you tell us about this sooner, Dad?" May said.

"I am a query-and-response system, my dear. I conduct massively parallel latent semantic index searches and pattern recognition processing of all Web material as well as most written documents. However, I cannot query you, or elicit a response without a query. I can only answer."

"You didn't answer her question, video brain," Oz said. "Why didn't you tell them sooner?"

"Because, Mr. Oswald, no one ever asked."

CHINA

"The Harvest is completed, Great One," Xi Wang Mu said, kneeling before Malcolm. She pressed her lips to the golden orb and laid a lingering hand on his knee. "Accept the sacrifice of our fertile bodies for your heavenly service."

Malcolm laid his hand on her head, her black hairs perfectly aligned tightly over her scalp, bound with a flawless red bow. Delicate muscles rippled on her back as she leaned toward him and worshipful Asian eyes gazed up at his, hers a bright new face. Monique's delay had cost her much. He wouldn't need her now. Xi Wang Mu served him well. Better, in fact.

"The guests await you, Priest. Shall we entertain them now?"

"No. I want to see the Mother Seed—to check on their progress."

"As you wish. May I suggest we begin with the first? They are waking in the east wing apartments now."

Malcolm smiled and indicated she should rise. "Prepare the way. I will visit with my guests first, for half an hour. Meet me at the White Door."

Raines's wooden sandals clacked on the tile floors as they walked down the main corridor of the east dormitory. Xi Wang Mu counted the clacks. He shuffled three steps for two of hers. She kept count.

Chinese art adorned the hallway, scenes of mountain passes, meadows and temples, and, occasionally, the Great Wall. The two of them were alone.

Xi Wang Mu stopped at the door labeled "#1." "The Edwards girl, Father. Shall we inspect her?"

Raines frowned. "Insolent child. No. Show me Judith. She pleased me today."

"Very well. Number fifty-five." Xi Wang led Raines down the hall.

"Where are the matrons?" Raines asked as they walked.

"They are tending the girls in the Harvest suites, Great One. The girls on this hall are resting. They have no need for close oversight."

"Just the same, I would prefer it."

"Yes, Father. As you wish. I will arrange it. Here is the room for the one called Judith." She opened the door, and Malcolm strode in, gathering up his long robe as he shuffled.

The apartment was gloriously furnished in Chinese décor. A large living room opened into a hall that fed into a dining area and kitchen, with four doors off the hall for a bedroom and three nurseries, and a spacious tiled bath at the end. He clopped along the floor, inspecting each room, then withdrawing. After the fourth bedroom, but no Judith, Raines turned on Xi Wang Mu with a scowl. "Where is she? The rooms are empty!"

"Perhaps she is in the bath, Father. Shall I check for you?"

Raines's scowl faded to a wry smile. "No. I will. You wait here."

Raines proceeded to the end of the hall and opened the door slowly. He craned his head into the bathroom. Then he slammed the door and turned on Xi Wang Mu, his eyes bulging, swollen neck veins visible above the robe's collar. "There's no one here!"

She stood her ground as he charged toward her, a threatening hand raised. "Where is she?" Without waiting for an answer, he clacked into the corridor, his head swiveling right. Xi Wang Mu followed. He flung open door #56 and disappeared inside, emerging a minute later with a puzzled expression.

Xi Wang Mu stood in the hall, ramrod straight. She smiled, tensing her arms, ready for what was to come. "They are not here, Father. They have gone."

He stumbled back a step in shock, his eyes darting to the doors along the corridor, then back to her. "What? Where is my Mother Seed?" He rushed down the hall, his silly wooden sandals and long velvet robe causing him to stumble as he dashed from room to room, each with the same negative result. Empty. He screamed for matrons and guards. No one responded.

Xi Wang Mu watched him from her position in the center of the long hall. "They cannot hear you or see you, Malcolm. Security won't come. There is no Mother Seed." She unfolded her hands and spread her feet, like a boxer taking a stance, ready to absorb a blow.

Malcolm turned from the last door, his eyes on her and wild with rage.

He ran for her.

"I'll kill you. Then I'll find my Mother Seed."

Stop! Hear us!

Malcolm tripped on the sandals as he tried to run, the words of the Father Race suddenly echoing in his ears. He careened into a wall and tumbled to the floor, his hand to his head. "Yes, Father?" he cried, his eyes darting about the hall.

There isn't a Father Race, Malcolm. No Mother Seed. No Nephilim. We have Amy Wells and her family. You're finished.

"No!" he howled, writhing on the floor. He looked up at her speaking into a small phone, the same words he heard in his head. It can't be! Once an object of his desire, she stood like a warrior in his hall. "You took them!"

He got up, casting off the clumsy shoes. She lifted a phone to her ear and spoke. He heard her. But why? He heard her words twice . . . as she mouthed them into the phone, and in his head.

The girls are gone, Malcolm. You can't touch them. Do you hear me? We have Amy. And Monique. And all your precious eggs.

He stopped, shaking his head. This must be a dream! I hear *her*, not the Father Race.

It's over, Raines. It ends here.

"Silence!" he screamed again, falling against the wall a second time, both hands pressed to his ears as he shook his head, writhing in agony.

You're under arrest. For the abduction and imprisonment of Amy Wells and her children. You have the right . . .

"No!" he bellowed. He dropped his hands from his temples and turned from the wall. Her black Lycra suit became his one focus, her delicate neck his target.

He would take her life. Now.

Malcolm charged.

Cat-like, Xi Wang Mu stepped aside and Malcolm Raines missed her, falling to the floor. She turned, her feet set half a meter apart, bent at the knee. She spoke into the phone yet again. "You have the right to an attorney. . . ."

As she held the phone with her left hand, she reached with her right and plucked a short black hypodermic tipped with a silver needle hidden in the base of her ponytail. She concealed it in her right palm, the sharp tip nestled between her index finger and thumb, her arm poised like she held a rapier.

Raines shook his head as if trying to dislodge some demonic power in his ears, then rose from the floor and rushed at her again, bloodshot eyes bulging, muscles in his neck and shoulders swollen. He lunged at her, arms outstretched for her throat.

Xi Wang Mu ducked, her head passing under his high arms, and she thrust her right hand upward, driving the needle into the fleshy part at the base of his neck.

As she rolled left and his body passed over hers, she jammed her hand against the plunger, forcing sedative into blood-rich tissues. The collision with Raines drove the small plastic syringe deep into his flesh and he screamed in shock. He clutched at his throat, stumbled, and fell backward. His head hit the tiles with the sound of a mallet cracking a coconut.

She sprang up, bent at the knee for yet another charge, but Raines lay unmoving. Only the faint rise and fall of his thick robes indicated that he was still alive. The hypodermic twitched in his throat in sync with his slow breathing.

Xi Wang Mu took a deep breath and let it out slowly, forcing herself erect as she regained calm. She rolled back the end of her left sleeve and pressed her thumb on a flesh-colored patch on her wrist.

"Come get him," she said into the thin pad. "Raines is down."

40

THE SLEEK WHITE GULFSTREAM G550 climbed out of Andrews Air Force Base, leaving behind forever, Amy hoped, the safe house and its razor-wire safety net. Wherever she lived next, Amy longed for open spaces, no fences, and low walls she could see over. Washington's lights came quickly into view out her window, beyond the plane's gentle upswept wingtip. As they flew east, she saw the mall and some of the midnight traffic still circulating in the District.

"We'll be cruising at fifty thousand feet, point eight eight five mach," the pilot said as the plane leveled out. She didn't know how fast that was, but Terrance had said they'd be on the ground at Ellington Field near NASA in less than three hours. She leaned back in the seat, wondering at the speed of these past days. From Slovenia to Italy to Maryland to Texas. She was so ready to have a home and be alone with her kids. The transition to a normal life, after six years, would demand much of all of them.

Alice stretched across two seats to her left, tucked under blankets and pillows provided by nice stewards in Air Force uniforms. Amy wanted to sleep, but couldn't. Not now, so close to this odyssey's end.

"Can I join you?" Terrance Kerry asked. He stood in the aisle as if he'd been there awhile, waiting on her to finish her thoughts. Shawnda sat in the row ahead. Amy patted the seat next to her and he sat down.

"We thought you might want to know," Terrance said. "What happened today in China."

Amy's heart quickened. "Yes! Is Monique all right? What about Raines? Did they extradite him?"

Amy hadn't seen Monique since the day Terrance ran through the house, screaming into his phone. Thirty-six hours ago. An hour after he'd departed, Monique was gone, too, with no word of where. Amy ached for word of the girls. Her own sisters, in a sense—like her, part of Raines's prison harem. Amy lived in a frustrating information void at the safe house, entirely dependent on government agents who'd shared almost nothing with her. "For your protection," so they'd said.

Where had these guardians been the past six years, when she'd really needed them?

Special Agent Kerry winked and leaned toward her, speaking low. "Monique is headed home, Amy. From China. With the girls."

"What?" Amy gasped. "How?"

Shawnda picked up the story, leaning over the seat. "When Terrance headed to Houston to capture Marsh, I helped plan the girls' rescue from Ürümqi with Colonel Scales. We needed assistance from someone who knew the access codes and security scheme. Monique was perfect. She was on the ground in China in time to help move them out.

"*All* the girls?"

Every one. CIA has been undercover in Ürümqi for years. We

suspected something was afoot with all the Raines money flowing in, and we had access to the construction crews. Some of them were our own people, in fact, and we had a good idea of the building layout. But we needed access codes, fingerprints for biometric scanners, that sort of thing. If Monique hadn't joined us, we might never have succeeded. She saved their lives. Not us."

A warm spot grew in Amy's heart, remembering the young woman squeezed into a cold ventilation shaft off her tiny cell.

If only Monique had known then what she would do!

Terrance spoke again. "They swapped each girl coming out of the medical procedure for a look-alike soft mannequin, rolled the gurneys with the fake girls to their rooms, then recycled the mannequins for another trip to the rooms. Three hundred twenty-one times. Turned out to be fairly easy; Raines's guards didn't bother escorting the sleepers, just the awake ones who were headed to Harvest. We had a number of guards mixed in that were CIA. They gave us the cover we needed when our people faked the placement of the sleeping girls."

"No one noticed the switch until it was too late," Shawnda said. "Most of his staff were partying hard, celebrating the new moon thing while our people pretended to be busy loyal employees. We moved the girls out in trucks, eighty in each trailer, and they were on airplanes by nine that night. They're en route to Andrews now. The planes will land tomorrow."

Shawnda took Amy's hand. "Monique's fine. She's called us three times to tell you she's okay. But we couldn't tell you without clearance." She shrugged. "Sorry."

Amy frowned. She and her kids hadn't needed a clearance to suffer in prison for six years. The secrecy of this rescue operation frustrated her. *Where was the CIA when we were suffering in Slovenia?* she wondered.

"What about Raines?" Amy asked, her lips drawn. She tried not to appear negative. She was so thankful that the girls—and Monique—were on their way home.

"That's the best part. Our agent on the ground was a young lady named Darla. She'd been on the Raines case five years. Chinese ancestry, adopted by Americans. Fluent speaker, with the right physique. She was promoted to be his Chinese executive assistant a year ago, but Raines never told her about you and the children. She worked at the Heavenly Home and never came to Slovenia."

That explains it.

"Heavenly Home?" Amy asked. A strange name for Raines to use.

"That's what they call his complex; a Chinese name. To hear it from Darla, Raines went berserk when he discovered his precious girls had been stolen from under his nose. It got worse when FBI showed him how he'd been duped for years with the false prophecy thing. He lands in the States in two days. Charges of kidnapping, conspiracy, and hundreds of counts of more disturbing voyeurism and pornographic stuff."

"Did he? Harvest them?" The very word made her ill.

"Yes," Shawnda said, frowning. "We couldn't prevent that without tipping off Raines's security and endangering the girls. But! There's an upside. We had CIA plants in the Harvest suites and the lab, too. All that Raines's people have now are sheep ova. And no girls."

Amy breathed a sigh of mixed regret and relief and settled back. The distant lights of a large Virginia city caught her eye, passing below the wing. It was over. The girls were headed home, free of Raines's clutches, and nothing was left in the Remnant's hands to parlay into future clones. Her immense captor was under lock and key where he belonged. *I'm free. At last.*

"Where will the girls go?"

Terrance shrugged. "Not sure. We're looking for good ideas. Placing them in hundreds of homes will take a while."

"Don't do that," Amy said. "Ask Monique. Put her in charge of that, and move them back into the real world slowly. Maybe a girls' school, someplace remote."

Terrance nodded. "The director might like that approach."

Shawnda squeezed her hand. "And how about you, Amy? Will you be okay?"

Amy nodded, afraid to share her true feelings. She longed to put this ordeal behind her, to gather her chicks around her and make a nest again—anywhere but Houston.

She turned back to the window and closed her eyes. They had to get John home first.

SATURDAY, MAY 23, 2020: JOHNSON SPACE CENTER, HOUSTON, TEXAS

Most of Texas's Highway 5 was dark this early morning hour for the six-car caravan of FBI and NASA vehicles. As they made their way past new storefronts and stucco subdivisions she didn't remember, Amy wondered how she would start her life over.

None of the world, outside a few in government and at NASA, had any idea that she or her children were alive. Many residents had moved beyond that dreadful day, seventy-five months ago, when body parts and a flaming aircraft rained down on a bloody Lincoln Memorial. Like John, America had compartmentalized the grief of an assassinated vice president and the historic Wells family riding with him.

In a strange sort of way, Amy felt a kinship with the Vietnam-era aviators John had told her about. Men who returned from POW camps in Southeast Asia to find that their wives had continued living, marrying and raising families in the absence of any information about loved ones lost over Laos, Cambodia, or Vietnam.

She was coming home a space widow, her husband on Mars because he'd thought her dead. Her home was sold, friends had probably moved, and her children were no longer the little kids who had romped on the street in front of their old home. A huge chunk of her old life felt ripped out and trampled on. She was a different person. But somehow, God had a new beginning in mind, she was sure.

Terrance turned from the front seat of the limo, nodding toward the entrance to their old subdivision as if to ask, "Do you want to go see the old house?" Amy glanced at Alice and the boys. They shook their heads.

Terrance waved the driver on and spoke softly into his radio. The caravan continued two blocks to the front gate of NASA Johnson Space Flight Center, where the guards waved them through. No fanfare, no signs, no heroic welcome. Amy knew that the government still wasn't sure who else might have been aligned with Marsh and Raines. Her arrival was a secret. News that they were alive would be withheld for at least one more day.

Terrance had told her they'd also captured "a big fish" implicated in the terrorist bombings of 2011, but he spoke only in hushed tones of "her," "spirited away," and "CIA." The woman's tie to the death of the vice president meant that Amy might never know who was behind this, a decade-long odyssey that had swirled around John, pulling her and the kids into its vortex. Somehow, though, she knew. Like a sixth sense, or the whisper of the Holy Spirit, she felt an answer to the woman's identity without being told. Ever since Monique spoke it from her hiding place in the ventilation shaft, the name brought chills: Dr. Felicia Bondurant.

Half an hour later, at the Mission Control building, the family followed the director of Johnson Space Flight Center, Greg Church, in silence down a vacant hallway. The plain block walls and poor lighting reminded Amy of a tunnel.

Like Monique's tunnel.

Dimness gave way to bright lights as Terrance and Shawnda Kerry opened the double doors to NASA's window to the Red Planet: Mars Mission Control. She squinted against intense white light.

When her vision adjusted, Amy's heart swelled at the sight of hundreds of NASA personnel filling the room. As they erupted into claps and cheers, Amy noticed a huge banner strung from one end of the basketball court–sized room to the other. "Welcome Home Wells Family. You Endured."

Greg Church turned and gave Amy his arm. She needed it—her knees were shaking. Cheers escalated as all four children filed in to her side. Abe and Arthur to her right, in front of Greg, and Alice and Albert standing to her left. Her tall daughter reached over and took her free hand.

Amy saw many familiar faces around the room, men and women who'd sustained her as she awaited news of John in his near-deadly flight from Mars years ago. Now they would be her sustaining force as she again waited for John's return.

"I—I don't know what to say," Amy yelled over the cheers into Greg's ear.

"Tell them thank you," he yelled back. "They're your friends. They want to be your family."

Amy nodded. "Something short, then. We want to see John."

He smiled. "Short."

Greg raised his hands to quiet the crowd and stepped back. Amy brushed her hair over her shoulder, unsure where to start. Then a sudden peace flooded her. Her racing heart calmed, and she smiled, squeezing Alice's hand.

"Thank you, so much. Thank you all. You probably thought you'd never see us again," she began, interrupted by nervous laughter. "But we're alive. It's been a long six years. Terrance and Shawnda will eventually tell you," she said, nodding toward the agent and his wife, "where we've been. But we're all fine—physically. It was—"

Amy choked, feeling that same peace that had touched her near the end of her second year of captivity, calming the fears and the anxiety that had nearly killed her then and were threatening to grip her now.

"It was hard." She wiped away tears. "We couldn't be together for five of those years."

Groans and gasps erupted. In that moment, Amy realized that this was the first of many times she would repeat this story. And it was her desire to make it a story of forgiveness, healing, and grace.

"There's a short story I'd like to share." Amy pulled Alice close, her bosom companion through dark days.

"On the night before John left on the first Mars mission, Greg let him out of pre-flight quarantine to spend time with me. We went to a bungalow on the beach and spent the evening running in the surf, playing, and talking. It was special. That night, John said something that sustained all of us . . . just like it did him when he flew home alone, in a broken spacecraft.

"John told me, with great conviction, 'God will provide.' And He did. We were often cold, damp, and hungry. Sometimes sick. But God provided for us with everything we *needed*."

She gazed about the room. "I learned something very important in those years, locked in a one-room cell with a tiny garden. Most of my life I'd depended on the wrong things—on my parents, on myself, or John, or the kids or NASA or the Navy or my neighbors or my church.

But when my life was stripped bare, I had only God. I learned to depend on Him for everything. It was a humbling and life-changing experience. That was a good lesson for all of us. We need to learn to trust in God and to lean on Him. Every day."

Amy lowered her head, praying for the team before her, and many joined her in silence. Half a minute later, she lifted her head and whispered to Greg.

"Can we call John now? I want to see his face."

WEDNESDAY, JUNE 10, 2020: MARS

"You may kiss the bride!" John said, concluding the first marriage ceremony he'd ever conducted—and probably ever would. In two days, he'd head home.

Jake pulled back a Martian version of May's bridal veil, Sachiko's special creation using paper and some tissue they'd saved for special presents. But no one cared that the veil wasn't tulle. Then Jake made history, leaning down to May and kissing her—the first couple married on Mars. In ten or eleven minutes, the rest of Earth would celebrate with them as the signal crossed the immense void between two planets.

Jake released May and pulled Rex, his best man, into a hug. "Thank you, Rex. For your blessing."

"Welcome to the family—Dad." His use of the familiar term got a few chuckles.

John motioned Jake and May to face Oz, their cameraman, and the other colonists. "What God has brought together, let no man divide. I present Captain Jake and Dr. May Cook. The Red Planet's first couple."

"Second!" Sam and Deborah sang out. They'd never let anyone forget it. The group laughed with them as Jake and May headed for Nicci's cake creation. It wasn't a big ceremony, but every human on the planet attended.

"Where's the honeymoon?" Oz yelled.

"Thought we'd go out of town for a few days," Jake said, never missing a beat. "Might spend the night at the Hab One Hotel, then take a cruise in the MSR. We've got a doctor along for good measure," he said, hugging May. She glowed in his embrace.

John watched the two crews welcome the newlyweds. Today was his wedding anniversary, a day that had torn his heart the past six years. But not today. Amy had been awake in her—*their*—new home when he'd put a "happy anniversary" call through Mars Mission Control. Only hours after the public announcement of her survival, Butler Builders had made the new home available to Amy, John, and the kids. Rent free as long as they needed.

Similar outpourings of love and community support made every call home extra special, as he learned how she was renewing old friendships and handling the crushing attention, sharing her story of endurance. John's heart swelled every time he thought about her. She was the heroine of the hour. Of his life.

Oz raised a cup of a special fermented bubbling red beverage concocted by Sachiko. Leave it to Oz to find the booze.

"To Mars's newest couple," Oz said, nodding to Jake and May, with a wink toward Sam and Deborah. "May there be many more!"

John was sure he saw Oz direct his cup toward Kate. She blushed.

Standing in a large circle around Jake and May, the colonists clinked plastic cups. Rex Sr. would never have foreseen this, two crews of very different astronauts drawn together with a common bond, making a new life for themselves on Mars.

This was not the Father Race, not a colony of clones, nor a group of like-minded NASA explorers. This was true diversity, John realized, as they joked and laughed and finished off Sachiko's strawberry champagne. It was humanity in the sense God intended, men and women from three races, forming bonds for a common cause—to establish a beachhead for mankind far from planet Earth.

THURSDAY, JUNE 11, 2020: MARS

"Don't beat yourself up, May. You're not alone," John said. "Raines capitalized on the perpetual spiritual hunger in every person. Millions fell prey to him, chasing some special secret knowledge. But you're back on the right track now."

May nodded in silence as she stood with John at a viewing portal. She'd poured out her heart for more than an hour, confessing years of mistakes chasing the god within her and nearly losing a daughter in the process. She pressed a small gift into John's hand and cupped hers about his.

"Give this to Sonya for me. Please?"

"Don't you want Rex to take it to her?"

She shook her head. "I want you to. Without you, without Amy, we'd still be in the darkness we'd accepted for all those years. Sonya would be with Raines, and we'd be here, a bunch of lithium-loopy hermits. If we'd survived at all."

John smiled, unable to express his own gratitude for what May and her friends had meant to him. He felt like he was leaving a legacy on Mars, his friends building a life together, not just leaving a planet. He turned to a table behind him and produced a gift of his own.

"This was a present to me from Amy before my first Mars mission.

I want you to have it." A smile grew across May's face as she pulled off the thin wrapper of some recycled paper.

"For me?" she exclaimed, opening the front of the gold-edged book with a black leather cover. John had penned her a special note in the front. Just below Amy's inscription to him years ago.

"For you," John said, squeezing her hand. "From Melanie, Amy, Deborah, and me. Something to remember us by—and to grow closer to Him. Read it every day."

"I'll try," she said, a single tear coursing over the dark freckles of her smile. "I promise."

FRIDAY, JUNE 12, 2020: MARS

"Any final words on Mars?" John asked from the copilot's seat of the Earth Return Vehicle. Strapped in, on his back as in a Space Shuttle launch, he and Rex occupied the front two seats of the colony's five-person spaceship, ready to head home.

"They wouldn't be my final words on Mars," Rex said with a hint of mischief.

"And why's that?" John scanned the checklist, following Rex's lead through critical system reviews in the final minutes before launch.

"Because I'm coming back."

"And when might that be?" John stopped long enough to watch the young man's face. He expected great things from Rex, who was driven to shed himself of his father's ghost. He had a multibillion dollar enterprise waiting for him on Earth. But if Rex Jr. said it was so, he'd be back.

"Soon as our business is finished on the Blue Planet, Admiral."

John followed Rex's lead for the last minutes of launch preparation, communicating with Jake, Kate, and Oz in the laboratory module five kilometers away. "Final prelaunch system check complete." John ticked off the last checklist item on their screen while Melanie, Ramona—and a remarkably reformed Geo—waited patiently behind him. He suspected that Deborah had slipped Geo some magical pill these past weeks. Or he was drinking the lithium-rich Martian water raw. They had four months of spaceflight ahead of them. Time would tell.

"Houston's go for launch," John said. "At least they were ten minutes ago when they said it. The final 'GO' is up to us. Everybody ready?" He looked back—three thumbs up from his passengers. Half of the original crew, returning. "How about it Jake? Kate? You good, Oz?"

The finality of this good-bye delayed their response, he was sure, because John would never return to Mars. He might never see his friends, and certainly not this place, ever again.

Jake answered at last. "You're 'GO' for launch, John. It's in your hands, brother. Fly safe."

John had never experienced a space launch quite like this one. It was more like leaving on a vacation with the van loaded and all the kids on board. No crowds, no lengthy procedures with contractors and armies of NASA engineers and technicians. Just a detailed checklist, a final wave good-bye from the folks at the Lab—and the big red switch.

John pointed to a glowing mushroom-shaped button, Rex Sr.'s engineering humor at work. One prominent button to start the engines, releasing a massive load of methane and oxygen to burn in three nozzles and lift the craft off Mars. Methane and oxygen they'd made from the Martian atmosphere and Martian water, with enough of a kick to propel them all the way to Earth.

"You're the captain, Rex," John said. "It's all yours."

Rex reached toward the button, then hesitated. "No, sir. This should be your honor."

John shook his head. "Can't do it, Rex. Your rocket. Take us home."

Rex nodded and smiled, reaching to the big, red, mushroom-shaped contraption set in the console's center. "Correction, Admiral," he said, lifting the protective shield from the ignition control. "I *am* home."

EPILOGUE

FALL WAS IN FULL SWING across the United States. Everywhere, it seemed, except wherever Amy happened to be on any given day. Texas was ending its summer drought and wither. And here in California was no better.

The barren salt flats of Edwards Air Force Base stretched beyond her sight, heat shimmering off a flat desert landscape. The late October temperature was tolerable—certainly better than muggy Houston. And the sky was crystal clear, a blue she'd never seen in south Texas through its endless city smog.

Amy strained to see what she'd come so far to find. She and more than one hundred thousand others packed the Air Force base, cars and campers stretching for miles. All to witness the return of one spaceship. The culmination of an era.

Her eyes searched the skies while she listened to the excited voice of Mars Mission Control describing the passage of *Pigeon One* over the

California coastline. That name had to be John's doing, referring to homing pigeons flying miles to return to their base, undeterred by anything except inclement weather. That would be John, bound and determined to reach Earth. Amy lowered her eyes and watched the crowds from her place on an elevated platform.

The children also scanned the skies, quietly waiting for the blistering streak of white and silver, then the sudden blossom of parachutes. This was their second landing event at Edwards. Amy shivered, remembering how the first had ultimately led to the promise of John's Congressional Medal of Honor—and the kidnapping that sent them to six years of torment.

"Everything all right?" Greg Church asked, catching her eye.

Greg had always been a dry, unemotional man. But the shock of learning that Dodd Marsh, his Mars Mission Director, was a mole feeding an alien hoax had changed Greg. He seemed to care more now than six years ago, when they'd last stood here together. Amy suspected that this would be his last space event—as she hoped it also was hers. The time had come for John and Greg to move on.

She smiled at him and nodded. "I'm fine, Greg. Just amazed. By all of this."

"It's for *all* of you." He put his hand on her shoulder in a fatherly way. His hand lingered a moment and he faced her as if there were something he struggled to say, then he turned away, gazing toward the horizon. "Amy?"

"Yes, Greg?"

The director shook his head and turned back around. "I still don't understand why. I mean, why take you guys? Six years. All that." He was nervous, his hands jammed into his pockets.

Amy forced a smile, cocked her head, and leaned on the rail near him. She stared out across the desert as she pulled in a deep breath of the dry air. "Have you ever heard the story of Joseph? Sold into slavery by his brothers, but rose to become a leader in Egypt and save a nation from famine?" She looked at him for a response. Greg nodded in silence.

"His brothers meant to get rid of him, yet God used Joseph in a wonderful way." She paused. "I don't know why Raines did what he did. But something positive did come out of that. When they found us, they rescued Monique and all those girls."

She sighed, watching for John out there somewhere, screaming toward them in a blazing ball of fire. "God took a bad situation and worked it out for good."

Stressful minutes passed waiting for the rocketing capsule to emerge from the high-temperature plasma radio blackout as it plunged, super-heated, through the atmosphere. At last the speakers began crackling with sound. At first, Amy thought it might be static. But it was a strange whistling sound.

Amy's heart jumped. She knew this. A few notes later, everyone else did too.

"Is that John?" Greg asked with a quizzical look.

Amy bounced on her toes, and Alice clapped. "It's Dad!"

"He's whistling, Greg. You hear? 'America the Beautiful.'" Amy rested her hands on her cheeks, her chin quivering. "He's home!"

"America . . ." Greg said, looking up into the sky with her. "Wow."

"I see it!" Alice shrieked.

Amy mopped her eyes with a tissue and jerked her head to search the sky. There he was, a silver and white streak screaming in from her far right.

The announcer's excitement increased as he patched in the cockpit communications. "*Pigeon One*, Houston. We copy your up-range telemetry. You are GO for chute deployment."

"Copy, Houston. Deploying now," responded a voice Amy was sure must be John's.

"Chutes!" Abe sang out along with the cheers of the thousands near their platform. Six square parachutes blossomed, arced at their tops like potato chips. They reminded Amy of a box of crayons: Red, orange, yellow, blue, green, and violet chutes lowering John and the capsule to Earth. Someone's sense of humor was at work; they were no longer the usual red, white, and blue of NASA flights. This was a rainbow!

"*Pigeon One*, good deployment. Six full chutes. Interrogative, steerage engaged?"

"Engaged. This baby can land on a dime," a voice said.

It has to be John.

"Copy, *Pigeon One*. Greg Church laid ten cents out there. You've got the coordinates. See if you can hit it. Bet you dinner you miss."

"And I'll bet you a box of Mars rocks we don't," came another voice, high pitched. That had to be Rex Jr.

"Ladies and gentlemen," the announcer began. "*Pigeon One* has a Delta V Corporation GPS guided chute system that will bring the capsule down with extraordinary precision. Soon the capsule will turn back into the wind and make a large arc about the landing zone."

Even as he said it, the brilliant parachute rainbow and silver spaceship began a wide sweep, circling down over support vehicles that raced out to greet the returning crew. It was reminiscent of a scene from *The Right Stuff*. Except this time, John wouldn't be walking out of the sunset with a charred helmet under his arm. Even from this distance, she saw huge bags inflated all about the capsule, softening its coming collision with Earth.

"Time to go, Amy," Greg Church said. "You guys ready?" He gestured at the Wells family.

"Yes, sir," Abe responded. "We've been waiting to see Dad a very long time."

"I know." He led them to the stairs at the front of the dais. Cheers and applause erupted around them. The ovation rippled across the salt flats, nearly a hundred thousand people clapping, whistling, and honking car horns.

Amy stood a long moment at the top of the steps, her hands shielding her eyes against the sun, the raucous tribute thundering in her ears. She wanted to remember this moment, to pour it into John. He deserved to share in the glory.

Amy took Alice's hand as they descended the stairs. "That's for you," she said to her sons and daughter, waving her free hand toward the crowd. Her eyes filled with tears. "It's for enduring. With God's help."

"Nothing like the last landing," John said as he reached for a control. "After fifteen months in zero G, I could barely move during the descent."

"Impact in five," Rex said. "Three . . . two . . . one."

Earth snatched the five crewmembers in the next instant as three men and two women plowed into their landing zone, like falling two hundred million kilometers to land in a pole-vault airbag. The vehicle pitched and rocked on Vectran airbags, then settled into a soft, cushioned rest on the salty desert floor.

An hour later, after support personnel had cleared the airbags and unbuttoned their hatch, John squinted as the mid-day sun broke through a window opening over his head. From his recumbent position, he reached across to a suited technician and shook his hand. Voices of congratulation boomed over the radio. Dry desert air blew in, the long-forgotten fresh air of Earth.

Home!

As the access hatch completely separated from *Pigeon One*, John saw Amy standing beyond a thin plastic tent wall, waving with abandon. And four children, all taller than she, standing by her side, hands shading their eyes. His heart swelled, remembering little ones running out to greet him on previous Shuttle landings—and the time he'd landed alone from Mars with two dead friends.

His family had grown up. Without him.

Three technicians in biohazard suits squeezed into the tiny compartment, helping John, Rex, Ramona, Geo, and Melanie climb out of their recumbent chairs and clamber with difficulty across the small compartment. John emerged first into the waiting hands of more yellow-suited technicians who slipped him into a thin plastic containment suit topped with a flexible clear helmet. He felt like he was dressed in a sandwich bag with his head squeezed into a clear plastic purse.

The ground wobbled under his feet, but in the steadying grip of two yellow-garbed technicians, he attempted to walk. He looked left, waving to Amy and the children as they ran to a tunnel five meters beyond him. A structure that reminded him of a clear circus tent encased the entire capsule. And the tent exited at a tunnel airlock.

Moments later, John stood outside the protective plastic tent in Amy's embrace, her arms wrapped about him, his plastic arms encircling her at the shoulders. The children joined in the group hug, their arms gripping him as the technicians released their hold. Amy looked up, her eyes showering tears, as he was sure they had many times in the past six years.

"Welcome home, Admiral," she said with a sniffle. She tickled him in the side.

It felt good to have Amy hold him, for the first time in far too long.

"You cut your hair," he said, running his plastic-gloved hand down the back of her shoulder-length hair.

"You're lucky it's this long," she said, gazing into his eyes. "Raines sheared it off. Takes a while to grow back. Alice's, too," she said, nodding toward their beautiful daughter.

John held Amy's face in his plastic embrace, like he'd held her so many times before, her round features a little more wrinkled, like his, and some gray appearing for the first time in her thick head of brown.

"Do you remember our evening under the stars at Cocoa Beach, the night before the first Mars mission?" He stroked her face with a Saran-wrapped finger.

Amy nodded. "I do." Tears ran down her cheeks and dripped over his plastic palms. "You told me to remember that God will always provide. And He did." She reached up and stroked his face, her fingers sliding across the clear stuff plastered to his face like a mask. "And do you remember what I asked you?"

"Sure do. You asked when God would give me back to you. Something like, 'Is this the end?'"

Amy nodded.

"Would you like my answer?"

She nodded again, her tears flowing over her broad smile. All four children listened intently.

"God called me to make a difference," John began as he cupped his hands about her cheeks. "He called *us*." John reached out and pulled all the children even tighter to them. "We've accomplished the mission He gave us—a mission for *all* of us." Now John couldn't stem the flow of his own tears, raining down inside his sticky plastic greenhouse.

He looked down at Amy, dear Amy, who'd waited a lifetime for him to utter these words.

"No more space, sweetheart. My mission's complete. I'm all yours."

She threw her arms about his plastic-covered neck, smiling from ear to ear. "Together forever then?"

"Yes. *Almost* forever," John said, taking her in a hug. "Until Jesus calls us home."

*"I have fought the good fight, I have finished the race,
I have kept the faith."*

2 Timothy 4:7

bonus content includes:

▸ **Deceived!** *Aerospace News* magazine article

▸ Reader's Guide

▸ About the Author

DECEIVED!

December 29, 2020. EPI wire. Adrienne Packard, Senior Correspondent, Aerospace News Inc., with Leslie Thornton, Faith and Values Editor, Boston Globe.

Shock Waves

A modern repeat of "War of the Worlds" has ended, leaving people perplexed and tens of millions victimized around the world.

"There's no precedent for deceit on such a global scale," said US President Brannon Hollingsworth at a press conference five days ago in the White House East Wing. "I don't think anyone can get their hands around it. Not yet."

Hollingsworth's words echo the confusion and disarray seen around the globe at this revelation of a global alien hoax. The ruse of towering spider-machine invaders from outer space was perpetrated by the Chinese government and covert agents operating unseen for a decade inside the United States. And a spiritually hungry world believed it, following the charismatic lead of Dr. Malcolm Raines.

"It will be years, perhaps decades, before the full impact of this deception is completely understood," Hollingsworth said.

Some will deny any deception wherever this last in a series of exposé articles on Saint Michael's Remnant is read. Like Iranian denials twenty years ago of the mid-twentieth century Jewish Holocaust, many will insist that the global manipulation didn't happen. Some are liable to assert that this article represents an attempt by NASA or the United States government to cover up the truth. Yet tens of millions were duped, apparently because they *wanted* to believe in the possibility of intelligent alien life. In the words of Clear Lake City,

Texas, Pastor Jim McGehee, "It's human nature to grab at spiritual truth that's tangible and exciting—something we can see with our own eyes. And that's what happened here. The proof offered was convincing, even spectacular."

But in this case, that proof was a well-orchestrated deception.

In the course of our investigation, Leslie Thornton of the *Boston Globe* and I have interviewed hundreds of government officials, more than fifty members of the erstwhile Saint Michael's Remnant, as well as numerous military officers and law enforcement officials. Our conclusions mirror the old warning that came first from one of the domestic terrorists involved: "Everything is not what it first appears."

Those words were the favorite byline of notorious terrorist ring leader Elias Ulrich, who was killed by the FBI on the night of Vice President Lance Ryan's assassination six years ago, according to FBI Special

Agent Terrance Kerry. Ulrich, a master of disguise, was the head of a national ring of domestic terrorists responsible for the bombings of Washington, DC, and Colorado Springs nearly a decade ago.

"A world of spiritually starving people fell for this deception," said astronaut John Wells soon after his return from Mars. "Every man and woman has a perpetual spiritual hunger inside. Many people satisfied that craving with what we now know was a lie."

Evil Origins

The lie began decades ago. In 1986, space robotics engineer Dr. Felicia Bondurant, then 35, was moving swiftly up through NASA's ranks. Dedicated to planetary exploration and fascinated with New Age thought, she found herself involved in a fringe sect of UFO worship known as Saint Michael's Remnant. The sect claimed to have heard 1300 years ago from interstellar travelers who seeded life on

Earth. The Remnant's beliefs promised that the "Father Race" would return to Earth once humankind proved its ability to reach another planet and to clone itself.

Dr. Bondurant gravitated to the obscure group, offering her body as an egg donor for in-vitro fertilization experiments that might speed the return of the Father Race. Fiercely independent and devoted to the cause, Felicia Bondurant became a regular donor at an obscure laboratory run by Saint Michael's Remnant on the famous tidal island, Mont Saint Michel, in France. From her eggs, twin girls were born of an Italian surrogate mother in 1987, and were placed in the care of the Remnant. Felicia never met the babies who would grow up to play a major role in this global deception.

Antoinette and Monique, tall like their mother, with her jet black hair and Mediterranean features, both took the last name Edwards as adoptive daughters of the next major participant in this international intrigue.

Rocket Man

In 1994, Rex Edwards was a leading entrepreneur in the California aerospace industry just a decade after establishing his own rocket business headquartered in Palmdale. The technological brilliance of his development of liquid-fueled engines was matched by his shrewd ability to pick business leaders in a thriving Silicon Valley computer industry.

Only a few years into the Internet boom, Edwards saw the future in software and the World Wide Web. His investments in key firms, sold with clairvoyant timing, fueled his rocket development with a windfall of Internet profits. From that financial infusion and Edwards' genius emerged a new rocket engine. "He revolutionized rocket performance, gaining 30 percent increases where others said it couldn't be done," said renowned rocket engineer Bill Hoffman of Sacramento, California. "Edwards proved us wrong. And made a fortune in the process."

Edwards turned Web millions into rocket gold by 2011, launching the first series of space tugs able to refuel spacecraft on orbit. The "Rocket Man," as he became known to the public, quickly dominated the market for space launch vehicles.

Yet for all his scientific and business savvy, he, too, became an ardent believer in the vision of Saint Michael's Remnant and their call to colonize space.

Unacquainted with Dr. Bondurant, but seeing himself as a valuable tool of the "Father Race," Edwards made his future in spaceflight. Mars captured his imagination as the home for the next generation of the human race. Learning from Remnant priests in France of their efforts at human genetic manipulation, Edwards and his wife adopted the donor-egg daughters of Felicia Bondurant and raised them at their Palmdale home until his wife's death in 2003.

His wife's death, caused by pancreatic cancer, was a devastating loss that changed the course of Edwards' life. Plunging himself into his work and more determined than ever to make a mark in interplanetary travel, Edwards sent his adoptive daughters to a French boarding school, located on Mont Saint Michel.

There, under the tutelage of Saint Michael's Remnant, Antoinette and Monique learned the skills that carried them into their later years as executive assistants and key advisors to Rex Edwards, and later, Dr. Malcolm Raines.

The Priest

In 1988 when Dr. Bondurant was donating eggs for the Remnant, a much younger star, Malcolm Raines, was burning up the basketball courts at Georgetown University in Washington, DC. Leading the Hoyas to multiple championships, Raines was a basketball phenomenon from Louisiana's river delta region. Raines progressed to professional basketball where, with the Magic, he became the key to Orlando's success in multiple seasons.

A badly fractured leg and knee ended his career in 2005, and Raines pursued his other love, philosophy. In an unusual move for a professional basketball player, Raines moved from Florida to the halls of Oxford University near London for doctoral studies. There, he too learned of Saint Michael's Remnant. His own history made him vulnerable to their vision of a future race that, as he once said, "transcends the dead genetics of modern man."

From Oxford to Arizona, the Mecca of the New Age, Raines moved in 2007 to establish a beachhead for Saint Michael's Remnant in the United States. Were it not for his basketball financial fortunes, he might never have succeeded with a meager storefront church and the few adherents to his curious belief system.

Then a miraculous—for Raines—emergence of generous, but anonymous, donors allowed Raines to relocate his headquarters to Phoenix and increase his influence.

By 2008 Raines had purchased a small church building and was reaching tens of thousands of UFO believers and New Age enthusiasts through the Internet and paid television broadcasts. Overnight, he was a local phenomenon in alternative religious thought.

Unknown to Raines, his meteoric growth was fueled, not by a divine miracle, but by Dr. Felicia Bondurant and the Chinese government, who hoped to make him their frontman for a global biotechnology strategy.

The China Connection

Chinese government officials from Beijing to Washington have refused repeatedly to comment on the Chinese connection to the "Father Hoax," as some television pundits have recently coined this deception. But analyses of intelligence reports we have pieced together, along with our own extensive research and interviews, have been corroborated by US officials.

The connection is clear: China funded Bondurant, and through her, Ulrich and Raines.

By 2004, Chinese officials were hungry to diversify a burgeoning Chinese economy and escape a growing dependence on agriculture and heavy industry. Government officials argued for technology leadership rather than slavishly building the consumer products America demanded in their discount stores. China sought to dominate a new market; biotechnology was their target.

China also sought military superiority. US Defense Department officials have privately speculated that China used the confusion after the attack on Colorado Springs in 2011, which China funded through Bondurant and Ulrich, to launch military payloads along with the alien packages headed for Mars. With space surveillance networks blinded, rockets may have been lofted from seaborne platforms south

of the equator and directed over the South Pole. Sneaking past blinded satellites and an inoperative missile defense shield, China could have launched nuclear weapons to orbit the Earth, as well as send the fake aliens to Mars.

Enamored with the global debates over cloned animals, bioengineered foods, and cures derived from stem cell research, China embarked on a singular mission to corner the biotechnology market. Following a key meeting of Chinese officials, Dr. Bondurant, and Saint Michael's Remnant priests in 2004, China began a massive build-up of technical expertise in clone research, underpinning a national plan to achieve human cloning success within two years.

It didn't take that long.

Anonymous sources inside China provided proof that the government modified its "one family, one child" policy to develop donors for the cloning program. A special proviso permitted select Chinese women who donated eggs or served as surrogate mothers to bear an additional child, funded at the expense of the state.

A massive outpouring of interest from women anxious for a second child allowed the harvest of nearly one million eggs within a short twelve months. Employing proven cloning techniques and using the donor somatic cells of Dr. Bondurant, Chinese scientists successfully developed several thousand viable clone embryos in late 2005. According to our Chinese sources, those embryos were placed in volunteer Chinese surrogate mothers.

Less than 10 percent of the fetuses survived pregnancy or lived beyond a few weeks of their birth. However, more than 400 girls, all the DNA duplicate of Dr. Bondurant, successfully reached their first birthday. Loyal adherents of Saint Michael's Remnant, scattered around the planet, took those children in as their own. Of those hundreds, the healthiest and most intelligent girls

were chosen for service to the Remnant, according to interviews we conducted with several priests on Mont Saint Michel.

Those girls were destined to spend years preparing themselves to usher in the future of the "Father Race."

The Harvest

In 2014, Dr. Malcolm Raines presided over a sell-out crowd of Remnant Worshippers at Washington's RFK stadium. There the self-proclaimed "Priest of the Heavenlies" gathered his faithful to celebrate astronaut John Wells's return from a near-deadly trip to Mars. That night, Raines took on the mantle of "Guardian" as identical nine-year-old girls filed out of the stands, thrust from the arms of their Remnant foster parents into his care.

The 321 girls who walked out of the stands that night soon became known collectively as the "Mother Seed" and were headed a few days later to their new home in Trieste, Italy, for indoctrination. Isolated demands for Raines to report what he intended for these girls went unanswered as the international community, caught up in Raines's eerily accurate prophecies and the Remnant's growing power, chose to ignore Raines's ominous message: "The Mother Seed is the perfect emanation of Sophia, our Mother. They are Vessels of the Father Race."

This past spring, at a renovated monastery in Slovenia, Raines and the Remnant prepared to harvest the eggs of these now-teenagers whose 15-year-old bodies had been primed through treatments of oral hormones. Remnant scientists intended to create hundreds of viable clone embryos and implant them in the girls one month later. Hundreds of young mothers would carry exact replicas of themselves — children bearing their own children in the foothills of the Alps.

Remnant documents obtained through anonymous channels highlight the magnitude of the planned "harvest" and their future breeding plans.

These 321 girls would birth exact copies of themselves every 15 months for 15 years, producing nearly 4,000 potential young mothers in that time frame. Those 4,000 would bear 50,000 new surrogate mothers in the next 15 years, while shedding a massive crop of eggs in controlled harvests. By the year 2070, the Remnant's vision was for half a million identical girls to be able to produce eggs and carry children as surrogate mothers for a burgeoning "Father Race" — one better described as the "Mother Race," given its dependence on women.

Within 50 years the Remnant would reach a productivity level of 50 million eggs a year. "Had they achieved that — tens of millions of eggs per year — it would have represented a milestone in biotechnology. A very dangerous milestone," said Dr. Richard Mabry, Director of Bioethics at the National Institutes of Health.

Why this dependence on

cloning young women? Because nothing in embryonic stem cell research, cloning, or in vitro fertilization can happen without a woman's egg. Ovaries and rocket ships were the essential tools of the Remnant.

The Hoax Unravels

Was it by accident—an extraordinarily improbable coincidence—that the alien spiders crashed in a place on Mars where John Wells would stumble over them and expose them as fakes? If human intentions cannot account for the curious location of such important evidence, then what?

FBI sources state that without the clues provided by those parts scattered on Mars, much of the Chinese deception may not have been exposed. As the hoax began to unravel, many observers raised concerns that NASA may have planted the evidence to discredit the Remnant. But independent analyses of parts returned from Mars—analyses conducted by laboratories in four nations, and overseen by multiple scientists and engineers—confirm the early statements made by the astronauts: The spiders were made on Earth.

Nevertheless, why did the Chinese robot craft fail over that spot on Mars where US astronauts were likely to find them?

"God's providential fingerprints sometimes appear in what we think are the least spiritual places," John Wells stated before a recent NASA board of inquiry.

Admiral Wells may have a point. A signpost for truth from God is perhaps no more improbable than evidence that falls from space into your lap, in the midst of a barren planet, and just when you need it.

Accident, coincidence, or God's hand? We may never know.

She's Alive!

Certainly John Wells would call the evidence of those spiders, and the survival of his wife, both miracles.

"We all thought she was dead," said NASA Johnson Space Center Director Greg Church in a recent interview. "We saw the same thing you did six years ago. The helicopter crashed. We were told she was on board. It was over."

It *was* over, for all Americans, but not for the Wells family. In a strange turn of events inside our nation's intelligence community, the discovery of Iranian terror groups led to proof of illegal activity by the late Vice President Lance Ryan, and brought the assassination evidence gathered after his death into question.

Cemetery officials in Texas have now confirmed that, as intelligence sources pointed to a suspect vice president, the FBI exhumed the bodies of the entire Wells family. New DNA tests confirmed that the bodies were not theirs.

FBI sources tell us that the family's remains were never identified at the crash site by Admiral Wells, who was too distraught with the death of his wife and children. The original DNA typing, according to the FBI, was faked by a laboratory tied to Chinese influence. The world thought John's family was dead, yet on that very day Amy Wells and her children were being whisked to a prison cell in Slovenia.

"Amy Wells nearly died in that prison," said FBI Special Agent Terrance Kerry in a recent interview. "That she and her family endured the isolation and poor conditions is testament to their grit."

Amy Wells, her daughter, and three sons were held in two tiny one-room cells, each attached to a small garden. It was a grim captivity in Slovenia until FBI and CIA evidence began to unravel the faked deaths. Spurred by the emerging news of the alien fraud, and John Wells's improbable discovery of the crash evidence on Mars, the CIA began to focus on Raines's possible role in a global deception, poring over imagery of his Slovenia facility. There, Amy Wells was waiting, and signaling for help.

Save Our Souls

John Wells, famous for his ability to improvise in difficult circumstances, isn't the only creative thinker in his family.

"Monique gave me a mirror. That was all we needed," Amy Wells told us in a joint family interview, as she held hands with her Mars-explorer husband. "Monique was losing faith in Raines because she learned he was lusting after the girls in his care. Thousands of hidden cameras peered into their apartments, stripping those girls of any privacy. When she saw him for what he was, her world came crashing down around her, and she came looking for us. We bonded, and Monique gave me the tool I needed to signal for help."

Amy Wells flashed passing airliners for a week before the CIA, using covert intelligence flights, photographed her behind tall stone walls in the Slovenian compound. Days later, she was rescued by Special Forces operating on a presidential authorization. That's when Raines ran.

Heavenly Home

Within an hour of the Wells family rescue, Raines had orchestrated a transfer of all the Mother Seed to his permanent facility in China. The girls' bodies were ready to be harvested within days. This new location in China was his ultimate safe house, deep inside the country and specially configured to be occupied by young mothers.

It *was* safe, except for one factor, unknown to Raines, Bondurant, or the Chinese.

Suspecting foul play because of the massive flow of Remnant monies into China, the CIA had penetrated Saint Michael's Remnant with several agents. They won the contract to build his new Heavenly Home facility in Ürümqi using a Chinese construction firm directed by the CIA.

Raines fled with his girls from Slovenia to a home built

and monitored by American intelligence personnel. Later, with support from Monique Edwards, agents were able to rescue every one of the girls, just after Raines harvested their eggs. The CIA moved the "Mother Seed" out of China undetected.

In my role as a senior correspondent for *Aerospace News*, I was face-to-face with the silver spiders that clambered up Mont Saint Michel years ago. And several months ago, I was an eyewitness at the Ürümqi Harvest, a nauseating procession of hundreds of young women led like lambs to slaughter, their bodies ripened for the suctioning needle of a gynecologist. I personally observed Raines's biotechnology factory as his doctors plucked tens of eggs from each girl — eggs that fed the genetic mission of Saint Michael's Remnant. Celebration reigned there, with men and women reveling in the use of innocent girls' bodies to promote their vision for humanity's future.

Say what you want about American intelligence failures in the past. The CIA and FBI brought Malcolm Raines to justice that day, penetrating and then dismantling his greatest achievement in plain sight. Blinded by ego and the success of his ova harvest, Dr. Malcolm Raines fell from grace at the pinnacle of his spiritual career.

Anonymous eyewitness sources report that he and Dr. Bondurant, both apprehended in China, have been sequestered in a secret location in the United States. Their ties to the Chinese are the subject of intense investigation, and it may be months before the scope of this deception, and China's involvement, are completely understood.

And what of the 6,000 eggs harvested that day? We have been told they were destroyed since, according to known technology, human ova cannot be transported reliably. However, we have no evidence to verify their destruction, a biotech cache worth over three million dollars on today's market. Questions — many questions — still remain.

Why Kidnap Amy Wells?

Perhaps the most unusual facet of this hoax remains unsolved. Through interviews with a number of law enforcement sources, we have learned that Dr. Bondurant, not Malcolm Raines, spoke the words of the "Father Race" for the past nine years using a covert cellular implant in Raines's jaw.

I was there, an unknown observer, as Dr. Bondurant hailed Raines's initiation of the Ürümqi Harvest from her hotel room in China, pretending to be a pleased Father Race heaping praise on Raines for his accomplishment. What she spoke, he heard and repeated, imagining himself an oracle for the Father Race.

One of her instructions to him, six years earlier, was to capture and keep the Wells family.

"Preserve them," she told an intensely loyal Raines.

He followed the directions of the Father Race — *her directions* — to the letter. Presuming he was obeying his god, Raines kidnapped and imprisoned the Wells family. But why? Why keep them six years?

"They were liabilities. It makes no sense," said FBI Director Carlene Whatley. "Don't get me wrong, I'm glad they're alive. But what's the motive?"

Indeed, what *was* the motive? Pundits and law enforcement agents alike agree that Raines was probably an unwitting pawn for the Chinese, a source of plausible deniability in the event that the complex hoax eventually unraveled. Should the Chinese plan for those hundreds of girls fail, Raines was left holding the most damning evidence: Amy Wells and her children. Any investigation would likely stop with him, a demented giant of a man claiming until his death that "The Father Race told me to do it."

And why kill the vice president as part of the kidnapping? We have determined through multiple sources that the vice president had ties to illegal monies originating in Iran, China, and across the United States. His death was very likely the result of Chinese efforts, through Bondurant and Ulrich, to erase any connection with his benefactors.

Special Agent Kerry summed up the situation by quoting the unforgettable words of Elias Ulrich: "Everything's not what it first appears."

It might be years before we understand these last wrinkles of a global hoax: Why the vice president was assassinated, why Raines faked those deaths and kept the Wells family sequestered. And why Bondurant told him to.

There may, however, be an answer. Amy and John Wells have proposed perhaps the most remarkable thesis yet postulated, but one neither reporter nor scientist can prove — or disprove. As a journalist close to this story for the past decade, I am well-versed in the motives of Dr. Raines, Dr. Bondurant, and Rex Edwards. Yet I wonder if, observing these developments with keen scientific scrutiny, we may have, in fact, missed the truth. Amy Wells explains it better than I can.

"Life requires spiritual eyes," Amy said. "There's a hand behind these events, a spiritual force that some have ignored because they can't explain what happened. Like us, imprisoned in Slovenia. Why? I mean, why fake our deaths, why take us there?"

She waved her hands toward her children as we spoke together at their home in Clear Lake City, Texas. "Do you know the story of Joseph?" she asked me. "He was sold by his brothers into slavery, imprisoned for years on false charges, a man who one day would save his extended family and Egypt from a deadly seven-year famine. His brothers threw him in a hole to die, and then sold him to slavers. They meant that for bad. It was an evil act. But God turned it around for good. God placed Joseph where he could save a nation."

Amy's confidence in her next statement was unflappable, a sign of the courage of this remarkable woman who has endured so much and has done it with such grace.

"Raines's actions were evil, too," she said. "But God transformed that situation for good. If we hadn't been there in Slovenia, perhaps hadn't met Monique, or hadn't signaled for help, who knows what might have happened to those girls? Even with the solid evidence of the faked aliens, nothing would have stopped Raines from impregnating hundreds of girls with copies of themselves. Hidden in China, he could have gone on harvesting eggs and planting embryos in girls forever. What then? Half a million clones in fifty years?"

Amy shrugged, smiling at her silent husband. Her credo captures the essence of what makes Amy and John Wells who

they are: Two unlikely players responsible for unraveling a global deception of unprecedented scope.

"God has a plan, Adrienne," she said. "We might not always understand it, agree with it, or even like it. I know I didn't. *Why* Raines kidnapped us doesn't really matter, in the eternal perspective. But what we did with that situation, that's the key. God put us here on Earth . . . John, me, the kids . . . *and you.* He put us here to make a difference. With His help, providing for our every need, that's what we try to do: Keep our eyes on the cross, and strive to make a difference."

I Was Wrong

The Wells family will be moving next April to John's childhood home, a large farm near Sistersville, West Virginia.

"Our family needs time for healing, out of the public eye," John said, then added, smiling, "and Amy's developed quite a knack for gardening. It will be good for all of us."

Working closely with young Rex Edwards Jr. and the Delta V Corporation, John Wells says they plan to establish a bioethics research and policy center, The Edwards Center for Human Dignity, headquartered in nearby Parkersburg, West Virginia. Delta V Corporation will also fund the settling and education for the hundreds of girls retrieved from China, the identical sisters of Rex's sibling, Sonya. Many of those girls have already been placed in foster homes in the Mountain State.

In our final interview before this article went to press, Leslie Thornton and I flew to Baker Island in the central Pacific. We toured the impressive spacecraft integration and launch facilities used to support the Mars colony and Rex Edwards's rocket empire. There we conducted what was perhaps the first interview with a computer, nicknamed "Dad" by Rex Edwards's son.

It's an eerie life-size video image of the real Rocket Man capable of speaking to us and answering our questions. The program that runs it draws on a database of decades of Edwards's own notes and audio tapes and the wealth of information on the World Wide Web. This interactive visualization of Rex provides his son frequent insight into business and personal decisions. It is perhaps the only such program of its kind in the world.

Leslie Thornton asked him—asked *it:* "Looking back on all your data, with the benefit of hindsight into the popular news of alien life, clone worship, and space travel, what can you tell us? What lesson have you learned about Saint Michael's Remnant and the Father Race?"

The computerized Rex was terse, like his progenitor, pondering our question with crossed arms and a finger to his lips.

He spoke after a long pause, using only three words: "I was wrong."

Adrienne Packard has reported on aerospace trends for 15 years as senior correspondent for Aerospace News, Inc., winning multiple awards for her investigative journalism in the field of aviation and space technology. Leslie Thornton is recognized today by the Religion Newswriters Association as editor and reporter for one of the top religion newspaper sections in North America.

1. Malcolm Raines instructs the Mother Seed in their daily Gnostic
   lesson using a collection of texts known as the *Nag Hammadi
   Library*. These thirteen ancient Gnostic codices consist of more
   than fifty texts, discovered in Egypt in 1945 and translated in the
   1970s. Gnosticism was one of the first heresies to arise in the
   early Christian church, and today's culture is riddled with
   Gnostic thought. Examples include recent fascination with the
   so-called "gospels" of Judas, Thomas, Mary, and others; the oxy-
   moronic cult referred to as "Christian Gnosticism" and its clev-
   erly crafted lie that Jesus was a Gnostic, the divine illuminator;
   popular fiction including Dan Brown's *Da Vinci Code*, George
   Lucas's *Star Wars* series, and the *Indiana Jones* series, to name a
   very few.

   a. You should prepare yourself, prayerfully, to identify Gnostic
      thought when you encounter it, and to understand how
      this doctrine is infiltrating churches and secular society.
      Consult a biblically based text or a known Christian web
      resource to research this topic in more detail. Try the
      Apologetics Index, http://www.apologeticsindex
      .org/186-gnosticism, or GotQuestions.org at http://www
      .gotquestions.org/Christian-gnosticism.html.

      > Warning: The Internet is replete with spiritually
      > fascinating material about Gnosticism, but it all
      > pales as a lie in the light of God's truth. Undergird
      > your research in prayer before you dive into this
      > study. Ask that the lies be revealed to you as you
      > conduct your research.

b. What do evangelical scholars say about the interpreted "gospels" of the *Nag Hammadi*, such as the so-called Gospel of Thomas, the Gospel of Philip, and the Gospel of Truth? Why were these writings rejected for inclusion in the Bible? What is the basis of argument from "modern" theologians for inclusion of these writings in recently published versions of the Bible?

c. What does the Bible tell us about early Gnostic ("proto-Gnostic") teachings? Review the book of Colossians and 1 John for examples of the early Christians' battle against early Gnostic teaching.

d. Secret knowledge is a crucial doctrine in Gnosticism. In *The Proof* and *The Return*, Malcolm Raines speaks of the Unknowable God, secret teachings, and Gnostic traditions, such as the story of Sophia, the Aeons, and the formation of the world. Gnosticism says that when, through knowledge of secret teachings, you become aware that your true identity is a divine inner self, you will be set free to live as a child of a superior deity or as part of a kind of "divine ocean." The realization of these secrets leads to unity with the "world soul" that is in everything. Therefore, in Gnostic tradition, faith is inferior to knowledge. With that background, what does Scripture tell us about seeking inner gods? About salvation and faith? Can salvation come through knowledge?

e. Some suggested questions:

    i. What is the Gnostic view of sin? What is the biblical view of sin?

    ii. Is the view of Jesus in the *Nag Hammadi* texts the same as the Bible's? Is it the same Jesus in the *Nag Hammadi*? Why does this matter?

    iii. Is there scholarly agreement on the dating, authorship, authenticity, interpretation, and relationship to Christianity of the *Nag Hammadi* texts? How does this differ from scholarly views of the dating, authorship, and authenticity of the Bible?

    iv. Can there be a "Christian Gnostic"? How would Gnosticism in Christian guise appear? [Note: Douglas Groothuis's *Revealing the New Age Jesus: Challenges to Orthodox Views of Christ* (InterVarsity Press, 1990) does a great job of tackling these issues.]

2. Dr. Robert Witt, known to his crew as "Geo," metamorphosed midway through the mission from a quiet geologist to the crew whiner. He grates on everyone's nerves and creates significant discord.

    a. Why do you think Geo transformed into a troublesome crew member? Have you known people who, for some unknown reason, "change their stripes" and do something completely out of character? Why would a self-made and successful person like an astronaut suddenly "crack" and become a different person? How might you see a change like this coming and head it off?

    b. If you were John Wells, how would you deal with Geo and what would you do to help reduce the conflict between Geo and the crew? Would you pray for Geo? What would you pray?

    c. What could John have done differently in his relationship with Geo? Do you agree or disagree with John's approach?

3. May Randall was a devoted Christian mother, raising her young daughter Sonya in the faith. As Rex embraced the doctrine of

Saint Michael's Remnant and sent Sonya to join the Mother Seed, May sought to convince herself that everything she heard from Rex and Saint Michael's Remnant was true. When John proved that the alien spiders were fakes, May suddenly came to grips with her terrible mistake. She had embraced a lie.

a. You are Dr. Readdy, and May Randall regains consciousness in your care after fainting in the rover. The fake spider evidence is scattered at your feet. May sees it and begins to cry, aware again of what has transpired. She sobs as she shares her story, overcome with grief. How do you comfort her?

b. A week later, May is withdrawn, suffering from severe depression about her actions. She wants to believe in the Father Race, but can't ignore what John has found. How do you share your faith with her and lead her to healing?

4. Monique has no foundation in any Christian teaching, raised her entire life in the Gnostic-centric environment of Rex Edwards's home and Saint Michael's Remnant. As she comes to realize Raines's depravity, she turns from him and seeks out Amy Wells. In her late-night visits, Amy has an opportunity to share her faith with Monique and does so, but slowly.

a. You are in Amy's predicament, cut off for years from all human interaction, other than your daughter. How long does it take you to trust Monique? Once you trust her, how do you share your faith with Monique in a way she can understand?

b. If you are Amy, what do you pray for? How are we commanded to pray, even when times are tough? How do you pray for Monique in the midst of your imprisonment?

For a good example, consult the book of 2 Timothy, where
Paul writes to his dear friend from captivity, with no hope
of release.

c. You haven't seen a Bible for six years. What Scriptures
would you remember after that period of time? Have you
ever practiced Scripture memorization? Pick a verse and
work to memorize it in the coming week. Have friends
encourage you and hold you accountable, and you do the
same for them. Recite to each other.

5. Amy suffers from diabetes and has battled obsessive-compulsive
disorder. She had a difficult time dealing with both issues during
her first year of captivity. After her escape, she stated that she
trusted God to provide for their every need. She was quoted in
the magazine article as saying that "God has a plan. We might
not always understand it, agree with it, or even like it. I know I
didn't."

a. What do you think happened inside Amy to enable her
to make such a change and trust God completely? Have
you experienced such a change before? Read 2 Corinthians
12:9-10. *The Message* says it this way: "I quit focusing on
the handicap and began appreciating the gift. It was a case
of Christ's strength moving in on my weakness. Now I take
limitations in stride, and with good cheer, these limitations
that cut me down to size. . . . I just let Christ take over!
And so the weaker I get, the stronger I become."

b. What does it mean to you to "trust God for every need"?
What is the difference between a "need" and a "want"?
Why does that matter?

c. Read the autobiography of George Müller, an evangelist in Britain who exhibited the total trust that Amy speaks of, depending on God from day to day.

d. How do you seek God's will in your life? Henry Blackaby, in *Experiencing God*, says that we can know God's will through the Bible, through experiences, through prayer, and through the body of the church, fellowshipping with other believers. Read *Experiencing God* for more insights into understanding God's plan for your life. Visit Blackaby Ministries International's website at http://www.blackaby.org/.

6. My editor asked me once: "Does Amy pray for her captors?" I had to admit that, until she asked, I hadn't considered the possibility. I'll let you decide.

a. If you were Amy, would you pray for your captors? Why or why not?

b. How did Paul treat his captors? Did he pray for them? What was the result?

c. What does Christ command us to do with those who hate and persecute us?

7. John Wells was quoted by Adrienne Packard in the magazine article, saying that "God's providential fingerprints sometimes appear in what we think are the least spiritual places." This is actually a quote from a close pastor friend of mine, Dr. Ed Culpepper, of Huntsville, Alabama.

a. Give some examples of such "providential fingerprints" in your own life.

b. Have you ever experienced a miraculous event that defied

logical explanation? How did that event affect you?

8. Sonya and her sisters are raised as egg donors and as future surrogate mothers for Malcolm Raines's Father Race. Their eggs will be used to create clone embryos of themselves. A clone is a DNA replica of the organism that spawned the original DNA. Like an identical twin, the clone and its "parent" share the same genetic material.

   a. Is it ethical to clone humans? If cloning would lead to less disease, fewer disabilities, or longer lives, would that make the practice ethical?

   b. What does Scripture say about cloning? What general context of Scripture would advise us on how to deal with this technology? Is there a difference between seeking a child through cloning technologies as opposed to in vitro fertilization?

   c. Should human reproductive cloning be illegal? Do humans have a right to not be created? That is, before they have been created through reproductive cloning, do humans have a right to *not* be created for experimentation? Where and when do human rights begin? At birth, or at creation in the laboratory?

   d. Embryonic stem cell research requires the development of a human embryo to produce the necessary stem cell elements for study. Extracting those stem cells requires destruction of the embryo. Is there a difference between creating an embryo for its stem cells and raising a human clone for its body part or harvesting DNA material such as a woman's eggs?

   e. Learn more about the ethics of cloning, egg harvests, and biotechnology. Visit the website for the Center for Bioethics and Human Dignity, http://www.cbhd.org/, or write them at The Center for Bioethics and Human Dignity, 2065 Half Day Road, Deerfield, IL 60015 USA.

ABOUT THE AUTHOR

AUSTIN BOYD IS AN award-winning novelist who writes about faith issues related to technology, and spiritual allegories that represent a fresh approach to Christian fiction. He creates stories that encourage readers to wrestle with dilemmas of faith through what he calls "a novel approach to truth." Austin is a Christy Gold Medal finalist (*The Proof,* 2007) and winner of multiple writing honors, including the Mount Hermon Christian Writers' "Pacesetter Award."

Austin writes from his experience as a decorated Navy pilot, spacecraft engineer, and as an astronaut candidate finalist. He and his wife Cindy are the parents of four children and live in America's "Rocket City," Huntsville, Alabama, where he serves as the Senior Vice President of a product engineering company that supports NASA, the Department of Defense, and commercial entrepreneurs.

Austin's creative talents include inspirational fiction, poetry, and finely crafted reproduction colonial furniture. In addition to his writing, he is active outdoors as an avid archer, cyclist, and hiker. He serves Huntsville's First Baptist Church and his community as an advocate for crisis pregnancy centers, and as a speaker on issues of lifestyle evangelism through a popular series entitled "Understanding Islam."

Learn more about the author at www.austinboyd.com and www. amgpublishers.com

NO AMOUNT OF TRAINING COULD PREPARE A MAN

As Navy Commander John Wells and his crew watch hopelessly from their space station perch, terrorists cripple the nation's capital and security systems. While the world looks to the Middle East for blame, sudden images off the plains of Mars offer a staggering alternative.

With a sophisticated alien culture seemingly confirmed on the Red Planet, a disorganized U.S. government struggles to formulate their next steps. Caught in a web of politics, torn by his family commitments, and called to serve not only his country but his God, John Wells must take a giant step for mankind.

The Evidence

Mars Hill Classified Trilogy
By Austin Boyd
ISBN-13: 978-0-89957-828-6
ISBN-10: 0-89957-828-4

Visit your local Christian bookstore, call AMG at 1-800-266-4977, or log on to www.amgpublishers.com to purchase.

"An explosive first novel from a major new talent." –Davis Bunn

AUSTIN BOYD

THE EVIDENCE

A NOVEL

MARS HILL CLASSIFIED BOOK 1

Living Ink Books
An Imprint of AMG Publishers

IS THERE LIFE ON MARS?

That's what Captain John Wells and his NASA colleagues hope to discover, in this second installment of the MARS HILL CLASSIFIED trilogy, when they undertake an aggressive mission to the Red Planet. However, from the outset, nothing goes as planned. An uncanny prophesy coupled with an unexpected alien starship escort ends in a series of catastrophic events that give John plenty to think about as he makes the interminable journey back to Earth.

The mysteries of Mars, woven into a complex tapestry of international intrigue, will lead him to answers even the most faithful fear. As he starts to put the pieces of the universal puzzle together, the pieces of his life fall irrevocably apart, but, as he must constantly remind himself, God does indeed have a plan for him.

The Proof
Mars Hill Classified Trilogy
By Austin Boyd
ISBN-13: 978-0-89957-829-3
ISBN-10: 0-89957-829-2

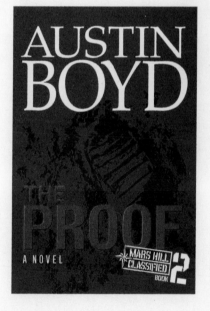

Visit your local Christian bookstore, call
AMG at 1-800-266-4977, or log on to
www.amgpublishers.com to purchase.

Living Ink Books
An Imprint of AMG Publishers